STORY TIME

BEHIND THE DOORS

STORY TIME

BEHIND THE DOORS

J. DOBSON

iUniverse®

STORY TIME BEHIND THE DOORS

iUniverse books may be ordered through booksellers or by contacting:

iUniverse
1663 Liberty Drive
Bloomington, IN 47403
www.iuniverse.com
1-800-Authors (1-800-288-4677)

ISBN: 978-1-4917-5086-5 (sc)
ISBN: 978-1-4917-5087-2 (hc)
ISBN: 978-1-4917-5088-9 (e)

Library of Congress Control Number: 2014918991

Printed in the United States of America.

iUniverse rev. date: 11/05/2014

For my children,
Bethany Marie, Jon James, and Thomas George,
and
in memory of "Sista" Joan Clare

Part One

WHERE DOES THIS STORY END
THE BAD MOON KNOWS
IT WAITS TO RISE AGAIN
THAT'S WHERE THE BAD MOON GOES

Prologue

Archie Cornati's hemorrhoids were burning as the little yellow and black school bus bumped along down Highway M-73. The early Stambaugh Grade School bus was little more than a paneled truck that was without shocks or suspension to speak of, much to the dismay of Archie's backside. Archie had the early afternoon run with kindergartners and a few first and second graders who lived along Highway M-73. His early turnaround run was tightly scheduled to get him back at Stambaugh High School when school let out at three forty-five.

Archie lived just down the hill from Stambaugh in Caspian. His little crook of the world was called New Caspian, which was across the Iron River and up the hill from Old Caspian. Like Stambaugh, New and Old Caspian were small iron ore mining towns in the Upper Peninsula of Michigan. More like rural villages, these haunts bore the vestige of a bleak era when mining companies took the city and miners for everything they had, sometimes taking life and property with them before hastily closing up shop and moving on to the next unsuspecting part of the world. It wasn't a pretty scene, but for some, this place was the only home they'd ever know.

Archie, in spite of his ancestors, didn't look like his Italian father or his Italian grandfather. He was not the swarthy dark-skinned, dark-haired third-generation Sicilian who had settled Caspian. He had thinning sandy-colored hair, fair skin, thick legs, and beefy arms that he often covered with a black and gold Stambaugh High

School jacket. Archie was one of those who would always call this bleak place home. His work overalls (which later would be known as carpenter jeans) were as old as the paneled truck he drove. Nineteen forty-four denim lasted forever; 1944 trucks, however, did not.

Even though he was plagued with painful hemorrhoids, Archie had a very jovial sense of humor, though he had a sarcastic side to him that helped him keep the kids he hauled to and from school in line. And maybe that's why he was respected by the kids. Archie was fond of those little snot-rags, as he called them. Always mindful of their safety and well-being, he was their favorite bus driver. Most found him funny and kind, though they didn't want to get on his bad side. Kids thought it a privilege when Archie gave them a nickname—a nickname that often lasted until the end of high school.

He was a good employee and mostly loved his job, except for his dislike of the early afternoon bus run and his unusual fear for the little Gehlhoff girl. Archie felt he fit in his niche as a satisfied, hardworking man. He and his wife, Mary, lived in a small home in New Caspian, and many of his neighbors were blood relatives (not many of the Cornatis moved far from home, you see). They had no children, which suited Archie just fine. If Mary never got pregnant, he was more than okay with that. He liked kids, and kids liked him, but nightmares about kids getting hurt or dying interrupted his sleep often enough to make him thankful he didn't have any of his own. Of all the kids he drove to and from school, Archie feared for eight-year-old Jane Gehlhoff most.

His first stop on M-73 at 3:10 p.m. was the middle of a hairpin curve intersecting with Stanley Lake Road. It was so dangerous a corner that he refused to stop in the middle of it to let Jane cross alone. Archie would turn down Stanley Lake Road to drop her off even though he knew this was not technically part of his route. Doing so had the potential to make him late getting back for his next run, in which case he would be criticized for not following the rules. He didn't care. Though she wasn't the first child to get off his bus at this stop, he still felt justified taking this extra step to keep her safe. Before letting her out the door, he always cautioned her to go straight home, no wasting time, no stopping on the way—none of that lollygagging that Jane was good at. Every afternoon she said, "Thank you, Mr. Archie. I will, I promise." And every afternoon as he watched her start the two-mile walk home, he worried. When he was tense, his butt crack would sweat, making his hemorrhoids burn even more. Making the U-turn to get back on M-73 caused him some difficulty because the road was narrow with deep ditches on each side. But Archie, having made the U-turn many times, was an old pro. Once back on M-73, he would glance out his rearview mirror to check Jane's progress.

Today, as always, he glimpsed her walking slowly up Stanley Lake Road, lollygagging and playing the whole way. "I wish that darn kid would listen to me," Archie cursed under his breath.

For absolutely no reason, Archie was more worried about her today than he had been yesterday. He was sorely tempted to pick her up again and bus her the two miles right to her doorstep so that he would know she was safe. But he knew that if he caved in to this unreasonable fear, he would be busing her home every afternoon. Losing his job for one student was not in Archie's future plans. Besides, he argued with himself, another driver would then get his route, and Jane would surely be walking the two miles anyway. As he was silently debating this, he noticed the time. Without other diversions, he would be on time for his second run. That decided it.

Jane was a pretty eight-year-old, dressed today in a rust-and-green plaid dress with a white collar and green knee socks. The day was warm, so she had forgotten her sweater on the back of her desk chair at school. The early fall days were like that in the Upper Peninsula—cool, crisp mornings with warm and even hot afternoons. Jane had brown hair twisted into two braids down either side of her head and straight-cut bangs that hung down to her eyes. By this time of the day, her braids were coming apart, and hair was sticking out all over. Below her bangs, she was blessed with big brown eyes—not hazel, not light brown, but a pure chocolate brown, the color of a Hershey's chocolate bar. A slight breeze lifted the hem of her skirt, revealing tan knobby knees, and she held tightly to her take-home school papers so they wouldn't blow away—again.

This October afternoon was the glorious reminder of a carefree summer. Not a cloud marred the azure sky. The hardwoods were a dazzling show of reds and yellows. Cicadas were singing their raspy, alluring song. Crows, high in the trees, were calling with acerbic, rakish boldness. Barbwire fencing ran up the right side of the hill beyond the scattered hardwood trees, just back from the deep ditch pasturing Maki's cows. The way home was simple for Jane. Walking up the long gradual hill was the hardest part. Down the other side was much faster. At the crest of the hill, she would be able to see all the way back to M-73 and all the way forward, down past her driveway, to the Camp Lake turnaround. Stanley Lake Road was covered in pea gravel that had been recently graded, though the coming winter and the plows would soon upset the smooth carpet of small rocks.

Unconcerned about her walk, Jane was happy it wasn't raining. Her take-home schoolwork would be safe. Humming and randomly breaking out into made-up songs, she made progress walking up the hill. As she looked at interesting rocks on the road, picking one up now and then, she knew she was wasting time. She was a daydreamer, and she found her daydreams interesting. Being easily distracted, she found that staying on task was difficult on her trips home. Walking up the isolated road, she dreamed of saving her little sister from drowning. Everyone would call her a hero. She would be famous, and the boys in her class would stop pulling her braids. All these thoughts occupied her as she finally crested the hill.

The drone of a fast-approaching car caught her attention, pulling her out of her daydream. Checking that she was walking on the right side of the road, she stopped and looked down the hill. She didn't often see cars on her walk home. The families living off Stanley Lake Road were few. Not seeing anything, she turned and continued walking. Then, as if out of nowhere, a red convertible slowed down as it passed her. Seated in the front were two men. The man in the passenger seat looked like her uncles and the daddies of her friends. She couldn't see the driver very well, but she couldn't help but notice his white wavy hair. The man in the passenger seat threw an empty beer bottle out of the car that landed a few feet in front of her. The copper-colored glass did not shatter, but the loud, scratchy thud it made as it hit the road startled her.

The man leaned out over the car door as it slowly passed her and yelled, "Looky here. Say, purty little gal, where you goin'?"

The car took off, spitting gravel everywhere. The man's piercing laugh echoed through silence that suddenly seemed so thick that not even the birds stirred from their high perches. Still watching the car pick up speed on the down side of the hill, she frowned and furrowed her brow. Jane wasn't normally afraid of adults. She didn't really have a frame of reference for fear of strangers in 1944, and her parents hadn't taught her to fear men, stranger or not. Was it intuition or a divine push that pulsed in her head as she watched the red car turnaround at the Camp Lake intersection? The car paused for a minute or so before starting back toward her—time enough for Jane to make a quick decision.

Leaving the road and dropping her school papers in the ditch, she hurried through the few trees to the barbwire fence. As she crawled under the second row of wire, her dress caught and then tore as she pulled it free. She could hear the car approaching—and fast. Running into the pasture, she lay down, face-first, behind a hillock not far from the fence. She was afraid now. Her little heart was hammering in her chest. Mewing and whimpering, her mind called silently for her momma and daddy. The car neared the top of the hill and stopped. Still, Jane didn't run. She stayed behind the hillock. For a few moments the violated October day was still, frozen in time. She held her breath and in her mind uttered a simple prayer, *oh God, oh God, oh God*, over and over.

Hidden by the grassy hillock Jane flinches as the car door screeched and crooned open, and the man in the passenger seat stepped out. He walked around the front of the car, saying, "I'll be damned. Where'd she go? I'll be damned—she disappeared." Trying to avoid eye contact with his new best friend, but unsure what to do next, he connected with the man's empty, dead-looking eyes. For a long moment Jane saw fear and dread spread across the man's face. With great effort he tore his eyes from the devil's grip. She was close enough to watch as he covered his eyes squealing in pain. The man in the driver's seat laughed hysterically.

Turning away from the car, he walked to the ditch. "Hey, girly, where'd you go? Come out, come out, wherever you are. Jus' wanna talk wit you. Give ya a ride," he said cajolingly.

Behind the hillock, a soft, loving peace stilled the fear driving Jane's knocking heart. She felt a gentle cover settle over her. The most love she would ever feel seeped into her being. The protective covering smelled like cleansing rain, and a feather tickled her nose. She wanted to giggle but dared not for fear that the man would hear her. A hand that was little more than a cool breeze lifted her chin so that she could see over the hillock. At her eye level she saw two scuffed cowboy boots. The man was standing inches from her face. Even so, the fear did not return.

"Can't find her!" the man yelled to his confederate. "Musta run to the Maki house. She's fast that girl, real fast," he said, turning back toward the car. Unzipping his pants, he fumbled out his erect penis and produced a long hot stream of yellow urine streaked with blood. When he was done, he walked back to the car, opened the screeching door, and got in, keeping his eyes on the road ahead.

Able to see the car now, Jane looked at the white-haired driver. He turned his head toward her, stared directly into her eyes, and opened his mouth. His long snakelike tongue flicked toward her. The words "next time" bit into her head, leaving behind a pinched headache. She continued to watch as he shifted the car and stomped on the gas pedal, leaving a cloud of gravel dust that followed the car down the hill. Jane didn't move. The tension and fear had returned as fast as it had left her. She couldn't move. Slowly and reluctantly, she stood. Turning around, she saw the logging road running through the forest that followed the road to her home. The same hand that had lifted her chin gently touched her back as she started walking down the forest road. She didn't look back to see what protected her.

I hear myself trying to yell out as the throngs of sleep paralysis restrict my movement and the sound that is trying so hard to escape from my mouth. I can feel the sleep witch sitting on my chest, suppressing my respirations. Struggling harder against the nightmare holding my mind, I'm finally able to move my head ending my terror. "It's 2005, not 1944, for God's sake!" I cry out.

Sitting up and drawing a gasping breath, I try to let the nightmare go back to my subconscious, where all these years I managed to keep the memory hidden. Clutching my head in my hands, I feel myself trying to slip back into the dream; a wish to know what it was that helped the little girl is the draw. Forcing my legs over the edge of the bed, I will reality to take hold.

My apartment is shrouded in darkness. Shadows of unfamiliar objects seem to leap out, causing my heart to lurch. The only light is from the window that reminds me dawn is still hours away. I reach for the bedside light. The light pushes back the monsters, and the bedroom becomes familiar again. Just like on any of my sleepless nights, I face the indecision of whether to try to go back to sleep or give in and get up. The decision to get up regardless of the hour is an easier one this night. I think this old heart is not capable of handling the nightmare's return. "I think I'll get a cup of coffee," I say to no one.

Chapter One

I probably will not get out of this, if I live, I realize as I sit in my senior citizen's apartment. My life is shallow, unfulfilled. Really, it's quite boring. I clean. I get the mail. I drink my iced tea mixed with lemonade in the evening. I try to write, but that's it. That's not living life, and that certainly isn't going to get this damn book done. The book. The stories I'm trying to write are muddled without substance. Pedestrian. The words I have written have no color. The pages have taken on the flavor of old-lady ramblings. And since all my friends are old ladies who ramble, I can't stand that my sacred words have taken on such a judgmental tone. Ah yes, the stories are as boring as my dry wrinkled skin and the aches and pains in my inflamed joints. *When did I become so old?* I wonder. Convinced I can change the sad, sorry state of my writings by leaving my safe, comfortable home, I've talked myself into leaving to find the stories that elude my pages. I will go back to the place I heard the stories in the first place, stories that have intrigued my overactive imagination like a gathering storm all these years since I retired.

Most of my nursing career after graduating from training was spent at Cre Falls Manor doing long-term care, from green nurse—one not used to the ropes, shall we say—to registered nurse, or rotten nurse, my family would tease; for twenty years I stashed away the tales told at the Manor about the townie's misdeeds. As the years passed, I became a white fixture that passed medication after eight in the evening to the round table of gossipy men. This is where the stories of the past were told. Times were relived. Always, their stories made my fingers itch to write. However, the flavor of those times has become a misty memory, kind of like what I had for lunch today: easily forgotten.

All who discover what I've done will likely declare "the plan" a sign of early dementia. They will shake their heads and say, "She couldn't help herself." When I really think about what I'm about to do, I know the probability of failure is high. The need to abort this insanity, put the typewriter away, and stay safe is pushing at the compulsive need for one last adventure.

I refuse to be impulsive and stupid. I detail the plan intending to tape the envelope to the bottom of my desk and hope—no, pray—it will miss discovery until this misadventure is over. By then, my smart kids will find it and rescue me. I am their mother after all, and since I rescued them from many of their adventures-gone-wrong, they can rescue me from mine. "Oh, please find me," I whisper as I groaningly kneel to tape the envelope to the underside of the desk. It's possible that after what I'm about to do, I will indeed be demented—or worse.

Now for the details; as I look at my list, my mind runs through the plan.

1. *Typewriter.* My old Underwood typewriter has been custom-modified to include a concealed space underneath, space enough to accommodate a manila envelope with two hundred thousand dollars, the balance of all the money I have left. The lock on the concealed bottom of the case has a thumbprint identification keypad that fits my thumb and my thumb alone.

2. *Suitcase.* I found a battered old suitcase under a pile of ancient ones at Goodwill and intend to pack as much clothes as I dare take, old clothes, in a much-used state with the labels removed.

3. *Car.* The 1990 car, for which I paid five hundred dollars cash, has no license plates and no registration, and the VIN number, I scratched to an unreadable state. It runs, rough, but I think it will get me where I want to go.

4. *Mail.* The post office will deliver my mail to an abandoned house I purchased for the price of the lot. There's a large slot in the door that should accommodate a year's worth of mail without

causing suspicion. I'll place a large "under construction" sign on the door.

5. *Bills.* All of my bank accounts are closed, and utilities and rent are paid in advance for a year. I even thought to cancel doctor appointments. I called the pharmacy to tell them I'd be away as well.

6. *Friends.* I went on and on to my friends about how I will be on an extended vacation—one long, last trip beginning in Florida to spend some time with my son George. It's a lie. Another mendacity I have repeated many times is that I will probably spend time in Italy for my daughter's last opera performance of this season. I have repeated my lie enough times that my friends have come to think what I'm doing is "oh so much fun!" They think I'm really striking out with independence. It's a lie. It's all a lie. Oh, if they only knew.

Maybe I can get this over with and actually make it to Italy, though, I think as I'm packing. I do love Puccini's *La Bohème*," and it would be such a treat to hear my daughter sing Musetta.

I have nice friends. We call ourselves "old creaks." The "M&M's" is the group of ladies I sing with. "Between menopause and Medicare" is our slogan. We eat together in our safe, clean, well-decorated dining room on special occasions, like every Friday. We have long discussions about our children, the weather, politics, aches and pains, and the never-ending rent increases. Oh yes, we also have discussions about "dribbling," especially after having several bladder-irritating cups of coffee. We can never agree on whether or not to wear pads or just put up with damp urine odor. I like my friends. I'm bored out of my skull sometimes with them, but I like them. I think they like me too, though sometimes I wonder. I'm just a little odd, my friend Ann likes to tease. And sometimes when I enter a room, the rest of them stop talking and just stare. Don't they know that staring is impolite? But I guess when you get old, you just don't care what's polite or impolite anymore.

My children approve of my safe, clean, well-decorated senior citizen apartment. I do too, I think. The bedroom is just about pace-worthy. Except for the bathroom, the rest of the space is the new open concept. Realtor-white walls, tan carpet, and cable TV. *This is as good as it gets,* I thought when I first looked at the place. This sounds a lot like old lady whining. I'm really not whining. I could easily live here for ten or more years. Except for this one thing I have to do. I promise I'll come back and play fair. *Just find the note, kids, will ya?* I think.

The message I record on my answering machine is my most difficult lie before turning the key on my apartment door, telling all who call, including my unsuspecting kids, that I plan to take an extended vacation for a year. "Please do not be concerned. I'm fine and will surely be in touch." The phone calls as they try to reach their always-at-home mother will become frantic. They love me and will be angry and very hurt. Can't help them there. I'm counting on their love, on their finding the envelope taped under my desk and coming to rescue me. *Oh dear God, please come and find me!* I think. *The three of you will be my only deliverance, my only way out of the mess I'm sure to find myself in.*

Fortune has it that my son George has taken a job in Florida and is not expected back for a long time. James is on sabbatical working on his PhD, and Marie will be singing with an Italian opera company in Oviedo for the better part of a year. It raises the hair on the back of my neck to realize it's now or never.

With a full tank of gas, the tires checked, and latex gloves on, I drive out of Green Bay, Wisconsin, praying this old Toyota will do the job. Wild-looking, wide-eyed, and nearly paralyzed with fear, I turn the corner toward Highway 29 with my few possessions and my Underwood typewriter. And we head north.

Chapter Two

The Crow's Nest Motel, with its cloying mixture of mold and body odor, some two hundred miles from the old 29 turnoff, is my destination. The rusty Toyota I purchased puddle-jumped up the highway from dusk into the dark of night. This blustery night smells like rain and, with it being this cold, possibly snow. Keeping to the back roads has been more of a problem than I anticipated. Upkeep on the once-familiar old roads going north has been pretty much nonexistent. Mile after mile of potholes and brush growing close on the shoulder has slowed my journey down to a crawl at times. Crazed, desperate not to get pulled over by a local constable, I push this old trap over one logging road after another. Snowflakes swirl in front of the slow-moving jalopy. White-knuckle driving has made the arthritic joints in my hand scream in pain. I have rheumatoid arthritis, and my usual painful joints are now howling. I'm going to have to sleep for a few hours. The car's exhaust could easily gas me. But going any farther is out of the question. I'm not making it to the motel anytime soon, so I better pull off.

Pulling over as far into the brush shoulder as I can, I rest my head in my arms on the steering wheel, feeling as though sleep is far away. But when I open my eyes again, I'm surprised to find it snowed at least an inch while I slept without dreams. Past the point of no return, and with no coherent thought process, I just pull back onto the road and automatically keep heading north to Cre Falls and the Crow's Nest Motel.

I barely remember stopping to sleep. Too numb to be surprised, at last I turn up the hill to the motel. I'm not even taken aback to see it standing much as I remember it. Putting the twenty-two dollars in the night cash box attached to the front office door, I retrieve the key to number six.

Sleep deprivation and dehydration feed my adrenaline. When I pick up the bedside lamp and slam it into the TV screen, I'm surprised that it explodes. Sparks, smoke, and glass shards fly back at me. Making as much noise as possible, I trash the small room. I roll up the bedding and toss it in the corner. The mattress and box spring, I move crosswise on the bed. While I was bumping up the road, I collected my urine and feces in a bucket, the contents of which now stain and puddle on the threadbare faded carpet. The room smells like an outhouse on a hot, humid summer day. Knowing adrenaline is my only source of energy, I smash the window with the 1950s pole lamp. Glass litters the floor.

I am dressed in a thin cotton shift that falls above my knobby arthritic knees, and my saggy breasts flop up and down as I jump. By now, half-crazy, I'm screaming in a loud-pitched wail. My hair is dry from over-perming and is standing around my head like a salt-and-pepper halo. It looks like ozone escaping the trashed TV screen has given it life.

Then I hear the siren. *Oh God, here they come!* The fear in my gut makes me feel faint. There's no turning back anymore. The siren howls as Cre Falls's black-and-white careens around the corner into the motel parking lot. Standing by the broken window, I get a good look at the faces of two young cops. I don't recognize either of them, but I bet I know their daddies. They certainly shouldn't know me. "Come and get me, boys. This wacky old lady is waiting!" I scream.

What looks like Cre Falls's finest rookie butts the door, breaking the frame. If he had turned the knob, the door would have opened. *Idiot*, I think. Ah, the enthusiasm of Cre Falls youth. Looks like the several hundred dollars I put under the Gideon Bible in the bedside drawer won't be enough to take care of this mess.

The rookie yells back at the other cop, "Jon, my God, I just stepped in shit! The frickin' smell in here is way bad. Get the old lady standing by the window. Her feet are bleeding pretty badly all over the place from broken glass. Jesus, this place is a fucking mess. What the hell? It looks like robbery."

Jon, seemingly the seasoned hard-ass, makes his way into the room. After gagging a couple of times, he vomits in my transport pail. Clearly reluctant to come any farther into the room, Jon orders the rookie, "Grab her before she bolts!"

If he puts his hands on me, I'll go berserk, I decide. Funny thing, I can't stop screaming. Got to run! Jumping Jesus, they'd better catch me before I have a heart attack. Just as I make it around the bed, I slip in urine mixed with bowel movement and fall hard. Out of breath, lying in urine, and still screaming at the top of my lungs is as nuts as I need to be.

The two officers finally grab me under my arms and haul me to my feet. Jon's green, pasty complexion, helped along by the looks of my bloody feet and urine-soaked nightgown, prompt him to say, "I don't know what happened here, but this screaming witch is nuts. I don't want her in my ride. Call County Rescue while I hold her. Lady, stop swinging your arms, goddamn it. Hurry, Dave, make the call. She's starting to scream again. Jesus, good thing we're wearing latex gloves. Too much who knows what flying around?"

I don't know how I could have done this differently. Incredibly, when I got into the car and headed north, it seemed as though some kind of influence was directing this outcome. I'm out of control now and totally exhausted. My throat is burning, and my head is pounding. The stabbing pain in my feet is probably why I can't stop screaming. I try to find the neat, proper old lady sitting contently with no worries some two hundred miles away, and she's not here in this wrecked motel room. I want to put my head on Jon, the cop's shoulder, and beg him to take care of me. I want him to call my children. My jaw is clenched. No words leak out of my mouth.

Dave comes back into the room. "They're here," he says tersely before heading back outside. Through the open door, I see the ambulance skid around the corner and into the parking lot of this wretched place, lights flashing and sirens wailing. Opening the back door of the rig, two EMTs jump out. Grabbing the gurney, they head for the open motel room door.

The cops let go of my arms. Before I can slip away, the EMTs put a gait belt around my waist. One has a stethoscope, and after placing the cold bell over my heart, he says, "She's pretty tacky." By this time my screaming has turned to whimpering. The squad boss assesses me for obvious broken bones. I'm as surprised as he is when he finds none. The squad boss yells over my screaming, "Let's put her back on the floor so we can get the backboard under her. What's her BP?"

The EMT with the cuff and the stethoscope yells, "She's back to screaming and I can't hear a thing. Get her strapped to the gurney and let the emergency room get her vitals."

Jon yells in the EMT's ear, "She must really be hurting. She's hardly stopped screaming since we got here. Boy, the fucking stench is getting to me." Without ceremony they put me on the gurney and strap me in, totally forgetting the backboard. Someone covers me with a blanket.

The EMT with the clipboard motions Jon outside the motel room. Neglecting to close the door, he says, "What do you have on her?"

Looking at his notebook, Jon says, "No name, no address, no identification on her; old beat-up suitcase with a few clothes, Underwood typewriter with some kind of locking mechanism, her ride was probably that old red Toyota over there. No license plate, and I can't find a registration. The damn VIN number is scratched out. I'll see if the fingerprint guy can lift her prints. I still can't figure out why she's wearing latex gloves. It must be a germ thing. She could have come in overnight because she didn't register at the Nest's office. Far as I can figure, she hasn't been robbed. Found several hundred dollars under the Gideon Bible in the room. Crazy Butch will want the money to pay for the mess, I suspect, but for now the money's going on my report and in the evidence bag. Dave and I will spend the rest of the shift trying to figure out who this old lady is. For now, though, she's a Jane Doe."

The other EMT, still standing beside me, yells from the room, "Let's get her out of here! Dr. Murray is on call in the ER. Let's do our best to spoil his night, eh? Say, cover her face; it's starting to rain. I call it just one more perfect night in Cre Falls."

Lying on the gurney in the parking lot, I can hear raindrops falling on the pavement. Struggling to get the blanket away from my face, I open my parched mouth to try to catch a few drops. I must look really loony now, with my arms in restraints and my mouth wildly open, searching for raindrops. *Classy*, I think. I can feel warm sticky liquid pooling under my feet, and I wonder how badly I'm cut. My insane act is hardly an act anymore. Oh, I'm afraid! I'm afraid they will find out who I am and somehow even more afraid that they won't, and I'll have to go through with this crazy plan. Somehow the doc has to send me to the nursing home and not to Marshfield Hospital's eighth-floor nutty ward. My throat hurts from screaming. Better keep screaming tonight, though, because nothing is coming out of my mouth tomorrow. I hope the EMTs take good care of my typewriter and the suitcase. Two, maybe three, minutes more pass. *Come on, come on!* I think. My butt and hip hurt from the fall. I really need something to help the burning in my feet. *Stop standing around talking, and get me there, you idiots*, I want to say. But all that comes out of my mouth is screaming.

The EMT with the clipboard calls over for my vitals to get recorded. "She's pretty tacky. BP is 170/90, pulse 102, and respirations are 22. I'm not sure I heard the BP right. Doc's gonna love this. Oh, ya gonna smell up the ER and make his night very interesting. Turning from mike he says to the driver, "Do you have all her stuff? Let's get out of here."

I have a life worth living. I have a life worth living. I have something I'm burning to do. Dear God, it's selfish and self-centered. "I will hang on a little longer" is the litany my brain keeps chanting. God, this was nuts, but it's working.

Chapter Three

"ETA three minutes. Bringing in a white, elderly female of undetermined age. Vitals stable. Bilateral lacerations to feet still actively bleeding. No identification. Jane Doe for now. Over … Yeah, that's her screaming. Except for her feet, no apparent physical reason. Has been screaming on and off since we picked her up. Out."

The ride to Cre Falls Memorial takes only long enough for the EMT to call in my stats. For me, it's long enough to really question my sanity. Now I'm screaming because I'm afraid and moaning because my feet burn with pain. I'm thirsty and exhausted. All I want is to be somewhere clean to rest. I'll die if I must, but please let it be warm and clean. My teeth are chattering. Likely, it's shock. Who will earn the fee tonight, God or the doctor?

On the count—one, two, three—the gurney is wheeled out of the ER garage and into the first bay. I think if I bang and shake the rails, maybe my feet won't hurt so much. Oh, bright lights. Bright lights and loud noises assault me as the privacy curtain is pulled.

The emergency room nurse is ready with all the pertinent questions. "What sewer did you find her in? Is she going to shut up long enough for the intake interview?"

The smart-ass EMT says, "She isn't applying for your job, Barb. So shut up and get to it, will you?"

A doctor pulls back the privacy curtain. He gets a good whiff of his new patient. Turning to Nurse Barb, he barks, "Get a couple of CNAs to clean her up and give that reeking blanket back to these fine heroes." He glares at the EMTs. "Oh, and Barb," he says from the other side of the curtain, "find out why she's screaming and clean the glass out of the cuts in her feet."

As predicted, two aides show up with a plastic pan of water, soap, and towels on a cart with clean linen. I think about how sorry I'm going to be. I could make this an easier job for them. Flailing my arms around, I continue to scream and moan. One aide attempts to hold my arms, cooing, "It's all right, dear. We're just trying to clean you up and get you into a dry gown." The water is warm, and their efficient hands quickly do the job. My filthy nightgown is removed, and a clean hospital gown is tied behind my neck. Warm blankets are tucked in around me. All of this care should be enough to quiet this old lady, but I have goals to attend to.

Nurse Barb now takes over the show and says, "I'm going to clean the wounds on your feet and dress them. Try to hold very still. It will take a while to get all the glass out. This is probably going to hurt. Boy, are they going to hurt tomorrow. Dr. Murray wants you to have a tetanus shot when I get done taking care of your feet."

Still moaning, I bend one leg and kick out, spraying blood on the front of Barb's uniform. Jumping back, she yells, "You old bag, look what you've done!" Poking her head out of the curtain, she demands an order from Dr. Murray for intramuscular Ativan. "Better make it two milligrams, stat, or this job will take all night."

The aide turns me on my side, and I feel the cold alcohol and then the sting of the needle deep in my gluteus maximus. Before I realize it, I'm being turned on my other side. Again the cold alcohol wipe and then the deep muscular burn of tetanus toxoid.

The overhead lights become fuzzy. The sounds around me have a hollow echo. I know I've stopped screaming. My body begins to sink into the gurney, muscles going flaccid. I try to focus on what Barb and the doctor are saying. With edginess in her voice, Barb says, "Do a history and physical and ship her to Cre Manor. Let them deal with her. They can do an emergency admit. If we ship her to Marshfield eighth floor, they'll just ship her back to the Manor anyway, especially if the diagnosis is dementia. You can write a psych consult. Do you think a recommendation of a bed on the behavior unit would appease the Manor staff? Less complicated, and it gets her out of our hair, at least until psychiatry makes a determination."

Looking annoyed, Dr. Murray obliges. "Call the Manor. Give them a heads-up. You know they hate these admits. Tell them she's coming with paperwork, and Barb, you have to let them know we don't have a name. Tell them the cops are working on it. Get Bill to x-ray that right hip."

Bill, the x-ray tech, soon pushes the curtain aside. "Is this Murray's old girl that needs a right hip film?"

Barb, pushing her weight around, stiffens up and says, "Yes, and read it stat. She's nursing home–bound before anyone changes their mind. Let me tell you, she moves that right leg just fine. That's what made a mess of my scrubs. At least the Ativan shut her up. For the record, she has no name for now. Use Jane Doe. Not my business, but who's paying for the ER? I suppose 'Little Sisters of the Rich' will cover this."

As Bill starts rolling the gurney, he says over his shoulder, "You had better watch your mouth, Barb. Little Sisters of the Poor signs your big checks."

Once in x-ray, Bill lines the gurney up with the x-ray table. "Okay, girly, just lie still." Bill puts my head and shoulders on the table first and then my hips and feet. Like all x-ray tables, this one is cold and hard. Bill is fast and efficient. Two films, and he is ready to read. He moves me back to the gurney thankfully avoiding bumping my feet. After reading my x-rays he pushes the gurney back out of x-ray to the emergency room, announcing, "Hip looks good. No fractures."

"I called County Rescue to transport her. All papers in the manila envelope are signed," Barb informs the ER staff. "CR should be here in minutes. If anyone is interested, I'm on break."

I try to stop a drunken smile. The Ativan has made me euphoric. I'm beyond caring that the trials have just begun. The County Rescue boys are back. Only six blocks to Cre Manor.

Chapter Four

I don't remember much of my ride to the nursing home. But I become aware of the conversation between the EMT and the Manor night nurse after being brought up by the elevator to the second floor.

The EMT pushes the papers into the hands of the night nurse, who says in a preachy tone, "No name except Jane Doe? We'll have to see about that! She can't stay here with no name or social security number. The state and our administration won't put up with that! No pay source, no room. That's the policy. I really shouldn't admit her except I have to follow Dr. Murray's orders. What did they give her? She's almost comatose."

The EMT smirks. "You know Barb. She likes the elderly rather subdued and cooperative, not farting around, causing her trouble. This one messed up Barb's uniform, and her screaming drove her up a wall. Murray didn't waste any time ordering two milligrams of Ativan, IM. Old girl will probably be out all day. Where do you want her, Laura?"

Laura looks up from my admission papers. "Put her in 802 with Lucy. That's the last bed I have behind the doors. Did she have stuff with her?"

"Yeah," the EMT calls over his shoulder, starting to roll the gurney down the hall. "A locked typewriter case, Underwood I think, and a battered suitcase with some pretty tattered clothes. Has her own teeth. Don't know where her shoes are. Cops picked her up at the Crow's Nest. Police report is attached to her papers. That's it!"

He rolls me through a set of double doors and into a room. Hands lift me into bed—three sets, I think. They are gentle, and I land softly. Pillows are fixed behind my head, and wonderfully warm blankets are pulled up to my chin. All of this kindness I'm aware of comes from a distant, out-of-body place.

An aide or maybe a nurse says, "The things in her suitcase can be marked on the day shift tomorrow. Her body audit can wait as well. Let's get out of here and let Miss Jane Doe sleep off the Ativan."

The light flicks out, and the door closes. All I can hear is some muttering down the hall. Otherwise, it's quiet as a tomb "behind the doors."

In the deep recesses of my foggy brain, I'm aware that I must get my head and body together enough to push my typewriter under my bed all the way to the wall. If I know the nursing home staff, they will try to force the lock while attempting to discover my identity. What they will find instead is all my money.

Pushing back the covers, I look at my right leg and will it over the side of the bed. Lying still with my eyes closed, I'm unaware of the passage of time. Did I fall back asleep? My gut fills with creeping panic. It's still dark in the room. I move my hips closer to the edge of the bed. My feet are burning as I lift my left leg over the side. With tremendous effort, I raise my upper half to a sitting position and nearly fall over head-first. I'm saved from falling on the floor by a half rail. Thinking I'll just lie down again for a little while, I almost reach for the pillow. But I cannot go back to sleep. The consequence of letting exhaustion and Ativan take over will be putting my Underwood and this whole plan at risk. I bang my left foot on the bed rail. The pain is as good as a slap on the face. The next challenge is to put both feet on the floor and stand. *Put your feet down now. Put your feet down. Now stand*, I tell myself. *Please, God*, I pray, *help my legs hold me up.* The typewriter case is next to my right foot. I try to push it, and ah, damn, I can't. I have to get down on my knees and push it. I have to do this. I try to remember, do dehydrated fools cry tears? I don't feel tears, but I think I'm crying. Beginning to bend my knees, I fall the rest of the way down to the floor. Sure that the grunt that escapes my mouth will bring staff on the run, I put my head on the typewriter case, waiting for the inevitable. No sound in the hall except some snoring and grunts, but no staff coming to investigate what's going down in room 802. The Ativan fog is catching up. I push the case and crawl forward. It moves a few inches. Inch by inch, I move the case slowly toward the head of the bed. Lying on the floor, I'm able to inch it under the bed. Now my head and shoulders are underneath. A giggle bubbles out of my mouth as I picture the back of the blasted hospital gown, with my white, saggy ass hanging out. What a sight! After pushing the case up to the wall, I'm ready to collapse. Next job is to back out and get into bed. But I inadvertently raise my head before it clears the bed rail. The blow to my head causes black dots and light flash across my visual field. Trying again to get back in bed, I grab the covers but bring them down on me instead. The last sound I'm aware of is my roommate, Lucy, shouting, "7-4-11-15 13-14-22!"

How long it takes exhaustion and Ativan to do their work, I'm not sure. Vague dreams, some half-awake hallucinations, and unsure touches of reality plague my nights and days. I am aware of strong arms helping me to walk on painful feet to the bathroom. I clutch strong hands that assist me to sit up and drink thick, sweet liquid. I'm also aware that my stomach doesn't always accept this nourishment. When I'm aware, my head hurts, the pain in my feet is excruciating, and this everlasting arthritic joint disease flares without mercy. The kindest state for me to be in is unconsciousness.

Chapter Five

Slowly my wrecked mind is coming awake and becoming aware of the nursing home around me. My first perception is pain. Not just lacerated-foot pain, but the sick ache of inflamed joints, a pain I've been familiar with for more than twenty-five years. Rheumatoid arthritis was the impetus, along with widowhood, for the move to the senior citizen apartment. I gently ask my body to move, and it answers with aching anguish. Putting my hand over my mouth to muffle the moan, I try to discover my surroundings. I'm not ready to have the staff know I'm among the living. My very next discovery is the overwhelming need to pee. Begging my bladder to calm down is no easy job.

My cervical neck joints are working without major stiffness. Able to turn my head to look at the bed opposite mine, I remember: Lucy. "Put her in with Lucy," the night nurse had said.

I'm startled to find Lucy boldly staring back at me. Two sterling-blue eyes with gray flecks meet mine. She is blessed with porcelain, pale skin and few age wrinkles. Her skin is so pale and thin that I can imagine blood coursing through the veins beneath. After her eyes, I notice the apple-dumpling cheeks. Her long, thin hair is snow-white and spreads out on her pillow. The rest of her body is covered from feet to chin with blankets. Lucy appears to be a tiny, thin woman. She doesn't speak as we survey each other. Raising my finger to my lips, I make a "shhh" sound. Amazingly, she understands and nods.

Not without trepidation, I'm becoming aware of the human smells of my surroundings; they press on my senses. Hot, acidic ammonia-urine smells filter in from the hallway. I think about how God gave us the gift of being able to tolerate the smell of our own body fluids, while making us absolutely intolerant of others' smells. The fecal smell overriding the now-innocent urine smell assaults my nostrils. The smell conjures brown, gaseous, purulent, fetid shit.

The fecal smell increases and changes. Fear crawls up my spine, and goose bumps rise on my arms. I smell an evil that thickens the air. As I look at Lucy, the same fear crosses her face.

Down the hall, an aide is exasperated. "Mr. Wirm, I can't stand this. You stink up the whole hall. Why can't you get to the bathroom? You manage to walk everywhere else for crying out loud!"

Mr. Wirm produces a hideous laugh in response to the whining aide and says, "All for you, my dear, and for the rest of my fellow demented brother, oh, my sisters too."

I remember from the old autopsy days that a smear of Vicks under the nose doesn't eliminate all odors, but it goes a long way to help. On my mental list I add a jar of Vicks.

Suddenly my bladder is in crisis. I must get out of bed and to the bathroom before I join the heavy wetter's club. Making all the right moves to sit up and get my legs over the edge of the bed is torture. My head begins swimming, so sitting on the edge of the bed before launching to my feet takes longer than I planned.

Lucy sounds the alarm—"8 13-4-4-3 7-4-11-15!"—with the cadence of a quarterback. She nearly scares the pee out of me. Before I can make myself move, the aide hits the door running.

"Okay, okay, Lucy, I got her. Oh no, you don't, Lady No-Name. No getting up on your own, nurses' orders. Put your hand on your head and feel the lump from your last midnight excursion," she orders.

I sort of remember banging my head on the bed frame while trying to get back in bed. For now, what I was doing on the floor escapes me. I gingerly touch the top of my head to find matted hair, a goose egg, and pain. "Ouch" escapes my mouth before I know better.

Now that they know I can talk, I say without caution, "Well, you had better get me to the bathroom before I'm in trouble and you have more work to do." She gets it, and painful step after painful step lands me on the throne of blessed relief.

"Around here you need to put on your call light to get help when you're done. Do you see the call light? Pull the string, and I'll be back to help you off as soon as I can. You're not my only resident, so you'll have to wait your turn."

"You'll have to wait your turn," I parrot when she is out of hearing. No sense in telling her she would save time waiting the few minutes to help me back to bed, assuming I wouldn't ignore her orders and get back to bed on my own. Oh, well. I spot a washcloth, towel, and soap and think it must be time for a damage assessment in the mirror. Using the handrail, I white-knuckle it to stand up and face the mirror. The first glimpse in the mirror takes my breath away. I expected unkempt, sunken eye sockets and dry wrinkled skin. Even the white hair framing my head like a halo isn't more than I expected, but the face that's so familiar has aged ten years since I closed the apartment door on my old life. I don't want to look like I belong here! As I look into the lost haunted eyes staring back at me, tears trickle down, making rivers on my dry cheeks. I want to give up, confess all, get on a bus, and go home. Before I have time to wash my face, I hear the aide enter, talking to Lucy. Quickly I hang up the wet washcloth and sit down on the toilet, trying to appear innocent.

"Oh, I see you've been at the sink washing up," she says with a smirk. You'll have to do what my nurse wants, or we'll put you in a chair with a clip alarm. Back to bed with you, and stay put. The nurse who will see you is Mary Olson. She'll be in after her medication pass. In the meantime, there's a breakfast tray with Jane Doe on the card. Guess that's you."

Back in the bed, the most intense hunger pains make me double up. Food, coffee, and juice cause the tears to overflow again. Until this moment, this very moment, I don't think I've ever felt hunger pain. Seeing the skin hang on my arms, and given the feel of hipbones and ribs, I know I have lost weight. Food has not been a consideration for longer than I can remember. That and dehydration account for the hollow cheeks. May I never forget this first sip of awful, wonderful nursing home coffee, a bite of toast that tastes sweet, a spoon of powered scrambled eggs that practically makes me swoon. My stomach lurches, but I'm determined to keep this offering down.

The aide is assisting Lucy with her oatmeal. Barely does Lucy swallow before she has another spoon filled and ready. I want to say, "Slow down," but I realize that Lucy is accustomed to eating fast. I want to ask the aide how long I've been out of it, but I decide to wait until the day nurse (what's her name, Mary Olson?) comes to see her latest and greatest "behind the doors" resident. I ask the aide for more coffee and another piece of toast.

"Now don't overdo it. It's been a while since you've had food. But I suppose more coffee and toast can't hurt." She picks up Lucy's tray, leaving Lucy and me alone. Lucy is still smacking on her last mouthful of oatmeal.

Returning with a cup and covered plate, she gives me a cautionary look. The aide fills Lucy's washbasin for morning cares. As she pulls down the bed linen, out wafts a strong urine odor that I just wasn't expecting. My stomach heaves, and without warning, I vomit breakfast all over my bedside table.

"I told you not to overeat," the aide says, scowling. "It's like talking to kids. I'll get you a basin, and you can clean up this mess. Hopefully, you'll get done before Mary gets here."

"I expect you to do your job," I answer, "and that includes cleaning up this mess." At this, Lucy's eyes twinkle, and she flashes me one of her first smiles. If the aide had pulled the privacy curtain before yanking down the urine-soaked linen, I probably would have kept my breakfast.

"If you're going to puke every time you smell pee in this place, you'll be puking all the time. Get used to it. Right, Lucy?"

"Lucy, my name is Jane Doe. I'm going to be your roommate, if you'll have me," I say. I ask the aide, "Why doesn't Lucy have language instead of shouting numbers? If she can't speak words, why doesn't she write the things she wants to say?"

"Your guess is as good as mine," the aide says while cleaning Lucy up. "Lucy came to us just the way she is now. As far as I know, she hasn't spoken a word or written one in the ten years she has been living here."

After finishing up Lucy, the aide begins to clean up my bedside table. "You're my partner's room. She'll be in for morning cares before too long. Remember, no walking around. Mary will about have a fit if you fall." As she heads out the door, she says, "Our Mary doesn't like extra work."

I have a feeling I'm going to hear this again and again. A nursing home's good resident is a dependent one, one who follows the rules. But I didn't come all this way not to do what I need done. I may have to manipulate the system some, but I will find a way to do what I came for.

"Lucy," I say, "If I write words down for you, can you read them and understand? I think if you can do this, it will help me understand your number communication. For instance, if the number one is 'A,' I could write it down, and you could nod if I'm right. That's the best idea I can offer this morning."

Lucy smiles and raises her eyebrows. I take the look to say, "Not a bad idea." I already have projects.

The nurse's aide who has our room comes in with her arms full of clean linens. "My name is Lois. I'll be your aide today. You, Jane Doe, I guess, have a bath scheduled. Pat, the bath aide, will be here to get you. She says around nine or so. Nurse says you need to drink a lot of fluids. Best get working on that. I'll make up your bed with clean linen while Pat is scrubbing you up. Lucy, you're mess is all mine."

She puts things in drawers and dust mops the floor. I feel some power return as she next cleans up my bedside table. "Don't get up without putting on your light for help, or you'll be put in a chair with a clip alarm," she admonishes me.

She's barely out the door when I start to get on my feet, groaning. "Now Lucy, take it easy. I just want to look around. Okay?" I say, begging her not to sound the alarm. "I'll be careful. I'll just walk over to the door and check out the hall … see what's going on. I need to see if my typewriter is where I put it."

Standing up is easier this time. My feet are sore, but the burning pain is less severe. There is no window in our room. The walls are wallpapered in small pink roses. Two small closets and two hospital beds are pretty much it. *At least we don't have to share the bathroom with other residents,* I think. Holding on to the side rails of my bed, I bend over far enough to see my typewriter. A flood of confidence moves me as I see the Underwood just where I pushed it and no scalp hair on the bed frame. Score two for the old wacky broad.

Lucy is silent as she watches me intensely. Her hair is now pulled back in a neat bun behind her head. The nurse's aide selected a blue print housedress, brown thigh-high cotton hose, and of course, the proverbially white sweater. Surprisingly, Lucy does not wear glasses. She looks like the quintessential nursing home resident, except for her startling clear blue eyes—no rummy, vague eyes like those I became accustomed to seeing as a nurse.

"Lucy, I'm just going to look out the door. I have to be careful that I don't let Mary catch me. I can't get myself confined to a chair. I have things to do, people to see, stories to write," I tell her with confidence that she won't tell on me.

Carefully shuffling, pushing the bedside table, I roll toward the door. Realizing the hospital gown I'm wearing flashes my backside, I give Lucy a "can't help it" shrug. Lucy is following me with her eyes and smirking. Pushing the bedside table aside and holding on the doorframe, I peek out. Our room is directly across from a small dining room. I can see round tables and chairs. A bank of windows is across the room.

No one is in the hallway except for the far end. I do recognize the person sitting in the hallway on his Adirondack chair. "For the love of Mike," I whisper before I can stop myself, "there sits Harold Brown." His legs are drawn under him as he rocks back and forth. A dizzy surge of déjà vu pulls me back twenty years. It is the same Harold—grayer, with a receding hairline, and thinner than I remember him, but definitely Harold. As he rocks and smiles his vacant smile, I hear him chant, "Do-da, do-da, Waupun bitties." It's as though the last twenty years never happened, and I'm still his nurse. I know Harold has no idea who the old lady is staring at him, but I wave. I'm not sure Harold was able to internalize the fact I left all those years ago. His physical changes don't appear to be all that dramatic. I, however, have totally changed from the forty-year-old nurse he knew then. Standing up taller, more hopeful, I realize tears are once more streaking down my face. Harold Brown is still here! God have mercy on his soul.

Bringing my attention to the double doors on the other side of the hall, I hear staff talking as the doors begin to open. Good guess, here comes Nurse Mary. Just in time, I duck back, but I try not to move too fast. Staying balanced, I'm able to get a hold of my bedside table. As I move one foot ahead of the other toward the bed, I can hear her chatting with the aide, Lois, who took care of us, She is saying something about "no name yet."

"We'll see about that," I hear the nurse say. Just in time, I'm safely sitting back on my bed, a little short of breath, but trying to look innocent.

Uniforms have changed from nurse whites to colored scrubs since my time. Mary is somewhat plump in her navy scrubs. She has an up-to-date look with short, streaked blond hair. She appears hurried and not happy with the extra admission work left from the night shift. The aide is with her to help with the body audit, I'm sure.

"So," she says as she enters the room, "Jane Doe is not a name I can accept. I have to have a social security number. Cre Nursing administration needs to bill you for services or arrange for a government agency to pay for your stay. This is not an option. Do you understand? Night shift left it up to me to get this information. What is your name?"

Giving her my name is out of the question. I just nod and look down. I've decided to speak as little as possible.

"What is your name? Do you have family or friends I can contact to get your information? Do they know where you are? Do you know where you are? I know you can talk," she says, giving the aide a conspiratorial look. "If you can talk to the aide, you can talk to me!"

Okay, time to take control! I slam my hand on the bedside table. "If I knew my name, I would have told you. Do you understand? I want to see the administrator after I'm made presentable. I want a shower. Get me an appointment today. Take care of my feet, and get me Tylenol for pain. My head hurts, and my hip is killing me! And I will not take any more Ativan."

Mary looks not threatened. "Okay, Jane Doe, I'll be happy to let administration deal with you. Best lie back. I have to change those dressings on your feet. Your aide will put plastic bags on your feet for your shower. If Tylenol is what you want, Tylenol is what you get. You get control of yourself, or I will be back with Ativan."

I lie back on the bed, steeling myself. Anticipating some pain as she cuts off the old dressings, I grip the side rail. I look at Lucy, who is taking all this in. She gives me a wink that I take as encouragement. The old dressings are stuck to the wounds. Marvelous Mary doesn't just pull them off. She floods the dressing with normal saline, waits a minute or so, and then slowly peels them off. I can tolerate the stinging. Relieved there's no active bleeding, I'm able to keep my feet still while she dresses them. While she's at it, I get looked over for bruising. The bruising she finds gets recorded on a body audit form.

Mary assesses the hematoma on the top of my head and says, "Where did you think you were going?" After that and neuro checks, she pronounces me "fit to live another day."

All through this exam, no privacy curtains are pulled. Lucy is once again subjected to the naked front and back of me. Maybe privacy is not an issue behind the doors. I decide to call Mary on this omission, just for a drill.

When I mention "behind the doors," Mary perks up. "How do you know to call this wing 'behind the doors'? It hasn't been called that for ten years. This wing is Perry's Alzheimer's Unit after Alice Perry, our founder and current administrator. So, Jane Doe, how is it that you know to call this 'behind the doors'?"

I dummy up, thinking I've made a large mistake. They will know I was here before the change if the name of this unit was changed ten years ago. They'll know there must be a record, or someone may recognize me. I knew Alice Perry twenty years ago. She must be over eighty years old, at least. If she is still running this place, there's a big chance she'll recognize me.

Breaking the silence, Mary says, "I'll bet that aide called this 'behind the doors.' She'll deny it, though. Perry should catch her. From now on, this is the PA Unit and only the PA."

Realizing I just got a very lucky break makes me weak with relief. I'm absolutely sure I will forget to call this hall "the PA Unit" the minute Mary walks out of my door, but she inadvertently gave me the perfect out. She knows the aides call this 'behind the doors' out of her hearing. If I get caught, I can always say "behind the doors" is what it's called by everyone who works back here. Before Mary gathers up her things and leaves, I find as strong a voice as I can. "On second thought, I think I need to see bookkeeping instead of bothering … who did you say? Ah, Mrs. Perry. Yes, bookkeeping will be able to help me."

"Whatever. Just get cleaned up before you gag Lucy. The aide will help you walk in the hall. If your gait is steady, and balance is good, you may be up ad lib in your room only. Your room only—is that clear?" Mary says, walking out the door.

I do not expect that Lucy understood the exchange between Mary and me, but she mumbles softly, "11-20-2-10-24, 11-20-2-10-24," and lets out a full belly laugh.

Stunned, I find myself laughing with her. "Lucy, I don't know what you're saying or how you managed to figure out the conversation, but I believe that somehow you also think my seeing Perry is a mistake."

Lucy nods. She knows.

Mary does return with two Tylenol and informs me that Stalinsky from accounting will see me after lunch. Basilar body function has taken such paramount focus, all I hear is "lunch." Mary places a water pitcher on my bedside table and says, "Drink or I will have to insert an IV," before leaving our room again. Being tied to an IV pole would be an unbelievable inconvenience. The water is cold and tastes sweet. Knowing what a medical crisis fluid overload is, I sip the water, restraining myself from chugging the whole pitcher. The source of my uncertainty is a failing body. My getting a grip on the slippery present blocks many pathways. Not knowing how long I was unaware of myself and surroundings poses many questions; when did I last have a bowel movement? Did I lose my shoes? How can I get the medication I need to control this rheumatoid arthritis I'm plagued with? I have money. Can I solicit the activity staff to buy me some decent clothes? So once the aide has checked my ability to walk unaided I'll be allowed up, ad lib, but in this room only. How long will it take before I get hallway privileges?

I expect to experience "prisoner syndrome": total dependence on "the joint" for all my needs (physical and emotional). Barriers exist: locked doors, twenty-four-hour monitoring, and rules, rules, rules. I know from past experience, from watching residents succumb to the will of the joint, how much mental focus it will take to overcome this disabling thought process. In order for my individuality to survive, I will need mental strength and will. Whenever someone says "nursing home patient," the image of a white-haired lady with glasses sitting in a wheelchair with a white cardigan sweater comes to mind. Never do you think of a well-dressed, independent, ambulating individual. Of course, the latter would not be confined to a nursing home—unless, the thought occurs to me, the latter patient has early dementia with periods of lucidness. Hopefully, that's how I will survive.

The next thought tugs at me, raising my anxiety. The money! If I go to accounting and plunk down full payment for my confinement in advance, I will certainly call unwanted attention to myself. Large amounts of cash can be traced. The fact-or-fiction mill will make all kinds of speculations. Where did the money come from? How much is left, and most importantly, where is the cash stashed? I will risk discovery. I didn't come this far to be defeated. Most of the money can't stay in my Underwood case beyond today. The housekeeper will find my case. I'll have to go to accounting with the cash and risk probable discovery. I'm stopped, trapped. I can't think of one safe way out of the overwhelming problem. I admit to being more than a little frightened. The local constabulary could incarcerate me, holding me for trial, where I would have to tell "the whole truth." That can't happen.

These thoughts swirl in my brain. Feeling like an old fool who has outsmarted herself, I curl in a fetal position on my bed. Nearly moaning out loud, I'm overcome by the willies. I cannot think beyond getting caught. If only Lucy could help me. But no, even if she could, I'd never be able to understand her.

Chapter Six

As if by magic, the bath aide appears, pushing a wheelchair into our room. Sounding a little apprehensive, she says, "Are you sick?" Knowing that word travels fast around here, I just shrug my shoulders. "Okay then, let's get you up. It will be lunchtime before we get this job finished. Roll over so I can put plastic bags over your foot dressings. First job is the hardest, so up you go and in the wheelchair. I'm reading here that Nurse Mary wrote in your chart, 'no ambulating in the halls.'" She eyes me with a certain knowing, like I'm the new troublemaker on the floor. "Are you going to talk to me, or do I get help to do this?" Again, I just shrug my shoulders since I don't feel like talking anyway. It's only ten in the morning, and already I'm ready for a nap, but if I don't speak up, I'll soon be in the shower, completely naked, with this know-nothing, pattering aide. That's certainly not going to happen. So I find my voice.

I grab her arm and pull her as close as I dare. Trying not to sound like I'm begging, I do my best to set her straight. "Let's understand this right off, you talkative little girl," I say in a whisper that only she can hear. "I'm *not* going to shower with you in there. Understand me? You get me there, and I'll wash myself." I manage to get the words out before dissolving into silent tears.

She wriggles free from my pathetic grasp. Who am I kidding, really, when it comes to arm strength? She eyes me again with that look before delivering her retort. "I will do whatever it takes to get the job done, Miss Doe." She leans in to whisper in my ear. "What I can promise is you will be clean when I'm done." And with that she helps me into the wheelchair, officially closing the argument. "Now don't be crazy and jump out of this wheelchair, Miss Doe. It doesn't make sense to get hurt, okay?"

The bath aide rolls me out the door and starts down the hall. I know the bath complex is off the unit, through the doors to the nurses' station and a few doors down the B-wing hall. Suddenly, I'm filled with panic and say out loud, "Stop! Take me back to my room. What if housekeeping comes?"

She turns the wheelchair to face her. "So what? I'm sure housekeeping can clean your room without your help. Besides, we won't be gone very long. If you're ever going to adjust to being here, you're going to have to trust me. The sooner we get done, the sooner you'll get back. Relax, nervous Nellie," she said, almost giggling.

My brain screams, and the interior scream comes right out of my mouth before I know what I'm doing. While I scream nonsense, inside my head I yell, *Oh yeah, maybe the housekeeper will steal the money, and they will put her in jail instead of me, or we'll both end up in a jail cell.* And now I'm the one giggling. First I'm screaming; then I'm laughing for no apparent reason. Maybe I do belong "behind the doors," for real. I've got to get control of this before I actually go crazy. I make a mental note to figure out how to keep sane as I get wheeled down the hallway.

The aide gives a big sigh behind me. She leans down as she pushes the chair and whispers, "I wonder when the psychiatrist makes rounds next. You need help."

I notice that there are no nurses behind the station as we pass the half door that leads to their desk and the med room. Ahead and to my left is the residents' lounge. Back when I was here, it was a smoking lounge, but I'll bet no longer. I wonder if the staff—probably the nursing aides—take residents outside to smoke. It might be worth taking up smoking just to get outside for fresh air. But what a hassle that would be. I think better of that decision. If I make it beyond today, my only goal is to avoid the lookie-loos. Again, I giggle out loud. The bath aide sighs again. I kind of like driving her crazy. It gives me something to do.

As I wait outside the bath complex while the bath aide gathers towels from a nearby linen cart, Mary the nurse walks by. "Pat, I want a good skin report before you go to lunch," she says without pausing. *Report? Ha!* I think. The definition of a report is no more than this: professional fact-gathering communication that often leads to giving false impressions of residents to influence nurses to act on information that's little more than gossip. For instance, Pat the bath aide might report, "Skin looks good, nervous attitude, inappropriate laughing, enjoyed shower, but not exactly a relaxing experience, unfriendly, but not combative, very, very dirty. Where *did* she come from?" And by this, she would mean, "What spaceship landed her here with me as her bath aide?"

Pat asks me to stay right where I am while she talks with the aide on B-wing about finding some clothes for after my shower. *Where would I go?* I think so loudly that I hope she can hear me. But I can think of many places I want to go—back to my room for one, to dig out my Underwood and run, Jane Doe, run. But I don't go anywhere. I just sit there with my head hanging down as though I'm really interested in my lap.

Pat returns and says, "We're in luck." I tear my mind away from the thought that this "luck" is probably that a resident about my size just died, and the family donated her clothes. I'm anxious to get on with it. She pushes me through the shower door. The walls are tiled in small squares of split-pea yellow with an occasional white one thrown in for decorative taste. Twelve-inch gray square tiles line the floor, and a shower chair with a handheld showerhead stands ready for me. *Oh joy*, I think. *Let the games begin.*

Pat turns the shower on to get the water warm and turns toward me with an expectant look. Now comes the disrobing. The vulnerability of nakedness in front of other humans causes me flaming indignity. I'm almost paralyzed with fear in the moments before the warm water covers nakedness and I let the embarrassment pass. Pat has removed the shower chair so that I can stand under the showerhead. She hands me a washcloth bubbly with soap and says, "I'll get your back." It's moments like this that make residents dependent. There is nothing more sticking than gratitude. We are so thankful for these human moments. So much so that I can feel this moment reduce me to dependence, the very dependence that I was fighting so hard against. The warm water and soap feel like no other gifts I've received in my life. And to my surprise, Pat is patient as my gift goes on and on, almost as long as I want. Fortunately for me, this isn't "splash-splash and you're done." But my time runs out eventually, and she signals my shower is coming to an end as she puts shampoo in my hair and rubs my scalp vigorously with her fingertips. I mumble feebly, "I need conditioner." Pat coos back gently, "The shampoo the nursing home uses has conditioner in it." Abruptly after the rinse of my hair, the water is turned off.

"All done," she says in a singsong way and puts a towel over my head. Pat tells me to step out of the shower stall and then wraps me in a bath blanket, sits me in the wheelchair, and kneels before me to cut my nails. She says, "How do you manage to cut them yourself? Your hands are so arthritic. They are practically paralyzed."

Looking her in the eyes, I say kind of menacingly, "I bite them." Did I imagine it, or did she flinch at the word "bite"?

She begins to blow-dry my hair. The B-wing aide arrives with my new-used clothes. Folded on top of a two-piece sweat suit are (I can't believe my eyes) an actual bra and white panties. If they anywhere near fit me, I'll be in ecstasy! Socks? I do believe I spot socks as well. Aloud I mumble, "Is that it?"

Pat replies in her most patronizing voice, "Yes, but to this you say thank you."

Dressed in clothes that cover most of my shyness, with clean skin and washed hair, I feel like a queen. If I didn't have this anxious knot swelling in my stomach, I would probably blubber and confess all. But the reality is that I'm so worried about where my typewriter—a.k.a money—is that I can only just restrain myself from getting up and running back the way I came. As I succumb to the urge to run and start to rise out of the wheelchair, Pat reads my mind and exclaims loudly, "Oh no, you don't! Not without me."

"I want to go back to my room now! I have to go back to my room, so get me there," I beg, stamping my feet up and down in spite of the pain it causes my cut-up feet.

"All right! All right! Just hold your shirt on, and we'll go. What's your hurry anyway? Your room is not going anywhere. It's still a half hour before lunch," she says, beginning to push me up the hall.

As we turn the corner by the nurses' station, a man walks toward me. He has a gait belt on, and a nurses' aide is assisting him as he "ambulates" in the hallway. The man is tall, maybe six feet. He has snowy white, wavy hair. Except for crow's feet that make his dark eyes seem humorous, his face is unlined. It's his ears that I can't take my eyes from. The pinnae come to a point much an elf's ears. As he passes me on my left, my heart flutters in terror, and I stop breathing for more than a few seconds. He turns to look at me, and there is no light in his eyes. They are as dead as a corpse. After seeing the horror in my own eyes, he laughs a hollow laugh and stage-whispers, "Boo!" I know my already pale face is blanched as I put my shaky hands to my mouth to muffle a scream.

"Don't scare the poor new lady, Joseph," says his aide, and they keep walking—thankfully, away from the direction my aide and I are going.

"Who is that man? Who is that man? Who is that man?" I stutter when I can speak.

Pat pats me on the back. "Not to worry. That's just Joseph Wirm. He has a room two doors down the hall from you and Lucy … Why, no-name Jane, you're shaking. Mr. Wirm isn't going to hurt you," she says as we go through the doors into the behavior unit.

As I round the corner to my room, all fear of Wirm vanishes. It's replaced by another fear. Sitting on my bedside table, out of my hiding place, is my Underwood.

"Well, here you are. She's all fluffed, dried, and folded, Lucy. Must say she smells a lot better—and just in time for lunch too. I'll just take you two to the dining room and get you set up."

Unable to stop myself, I shout, "No dining room!" I shout it so loud that Lucy jumps in her wheelchair. Pat backs out of the door without another word. She's probably off to get the nurse. "Oh, shit," I hiss. "Now I've done it, Lucy. It was nice knowing you."

Sure enough, no sooner than the thought crosses my mind, Mary shows up with a small white tablet cupped in one hand and a

Dixie cup of water in the other. I don't have to guess to know what's in the medication cup: Ativan.

"A little out of control, are you? This will settle you down." She holds out the medication.

I realize that I could knock it out of her hand, but knowing the routine, she would be back with two aides to hold me still while she injected Ativan right into my deltoid. I'd be out before they got me in bed and be out for at least all day. I may not come to until tomorrow morning, the typewriter case left vulnerable for anyone to tamper with, the money left unprotected, and no appointment with accounting to get on with this madness; and to my rumbling gut's dismay, no lunch and maybe no supper as well. It would be like being a naughty little kid, sent to my room with no supper. I weigh my options and decide that under no circumstances is that medication entering this old lady's body.

Attempting to disarm Mary, I say in my calmest, sweetest voice, "I don't think that will be necessary. I'm really okay. I just don't want to eat in the dining room today. I don't want to miss my appointment with accounting, and the aide said I should wait here. I have to be here when she comes for me, don't I? What I could use is a couple of Tylenol. My feet are starting to hurt. That's what is making me so jumpy."

It works. Thank the heavens the dummy buys it, though she looks doubtful. She heads out the door to get the Tylenol or to blow my cover and ask the aide what she might have said. Either way I have a moment, and that's all I need to survey the damage.

Walking over to inspect the Underwood's case, I ask Lucy, "Did anyone open this case while I was gone?" No answer, of course. Lucy looks at me with her piercing blue eyes. "I'm sorry I yelled and scared you, Lucy. I didn't mean to, honestly." With sort of a nod of appreciation, Lucy seems to accept my apology.

Mary shows up with the Tylenol. She doesn't say anything as she wheels Lucy out of the room to the dining room across the hall. From the wonderful smells wafting across hallway, I know the food trays must be up from the kitchen.

Of course, my first impulse is to open the Underwood's locked chamber to see if the money remains undiscovered, but knowing my lunch tray will soon be coming through the door to my room, I move the case onto my bed instead. I take in every inch of the cover, and my breath catches. I notice scratch marks by the lock—scratch marks I don't remember being there—and it makes my heart hammer against my chest. The possibility that the money is still there now seems remote. What will I do if the money comes up missing? Where would I go from here with no money and no identification? The acid fear in my gut is replaced by bright red anger. Gone is the sloppy apathy induced by my shower. The "help me, help me, hide me" feelings that I overcame when I closed the door of that old jalopy and headed north are once again renewed. Anger, pushing fear from my psyche, prompts me to act. Hands shaking, with no thought of the aide bringing lunch any minute, I fit my right thumb on the hook-lock that reads my thumbprint. I did this countless times back in my apartment, practicing for this moment. I hear the lock click just as the aide arrives with lunch. With my back to her, covering most of what I'm doing, I tell her in the calmest voice possible, "Please leave the tray on the bedside table."

She says idly, almost like a hash and egg waitress, "Do you want coffee with lunch?"

Even though my mouth waters yes, I can only focus on getting her to leave my room. "No. No, thank you."

Leaving the room without even turning back, she says over her shoulder, "Well, okay. If you need anything, put your light on."

Need anything? I need the money, all two hundred thousand of it, to be there under the fake bottom of my typewriter in the manila envelope, untouched. My acid anger can only be quenched by a "calm down and eat your lunch" approach. For the moment, while I eat lunch, I will try to forget the money. I will do what's needed most. I will calmly eat lunch. Chortling out loud, I ignore the unlocked case and open my napkin, pick up my fork, and pause to give thanks. Ambrosia, food of the gods, sustenance—I marvel at how my anxiety is placated by food.

I'm the plump elder always wishing away twenty extra pounds. Feeling my abdomen, a once tubby tummy, I sense the recent weight loss. There on the tray, in my state of mind, is food I would pay a lot of money for. Lord love a duck. I might as well enjoy the chicken, the creamy sliced potatoes, the green beans, the roll, and a slice of apple pie. At peace with my ever-pressing problems, I will try to make lunch last. I put off for later all the things that press in on my future.

I eat most of the chicken, some of the potatoes, and all of the green beans and leave the roll. So unlike me, I have no room for the pie. I drink the glass of water and sip some kind of red juice—cranberry, I think. I am satiated for the first time since leaving my "eat anytime I want" other life.

Just as I turn my attention to the matter of the money, an aide arrives, quickly picking up my tray as she asks, "Have enough?" Before I can answer, she's gone.

So much for "I'll have the pie later," I think as she disappears with my tray.

Relieved that the thumbprint lock worked like a charm, I click open the case. I have to stand to remove the Underwood typewriter and the false bottom. There below is the stuffed manila envelope, just as I last saw it back when I made all these careful plans. The seal on the envelope is innocent looking. Breaking the seal, I peer in at the money that not fifteen minutes ago was making me crazy. I paper-clipped bills to equal a thousand dollars and rubber-banded twenty packs together, and the packs are all there. These twenty packs equal all the savings I have. Now, not only do I have to give most of it away; I have to convince the accounting person to accept it as a payment for one year of nursing home room and board. I pray I have covered all of my bases, and the money is not traceable. When I started this cloak-and-dagger adventure, I split the two hundred thousand between ten banks and slowly, over roughly a year's time, withdrew two thousand dollars a month from each. From a bank's accounting perspective, I was merely supplementing my social security with a few thousand a month. With the extra money I took from an additional savings account, I paid five hundred cash for the car and an additional fifteen thousand for the run-down house that

I'm using as a mailbox. Twenty-three thousand, I left taped with the note under my desk—insurance money, I call it. And the few hundred I intended to leave at the Crow's nest left the balance of two thousand I put in the bottom of my typewriter. I feel confident none of the money can be traced: maybe not 100 percent confident, but surely 90 percent.

I have no clue how I will convince accounting to accept this payment. I feel pressed to come up with a workable plan before the question is broached. The intent to pull this off will have to be laced with some convincing craziness. Without a doubt, too much, and I'll be shipped out of here. Too little, and I may not be able to push her into accepting the plan. Half-sane, that's the key. Half-crazy is more like it.

I walk over to the door of my room and lean out. "Hello, I'm ready! Where's my escort?" I shout down the hall. Clutching the manila envelope to my chest, I stand poised by the door to wait. A nurses' aide wheels Lucy across the hall from the dining room and parks her by her bed. When she starts to leave, I get impatient with her lack of skills. I step in front of the door before she can step out of it and admonish her, "You will toilet Lucy before you leave, right?"

The aide gives me an "I can just tolerate you" look. She says, "Lucy wears a brief, a diaper. Get it? She will be changed before her aide lays her down for naptime. Now out of my way. I'm in a hurry."

Calmly, I try for a teaching moment. "If you toilet her now, she probably won't have to be changed later. So do yourself a favor. Save time and Lucy's dignity. I think that's called a twofer," I retort, still standing in the doorway.

Just as I'm preparing myself for more bullying, another aide appears behind me. "Are you ready to meet the lady who takes care of kicking freeloaders out of the nursing home?"

Startled, I exclaim, "We'll see about that!"

The aide who delivered Lucy takes this chance to leave. Walking past me, she grumbles, "Who are you anyway?"

Not to be daunted, I get the last word in before stepping into the hallway. "I see I have work to do here."

Chapter Seven

I remember now that accounting is in another building. The aide walks me through the doors of the behavior unit, past the nurses' station, and down the 600s hall to a set of doors leading outside. As she punches the keyed alarm, I try to memorize the code, but her fingers move too fast. Damn! We move through this set of doors to the exit foyer, and then she pushes a second set of doors to the outside.

I have forgotten its spring. How did I forget so easily what time of year it is? It's a coveted warm April day. I stand still for a moment, just breathing the fresh air. Right here in this moment, unlocked, is the one last chance that I have to fess up and escape. I could take my identity back and be gone before supper. But how could I undo all that I did while driving the back roads to get here—mile by mile, shedding my other self, brainwashing my mind for survival? I just can't go back to doing nothing until I die. Doing what I started is the only way to stave off death for another year, maybe not the lying-in-a-coffin kind of death, but the death of my creative self. This adventure, as crazy as it seems, is my one moment to write my name on something: to set the record straight on this small town.

"My instructions are to get you there. The rest of my work is being done for me, so if all you want to do is daydream in the sun, have at it. I couldn't care less." The aide's diatribe jerks me back to here and now.

I remember as I gaze at the next set of doors. It's all coming back to me now. The small brown building houses bookkeeping on the first floor. On the second floor is Perry's apartment when she's in town. Realizing it would be prudent to get out of sight of the apartment windows and into the accounting office with the doors closed, I walk as fast as my injured feet will go. When the sidewalk splits, I take the right one leading to the back side door.

The aide walks me through the door into the small office. Sitting at the desk facing me is someone I know, or knew twenty years ago. I don't recognize the name on the name tag. I don't know a Mrs. Stalinsky, but I'm almost sure this woman was the scheduling aide twenty years ago. Expecting her to look up, say my name, call my bluff, and announce game over, I stand barely breathing. She looks up from the figures she's adding and says, "What can I do for you?"

I make an attempt at coherent speech, but I utter a sort of squawk instead. I take a deep breath. Starting over, I say, "To start with, you can ask this aide to leave. This is a private conversation." I plunk down in the chair across from her and hang my head, staring at the manila envelope in my lap.

"Okay, Jean, but don't go very far in case I need you," Mrs. Stalinsky says without sounding unkind. "Shut the door while you're at it."

I first make sure the door closes, and then while I still have the nerve, I say with all the confidence I can muster, "I'm here to give you enough money to pay for a year in advance for room, board, and nursing care at Cre Falls Nursing Home." Opening my envelope, I put all the money in front of me on the desk.

Everything I did to get here is now on the line. Everything. It now lays in the hands of this woman, a woman who makes decisions based on policy and procedures and not on frantic-looking residents who present cash and outrageous requests. During my life I have struggled with less money more often than I have felt at ease with enough of the stuff. My money philosophy has been that money is only worth using to buy what you want, not for squirreling away for a time of need. My late husband managed to keep enough money out of my hands to have a house to sell for the cash, and the children said, "There, you have enough, if you're conservative for the rest of your life." I rented a nice, safe apartment where I did nice, safe things until enviably I would die with money left over. Knowing this has pushed me toward this risky gamble with my future. And it is mostly the reason I'm sitting in this chair, waiting for this woman to decide my fate like a judge.

Whether anyone reads this story I will write matters little to me. What matters is that I actually write the tale in my own words. Accomplishing this feat of literary skill is about to cost me two hundred thousand dollars. It's really no large fortune, but it's my fortune, the largest I've ever amassed. Never before in my sixty-seven years have I had to second-guess decisions or feel anxious about whether or not I can physically cope. Therefore, my not snatching back the money and making a run (maybe not a run, but at least a walk) for the door tells, I think, of my courage. At the very least it tells of my desperation to finish what I came to do.

Stalinsky looks at me over her cheaters. "I can do what for you? Are you going to tell me about all this money, or should I call security so you can tell them?"

I pop up out of the chair. Leaning over her desk, I say, "Don't rush me and don't get grabby. I have something to say, and I have conditions. You can take fifteen minutes to do right by me, or I'll take my money up the highway to Perry's competitor. What do you say? Do you have fifteen minutes?"

Stalinsky puts up her hand and says, "Calm down!" Her face is flushed, and the hand she holds out is shaking a little. She reaches for the phone. I realize that, knowing the residents of "behind the doors" have a reputation for occasionally being out of control, she isn't taking any chances.

"Okay, okay. Please, hear me out. Put down the phone. I'm here to solve your problem and mine. I don't want you to mistrust me. Please!" I beg. Sitting back down in the chair, I put my face in my hands, managing real tears.

Taking her hands from the phone, she calmly says, "Let's start over. What can I do for you?"

I imagine I've never looked more pathetic or so old. My hands are gnarled with arthritis, and tears are making tracks down my lined face. My hair is sticking up in a fuzzy halo around my head, and I'm wearing some dead resident's clothes. Taking a deep breath,

I say again, "I want to make payment in full for one year of room and board behind the doors in the behavioral unit." Saying this out loud sounds crazy, but there it is.

"Do you know that private-pay, double-room occupancy is four hundred dollars a day? That's two thousand eight hundred dollars a week. You would have to give me, let's see … twenty-eight hundred times fifty-two weeks is $145,600. Why would you want to use all of your money doing this?"

I shrug my shoulders. I can't at that moment give her a reason, even though thousands of reasons instantly race through my mind.

"Well, give me your name and social security number, and I can at least get you ninety days Medicare-paid. If you insist on being private pay, I could get you another room on a different wing, possibly even a private room. I really can't accept all your money in advance. Not even creative bookkeeping can change this state-mandated rule. The one thing I can do is put your money in the safe for two weeks. Then you'll have to get it and make other arrangements."

I thought this might happen. It's funny how rules can be so set in stone. With experience on my side, it's now my turn. I have to win her over, armed with one possible way to accomplish the impossible. "You could set up a trust account. The nursing home could become guardian administrators of my account. The National Bank could make automatic monthly payments to the nursing home from this account, sending statements to me using my room number. The state will accept these arrangements."

She is clearly surprised by this proposal, but still I can see that she is weighing it as a possibility. "It won't be as simple as you think," Stalinsky challenges. "I will have to get authorizations from the administrator, and you will have to sign guardianship papers. This also requires a witness to your signature who is not an employee of the nursing home."

I didn't think about this detail, which puts me a box: a box with no airholes. What can I possibly do? Keeping my true identity secret is one of the most important aspects, if not the single most important, of this whole plan. My mind just won't come up with an answer. I'm an old lady with an old brain, and I'm stuck.

Stalinsky breaks the silence. "There is one option. I could call activities and get a volunteer over here to be a witness. I do have guardianship forms and the necessary asset account forms that can be filed with the National Bank. We could, as you stated, do an automatic withdrawal. Keep in mind, if the room fees go up, we would have to redo the agreement. Bank statements would be sent to you, as you say. This is an unusual arrangement and might raise flags, so it's up to you if you want to proceed."

I can see she's getting nervous. I also can see I'm pushing too hard, beginning to appear too "with it." "Yes, get a volunteer." Putting my pitiful gnarled hands over my eyes, I beg, "Please, I can't stand all these complications. Help me solve this problem. I know I can't do this without your help."

With this, I crack her. No one likes to see an old lady cry. Coming around her desk, Stalinsky puts her arms around me. "We can get this done right now. I'll make some phone calls to get the ball rolling. Would you like something to drink while you're waiting?"

Thinking about the coffee that I didn't get at lunch, I mumble, "Coffee would be nice." Before she summons the aide, I put the money back in the manila envelope. By this time my backside is numb, so I stand up to let the blood circulate. Pacing the office, I notice that instead of art prints, Stalinsky has chosen personal pictures to make the walls of her office interesting. I recognize a picture taken some years ago of her and two young children. There's another of her accepting an award from none other than Perry.

Coffee arrives in the hands of Jean, in one of those hospital-grade brown plastic cups. What I wouldn't do for a proper glass mug with a large handle that allows me to get my gnarled fingers around it. It's these thoughts that make me appear absorbed in my coffee. Picking up the phone, Stalinsky has a short conversation with activities. "Send a volunteer over to the accounting office as soon as possible. After a pause she says, "Yes Maureen will do." She hangs up without a good-bye. Then she puts the receiver back up to her ear as she punches the keypad again. I count the finger punches: the number nine for an outside line and seven more numbers. A brief conversation with the bank confirms the information she gave me about the account setup. One more phone call to make. When I realize that she is beginning to dial Perry's extension, I put my hand over the phone's hang-up, ending her connection.

"No one—I mean, no one—is to know of this confidential meeting or its outcome. What information I have given you is between you and me. I must exercise my state-given right to privacy. I want a signed statement that states my right to confidentiality, signed by you and the volunteer you just summoned. I will write a similar statement that gives you specific information you can use about this meeting. It won't stop gossip, but gossip without facts will go away as it always does in time."

Stalinsky hesitates, her eyes narrowing slightly as she hangs up the phone. I expect the next words out of her mouth to be "This meeting is over." Waiting without breathing is too much for this old lady. So I say as humbly as I can muster, "Please." I know very well that a decision involving two hundred thousand dollars must be approved by Perry. I also know my privacy is mandated by the state. "You may have to expose the receipt of the money, but you can keep the rest of my information confidential. You don't have to reveal admission information, what I look like, or any pertinent information that might identify me. I know this is part of the nursing home's policy."

Stalinsky rubs her forehead as if trying to stop a headache. The silence seems to stretch on for hours. Finally Stalinsky admits defeat. "I will go along with this nursing home guardianship just as planned, but I will not withhold the receipt of this sum of money from administration, a.k.a. Mrs. Perry. As a matter of fact, I would call her right now in spite of your threats about your rights except I just remembered she already left for Guadalajara yesterday for her annual three-month vacation. You can rest assured that when she returns, all this will be reported. In the meantime, I will be talking to the assistant administrator, Anthony Haffel. You are a resident here, you occupy a room, and you have the money, so you will pay. The means by which this is accomplished will be exactly as we discussed. It's as simple as that."

Just as she is making life clear for me, there's a knock on the door—the volunteer, I suppose. All this business is making me so exhausted that my thinking is getting murky. Keeping all my ducks in a row is getting difficult. The soft knock on the door opens to a stocky, grey haired woman with a flat open face. A trusting smile and twinkling blue eyes completes the image of Mrs. Santa Clause.

"Come in, Maureen," Stalinsky calls to the woman already in the office. "To explain why you're here, I need you to witness this resident's signature on this guardianship paper. There's a statement that you are not an employee of Cre Nursing Home. The resident signs on this line, and you sign on the line below her signature." As Stalinsky slides the paper across the desk in front of me, I take a deep breath.

Hoping for the best, I pick up the pen and mark an "X" on the line. Maureen takes the pen and signs on the line under mine and then hands the paper to Stalinsky. My brain stutters as the expected roar comes out of Stalinsky's mouth.

"Oh good God, will you stop wasting my time? An 'X' is not your name. If you can't write your name, tell me what it is, and I'll write it for you below the 'X.'" Stalinsky clenches her teeth, waiting for my cooperation.

"I can't. I don't … I don't know …" I trail off, wailing and looking pathetic with my hand over my mouth.

"That's okay, honey," Maureen says, patting my shoulder. "A lot of seniors your age can't write, or did you forget how? Did you forget your name?"

Face flushed and appearing at the end of her rope, Stalinsky exhales loudly. "I'll take care of this, Maureen. Thank you for helping out." She gets up and leads Maureen out the door. After pausing for a moment, she calmly shuts the door again.

While settling back in her chair, she says, practically hissing, "If this is a game, it seems you've won. Hand me the manila envelope." Taking the money out, she stacks it in thousands, hundreds, fifties, and twenties. "You know a trace has to be put on this money? In the meantime, it will be banked subject to Mr. Haffel's approval." She counts out $145,600. "You have $54,400 left. What am I supposed to do with the balance?"

"If it wouldn't be too much trouble, my account needs to pay for prescription medication, doctor visits, and other medical needs. I also have a list of personal things that activities should purchase for me. The account balance will cover all of my needs. I need shoes. Seems I lost mine. I'll also need clothes, underwear, lotion, and stuff. It's all on the list," I say, taking a list out of my sweat suit pocket. "I'm sorry for adding to your bookkeeping, but I don't feel comfortable having money in my room. Oh, and one more thing. I will not change rooms. I need to be behind the doors. The emergency room doctor said I have difficulty controlling myself during emotional situations. He said I will benefit from the lack of stress. Living in the behavior unit rather than in the mainstream nursing home will provide that." I slide my list across to her and almost snicker.

By this time, Stalinsky looks thoroughly annoyed. "This is how this will go," she says, pushing the list back my direction. "I'll contact activities about your needs. They will get in touch with you. I'll authorize money from your account for payment. Medical and prescription bills will be paid from this office. Last, your room and board will be deducted monthly." She counts the money again and writes a receipt while we sit in total silence except for the sounds outside the window. *The birds are singing*, I note mentally. *The orioles and grosbeaks, finches, and water birds will all be coming back soon.* Tearing the receipt out of a book and tearing me away from my daydream, she sets the receipt on the desk where I can reach it. This concludes our meeting, obviously.

Feeling I just skated through by my skinny, skin, skin, I decide a rapid exit is prudent. "Thank you for helping me. Now I have to pee. Please call the aide." All this I say while getting out of my chair with difficulty. Pee—you would think it would be like an express calling card, but when you're old, and you gotta go, everyone but nursing pays attention.

As predicted, Stalinsky takes her time getting out of her chair and calling for Jean. "Take Madam X to the bathroom and then stop at activities before getting her back to her room. Thank you."

Stepping over to a door in the hall, Jean responds, "Aw, sure." She gives me a "get in there" gesture with a slight bow. With the air of "thank you very much," I half-bow back. I'm sure this enrages Stalinsky, but what's done is done. She can't go back now. Besides, one year, paid in full. Stalinsky will get a pat on the back, and I'll get exactly the time I need. It's a win-win.

The coffee is doing a number on my bladder, so I scurry to the bathroom. Feeling pretty smug that I managed to put the money in a safe place and have arranged to get medication for this damn arthritis, not to mention the upgrade in my wardrobe, I'm ready. Really ready to search out the stories and write the book that has been rattling around in my brain for the past twenty years. Heading out the door after I finish in the bathroom, I turn to Jean and tell her I have two more stops to make.

"You better make it snappy," she says. "Its two thirty and I'm off at three. Where do you have to go?"

"I'm too exhausted for this outing to take much longer," I say with a loud exhale. "But next we have to stop by the activities department and then a quick stop at the beauty shop. I'll be out of your hair well before you need to punch out." The manila envelope clutched in my gnarled hands now contains a few twenty-dollar bills and the shopping list. On the back of the needs list, Stalinsky wrote instructions for payment.

Jean and I walk in silence. She leads me around to the first-floor main entrance and down the hall to activities. The activity aide is busy cleaning up a recent project. I take out my list and tell her if she has any questions, I'll be in my room. I say with a smile, "That's the PA Unit, room number 802. You know, I'm in with Lucy."

Looking at the list, she says without looking up, "You mean 'behind the doors" "This is a pretty long list. You sure you can pay for this? I'll need sizes. Hope you don't need this by tomorrow."

Sighing, I tell her to see me in my room or talk to Stalinsky about more money. "I don't need this stuff tomorrow, but I do need shoes very soon. I'm outta here."

The elevator is just down the hall past the first-floor nurses' station. I realize I'm just going to make it. My feet are aching, and my right hip joint is starting to scream. After pushing the second-floor button, Jean turns to me. "You look beat. I'll drop off your money at the beauty shop, but you better get off your feet, the sooner the better.

Digging the last twenty out, I hold fast to the envelope. Who knows, it may come in handy. It may even hold pages of a book in progress soon. Smiling at that thought, I hand Jean the last of my money.

"You look pleased with yourself," she says, arching her eyebrows, "and I must say done in. Not much further to go."

The elevator arrives at the second floor, and the doors open. Passing through the doors, I touch her arm lightly. "I can take it from here. Thank you for being so patient with me. Mission accomplished. Just in time for you to punch out. I'm on my way to a nap." Turning, I head down the hall.

The door to our room is open. Lucy looks peaceful, sleeping. I quietly close the door so that I don't disturb her and climb into bed with a deep sigh. I think I'll fall asleep before my brain can utter one more thought. So for the next two hours, I sleep the sleep of the self-satisfied.

Chapter Eight

Slowly pushing my way out of foggy sleep, I become aware of being watched. Lucy is up in her wheelchair, sitting at the foot of my bed. She looks anxious and a little fearful. Yawning and stretching, I tell Lucy everything worked out just fine. But I didn't tell her what I had to do or about the money, so why do I suppose she knows? Could be she heard what the aide said about my getting kicked out of the nursing home if I was a freeloader. Lucy looks expectant, like she wants to tell me something. Once again, I wonder what trauma has left Lucy with only numbers as speech. It's her only way of communicating. Revelation thuds me on the head. That's exactly it! Her numbers are words or, at the very least, something like words. By her body language, I can tell she has a lot to say.

Just as I am about to explore where this could be going, an aide pops her head in the door to announce supper trays are up. At the mention of food, I'm on the move toward the bathroom to tidy up my bed head, splash some cold water on my face, and wash my hands. I push Lucy to the dining room to have supper with her at her table. I'm looking forward to having my first look at my hall mates anyway. Now that I know I'll be here for at least the next eleven months, I might as well get acquainted with my neighbors.

Aware that I'm probably breaking the rules by pushing Lucy's wheelchair, I still wheel her into the dining room, saying, "Where does Lucy sit?"

Most everyone looks up, and for an awkward moment, the dining room is silent. Then that man, that Joseph Wirm, stands and points to the chair next to his. He says, "Why, Lucy is privileged to sit at my table. Isn't that so, Lucy?"

Lucy squirms in her wheelchair, trying to see my face, and moans softly. So quietly I barely hear her, she hisses, "7-4-11-11 13-14." Able to see the distressed look on her face, I get the message.

"I'm with you, Lucy," I say, spotting another table across the room from Wirm. "We'll sit with this other gentleman unless we're told to move." As we approach the other table, Lucy reaches out. She and the other resident touch hands lightly. By the smile she gives him, I'm guessing they know each other, and Lucy is comfortable with his company. Sitting, I announce to the table, "I'm Jane Doe, the newest resident around here." I notice the aide uses a marker to add Lucy and my name to the table assignment sheet.

Lucy's friend searches my face like he's choosing his words. "Jesus Christ," he says with a very questioning tone. I'm absolutely speechless. Trying to keep in mind we're all living "behind the doors," and aberrant behavior is often the rule, I'm still stunned. Thinking I've been somehow insulted or he's angry because I'm inviting myself into his space, I start to stand. Lucy puts her hand on my arm to restrain me. Our man at the table has brown hair with a receding hairline. His face is pale with a noticeable five o'clock shadow. Bushy eyebrows arch above warm brown eyes. Laugh lines wrinkle the corners of his eyes, and I notice that the left side of his mouth is pulled down, indicating perhaps a stroke. It appears that his left hand is splinted because of contractures. It's difficult to estimate how tall he is because he is stooped in his chair. His right hand rests on a quad cane.

He smiles at Lucy and says in the most welcoming voice, "Jesus Christ." Lucy giggles and gives me a knowing look.

I extend my right hand, and he firmly shakes. "I hope you don't mind company for supper?"

He nods, leans his head forward, and says, "Mm, Jesus Christ," apparently indicating that our being at his table is okay.

My first impression was that Jesus Christ is his name, but I see my mistake now. "Jesus Christ" is how he communicates. Unlike Lucy, who I'm sure did not have a stroke, I think our tablemate presents with a very unusual aphasia.

A nurses' aide delivers Lucy's supper tray and prepares to sit down to feed her. Lucy stares at her face and shakes her head. The aide sizes her up. "What's the matter, Lucy? You're not hungry?"

"If you don't mind, I'll help Lucy with supper," I say, jumping at the opportunity for the three of us to be alone. I'm sure there must be rules against my feeding Lucy, but she doesn't have any choking problems. "I really don't mind."

"The nurse is on her way in with medication; ask her," the aide says while walking away. "I'm pretty sure a resident can't feed another resident, especially on this wing."

I'm betting she will say no, but it never hurts to ask. If you don't ask, the answer is always no after all.

The evening nurse, one I've not met, pushes her medication cart through the door. The aide gets her attention and speaks to her loud enough for me to hear the conversation. "Sally, that resident sitting next to Lucy wants to feed her. I told her you had to give her permission first."

"Nice try, but absolutely not," she answers. "Besides, Lucy needs to be encouraged to feed herself. She can do finger foods at least."

Leaving the med cart, Sally comes over to our table and stands over me like a teacher over her kindergarten class. "I want Lucy to try to help herself," she says so loudly that I'm tempted to tell her that I'm crippled, not deaf. Looking at me, she again says, "I'm told you can have Tylenol every four hours if you need it until the doctor calls in orders for something better." She puts two oblong white pills in a med cup on my tray and walks away.

Supper is soup and a full sandwich, some fruit, milk, and a cup of coffee. I notice a cookie in a bag. I pick up one half of Lucy's sandwich and put it in her hand, telling her, "Take a bite. Nurse Sally says it's in your care plan." Lucy smirks. Holding her sandwich, she does just that. The aide looks like she is about to repeat what the nurse said, but before she can scold me, I shrug. "I'm not feeding her. See, she's doing it herself."

Mr. Jesus Christ man snorts out a kind of laugh. The aide snorts back, "Oh, stop encouraging her, Otto. What's with this table tonight? You must be showing off for the new lady."

Otto smiles and through a pinched face gets out a rather singsong "Jesus Christ." It would have been a wolf whistle if he could pucker his lips.

I decided that particular "Jesus Christ" was meant for me, so I blow him a kiss. He blushes almost immediately, and I don't miss the twinkle in his eyes. The identification card on his tray says his name is Otto Jener. Glancing back at Lucy, I notice she has finished almost half the sandwich. I give her a look that indicates "more," and she immediately nods. By now the aide isn't paying attention, so I give Lucy a long swallow of milk. I'm just thinking about how to spoon the soup without getting in trouble when the aide, without even looking at me, says, "Don't even think about it, Jane." I stare at the back of her head and try to burn the word "fine" into her skull. I'm close to sticking out my tongue at her when I think better of it.

As I eat, I become aware of the other residents in the room. Wirm is being boisterous. He has a deep growl to his voice that conjures the image of an angry dog. I notice another aide sitting at his table, encouraging him to keep eating. It could also be a way to keep his voice down. If his mouth is full, then he can't raise hell as loud as when it's empty. Well, maybe he could. He seems like the type who could raise hell mouth full or not.

Without counting the tables, I approximate there to be at least twelve. Some of the tables are empty. More than half have just two residents. Many residents are eating independently, but some require assistance by an aide. The room has nice windows, and I can see trees across the parking lot outside. The walls are covered with homely wallpaper: yellow with a very narrow, off-white pinstripe. It's peeling, revealing cracked glue and old plaster. On the wall by the door is a small refrigerator, a small cupboard, and a coffeepot sitting on the countertop.

Here, by the cracking glue and peeling wallpaper, is where I'll make my writing corner. I can push Lucy over here to sit by the window, and she'll watch the world while I write about another world entirely different from this one. Eyeing Lucy as she fumbles with her other half of sandwich, I sigh internally. It's unhealthy for Lucy and me to be without fresh air and natural light. Not to mention the lack of brain stimulation with nothing to do but look at each other.

Down the hall, I can hear Harold protesting his supper. Lots of "do-das" and "Waupun bitties" and "get a gun" babbling. He'll probably have the aide so frustrated she'll leave her post long before he has had enough to eat. I couldn't help but notice how much thinner he looks now (than my memory of him) when I saw him sitting in the hall on his Adirondack chair. I'm very curious about whether he'll remember me, but I can't imagine he will after all this time, especially in light of his cognitive difficulties that has necessitate a life at Cre Manor.

Otto, apparently finished with supper, is being helped to his feet by the aide. With his quad cane and the aide close by, Otto drags his left paralyzed leg, thumping out of the dining room. A disdainful "Jesus Christ" echoes down the hall. The look on Lucy's face is sad, obviously concerned.

Sipping my coffee and eyeing the homemade cookie on my tray, I'm content to just let the evening slip away. I'm not looking forward to the aide coming back to dispel this peaceful moment. What will Lucy and I do with the hours before sleep? I won't pull out the Underwood tonight, but I may make some notes. I'll prepare Lucy for my plans to write and give her the gist of the story. Maybe we'll take a walk downstairs to see what's going on.

As Lucy and I are stepping out of the dining room, Sally the evening nurse comes down the hall. "Two things," she says. "I need to change the dressings on your feet, and you have a doctor appointment tomorrow at ten o'clock at the clinic. I'll arrange transportation. Oh, and one more thing, just to let you know, the psychiatrist will be making rounds next week. Being a resident on the PA Unit requires you see him." Once again she makes me feel like she's a rather strict teacher, and I'm a student who used too much glue on my arts and craft project. I nod without a word escaping my pursed lips.

I lean over Lucy's shoulder as I push her down the hallway. "Suddenly, I'm getting popular and rather visible, Lucy." I can't help but wonder whether, after the psychiatrist sees me, I'll be confined to our room in a drooling stupor. It's hard to fool Mother Nature, even harder to fool a psychiatrist. That was my experience as a nurse. Patients are usually putty in their hands, and they're quick to write mind-numbing prescriptions. I'll have to avoid taking that class of medication. The Ativan episodes were enough.

"After I get my feet redressed, what do you say to a wheel around the joint? I'll even ask permission from the nurse. We could stop in the lounge to watch the news on TV. I'm so out of touch. Of course, I get all the news I want from the weather report, as the saying goes."

Wirm bellows behind me, "You better watch out! Psychiatrist gonna get you, new lady!" He releases a howling laugh as he and the aide walk down the hall. He wasn't anywhere within hearing distance when the nurse was talking to me. Maybe the aide said something. I'll have to remember to ask her whether she passed on my information to him.

Lucy turns her head and watches him walk down the hall. Panic and dread pass across her face. She mumbles, "7-4-18 18-2-0-17-4-18 12-4." I am now certain that Lucy's groupings of numbers represent words. As sure as I know this, it also occurs to me that Lucy and Joseph Wirm have history. From the body language, none of that history could have been pleasant. Once again, I resolve to learn to interpret her way of communicating. Putting my hand comfortingly on her arm, I turn her wheelchair away from the far hall and toward the doors.

"We'd better go in before Nurse Sally wants my head as well as my feet." I notice Lucy's sense of humor has not returned.

I put on Lucy's call light before lying down, providing easy access to my bandaged feet. With my eyes closed, I slip into deep thought about how Lucy communicates and about Joseph Wirm. I'm startled when someone touches my leg.

"Sorry I frightened you, Miss Doe," says Sally. "Why is Lucy's light on? Since she never puts her call light on, you must have. Lucy's aide will get to her when it's time for cares. You don't need to do that for her."

Sighing, I repeat the conversation I had this morning with Lucy's aide. "Isn't toileting also part of her care plan?" I say. "Why should she be expected to be incontinent? Busy or not, I think an effort should be made to keep her dry. If her aide can't get in here to do this, I wish you would give me permission to do this for her."

Sally appears to be thinking about this as she removes the old dressings from my feet. "Just as you may not feed her, you also may not transfer Lucy from her wheelchair to the toilet. The nursing home would be liable if Lucy or you got hurt. If you cannot restrain yourself from these activities, I'll have to change your room. It's your call. By the way, what do you know about care plans?"

"Nothing, actually. I'll behave. I don't want to change rooms or roommates," I say quietly.

The aide hustles in with an armload of clean linens. "What's Lucy's call light on for? Sally, do you need something?"

"Yes, I want Lucy toileted last rounds by night shift, before morning cares, after meals, and before evening cares. And … and her incontinence given during shift report. This will be added to her care plan," Sally asserts. "Start by toileting her now, thank you."

"Okay, sure. How do we know she has to go? You know she can't tell us," the aide complains as she pushes Lucy's wheelchair to the bathroom door.

"We're going to anticipate her toileting needs. Starting now," Sally says.

"Wow, I'm really impressed," I whisper. "Thank you. I'm sure Lucy appreciates your intervening. Oh, one other thing. Can I take Lucy for a wheelchair ride off the unit? It will be good exercise for my stiff joints and give her a change of scenery. What do you say? We could catch the news on TV in the lounge," I say, finding it remarkable that her redressing of my feet doesn't sting at all.

Gathering her supplies, Sally says, "Doctor will probably discontinue the dressings on your feet tomorrow. The lacerations look healed. You and Lucy, out of your room, second floor only, can't hurt either of you to get out of this room for a while."

Looking over at Lucy as the aide wheels her out of the bathroom, I give her a thumbs-up. Lucy snickers and rolls her eyes. I would say, all in all, I've had a successful day. The money's taken care of, I'm set up to get some decent clothes, the doctor will see me tomorrow, my feet are just about healed, and I've made headway advocating for Lucy. Can't forget I actually got a shower, and my typewriter is ready to roll. Not bad for a first day.

As much as I feel like gloating, a sudden chill worms up my back, sapping some of my confidence. I have a sudden feeling that something hideous is hiding just where I can't see it. My brain stutters. After a moment of confusion, I start coming back to myself. Where did that come from? Back from woolgathering, I rationalize it must be the latent effects of dehydration and Ativan.

Sitting up and putting on my new-used socks, I ask Lucy if she's ready for a spin around the second floor. Could be I'll ask the aide to get us a couple of sodas for our TV watching in the lounge. Telling Lucy that if she gets tired, she should let me know, I push her down the hall through the doors and past the nurses' station. I walk Lucy slowly down 700s hall. Stopping at the bath complex to say hello to the bath aide, I explain that Sally has given permission for Lucy and me to be out from behind the doors. We wander to the end of 700s hall to the exit door turn and start back. Halfway down the hall, a man is walking with his walker. As we pass, he says hello to Lucy. She nods and smiles.

Wanting to talk to someone who knows Lucy, I say, "Have you known Lucy for a long time?"

"Oh yes," he says with a smile. "Everyone in town knows Lucy. Why, she was the town's only switchboard operator for many years before telephones went automated."

I hold in my astonished questions until I find a chair in the lounge, and then I position Lucy so she is facing me. "Lucy, you were the telephone operator in this berg before Ma Bell went voiceless! How many years did Cre Fallians hear you say, 'Number please,' whenever they picked up their phones? Must have been in the thirties, forties, fifties, maybe even the early sixties before dial phones got up this far. You must have been in your twenties when you started talking to the townies. That must make you … near ninety now!"

She gets a very distant faraway look in her eyes. With a sweet smile on her lips the memory must be a very pleasant one.

"Lucy," I mused, "I didn't know you back when I lived out at the farm. There were a lot of people I didn't know. I sort of stayed to myself raising the kids; did a little farming. No one ever mentioned your name. I wasn't aware of when dial phones hit town. Doctor and I bought the farm in seventy-nine."

I have so many questions to ask her. She seems to be my link, my key, to this place and the key to unlocking its secrets. I've just got to crack her code, and we're in like Flynn. "Did you have a stroke like Otto?" She smiles and shakes her head no, but I am already halfway into my next question when she does. "Does that explain the number thing, Lucy?"

Her face flushes, and she looks angry. She sits up straight, shoulders back, and shakes her head. With nostrils flaring, she says, "19-7-8-18 8-18 19-7-4 22-0-24 8 18-15-4-0-10!"

"If your numbers are words, I don't get what, say, 15 means. Fifteen would be, let's see … oh, I'll never get anywhere counting on my fingers. I need to write it down. Tomorrow I'll get a notebook and a pencil. We'll have Lucy language hour. I'll get it, Lucy. I will."

The other residents in the lounge seem intent on watching a game show on TV. I watch for a while without much interest. Distracted and yawning, Lucy looks toward the door. She must be tired. It must be time to head back. As I wheel her through the doors, Wirm's barking voice assaults the hall. *What is it about that man I find so offensive?* I wonder. I know Lucy gets very apprehensive when he's around.

Parking Lucy by her bed, I put on her call light. I get out my hospital gown, and heading for the bathroom, I say, "It's been a long day, Lucy."

I wash up, brush my teeth, and do the necessary things so that by the time I'm finished with the bathroom, Lucy's aide is wheeling her in.

When I get settled in bed, Lucy is out of the bathroom and being transferred into bed. The aide turns the light out. This long day is finished. "Good night, Lucy."

Part Two

The Cast

"Send in the clowns."
—Stephen Sondheim, *A Little Night Music*

Chapter Nine

The activity aide, with my clothes wish list in hand, chooses breakfast the next day to make notes of exact sizes, colors, and preferences. She tells me that Mark from Cre Falls's only shoe store will come to the nursing home to fit my feet with shoes and slippers. She says I can expect something decent and new to wear by lunch. All that plus shampoo, lotion, a comb and brush, toothpaste and toothbrush, and I will have everything I need. I do have one more request, I tell her; I want a ream of white typing paper, another typewriter ribbon, yellow legal pads, pens, and pencils. With this supply request filled, I'll be ready to push my over-the-bed table across to the dining room to make a serious attempt at writing.

At nine thirty, my ride picks me up to see the doctor. *I shouldn't have any trouble convincing him I'm a rheumatoid*, I think on the way. *He won't like being manipulated into writing prescriptions, but maybe I can make suggestions.* In reality there are few medications that really help my symptoms. The most disabling symptom is chronic, joint-crunching pain. I often suppose the small joints in my fingers and toes are by far the most excruciating, preventing my ability to touch any object without crying out when they are inflamed. The most disabling symptoms, though, are in the weight-bearing joints: hips, knees, and ankle joints that become stiff and feel like broken bones when I try to move. I imagine the pain of being on a medieval rack, being stretched beyond endurance with every turn of a wooden crank, every movement filled with gnawing and grinding pain. That is the kind of extreme pain this disease has plagued me with in the twenty-six years since it reared its ugly head. Kingsley said it best: "Pain is no evil, unless it conquers us." So I have not let it conquer me. It's an unavoidable part of who I am now, and definitely who I am has given me understanding of other peoples' pain. In the past, I have refused narcotics to gain relief. I refuse to be fogged out. Actually, truth be known, I've always been afraid narcotics would make me feel too good; the addictive need for more and more. When I see the doctor, I will steer him away from the traditional narcotics they all want to give me and hope he will be conservative. Prednisone used in crisis has saved me a number of times. I will push for a dose pack to use as needed. Even with the horrendous side effects, prednisone is my crisis drug of choice.

I am much more concerned about seeing the psychiatrist. He is very powerful here and well known behind the doors. Management of escalating combative dementia is always done with psychotropic drugs. Nursing can be an indiscriminative influence on how a psychiatrist manages client behavior. The "behind the doors" residents are treated to Chemical Behavior Management 101. I'm caught between a rock and a hard place or really, in this case, between keeping my sanity and losing my marbles: If I convince him of my mental instability (prerequisite to life 'behind the doors'), he will order drugs to control any antisocial behavior that nursing reports. Maybe the only solution I will have is to palm the drug he prescribes. I see this as my next colossal challenge, perhaps in as soon as two weeks.

With the successes I've already accomplished, I'm in an expansive mood this morning, making plans to begin writing after getting the doctor appointment out of the way.

The morning of another day of my internment passes without problematic events. The clinic MD is kind and helpful. New clothes (that mostly fit), new shoes (rather orthopedic-looking), and all the other items on my list show up in my room before lunch as promised.

As soon as the dining room clears after lunch, I amble across with my typewriter and paper to begin the daunting task. Clearing my head and staring out the window, I search for the words that will become the first sentence and finally start writing.

It's nearly impossible to imagine I'm amused at the situation I intentionally find myself in. While most, and I can write this with certainty, elderly find because of physical or mental frailty the need of nursing home admission come digging in their heels and yelling their heads off. I, on the other hand, came to admission "behind the doors" fighting to get in. Going so far as to erasing my identity and becoming a missing person, I acted on this decision, not because of delusional fugue, but with the burning need to write the stories only this place can tell before I die without one last hurrah.

I begin my story really where it will, if I do this right, end........ ...

The hours flee, and before I willingly look up, the dining room door opens, and smells of supper fills the room. Guiltily, I realize that I haven't seen or talked with Lucy since breakfast, or was it before leaving for the clinic? Packing up my work, I head for our room, excited to tell Lucy what I've been up to all afternoon. I'm surprised to find our room empty. I quickly wash up for supper and decide to wait for Lucy to show up.

An aide says as she passes our room, "Are you coming in to supper or eating in your room?"

"I'll eat in the dining room, thanks. Do you know where Lucy is?"

"She's down visiting with Harold Brown," she says. "Or at least they're sitting next to each other having a silent conversation."

I look down the hall as I walk to the dining room, and sure enough, Lucy is sitting next to Harold in the hallway, looking kindly and concerned. Forgetting supper for the moment, I walk toward them.

"Lucy, is everything okay? Is Harold all right?" I ask, aware that the look on Lucy's face is dread or maybe fear.

Harold's pale gray eyes stare at me, unblinking. He is so thin that his skin seems stretched over his skeletal facial bones. He is sitting on his Adirondack chair with his legs curled underneath him just as I remember from a whole lifetime ago. He grins, and the effect is unnerving. I am about to break the silence and ask Lucy to supper when Harold says with more than a whisper, "You're here." When I ask Harold if he knows me or rather remembers me, he chants, "Do-da, do-da, Waupun bitty," in a singsong, agitated voice. His mind was clear a moment ago, and now it isn't. Lucy puts her hand on mine and shakes her head as if to say, "No more."

Confused by Harold's whispered words, "You're here," I want to ask Lucy what he meant. Until I can understand Lucy's language, asking Lucy questions that require more than a nod is hopeless. Nevertheless, while pushing Lucy down to supper, I say, "Lucy, do you think Harold knew that I would be coming back here? Do you think Harold recognized me from so long ago?" Of course she has no response. No numbers either. I'm determined to work on breaking Lucy's code after supper. I want to know what Lucy knows.

Harold must be nearly eighty, more or less now. When I started working as a nurse at Cre Manor, Harold was in his early forties. I don't know whether Harold's story as told to me by Perry herself is true, but I certainly have no reason not to believe her.

Harold was homeless back then, sleeping in doorways on Main Street and often in a pew at St. Mary of Perpetual Help Catholic Church. He came to the nursing home looking for food or other handouts. Perry took an interest in him when she found out Harold was a diabetic. The pharmacist at the local drug store was checking Harold's blood glucose and giving him insulin as often as he would show up. Perry convinced Harold, after he came to her hypoglycemic one morning; she would give him insulin and promised him regular meals at the nursing home if he would come to her office by eight in the morning. That was the beginning of Harold's relationship with Perry and the nursing home.

I'm not sure whether Harold was naturally mentally slow or the regular abuse from his father caused him head injuries. No one I talked to seemed to know the answer to that. He spent two years at Waupun prison for allegedly beating his father outside one of the local downtown bars. Perry said it was while he was in Waupun that Harold was diagnosed with diabetes.

When I started working as a nurse at Cre Manor, Harold was my resident, already living behind the doors. He was diagnosed with antisocial behavior and thought to be developmentally disabled. His diabetes was out of control, and his gait was unsteady and ataxic from psychotropic medication. They used those meds to keep his escalating behaviors in check. Whether from agitation or tardive dyskinesia (impairment of voluntary movement), his extremities were rigid.

Harold is now thin with an impish, wizened look, looking much the same way as he did nearly twenty years earlier. He always sat in his room or at the end of the hall in his Adirondack chair back then, constantly rubbing his hands back and forth on the arms until the wood was worn and smooth.

The opinion I held then and hold to this day is that Harold's agitation and subsequent cognitive failure were in large part due to antipsychotic medication ordered by psychiatry. The very medication ordered to control his escalating behaviors caused Harold to act out his aggression. So for the more than twenty years I was Harold's nurse, his mental and physical well-being declined.

Harold had times, brief as they were, of astounding clarity. He would become acutely aware of his environment. He would speak clearly, as he did just now when he whispered, "You're here." He had a lively sense of humor and could be heard joking with the nurses' aides. He would make odd requests like "I want white ice cream and Betty Grable to serve it" or "Find my pipe and light me." At other, dark times, Harold was the little boy crying, "Daddy, daddy, don't hurt Harold." Often when he was most aggressive and agitated, he chanted over and over, "Do-da, do-da, get a gun," and remembering when he was imprisoned, he'd call out, "Waupun bitties."

As a nurse, I found that controlling his diabetes was next to impossible because of his erratic eating behaviors. More suppers than not, I spent coaxing nutrition into him. Many suppers I failed and then tested for the inevitable insulin reaction. The orange juice the orderly and I forced him to swallow was to keep hypoglycemia at bay. The troublesome IV needle insertions and instillation of antibiotics to cure urinary tract infections were (in twenty years) some of my most difficult nursing procedures. Still, as I remember Harold, I smile.

All of Harold Brown's past, I remember as I wheel Lucy to supper. All of my memories of him are as vivid as yesterday. Lucy and Harold are linked somehow, I'm sure, and I intend to discover just how. Lucy, the telephone operator, and Harold, the homeless young man, are somehow connected in some bizarre way. I know this like I know rain is coming, causing my joints to ache.

Lucy and I have supper. We spend more than an hour after supper working on breaking Lucy's code. Over and over, I try different letters and words for her numbers. Over and over, I fail to get it. Lucy begins to look exasperated and tired, so I resolve to try again tomorrow.

Back in our room with the lights finally out, my mind refuses to give up, and I continue to do number associations long into the night. The rest of the night, mystery spills over in restless dreams. I race down the potholed road in my old Toyota toward what will surely be death without ever understanding what I'm looking for. All of the dreams are tied to Lucy the telephone operator, no-name Jane, and Harold sitting down the hall, chanting, "Do-da, do-da."

The nursing home days come and go. I spend afternoons writing and the hours after supper working on Lucy's code. I begin to spend time with Lucy and Harold just sitting quietly at the end of the hall, waiting for the next clear word Harold may utter. And the nights I spend in my mind, either awake or asleep. But it's the sleeping hours that haunt me most.

Chapter Ten

Three weeks fly by without a decoding clue. The writing is going way better than "18-19-14-17-24," the latest series of numbers Lucy gave me to work on. She will not or cannot help me. I'm not sure why this is so hard, or why it's necessary for me to struggle with this impossible task. Lucy is much more patient than I am, encouraging me on. It has occurred to me, why can't Lucy just be my silent friend? That's when I'm reminded of my conviction that Lucy is somehow a key, and opening that lock will be an epiphany, confirming why I'm here and the connection between Lucy, Harold, and Joseph Wirm.

At least three times a week, I push Lucy outside when the aides go out for supper. I usually push Lucy by the flowerbeds so she can admire them, and I sit there on a bench while my arthritic joints soak up the sun's warmth.

This time, instead of following the aides to the elevator, I detour into the first-floor dining room. Taking a chance by being on the first floor without the nurse's permission, I put Lucy at a small table near the large round table that the men usually occupy. Telling Lucy I'll be right back, I walk out to the nurses' station.

"Sue, would you tell the nurse on two that I'm down here with Lucy having a soda? Just want a change of scene." To show off I say, "Lucy's not a diabetic, so she can have a soda too."

Not waiting for an answer, I walk back, fishing quarters out of my pocket. Lucy looks like a root beer kind of gal, I decide. After getting two cans out of the soda machine, I walk back to the table. Lucy spots the soda I'm carrying and makes a content humming in her throat. Her eyes twinkle. She looks positively delighted. If I knew all it took to please Lucy was a soda, I'd have taken the first-floor risk a lot sooner. I open a can and set it in front of her. She easily lifts the can and takes a swig.

"Take it easy, Luce. This is wild fizzy stuff, you know." Lucy continues her humming, totally engrossed in her can of root beer.

The first-floor men wander in one at a time, taking a seat at the round table. It looks like they will be hanging around for a while since one of them has a deck of cards. In no time, eight old codgers fill the chairs. Their moaning and groaning about their aches and pains, the rotten food, their sick roommates, and no rain for more than a week makes twenty years ago seem like yesterday. That nothing had changed was what I prayed for while I was bumping up the back Wisconsin roads in my Toyota. I'm ecstatic that some things in this world can still be predictable, such as the men of the first floor taking up space at the large round table in dining room one.

My plan is to inject a comment about one of the townie stories to see if they will take the bait and run with it. I will have to just listen and remember. Paper and pencil are for next time. Also, I don't want to inhibit the free flow of the tale.

I whisper to Lucy, "Are you okay with sitting for a while? You know these guys are long-winded." Lucy makes a funny, crooked Charlie Brown–like smile and goes back to being engrossed in her soda.

How easily recognized is the apparent pecking order in a group of elderly gents. The boss, or leader, of the group is the only one who walked in unaided by a walker or wheelchair. He is not very tall, maybe five-six or five-seven. He has a barrel chest on top of short legs that I notice are bowed. He is wearing a red plaid flannel shirt and wool hunting pants held up by black suspenders. My amused guess is that under those wool pants are long johns. Last I looked, this was July. He has tufts of gray hair above his ears that circle around the nape of his neck. The rest of his head is waxy, shiny bald. He has bushy eyebrows and rheumy eyes behind his gray metal–framed glasses. His large, lumpy red drinker's nose runs a little. There are no teeth to fill out his sunken mouth. *Probably took out his dentures after supper, storing them in a glass of water*, I guess.

These same men sat at this table not an hour ago eating supper, so there is little small talk. Boss man says, "You gonna deal the cards or eat 'em, Charlie?"

Charlie, a tall skinny guy with a hooked nose, bites back. "Keep your shirt on, Fred. What's your hurry? Got a hot date?"

The rest of the men giggle like a bunch of teenage girls, and one mumbles, "Don't he wish?"

Fred silences them with an impatient look and retorts, "If you yokels have nothing better to do, I can fucking wait." Seeing Lucy and me for the first time, he winks. "Sorry for burning your ears with the nasty word, ladies. Oh, Lucy, what are you doing down here? … Yeah, I forgot you don't speak. Nothing to say? Not like these guys, running off at the mouth all the time. Your friend got a name?"

My chance to get the old guys talking has come more easily than I thought it would. "I'm Lucy's roommate. The staff here calls me Jane Doe because I can't remember my name. I know none of you gentlemen have a problem with remembering, right? Lucy and I are here to be entertained with your stories about Cre Falls's past misdeeds. You know, the stories the law did nothing about. The ones the townies can't forget."

That gets them all talking at once. "Now hold up!" Fred shouts, pressing his arms down to signal the guys to pipe down. "What's your interest? You don't look like that detective on *Murder, She Wrote*."

How perceptive of him; until this moment I had never thought of myself as, oh, what's her name—Angela Lansbury. "Nah, I can't sing," I answer. That gets a laugh. "Besides, she's too prissy, right, Lucy?" Lucy is still not paying much attention, enjoying her soda. "Still," I say, "nothing better to do on a rainy night in Cre Falls."

"Rainy night lady, you got that wrong. We haven't had rain for more than a week," Fred says, pointing to the door.

"If it isn't raining out there, I'll be damned. My joints never lie. There's nothing like arthritis to give you heads-up when it's going to rain." To prove I'm right, a rumble of thunder booms like an exclamation point.

Several of the men agree with me. Having an inkling that rain is coming is maybe the only benefit to suffering from achy knees.

Charlie laughs, almost with disbelief. "Best weatherman I know. So lady, or Miss Doe or whatever, which dark story do you want to hear? Which story is ladylike for your delicate ears?" The others laugh.

"In that case," Fred chimes in, "she can't hear any of the ones I know. All of them are X-rated for sure."

"Come on, guys. I wasn't born yesterday, the day before yesterday maybe. How about that one from the forties? You know, the one about that bastard in Sawyerville."

Hearing this pulls Lucy's attention from the root beer she has been enjoying. She gives me a censuring look and nods her head at one of the men.

"Okay, Lucy, I guess I know this one best. I lived with my folks near that house in Sawyerville. I'm Jim Lefdal, by the way." I swear he would have tipped his hat if he were wearing one.

Jim relaxes into his story. "Like you say, it happened in the forties, or at least that's what my dad said. The Heyfelds—that was their name—had a shanty back in the woods north of Sawyerville, really just a shack. Old man Heyfeld made good money for those days, logging for Bittercreek Lumber Company. Most of the money he made went for whiskey. Dad said very little of the money made it to his wife. Like you say, he was a mean bastard—meaner when he was drunk, and that was most nights. He was always beating up on that skinny little wife of his."

Jim has a haunted look on his face as he recalls the story. Lucy now stares at him, two shades paler than her usual ivory pallor. Actually, she appears rather green. I understand from watching her that she knows this story, probably better than Jim. I guess both of us know what is coming, but that doesn't make it easier to hear. The other men at the table are unusually quiet.

"He had two daughters," Jim continues. "I take it the oldest one was in her teens. She was really pretty, or so my father said: A shy girl. She was almost never seen in town. When the folks would talk about her, they would say her hair was so blond it was almost white, with stirring blue eyes. As I say, real pretty. The other girl was a few years younger than her. Not many people knew much about her. Only a few folks knew what she looked like.

"Story is that their bastard father got the older girl pregnant. I know that part of the story is true because word has it that the priest told the sheriff. Father O'Brian said the mother came to him nearly hysterical. She was afraid the old man would give her the beating of her life if she went to the law. The sheriff went up to the shack, called Heyfeld out, and demanded to see his girl. Heyfeld said his family was his business and none of their business. He said if the law wanted to be doing something; it could find the fucker that got his girl in a family way. If the sheriff couldn't do that, then he would find the son of a bitch and kill him.

"That was that. Months later, Dad said, Heyfeld's daughter turned up downtown at the grocery with no baby bump, if you catch my meaning. Father O'Brian got wind of it and went out there to find out if there was a baby to baptize. Low and fucking behold, no baby! None of the Heyfelds had anything to say. Old man Heyfeld was as rude to Father as he was to the sheriff. Father O'Brian did say the older daughter hid her face and wouldn't look him in the eyes while he was talking to her father.

"No one to this day knows where the baby went. The story goes, old man Heyfeld buried the babies in the woods in galvanized pails. Yup, you heard me right. I said babies, plural. Thing is no one went out there to find out. I still hear rumors that the oldest daughter came up pregnant again, same for the younger girl. I don't think any of the townsfolk knew for sure. The girls never did go to school or have anything to do with the young people in town."

"Would you say that's the story you know?" Jim looks around the table, but there is a long, turbid silence from the gossipy old men. The only sounds are the booms of thunder and the rain hitting the large window in the dining room.

"Whatever happened to that family, Jim?" I ask. "Why didn't the law actually go out there and investigate? You're telling me no one knows the truth?"

"This town has always been like that, missy: Sweeps its sins under the pine needles. I'll tell you, it's like that today. Ask that fellow Wirm upstairs. He knows more than the eight of us put together. That's one weird son of a bitch. I'll never know why Perry lets him live here. I suppose money talks."

Lucy is fiddling with her empty soda can, trying to get my attention. "Right, Lucy. Time to get upstairs before the nurse is breathing down our necks. Good night, fellas. See you again on another rainy night."

"Don't wait until it rains, lady. It rains less and less in Cre Falls," Fred says. "Well, we going to play a hand or not? It's getting past my bedtime."

Several more decks of cards appear out of pockets. Apparently, they play canasta or some rummy game. I push Lucy out of the dining room to the elevator.

"Good, Lucy, you still have your empty soda can. We may have to show evidence of where we've been to Sally. Some story, huh? I bet you know all of the Cre Falls stories. Right?" There is only silence as we ascend to the second floor. I resolve again that I will be able to communicate with my friend Lucy one day. One day very soon.

Trying to scoot Lucy through the doors before catching the attention of the evening nurse, I almost make it behind the doors before we're busted. Sally sighs. "About time you show up. Stop back at the desk and get your meds. I'm not walking all the way to your room again. I'll take that soda can you're holding, Lucy. You two are becoming a thorn in my butt," she says.

I spread my hands apart in front of me, and dear Lucy belly-laughs. "Just about that wide," I whisper. Sally hands us our med cups and enough water to just wash the pills down, barely enough.

"The psychiatrist is here next week, sister. I hope he gives you sodium pentothal to dig your name out of your brain, or at least gives you a pill to tame your sassy mouth," Sally says, walking away.

"Fat chance, Sally, fat chance," I retort, moving through the doors. "Don't worry, Lucy. I've got a plan!" At this minute my plan is getting in bed. I'm bushed.

I'm still awake when I hear the aides making midnight rounds. Since putting Lucy on a toileting schedule, they don't come in our room until around six in the morning, and this night I need help. As I try to reach my call button, I remember hooking it on my bedside lampshade, out of reach. I would shout to attract attention, but I'm choked by a viper of agony.

The gnawing pain in my left hip and knee is horrendous. My right shoulder and wrist are festering with the promise of greater agony to come. I'm being swept away on a rush tide of torture. Hissing through my teeth, I feel myself losing control. Rapid breathing and irregular heartbeat are the gifts of this pain. With this much inflammation, it's like a walk in hell. Every time an acute arthritic flare-up assaults me, I'm sure this is the last time my body, mind, and spirit will survive. My mind is screeching the worn-out litany, *God, help me through this. God, help me through this.* Sobbing out loud, I moan, "Please, God, send someone to help me. I can't do this alone!" *Please*, my mind begs, *where are my children? Why aren't they here to help me? Oh, they don't know where I am!* The pain comes in spasms with hardly a second between them. Surely this time is worse than ever. This time my body will fail.

Suddenly, he's close, very close, to my bed. His hand is shaking my bed rail. Opening my mouth to scream, I get out only a huffing sound as his hand covers my mouth. He's standing over me. I can smell his fetid breath on my face. Paralyzed with fear and pain, I struggle to breathe through my nose. He whispers, "Just let go and die. You know you want to. No one will help you here. You came here for nothing, Jane. You'll never make a difference. No one will listen to you or the fools that think they've been waiting for you."

Reaching up through my right wrist pain, I wrestle his hand off my mouth.

"Lucy, Lucy!" I cry. "Wirm is here, Lucy. Help me!"

"7-4-11-15!" Lucy bleats. "7-4-11-15!" This time her alarm is earsplitting.

Wirm hisses, "Damn that interfering woman. I'll see both of you in hell. You think you have pain now—just wait." Heading out the door, he says, "I'll fuck you where the Wirm never dies."

Lucy's cry brings Mary and two night aides on the run. Mary turns on the overhead light and rushes to Lucy's bedside in a blur of blue scrubs. Lucy nods her head at me and moans softly. Mary approaches my bed, not missing the fear and anguish on my face.

"I have a feeling you're going to tell me exactly what you need to back off this joint crisis you're in," Mary says, seeing my swollen, inflamed right elbow joint.

Through the irascible pain, I manage to speak. "Prednisone, twenty-five milligrams now, twenty milligrams for three days, and titrate down to two and one-half milligrams after that. Doctor gave an as-needed order. There's prednisone in contingency. He also ordered two Darvocet every four hours. I'll take two now. I need the aides to position me on my right side with pillows for support. Thank you."

Before the aides have me positioned, Mary is back, holding out five 5-milligram tablets of prednisone and two pain pills. Lois, the aide, helps lift my head high enough to swallow the medication. If I am still lucky, the prednisone will work its magic by morning, and the pain pills will take the edge off the pain, making the balance of the night almost tolerable. It is going to be a long night.

Before Mary gets out the door, I say, "I don't want Joseph Wirm in my room again! If I have to, I'll call the ombudsman and petition to have his evil ass thrown out of here! He threatened Lucy and me. You do a behavior flow sheet and have the aides check on him every fifteen minutes."

"I'm sorry. I didn't know he was in here," Mary says. Putting my call button where I can easily reach it, she asks, "Is that what Lucy was alarmed about?"

"Yes, I'm sure," I say. "I didn't have any power in my voice, so I got Lucy's attention. Thank God for Lucy," I say, sobbing. Tears spill down my face.

Mary hands me a tissue. "Okay, I'll do everything I can to keep him out of this room. Are you positive you weren't dreaming? As a matter of fact, I have an orderly, Donald, on 700s hall. I'll put him on a chair outside of Wirm's room so you can rest easy tonight. Day shift will get a full report. By tomorrow night, I'm sure they will have a protection plan in place."

Mary turns out the light, leaving me to battle a familiar enemy: pain. I know Lucy is still awake. "That was close, Lucy," I say. "I think he means to hurt us, or scare us to death. The staff will help us for now. Tomorrow when I can think straight, you and I have to have a powwow, my dear. I know what 7-4-11-15 means. I know that means 'help.' Tomorrow we talk!"

Someone is in the dining room, scraping a chair across the room. I assume Donald has arrived to take up his post. The propox is beginning to take the edge off the pain, and I think maybe I'll at least be able to rest some. But the storm has become a real downpour, the thunder is loud, and the lightning strikes seem near.

Just as I'm certain I will never be able to sleep this night, the medication kicks in, and I do.

Part Three

The Ectomorphic Wirm

And his eyes have all the seeming of a
Demon that is dreaming,
And the lamp-light o'er his streaming
throws his shadow on the floor;
And my soul from on the floor
Shall be lifted—nevermore!

—Edgar Allan Poe, "The Raven"

Chapter Eleven

"That interfering bitch!" Wirm roars as he crosses the Highway 42 Bridge, cloaked in mill muck from the rain pushing down air pollutants from the mostly illegal smokestack. The thick fog shrouds him as he passes the Cre Falls Mill. "Should have killed that bitch years ago when she was the voice on the phone," he rages. "Harold Brown, I'll get you for saving her. You fucking moron. I'll get both of you!"

The black suit coat covering the nursing home gown he is still wearing is tight across his back and shoulders. The sleeves are too short, and his large, mitt-like hands and thick fingers protrude. His hairy legs are bare. Nursing home slippers, nothing more than paper with plastic soles, flaps on his feet. Little more than a block from his escape, he is already soaked with rain.

He shakes his fists at the night sky and punches at the air as he continues to rage at the storm, at Lucy, at Harold, and at the woman whose name he cannot see.

Why can't he see her name? He could have exposed her to Perry. Perry would have made her leave, and "behind the doors" would once more belong to him. He should go back before the staff finds him missing, but he's too mad to go back now. He knows she is strong enough to expose his past involvement in Cre Falls's crimes. Then who knows what will happen to him? Surely, he will be left without a purpose, to be forced back into the blackness. He pounds the sides of his head, trying to shake his second sight alive.

Needing to get off the bridge, he shuffles down the highway. He has walked this way many times, spreading angst like seeds. One more block, and his trail will vanish.

Maud's boarded-up tavern on the corner of the Highway 42 and Main Street has been his shelter ever since Maud was beaten to death by that woman. What was her name? Lynn Frisk. Oh yeah, he had something to do with that too. All that Lynn wanted from old Maud was money to feed her kids and pay her bills. It was almost bar time, and old Maud wanted to close up and take her sore feet upstairs to bed. Business was always steady all night long, with mill workers having a few after their shift. There was almost two thousand dollars in the till that night.

Lynn had worked the afternoon shift as a housekeeper at the motel. During the nights, she tended bar at Maud's. Neither job paid very well, but it was something. Before she left work, her boss at the motel had caught up with her. "Don't bother coming back tomorrow. Business is slow, and I don't need two women cleaning. Besides, Polly is a better worker than you." Lynn had only two days pay coming, and she barely made minimum wage. Her husband had been laid off, so she needed money, and the fool thought old Maud would lend her some.

Maud hadn't locked the back door of the bar, so Lynn let herself in from the back parking lot. The smell of beer and cigarettes was almost as overwhelming as the strong urine odor wafting from the toilets. Lynn walked down the dark hall and approached the bar.

Maud was startled to see someone coming from the back hall. She had already locked the front door and shut off the lights. The only lights were the beer advertising signs behind the bar. Maud had a whiskey-rough voice with a demeanor to go with it. Lynn flinched when Maud said, "What are you doing here? The bar is closed."

Maud had no need for a strong-arm bouncer. Most of the men and all of the women who were patrons of the bar feared her. She was charmed by no one. Standing barely five feet tall and just as round, Maud had to be in her eighties. This place had been her gold mine for forty years, hers since Fred, her husband, had died of a mysterious fall down the stairs from the second-floor apartment above the bar they called home. The day her husband died, Maud had opened the bar before mill night shift punched out and had opened the same time seven days a week since. Some said she was worth a fortune. There had never been hard times on the corner of Highway 42 and Main Street.

What can Maud do to me? thought Lynn. *She can't hurt me. All she can do is say no.* Still, fear constricted her throat and caused her heart to hammer. Some inner voice told her to run out the back door she'd come in. Her need to feed her kids and pay the utility bill pushed the terror back. Still her hands were sweaty and trembling, so she held tightly to the back of the bar stool nearby.

Lynn's need for money and the loss of her job gave her disparate courage. "It's me, Lynn Frisk, Maud. I was wondering if you would lend me some money. I got laid off from the motel tonight and need money for groceries and some bills I have to pay today. Three or four hundred would be enough. I will pay you back as soon as I get another job," she said.

Maud started to laugh. She laughed until tears streamed down her face. Catching her breath, Maud said, "You fool. What makes you think I would lend you money to feed your snot-nosed kids? Do I look like a bank?" She turned her back on Lynn.

He was standing in the dark by the front door, listening to Maud give Lynn the boot. A cold breeze seemed to cross Lynn's face, and on that breeze a whisper said, "Just kill her and take the money you need. You deserve that money for your kids. Kill her and take the money." Lynn started to cry. Picking up the stool at the end of the bar, she rushed up to Maud. Screaming, she raised the stool over her head and brought it down on the back of Maud's head, knocking her down to the floor. Maud moaned and turned over, facing Lynn. Picking up a leg from the broken stool, Lynn began beating Maud in the face and didn't stop until her face was a bleeding pulp. Still, Maud was breathing. Lynn beat her across the sternum, breaking several ribs, which punctured her left lung. The gurgling, labored breaths lasted for a couple of minutes. Sure that Maud was dead, Lynn headed behind the bar to the cash register. She emptied the money into a bottle takeout bag and hurried out the door through which she'd entered.

Following her down the hall was a strange, dark form and a strange, hollow cackling of something or someone evil. Lynn ran to her car, opened the trunk with shaky hands, and threw in the broken leg of the stool covered with Maud's blood. Squealing the wheels as she left the parking lot, she raced up Highway 42, past the mill, past the nursing home, past the funeral home, and out of town, heading to a place in the woods to hide.

Joseph Wirm peered down at Maud's beaten face, feeling joy and pride in a job well done. An evil smile pushed up the corners of his mouth, showing small, white, pointy teeth. Cooing, he said, "You shouldn't have laughed at her, Maud. Not to worry. The cops will catch her. She won't have any money worries for the rest of her life in prison. You don't mind if I use your place to hang out, do you? You old cunt?" Pleased with himself, he sat down at a table, putting his feet up on a chair to wait for the cops to come.

He would blend in with the crowd of townsfolk who would come to see old Maud take her final trip to the small morgue in the Bayles' Funeral Home hearse.

Come they did. Catch Lynn they did. That's how Joseph Wirm came to hanging out at Maud's Bar, when he needed to, for a long time after Lynn was sentenced to life for killing Maud.

Remembering all this, Wirm shuffles to the boarded-up back door of Maud's Bar. With a pound of his fist, he easily pops the top board off and goes on to the next until the locked door stands in front of him. Putting his hand over the bolt lock, he pushes until the lock turns. Whistling, he turns the doorknob and opens the door into the black hall leading to the bar. "It's like coming home, Maud darling," he thinks out loud. "Too bad you're not here to draw me a cold one. You shouldn't have laughed at her. Isn't that what I told you, Maud?"

Shuffling across the bar to his favorite table, his paper slippers hanging on by only a thread, he sits to wait for Harold Brown and that stupid woman he's been waiting for.

Part Four

Lucy's Bane: The Worm in the Apple

Dire overthrow, and yet how high
The re-ascent in sanctity!
From fair to fairer; day by day
A more divine and loftier way!
Even such this blessed Pilgrim trod,
By sorrow lifted towards her God;
Uplifted to the purest sky
Of undisturbed and mortality.
Her own thoughts loved she; and could bend
A dear look to her lowly friend;

—William Wordsworth, "The White Doe of Rylstone"

Chapter Twelve

The room is as black as a tunnel, lifting her hand and wiggling her fingers; nothing. All she can see is a faint strip of hall light on the underside of the door. On this side of the hall, the side with no windows, she has been able to sense Wirm better. There is something about being just down the hall on his same side that makes her able to concentrate and know where he is.

She missed Wirm earlier because of Jane's horrible pain. While she was unable to think of anything else, Wirm slipped off of her radar, made his way to their room, and was about to hurt her. This cannot happen again. She has to be more vigilant. If anything happens to Jane all will be lost. So she is still awake, listening. Jane's breathing is soft, even. The pain pills must have worked, and she is able to sleep.

Lucy thinks of her as Jane even though, like Wirm, she cannot see her name. She thinks Harold can, but he has said nothing except "You're here." Knowing her name isn't important. Knowing why she is here is all she needs for now. She thinks maybe Wirm could force her to tell him.

She closes her eyes and can sense Donald sitting on a chair outside Wirm's room. Lucy knows that will not stop Wirm from getting out of his room. As a matter of fact, she senses Wirm passing through the nursing home wall, walking down the walk toward the highway. He's out! Soon she will lose him in the storm. She is afraid of just this. Wirm out and about is so dangerous.

She is always afraid now. It wasn't like this when she was younger. Then she was the voice on the phone, summoning help for a caller who needed her; finding the doctor when a mother was in labor, sending the police to a car accident, trying to calm a father who couldn't find his child, just being the friendly operator when a Ma Bell customer needed someone to listen. From her little hovel office that housed the switchboard with its lifeline trunks to everyone in town who had a phone, and that was nearly everyone, she answered their calls twenty-four hours a day, seven days a week. When the answer was "number please," they all knew it was her voice on the line. There was a substitute available, but she was rarely needed. The hovel office was in a small cottage home on Pine Street, two blocks west of Highway 42.

The local grocery store delivered the food she ordered, and the clothes she needed were delivered by the post office from Sears Roebuck.

Everyone knew she attended mass at eight o'clock Sunday morning, and for that hour and a half, she did not answer their calls. Cre Falls customers were okay with that because at nine thirty they knew she would be there. All of this is why one day, twenty years ago, the town was in a panic. She wasn't there to take the calls, and no one knew why.

Lucy's long- and short-term memory is intact and as sharp as when she was a girl. Her total recall gives her hours of pleasure and terror that consume most of her waking time and often her sleeping time too, in the form of nightmares. It's because of her never-failing memory that the nursing home has become her only safe haven.

Even after Wirm attacked her and Harold saved her (until blocking him with her numbers) he shadowed her every move. Finally, when Harold was unable to care for both of them, the nursing home became the only place that could. Harold's diabetes was out of control. He was much thinner, weak, and losing physical and mental strength before she was able to convince him that where they were hiding wasn't safe anymore.

Fear became her diligent companion, always a warning beacon. Fearing that Wirm could read her thoughts, she devised the number-code language to safeguard her knowledge of the evil deeds that he had inflicted on the people of Cre Falls. Only Harold knows what she has been unable to say. Only Harold has protected her sanity and given her hope of a peaceful death. That is her quest now—that and helping Jane understand why she came to Cre Falls and what she must finally do. Harold told her about the need to wait for Jane and about all the things Jane would need to know. Harold's last words to Lucy were "Know her timing will be perfect and that you will never forget me." After he said those words, they walked into the nursing home hand in hand where he watched them admitted her to a room behind the doors. That is where like Harold she begins to wait.

Harold's health was never stable, and through the years it worsened. His mental health was just as precarious, or so the staff thought. She knew, however, that Harold was hiding, just as she was—hiding from Wirm.

When Wirm managed to get himself admitted behind the doors, she and Harold agreed it was a good thing. They have since been better able to track his movements, especially at night. It is now getting more difficult for him to project himself through the wall and be the night stalker he was, but then everyone gets older, lazier, more willing to take the easy way, even the evil Joseph Wirm.

She likes to remember the past: mostly the time when she was Ma Bell's hello girl. She likes to recall the cozy little one-bedroom cottage given to her by the phone company to live in as long as she worked for them. That same cottage belonged to the operator before her. After telephone connections became automated, the company must have sold the little blue cottage. It saddens her to think there is no human link on the telephone now when Cre Falls citizens ring.

The switchboard where she worked was in the office room. The Cre Falls mainframe was built in behind the closet and hidden when the closet doors were closed. From her position at the switchboard, she could look out the window and admire the Cre River and the busy wood yard that belonged to the mill. The bathroom was in the office, and the kitchen just a few steps away. The phone company rigged up a buzzer in her bedroom that alerted her to night calls.

That was all there was to her little home, except for an enclosed back porch with a door opening to the office.

She was always a thin woman and just over five feet tall, with round perky breasts that rarely needed a bra. She had a short torso, which made her look leggy. The townies thought she was a "looker" with a pageboy haircut and good skin that required almost no makeup. Her most remarkable feature was the sky-blue color of her eyes, ringed with a dark navy blue. In spite of many offers, there had been only one man in her life, a lumberjack who had died in a logging accident back in 1949. No man ever came close to winning her heart again, though many tried. Steve was her first passionate love, and his death closed her heart, leaving no room for anyone else.

The calls started shortly after Steve died. At first the call would buzz on her switchboard. When she plugged in and said, "Number please," the line sounded hollow. As she listened, she heard a far-off babbling that didn't sound like language and then screaming and calls for help. Frightened, she called the sheriff, but as the calls became more frequent, he was never able to trace their origins. There were months between calls with no change, and then one night after midnight, she heard the same babbling and cries for help, and this time as she listened, a cloying male voice said, "Do you want to know who died and how?"

Her throat was so dry she could hardly squeak out the words "Do you want to tell me?"

Many times he called after midnight telling her of murdered people, and when she would ask "Do you want to tell me who," he would laugh and say, "No."

Then one night he said, "Read the newspaper, you dumb bitch, and find out for yourself! The newspaper must have nothing interesting to print. This old story was up on that water flowage—a nice schoolmarm with one in the oven."

His mocking laugh filled her headset, making her heart beat wildly before she pulled the trunk from her switchboard. Shaking, she reported the call to Sheriff Becker. Becker took her call and sent two deputies, sirens blaring, north to the small village bordering the lake connected to the flowage. Not able to locate the schoolteacher who lived with the Nevels, a search party of men formed and at first light began scrutinizing the woods and the lake's shoreline. They found her in the lake wrapped in a deerskin coat, with rocks holding her on the bottom, the front of her dress soaked with blood. Her throat had been slashed, exposing her cervical spine. One more thrust, and she would have been beheaded. The baby she had carried had been carved out of her uterus. More than one of the searchers made for the brush, unable to stomach the bloody scent.

That was the first night of terror for Lucy, and she was right to think that it would not be the last. Becker's investigation did not lead to the arrest of the butcher who killed Miss Haver and her unborn infant up on the flowage. As the months and then years slipped by, the murders and misdeeds multiplied, as did her terror. Now when the switchboard rang after midnight, her terror was palpable. Convinced she was a conduit for a serial killer who managed to slip by the law each time she called to report his latest afflictive evil, she was positive this time he would be captured. Every time the law came up empty-handed, her fear for who was next filled her with trepidation, or maybe the next time he called, it would be her turn.

She thought of moving—no, running—away, but over the years none of her relatives had survived. She had a lot of acquaintances and knew practically everyone in Cre Falls, but she really had no close friends. The switchboard had kept her attached to the job. In the end she did not run but stayed at the job, waiting.

The call came at midnight nearly ten years after the last attempt to solve Haver's murder, he simply chuckled and said, "Your turn." Her headset went dead. She tried to dial the police station for help, but the mainframe was dead as well. She started to run out her back door, but she knew at once it was useless. She could not get away. It was her turn to die at the hands of the man she called the "Bad Moon Killer." There was no clear reason for that name. It was just a name that had come out of the recess of her mind. Cre Falls had not adopted the name because Cre Falls refused to believe the killer existed.

She remembered Edgar Allan Poe's "Shadow: A Parable"—"The year had been a year of terror, and of feelings more intense than terror for which there is no name upon the earth."

When he slid through the door, she was standing to face him with resolve and courage. But oh, she was afraid. She feared her bladder would fail or, worse, her watery bowels would betray her. There he was at last: handsome and tall, with a winsome smile turning up his mouth, wavy white hair, wide shoulders, and a narrow waist. He was dressed in fashionable clothes. His puissant, dead, black eyes sucked her gaze down into the well of his purulent nature. Knowing her mind would save her from feeling the evil attack, she prayed for insanity to take her

"Oh no, you don't. Look away. No hiding behind insanity," he said, reading her thoughts. "I want this to be our special moment, Lucy," he said cajolingly.

Wirm took a step toward her, shortening the space between them. She stepped back, but the wall of her office was directly behind her. With no place to go and no hope of helping herself, she pleaded, "God help me."

His hands slid around her neck, and he pulled her to him. She tried to breathe through her mouth to avoid the stench of his clothes. He smelled of smoky campfires, old blood, and fresh urine. His acidic body odor coated her throat, making her feel faint. Forcibly pressed against his hard erection, she realized, *God, he means to rape me.*

"Come on, Lucy," he whispered against her cheek. "You've been waiting for me, and I've been dreaming of having you. Love your lover, Lucy."

Somewhere in her scorched mind, she found the will to resist. As she tried to pull her face away from his lips and putrid breath, his hands tightened around her neck. He shook her slowly like a rag doll.

"I will have you dead or alive," he seethed. Frothy saliva struck her chin and neck. "Did you think I called you all this time just so you could tell the sheriff about me? I called you to hear your sexy voice, ready to scream my name. You made me want your cunt. I'll give you my number, and you'll never forget it," he said, his face darkened with rage. "Say my name, Lucy. Say my name Joseph

Wirm with your lovely mouth before I stick my cock in it," said Joseph Wirm.

A fatalistic calm stole over her fear. Prying his hands away with the strength that comes with a whopping surge of adrenaline, she managed to shout, "Never! I will never utter your evil name or be any more than a lifeless corpse for whatever heinous sexual corruption fills your needs!" Her words seemed to stab his black heart like a knife. Inarticulate with rage, he lifted her by her neck, choking off her oxygen completely. Her last desperate thought before passing out was triumph. *I've won!*

The next thing she was aware of was being lifted off the floor, air expanding her seared lungs. An urgent voice said, "That's it, Lucy—breathe. We have to get out of here! Lean on me. Can you walk?"

She did lean against his thin chest, inhaling one raspy breath after another, sending oxygen to her numb feet and legs. Panic gripped her heart like a vise. "Run? Run where?" *He'll find me,* she thought, *and this nightmare will brutalize me again.* "I can't do this twice, whoever you are. Let me die. Please, I'd rather die," she wailed.

"No, if you move now, we can get away. I know a place," he said, pushing her toward the door.

He tugged on her arm, urging her to hurry, but she turned for one last look. All of the small green lights on the switchboard that represented all the telephones in Cre Falls were dead; the red lights, which were trunk lines (the "number please" lines), were out as well. Her heart felt as dead as the switchboard.

Wirm was lying on the floor by the closet's open door to the mainframe, the back of his head bleeding. He looked awkward with his hands behind his back, handcuffed. Thin drapery roping circled his neck, tied with a slipknot, and the opposite end was attached to the leg of the mainframe. Already he was struggling, tightening the rope around his neck. He was conscious, mumbling the strange language she had heard through her headset so many times.

The tugging on her arm stopped. Taking her by the shoulders, the stranger turned her to face him. "He's not going to die. He never does. We have ten, maybe fifteen minutes before he's on our trail like a bloodhound. We need to leave now and fast if we're all about living!"

"Who are you? Why? How did you save me? Why don't we get the police? Where are we going?" she said in a blur of words. Looking into his pale gray-blue eyes, she could sense the frustration and urgency he was feeling.

"Not now, Lucy. Later, when we're away from here, I'll try to tell you everything. Let's go," he said, taking her hand and starting off on Pine Street.

The night was clear and cool, with a full moon casting their shadows in front of them. He moved fast, but she was able to keep up. Confused and disoriented, she soon realized they had turned the corner and were headed down Ice House Street toward the Cre Falls Mill dam.

Knowing it was impossible to get across the river using the dam, she couldn't understand how they would be able to escape going this way. When they arrived at the dam, her rescuer climbed up the cement buttress using hand- and footholds he had obviously used many times before. He scaled the buttress to the top without difficulty and motioned for her to do the same.

"I can't do that. I could never do that," she said with a quiver of anxiety in her voice.

"You have to, Lucy," he called down to her. "Pull yourself up and don't look down."

New terror flooded her traumatized mind. Could she get to the top without falling, and could she get there before Wirm pulled her back? Knowing she had to try to save herself, she tucked the skirt of her dress into her white cotton underwear. She put her feet in the first footholds, and they immediately slipped out. Removing her shoes and putting them inside the front of her dress, she started again. She began counting the number of times she moved her feet higher up on the cement buttress. Finding it unbelievable when the count was only ten, she made an effort to go faster. Her bare knees were already rubbed raw from scraping against the cement. The full moon gave enough light for her to see the places to put her feet and the handholds to pull herself up, but she knew Wirm would see her the minute he turned the corner on Ice House Street. If she was going to get away, getting off the dam buttress was imperative, even though she was sure escaping Wirm was an exercise in futility.

Keeping her eyes on her savior, far above her, outlined in the moonlight, she felt an imaginary strength seep into her shaking leg muscles. Even though he did not yell down to her, she could feel him urging her on. She reached the count of twenty and was sure muscle fatigue would be her undoing. Leaning her cheek against the cold cement, the only prayer that came to mind was "Count with me, Lord." *Twenty-one, twenty-two, twenty ...* At last her right hand reached out and touched the steel bar of a railing. Finding one more foothold, her left hand grabbed on as well. His hand was there to help pull her over the railing bars. With legs unable to hold her upright, she collapsed on the train trestle.

"You made it, Lucy," he whispered, kneeling on the trestle. "The hardest part is over. Stand up. We'll walk the rest of the way together. Hold on to the crossbars and move your feet on the train tracks. The way down on the other side is simple, just stairs."

For the first time since Wirm's call, she started to sob, the tears forging rivers down her cheeks. He reached out and patted her back, as if comforting a child. His kindness made her sob all the more. Getting her feet under her and wiping her nose on her sleeve, she took the hand he offered and made her way across the train trestle. The dam beneath was turbid. Frothy river water drummed over the dam by the thousands of gallons. The noise was vociferous. The dizzying, turbid water left her with an overwhelming desire to jump over the railing. Focusing on the back of his neck, she continued the walk to the other side. Just as he said, there was, on the east side of the trestle, stairs and a railing to hold on to.

Once off the dam, they followed the Cre River. At times the footing was boggy, and it was difficult to find the next part of the dry path. River rushes made their progress congested and slow, but he moved the obstacles out of her way the best he could. More than once, some creature slithered over her feet. She felt, rather than knew, that they were headed out of town too.

They turned on a logging road called Grassy Road by the locals. This is where she had picked berries in the recent past. As they left the river, the footing got easier. He picked up the pace without looking back to see whether she was following. She was exhausted and found it difficult to catch her breath. She stopped briefly and bent over to relieve a stitch in her side. She pleaded for a rest break.

He looked back without slowing his pace and said, "We can't stop now. We're almost there, Lucy. Please, keep up."

She wanted to ask him where they were going, but he turned forward before she had a deep enough breath to speak. The pervasive evil of Wirm seemed to follow behind them down the road. The sensation that he was close enough to touch her back propelled her forward. Loss ate at her heart—loss of her lifetime job, loss of her once-safe home, mostly loss in the belief she could always care for herself. Knowing none of these safe havens would be hers again left her without an identity. From this night forward, she would always think of herself as Wirm's victim. Fury that she would never be the same sullied her belief in what was good in her life. Live or die, her life was now inexorably tied with Wirm. With all of her being she repudiated this evil plunder of herself.

Abruptly, her companion veered off the logging road and onto a dark path shadowed from the moon by trees. Into the path a few feet, he stopped. Hugging a tree, he breathed heavily. Perspiration glistened on his face, which was now ghostly pale.

"Why have we stopped? Oh, you're sick," she said, putting a hand to his forehead. "Your shirt is soaked with sweat. Tell me what's wrong."

"I'm having an insulin reaction from too much running and no food since noon yesterday," he said, his voice quivering. "Help me get to the shack. I have food stashed there. We'd better not waste time. I'm close to fainting. Stay on the path for about a hundred feet. You'll see the shack on your left."

She extracted his arms from the tree and put her arm around him. As he leaned against her, she mostly dragged him down the path. "Please don't go unconscious. I don't even know your name. I don't know how to help you."

"Lucy, don't talk so much," he said weakly. "Save your breath. We'll get there."

Looking to her left, she saw the form of a shack mostly hidden by trees and underbrush. Pulling him through the underbrush, she gently lowered him to the ground in front of an open door. The wind eerily swung the door on rusty hinges, making a screeching noise in the quiet forest.

Weak and almost comatose, he muttered, "On the table. Sweet stuff. Hurry!"

Reluctantly, she stepped through the door of the darkened cabin. There on the table was a rucksack with bulging sides. Quickly opening it, she grabbed a bottle of juice and two packages of sugar. Finding a cup, she dissolved the sugar in the juice and hurried to where he lay, hoping he could still swallow. "Hey, look at me," she said breathlessly. She lifted his head to her lap and let some juice trickle in his mouth. She massaged his throat and felt him swallow. Repeating this until the juice was gone, she prayed that what she'd given him was enough. She held his head on her lap, waiting for the crisis to pass, with only the screeching door for company.

Fifteen, maybe twenty, minutes of anxious prayer gave way to fear that she was too late. Sure he had succumbed to this terrible disease while bravely trying to save her from Wirm, she could hardly endure the thought. Mourning her defender, she stretched out by his side, holding him in her arms. She slipped into sleep as easily as he succumbed to twilight coma. She was lightly aware of the night, but did not care.

Sometime later, she stirred. Thinking she was back by her switchboard, and Wirm was pushing her against the wall, she came awake batting at the air and screaming. It took several moments for her to realize she was sitting on the ground next to her defender, and to her astonished relief he's alive. She squeals with delight as he stands and offered her a hand up. The sky was streaked with gray as dawn pushed away feral darkness.

They turned in unison toward the door of the cabin. He took hold of the swing door and let her pass into the maw of the ancient shack: one room, one table, one fireplace, two small windows. That was it. The smell was acidic, wet burned wood and dust. With no apparent place to sit, she stood by the table. He came to her side, grabbed the rucksack, and knelt in the center of the floor, feeling for a latch. Pulling up the cellar door, he felt in the rucksack for a flashlight. In the pitch-black, the dim glow barely revealed the steps that led to the cave below.

He motioned for her to lead down the stairs. Finding no railing to hold on to, she leaned against the wood wall and was able to take several steps. Overhead he pulled the trap door down. Using the weak light of his flashlight, he pushed a steel bar across the trap door, locking them in the cellar.

"Let me go in front of you," he said. "Don't be afraid. I'll shine the light on the steps so you won't fall."

Coming away from the wall, she took his offered hand. Step by step, they made it to the bottom. It was cool and humid and smelled like a root cellar. He handed over the flashlight and disappeared into the black room. She attempted to examine the space before her, but the pitch-blackness of the cellar rendered the weak light inadequate. She heard him stumbling around in the dark, whistling a tuneless melody.

"How can he be so calm?" she thought out loud. "Wirm on our scent, barred in this root cellar with no light, and probably nothing else to help us survive, and he's calm enough to whistle. Out of tune at that." She suddenly smelled something suspiciously like kerosene. With a sudden flare of a match, the cave burst into light.

The room was small with rock walls and a packed dirt floor. In the middle of the room was an oak table and two chairs excoriated by age. On the right side against the wall was a homemade bed frame with a surprisingly clean mattress. A blanket was folded neatly on top of a pillow. She realized he must have stocked up on supplies; there on the shelves to her left were cans of food, a jar of peanut butter, and a loaf of bread. Astonished at his resourcefulness, she felt suddenly jarred by reality. He had planned her rescue, planned her escape, and made plans to help her survive. Had he followed Wirm to her house? How? How did he know? She looked at him, puzzled.

He put a hand up to stop her. "First, come and sit down," he said. "I have to take some insulin and then make us something to eat. You must be starved and tired. I'll explain everything after you've eaten and had a cup of coffee." Pouring coffee from a thermos into two cups, he retrieved the peanut butter and bread off the shelf. "Here, you make the sandwiches. Come, Lucy, sit."

Sitting at the table, she took the butter knife from him and began spreading peanut butter on the bread. The coffee was more than a marvel. It was a spiritual offering. Watching him closely as he cleansed an area on his abdominal fold with an alcohol pad and injected insulin from a syringe with the expertise of someone who had done this often, she grimaced for him.

"I want to know your name. I want to know how you knew Wirm would come for me. I want to know where I am and what makes you think we're safe here. I want to know if you're evil like Wirm or a holy saint," she said, letting the tears drip off her nose and fall onto the sandwich in front of her.

Sipping his coffee and taking a bite of sandwich, he sighed. "My name is Harold Brown. The reason you don't know me is I have been living at the nursing home. I know Wirm better than I knew my own father. As a matter of fact, Wirm and my father were buddies. Close buddies. They took turns abusing me when I was too young and weak to fight back. I killed my father right here in this cabin and went to prison for five years until the judge set me free because of evidence against my father. After that, I couldn't get anyone to hire me. I lived on the streets. Here in the woods in the summer. I've been spending most of my time tracking Wirm, on foot and in my mind. When I didn't take care of getting insulin every day, Alice Perry at the nursing home decided to help me. So I ended up in the nursing home, watching the streets, watching Wirm. I don't have to follow him on foot anymore. I just know where he is. Don't scream or anything, but right now he's looking in the shack window."

Heart thudding against her chest wall, she lifted her eyes from Harold to the ceiling. "Why have you trapped us down here? How can we possibly be safe here? Oh, what have you done?" Her words came out like a hiss.

He put his hand on the table over hers and said, "Please trust me. Wirm won't cross the threshold of that squeaky door. I think it has something to do with the night I bashed in my father's head. He was here standing in the doorway that night. He didn't lift a hand to help ol' Brown the Terrible. After I hit my father the second time, he staggered over to Wirm, spitting blood all over his face. Wirm started to scream, yelling something about the blood burning him, and took off down the path. I know he's wanted to come in the cabin after me since, but he can't pass by the bloodstains on the doorpost. That's why we're here. That's why we're safe."

"One more question, Harold Brown." Lucy's mind was foggy from the events of the last twelve or so hours. "Why did you save me?"

Sighing as though all this talking was more conversation than he had engaged in a long time, he said, "I need you to help get rid of Wirm once and for all when the time comes. I know it is too early for her to come back. I haven't been able to help the others Wirm has had a part in killing. You know, I'm just a voyeur with my hands tied. When I knew he was going to hurt you, Lucy, I had a breakthrough. Because of all the midnight phone calls, you think Wirm did the actual murdering. But it has always been his evil mind that has influenced the doer. Without Wirm, most of the crimes he called you about would not have happened. I knew he wouldn't be able to resist coming for you. He had to destroy your goodness, your purity, your beautiful soul. He was drawn to your shining spirit. But I was almost too late. I got hung up by the night nurse before coming out. She was making quality-care checks of all things."

Lucy was hardly breathing by this point. Her words took a while to come out right. "Harold, how were you able to get out of the nursing home, and how do you know all this about Joseph Wirm?"

Looking to the small twin bed, he laughed. "That will have to wait until later, dear Lucy. It looks like you and I are sharing this bed."

Grabbing his hand and pulling him back from his descent onto the bed, she said, "Thank you for my life, Harold. Thank you."

They curled up, spoon fashion, on the narrow bed. She fell asleep before three thoughts crossed her mind. Innocent of all the evils of their world, their sleep is dreamless.

Above them, Wirm circled the cabin, snarling. Losing his moment with Lucy sustained his hateful rage. Losing to Harold Brown on top of that was insufferable. The damnable bloodstain on the doorpost was, after all these years, the effective barricade that kept him from squashing him once and for all. This single-minded angst preoccupied Wirm as he spread his evil through the night. He could sense their combined power against him from beneath the earth. He was consumed with the need to kill, and it fed his temper tantrum. When the sky began to turn gray, he slithered down the path, whimpering.

Lucy came awake with a start, feeling a brick leaving her chest. At once she felt safer. And she felt her bladder nudge her too. Extracting herself from Harold's limbs, she made for the steps. The kerosene lantern was burning low, giving off a weak beacon. Negotiating the steps that were so narrow she barely had room to place her foot, she reached the top. The iron bar was her next obstacle. Pushing it aside proved too difficult. She was forced to call for Harold's help. At once, he was looking up at her from the bottom, fear exaggerating his skeletal features.

"Don't open that trap door, Lucy," he seethed. "I didn't go through all this for you to walk into Wirm's arms. Wirm reads your mind like a book."

"I have to go to the bathroom," she moaned. "Besides, I think Wirm is gone for now."

"Come back down here and use the commode I set up for you. Didn't you see the curtained-off corner?"

His instructions were more demands than requests. Making her way back down the stairs, she thought her bladder might burst. He was fixing the lantern with his back to her, so she quickly scooted to the curtained corner.

"How was I to know where to go if you didn't tell me?" she mumbled under her breath. Pulling the curtain aside, she realized he had planned for her comfort. On a small table next to the commode was a washbasin filled with water and a cloth.

Just before she pulled the curtain closed, she noticed him hanging his head and rubbing it as if trying to figure out the solution to a very difficult problem. While she was washing up, he said, "We have to find a way to block Wirm from reading your thoughts, any ideas?"

She came back out from behind the curtain, and he looked up at her with expectant eyes, as if pleading for her help.

"I don't know. Numbers have been my entire focus for so many years. They're about all I know."

"Numbers, numbers. Sure, yeah, why not numbers?" he said, but his voice gave away his uncertainty.

She sat at the table, watching him take insulin. Of course, food would be next. Looking at their meager supplies, she worried about where they would get more. They would have to leave this cellar, and then what?

It seemed it wasn't just Wirm who was in her head. "Okay. What happens when we run out of food, Harold?"

She expected him to have worked out the answer to her concern, but he shrugged. "I don't know. I'll have to face that when it happens."

"You know we can't leave the lack of food for when we have none. We must come up with some plan before it's a crisis," she huffed.

"Let's table that thought and spend some time working out a number thing to confuse Wirm. Can you fill your mind with numbers that mean something to you and actually no one else?"

"Do you mean phone numbers? I can't see how they would mean much to me. Do you?"

"If we could just figure out a code for words—like eleven means hello or something along those lines."

"That's not practical, Harold. I would have to have a number for each word I know. That would be thousands and thousands. Are you saying I have to give up speaking words entirely?"

"Yes, Lucy. I know that will be next to impossible for you, but if you and I are going to survive, I think you'll have to find a way to do this. You need to figure out a way to replace your thoughts as well as your speech with something else, something that only makes sense to you. If you can do that, we might have a chance to get out of here. Lucky for me, he can't get into my head."

"I get where you're going, Harold. If I can't do this, we don't get out to get more supplies. We just die, right?"

She looked at the shelf with their meager food supplies. Three cans of soup, one can of pork and beans, half a bottle of juice, a gallon of water, the peanut butter, and half a loaf of bread. She would have to solve the number problem, memorize it, and be ready to walk out of here in less than three days. She could ration how much she ate, but Harold couldn't.

She spent the rest of the day, and long after Harold went to sleep, trying to come up with a workable code. A number code would probably keep Wirm out of her mind. She had faith in Harold, but she also knew that never again, for as long as God allowed her to live in this world, would another soul converse with her. The packed-earth floor made a suitable blackboard. Using a stick Harold found, she scratched out a failed attempt and tried again. How to make words out of numbers? How to easily memorize the number code? How to keep the code safely locked in her mind?

"One could be the letter A," she mumbled as she worked, "No, way too simple. Two could be A. Too easy to think forward."

So the scratching went on through the night. By the time she could not keep her eyes open any longer, the entire floor was scratched with numbers and letters. Convinced she was not smart enough to come up with a code, she put the stick down. Too tired to make room on the bed, she rested her head on the table, using her arms for a pillow. She murmured a silent prayer to the Holy Spirit to open her mind or to simply leave her life in God's hands. A little drool escaped her mouth and puddled on her arm as she easily slipped into sleep.

She felt Harold wrap the blanket over her shoulders. Grateful for its warmth, she kept her eyes closed for a time, reluctant to give up the illusion of comfort. She searched her mind for a solution that might have been given to her while she was asleep. No more of an answer blazed in her mind than before. Harold was busy with morning needs.

"Harold," she said, yawning, "we can't stay here even if we're able to get more food. Can you think of another place where we can be safe and survive? Even if—and Harold, that's a big if—I can come up with a number code to confuse Wirm, we still can't stay here."

"Don't you think I know that, Lucy?" he said. He was not angry. "We have to come up with the number thing before walking up those steps. We can make it to the Catholic Church, I think. Father Jim will help us. He drives to the nursing home at noon on Wednesday. If we can block Wirm from reading your mind, I think we can make it there. The safe thing about the nursing home is all the people, all the time. We'll be warm and fed. You know, Lucy, we're making this number code too complicated. Let's try an easier approach."

They sat across from each other, smiling. A certain renewal of determination melded their minds. Going to the nursing home was brilliant. It is an easy walk to the church now that they were on this side of the river.

"All I have to do is look vacant and spout numbers. Not only will Father help us, but the nursing home will admit us in a minute," Lucy said, almost laughing. Her eyes were wide with excitement. Grabbing his hands, she stared deeply into his eyes. At once she knew the answer. The code immediately became part of her memory. She attempted to tell Harold, but the words that fell out of her mouth were numbers. "22-4 13-4 4-3 19-14 11-4-0-21-4 13-14-22." *Oh God help me, it worked, she thought.*

Kneeling next to her chair, Harold held her in his arms, allowing her as much comfort as he had to give. This was Lucy's ultimate sacrifice. No more words. Only numbers for as long as Wirm was able to spread his brand of evil on Cre Falls, only numbers.

Now, while Lucy was looking vacant and whispering the numbers that would be her new language, he decided to tell her what he knew about the woman who would come one day. Quietly, while still holding her head to his chest, he told her, like a father tells a child a bedtime story. "A woman everyone will call Jane will come to Cre Falls for the second time. She'll be searching for the truth of the stories you and I know. She will find a way to break this number code, and you will help her understand the real reason she risked everything to come here. You will be her guardian against Wirm.

Your numbers will block Wirm from your mind. He will not be able to stop you from reading his thoughts, but he will not be able to read yours. Give me your hand, Lucy. You don't need to be afraid. Let's get out of this prison and go find Father Jim. He has helped me in the past, and I know he will again."

Taking her hand, he led her up the stairs, lifted the iron bar barrier, and raised the trap door. The sun was still weak, with the dawn coming on slowly. He prayed he wasn't overestimating Lucy's ability to confuse Wirm with numbers. There was no sign of him lurking around the shack.

"He thinks we don't need to run yet, but if we have to, I hope it's not until we're getting close to town. There's lots of traffic heading out of town. First thing we have to do is get off the woods trail and the logging road. Too many places we can get ambushed."

Harold was thinking out loud to comfort Lucy. As soon as he hatched his plan, the pale skin of Lucy's face blanched two more shades, and her hand quivered in his. He could see she was afraid. The cicadas were singing their discordant summer chorus. In the canopy of trees overhead, morning songbirds were singing with kinetic energy. These sounds were so loud compared with the silence of the cellar that Harold's ears felt assaulted. As they headed south on the logging road, he knew it was now that Lucy's numbers would be most tested.

Lucy knew exactly where they were and was prepared to walk. She could see the Catholic Church steeple from the logging road. There was a sidewalk in front of the church, so they were once again walking side by side. Harold held her hand, giving it an encouraging squeeze, and steered her into the parking lot between the church and rectory. There, standing next to his car, still in his chasuble from eight o'clock mass, Father appeared to be having an argument with Wirm.

The priest was a tall, round friar. His head was totally bald, and the luminous dome gave his whole head radiance. His kindly face had plenty of laugh lines. He wore his firm faith in God like a bulletproof vest.

At this moment he appeared as angry as Harold had ever seen him. Waving his arms and shouting, he fearlessly stepped closer to

Wirm. Now almost nose-to-nose with Wirm, he raised the stole, still around his neck from earlier confessions, and touched Wirm's chest. Wirm jumped back as if he had received a shock.

He turned and ran from the parking lot, yelling, "You know where they are. You can't hide them from me forever, priest!"

From the bushes where they were hiding, Harold counted them lucky that Wirm couldn't find Lucy's mind.

"See, Lucy, the numbers work," he said. "We'll wait until Wirm is out of sight and catch Father in the church. Wirm is very afraid of going in the church."

A few minutes later, Lucy and Harold entered the cool, dark church. Father Jim was kneeling in front of the altar, head bowed in silent prayer. Quietly slipping into a pew behind him, they kneeled and said a prayer for deliverance from the evil that was chasing them. As the priest turned to them, his face registered surprise and immediately relief.

"Harold. Lucy. Praise God you're safe. Lucy, the whole town is looking for you. Seems the phone system is still down. I chased Wirm off, but I'm sure he'll be back. Come to the rectory and have breakfast with me."

During breakfast Harold retold the whole story, from Wirm's attack on Lucy to where they had been hiding, to coming to the church and seeing Father run off Wirm. Of course, Lucy didn't utter a word. Finally, Father asked whether the trauma had left Lucy speechless. Harold explained the need for a number code to confuse Wirm. Father looked incredulously at Harold.

"I know you, Harold, and have come to accept your gifts," he said. "I also believe they're God-given. Now, how can I help the two of you?"

Harold wiped his mouth and folded the napkin he was holding in a steady, slow way. "We have to get to the nursing home without being too exposed. When you go there to say mass this morning, we want to catch a ride. We'll be safe there and taken care of, especially if we're admitted behind the doors on the second floor."

"Yes," Father said, breathing out what sounded like a sigh of relief. "Finish your breakfast while I gather the mass things I need. I think this idea of yours is a good one, Harold."

They had no problem migrating to Father's car. Father put a small bottle of holy water on the dash for use as a weapon. The ride to the nursing home took only ten minutes. Lucy was all eyes, staring out the window, since this might be the last time she would see the streets of Cre Falls.

Arriving at the nursing home, they let Father go ahead up the sidewalk. Harold took Lucy's hand and tried to comfort her. "We're together until the end, Lucy."

Walking through the doors on that day, Lucy was seventy-two years old, and Harold was fifty-nine. Thinking in unison, they pleaded with God to have the woman come soon.

Part Five

Her Brutal Belief

"They can because they think they can."

—Virgil

Chapter Thirteen

I don't startle awake, remembering Wirm's threat. I chug up from the fog slowly, remembering Arthur. It is the memory that always punches fear into my semi consciousness, the devil Arthur, the pet name given to this damn disease. This will be the time prednisone doesn't work. This is the end of my mobility, the end of hand use. This is the time I'm forever a nursing home cripple, or will the miracle happen once more? Fear of Wirm is a distant nag. Fear of Arthur is conditioning, like Pavlov's dog.

Not moving any part that may hurt, I blink open my crusty eyes. On one of my many office visits, a rheumatologist added my eyes to my list of possible deformities. Rheumatoid arthritis severely robs eyes of moisture, making tearing impossible, interfering with vision, and causing repeated eye infections. My eyes are open now, recording the new day. My ability to move my mouth indicates inflammation has not locked the mandibular joints. These are the baby steps I take before summoning the courage to try out hands, wrists, elbows, and shoulders, the litany of joints that could end my ability to function. *Arthur the demon is in the building*, my mind sings. Truth be known, this is one more episode (one more event) toward inevitable crippling. No amount of prednisone changes that reality. Carpe diem. Pluck the day. Let the struggles begin. Push Arthur back. Today I refuse to be identified as the arthritic. Please let me be the mysterious Jane Doe, the fearless writer from behind the doors.

Then Lucy's code comes to mind, and a smile twitches at the corners of my mouth. Yup, today I will understand Lucy's numbers.

Lucy and I will embrace conversation as we haven't been able to do since being admitted here. Anxious for that moment, I find the motivation to move my hands. Fingers and wrists are sore, but movement happens. Up the arms and down to the walking joints, I take inventory. There's pain, but not the irascible pain of midnight, no longer the hope-stealing pain. The familiar little red engine, "I think I can, I think I can," is what pushes the demon Arthur back. He's there, sharing a place with Wirm as a distant threat in my mind. From this place I know they will fight for supremacy to be my worst enemy.

Pulling myself up using my elbows, I peer over at Lucy. Lucy is already up, dressed, and in her wheelchair. Her arms are folded in front on her bedside table, making a pillow for her head. She appears to be sleeping. Thinking the past night has taken its toll on Lucy, I'm reluctant to disturb her. Using the bed railing, I pull my upper body to a sitting position. Thinking it must be very early and wondering what Lucy is doing up already, I bend over to cushion my painful arms. In the early dawn stillness, I hear Lucy sobbing quietly in her folded arms.

"Lucy, for heaven's sake, what's wrong?" I ask, alarmed.

Increasing my terror, Lucy does not lift her head or give any indication she has heard me. Thoughts of possible abuse or, God forbid, Wirm make breathing difficult.

"Lucy, please, look at me and tell me what's wrong," I say, pleading. "I'll understand. I can now. Are you hurt?"

Swinging my legs over the side of my bed, I stand without my knees giving away. Using my bed for support, I make my way to Lucy's side. Feeling secure holding on to Lucy's wheelchair, I pause to steady myself. Slowly Lucy raises her head, turns, and looks into my eyes. Surprise sticks in my throat. I do not read sadness in those blue, blue eyes, but seething, bristling anger. These are tears wrought by seething anger.

Flinching, I say, "What … what's this all about? Who has made you so mad? Tell me so I can fix it."

"7 -14-22 2-0-13 24-14-20 1-4 19-7-4 14-13-4. 24-14-20 0-17-4 19-14-14 22-4-0-10 19-14 7-4-11-15 7-0-17-14-11-3 18-19-14-15 22-8-17-12."

"Wait, you're going too fast! I need to write the numbers down, or I'll never understand what you're saying. I'll get something to write with. Please give me a chance."

I make my way back to my bedside table and return with paper and pen. At the top of my paper I write the alphabet and give each letter a number, just the way I saw the code during my screaming night of pain. "Okay, Lucy, once more, only this time slower."

Lucy starts again, and I write the numbers down. This is going to take time, I realize, and if Lucy gets too frustrated, she will clam up. Still, what else do we have to do this morning but learn to talk to each other?

"6-4-19 0 2-7-0-8-17. 24-14-20 13-4-4-3 19-14 18-8-19."

Quickly I note the first letter of each word and get the gist of what Lucy is saying. Pushing my chair in front of Lucy's bedside table, I gladly sit with a grimace of knee pain. "Okay, I'm ready. Tell me again why you're so mad at me."

Before starting to speak, Lucy puts her hand over the top of mine. "7-14-22 2-0-13 24-14-20 1-4 19-7-4 14-13-4? 24-14-20 0-17-4 19-14-14 22-4-0-10 19-14 7-4-11-15 7-0-17-14-11-3 18-19-14-15 22-8-17-12." She enunciates each number like she is speaking to a child.

Matching the numbers with what I believe is the correct letters seems to take forever. I can't come up with a shortcut to make the process faster. After relaxing for a moment to clear my mind, I begin again, calmer. I determine that her first sentence is "How can you be the one?" The one? Which one does she think I am? I move to the next sentence: "You're too weak to help Harold stop Wirm."

"Harold?" I say, looking up at Lucy. "Harold is going to stop Wirm from doing what? Lucy, why are you angry with me if I'm not the one? Or if I'm the one and can't help Harold? Lucy, I just don't understand. Stop Wirm from doing what? If I'm too weak, or you mean too sick, I'm here to tell you, girl, Harold's not in top shape himself, if you haven't noticed."

I'm rambling. This is not at all what I thought our first conversation would be about. I thought a hello or a "how are you feeling?" would be the first numbered words she would spell out for me. But this! Telling me I'm not "the one"?

Lucy begins again, and I snap out of my confusion to jot down the numbers. "24-14-20-17 9-0-13-4 19-7-4 14-13-4 7-0-17-14-11-3 18-0-8-3 22-14-20-11-3 2-4-12-4 18-19-14-15 0-13 19-14 22-8-17-12, 14-13-11-24 22-0-24."

"Lucy, I think you and Harold have the wrong Jane! I think either one or both of you have caught 'behind the doors' syndrome. If you have a case against Wirm, you should call the cops," I say.

"2-0-11-11 19-7-4 2-14-15-18! 11-14-14-10 0-19 12-4 13-14-19 11-8-10-4-11-24!"

"Okay, I get it! You can't call the cops, but why do you want Wirm dead? Isn't that a little drastic? And you think I should be the one to do just that?" I let incredulity slip into my voice.

"7-0-17-14-11-3 18-0-8-3 24-14-20-17 19-7-4 14-13-4 18-14 24-14-20-17 19-7-4 14-13-4," she says, slapping her hand on the bedside table.

"Listen, sister," I say with a laugh that sounds like misery.

Lucy and I are having our first fight. We sound like two old hags arguing about which exit we should take off the freeway. Here we are flinging words and numbers back and forth like inmates with a diagnosis of dementia. She actually thinks I should kill Wirm. *Oh, Lucy, you're losing it*, I think.

"8 2-0-13-19 18-0-24 19-7-4 22-14-17-3-18 19-14 12-0-10-4 24-14-20 20-13-3-4-17-18-19-0-13-3. 15-11-4-0-18-4 19-17-20-18-19 12-4," she says meekly.

Lucy is bristling. I can tell she has taken offense at my moment of mirth. "Okay, Lucy, let's shelve this until later. Don't be mad at me. I'll try to be better at this. Later this morning, after the medical records secretary goes on break, I want to sneak my manuscript pages in the file drawer where she keeps the deceased records. Will you be my lookout?"

Examining Lucy closely, I see that she apparently is no longer angry. She appears exhausted instead. She is visibly frailer, diminished in some way. Gone is her pugnacity. The long night awake and the emotional morning have sucked vitality from her spirit, I fear. She sits slumped in her wheelchair, head down, and chin resting on her chest. I'm afraid Lucy is having a medical crisis. Lifting her hands, she pushes up her head, murmuring some numerical whispers I can't distinguish. The numbers are musical and sound like a chant or prayer.

Instead of putting on my call light and waiting twenty minutes for help, I gingerly make my way to the door, thinking Lucy is so much better than I at attracting attention. Determined to find an aide and bully her into helping Lucy, I manage to get myself into the hallway. Leaning against the wall to steady my aching joints, I wail, "Help!" Thinking that Lucy is having serious health issues dries up all the spit in my mouth. Standing on trembling knees, I yell, "Help, I'm going to fall!"

Probably the most overused word in the nursing home is "help." Residents cry help, yell help, demand help, and plea for help whether they need it or not. Nurses call for help when they need extra hands during a procedure or while attempting to handle a combative resident. All employees of the nursing home call for an aide's help when what they're doing falls below the imagined scope of their practice. But the call "Help, I'm falling" sends a current of immediate response from the staff. The state agency governing nursing homes frowns on resident falls, and they create reams of paperwork for nursing.

They hear me. Out of a resident's room tear two aides to the rescue along with Donald (the Wirm-watch orderly). I mouth the words I inevitably know are coming. *What are you doing out here?*

"What are you doing out here, Ms. Doe?" The first aide with the fastest sneakers is the one admonishing me. "I can't believe after last night you're walking out in the hall. What are you thinking?"

All three stumble over each other in an effort to get me safely back to bed. I almost get tripped. A fall could be a real possibility here.

"It's Lucy—you have to get Lucy back to bed. Something is really wrong with her. Call the nurse," I say, pumping anxiety into the mix.

I watch them gently lift Lucy from her chair to the bed. She doesn't lift an eyelid to peek. I can barely see the rise and fall of her chest. Her breaths are shallow.

Donald calls out, "Get Mary, quick!"

Donald stands by Lucy's bedside, calling her name. Anxiety has me dumbstruck. I see no response from Lucy. Not a flicker, nothing except regular shallow breathing. Where in the heck is Mary, for crying out loud? Surely seconds, not minutes, have passed, but it feels like the latter. Just as I'm about to head up the hall, Mary appears in the doorway, taking her sweet time.

"Did you call the doctor or the ambulance?" I ask. The frantic pitch of my voice makes me sound like a teenage boy.

"You last night, Lucy this morning. If I didn't know better, I'd think there was bad juju in this room," she says. "Lucy has had TIA in the past. That's small strokes. If she comes out of this as before, good. Doctor has an order on her chart for 'No hospitalization.' Her vitals are stable. So we wait and see." Leaving, she turns to the aide. "See that Lucy is kept comfortable and her roommate stops hovering over her."

The aide catches the look in my eyes, and realizing that saying nothing is a sagacious approach, she leaves to catch up on her morning work. Donald leaves as well after he gives my shoulder a reassuring pat.

Pushing Lucy's wheelchair close enough, I sit to take up the position of "wait and see." I mutter prayers to God, the advocate of geriatric earthbound angels. *Please, I need her too*, I pray. Out loud I say, "Lucy, don't give up on me, you hear!"

After taking medication at eight and ignoring my breakfast tray, I prepare myself for the long hours ahead. After some time, I realize I've been talking out loud to Lucy about our early morning number session, trying to make sense of what she said and how her anger might have brought on the TIA (transient ischemic attack). I'm well aware that past TIA attacks often precede a full-blown stroke, and I look for signs that this has happened. Getting out my flashlight, I look for right or left fixed pupils indicating a complete stroke. As Mary said, we wait and see. We wait until Lucy opens her eyes and then see what function she has left.

Talking quietly to Lucy has the remarkable effect of calming my anxiety. I lull myself with memories of our first days together and how, when I needed her, she was my loud Lucy. I whisper how I need her to help me understand all that she knows. I tell her again of my plan to take the pages of my book to Medical Records across the hall and put them in the deceased file when Janet, the medical records secretary, is on break. On and on, I have a one-sided conversation with Lucy, not especially different from before I knew her code. Only now I plead with her to come back to me. The hours pass, and lunch trays are up. I pick the cup of coffee off my tray and once again sit in Lucy's wheelchair, sipping it and telling her how wonderfully awful it is, as always. I put my head down on her bed and doze, lightly at first, before slipping into sound sleep.

I awaken with a start when the day aides come in to change Lucy's linens and reposition her. They say I have to sit on the other side of the room behind the privacy curtain while the job is being done. Jean, the aide who escorted me to accounting, says she will take Lucy's vitals and let me know what they are. Feeling like a zombie, I walk down the hall to work out the stiffness in my joints. Mary is coming through the doors with none other than Wirm in tow.

Mary says cheerfully, "Look who's back, will you? Poor man is so upset that he frightened you and Lucy. He says he went in your room because he was concerned that you were sick. When Lucy sounded the alarm, his only thought was to get out, so he went out the door in the confusion. He's back now and better for it."

"Don't believe him, Mary," I mordantly say, staring Wirm right in his dead-fish eyes. "He's here to do no good, and I will be ready for his next move. You'll be sure to tell him what will happen if he goes near Lucy! Instead of spending your precious time taking care of that evil idiot, you should be concerned with Lucy."

Wirm looks over his shoulder with an insidious grin as he continues down the hall with Mary. He makes a threatening fist and shakes it as he passes our door.

Following Wirm's progress down the hall, I notice Harold sitting in the hall with escalating agitation, repeating, "Do-da, do-da geta gun." I really want to tell him about Lucy, but I know it will be prudent to wait until his aggressive behavior calms down. Maybe bedtime will be a better time.

Meeting me at the door, Jean says with a helpless shrug, "Her vitals are on the low side, but they seem stable. She didn't open her eyes or acknowledge she knew we were cleaning her up or repositioning her. I took care of her the last time this happened. This time is different. I wonder if she has just given up. Keep talking to her. If she hears anyone, it will be you."

Going back in our room, I take up my vigil at her bedside. I can't help wondering what Wirm being back might have to do with Lucy's unconsciousness. What I do know is that she fears him above all else. He is her bête noire like no other—Wirm the beast out of the past.

If only Harold would talk to me, I muse. I decide I'll take his supper tray down to him. Maybe while I'm feeding him, he'll say something useful.

"Lucy, Lucy, please wake up. Tell me how to be the one against Wirm," I say, holding her hand.

Lucy's breathing hasn't changed since this morning, still shallow and regular. I check her pulse every fifteen minutes. So far no apnea or mottling of her extremities. No indication that she has moved closer to morbidity. One change I do notice is rapid eye movement under her eyelids, a sure sign of dreaming. Watching the movement of her closed eyes, which has not even slowed in the past hour, I know the dream she is having must be vivid. I didn't notice this before meeting Wirm in the hallway. If Lucy is dreaming of Wirm, I'm afraid she is experiencing terror.

Donna, the evening nurse, arrives during required rounds to those residents who are in crisis. She asks me to move once again while she assesses Lucy's status. I again wonder why they are not sending Lucy to the hospital.

Before she leaves the room, I ask, "Who decided on no hospitalization for Lucy?"

Donna answers without looking up from the chart she is writing in. "Her doctor. Who else?"

"So Lucy didn't have a choice? Would she go to the hospital if she had broken her leg?"

Exasperated, Donna turns to me. "Of course that's an emergency. Do you know the difference?"

"A brain injury is not an emergency?" I charge back, ready for an argument.

Avoiding an answer, Donna begins to close the door. I follow her out of our room. Walking down the hall, I hear Donna give voice to the one argument I find the hardest to accept. "TIA is a preexisting condition. The doctor has decided that Lucy is not to be hospitalized if she has another episode."

I need something to distract me from my fears. Feeling helpless, I cross the hall into the dining room. The new resident admitted this morning is sitting in a wheelchair near the window. I heard the aides discussing her when she came in, but I was too preoccupied to pay much attention. I do remember the aide calling her the "Shun Lady."

Pulling a chair over to sit facing her, I say, "Hello, my name is Ms. Doe, or everyone calls me Jane Doe, that is."

Her posture is erect and straight as a board. Her face is skeletal, with eyes wide open, giving her the appearance of being startled. Before I can say anything else, she says, "Starvation, mastication, liquidation."

So this is the "shun" in "Shun Lady," I realize. "I get it. You're hungry! Supper trays will be up soon. Can I get you a drink of water in the meantime?"

There is no comment from her, so I take a chance and get her a drink. When I hold the glass in front of her, she makes no movement to grasp it.

"Micturition," she says with urgency.

Leaving the dining room to get an aide, I flag Sara down in the hall. "Our new lady has to go to the bathroom."

"Yeah, sure," says Sara. "You just made that up. Our new lady doesn't make sense. Got you this time, Doe girl."

Low on patience, I exhale. "Micturition. Micturition, for your information, is urination. She has to go."

Putting up a stop hand and looking rather annoyed, she says, "Okay, okay, I'm going."

The new resident says as the aide approaches her, "Salutations, micturition, gratification."

When Sara returns our new resident to the dining room, I say, "I'll feed Harold his supper. Would you bring my tray down to his room as well?"

Sara curtsies. "Yes, Queeny. Try to avoid food splatter when he throws his tray at you. He's pretty agitated tonight."

Stopping in to check on Lucy, I find her current condition has not changed. It's been ten hours since I summoned help for her. I know the effects of TIA can last over twenty-four hours. I also know that as the coma deepens, the more vulnerable the brain becomes to injury.

"That's enough, Lucy," I say. "Open your baby blues and take a peek at the wonderful world. You're really warring on me, you know."

No response, nada. The rapid eye movement and shallow breathing remain the only visible signs of life.

"Mary says the psychiatrist makes rounds day after tomorrow. Do you think you might come to and help me with that?" Still, there's no miracle response, just apparent dreaming out of Lucy.

"I'm going down the hall to feed Harold. I hope he's less agitated. If you were with me, I know you could calm him down," I say, walking into the bathroom to wash my hands. I then cross the room to the door to see whether trays are up. With my back to the room, I hear a faint whisper: "3-17-4-0-12 14-21-4-17."

Hardly believing what I'm hearing, I turn to see Lucy's blue eyes open and a slight grin on her face. I stagger against the doorframe, crying out, "Lucy, you old bag, you didn't leave me after all!"

On unsteady legs, I return to my bedside vigil chair and take her hand in mine. My other hand over my mouth in awe, I find no voice or question worthy of asking. After I thank God for returning my friend to me, my very next prayer is for Lucy to be as she left me.

Lucy seems to find my concern pedantic. The amused look on her face tells me all is well and my concern is ill founded. She looks pale, her pallor blanched more than usual, and the hand I hold is without enough strength to pull from mine. Still speechless, I retrieve my water pitcher and pour Lucy a glass. As I support her head, she drinks deeply. With no coughing and no choking, she swallows without difficulty. Next I hold both of her hands in mine and squeeze. Her grasp is light, but definitely equal. I cannot discern any facial droop. Lucy is back, weaker, but back from wherever her frantic dream held her.

"7-20-13-6-17-24."

"Would you like some soup and more to drink? How about some fruit or ice cream? Can I feel safe leaving you while I get you a tray?" I say. How easily I understand her by just picking out the first couple of letters.

Lucy sighed. "24-4-18 15-11-4-0-18-4."

"I'll let the powers that be know you're awake and hungry," I say. "I was going to help Harold eat, but I think I'll hang out with you for now."

"24-14-20 13-4-4-3 6-14 19-14 7-0-17-14-11-3-18 17-14-14-12 0-5-19-4-17 12-8-3-13-8-6-7-19 17-14-20-13-3-18," she says, a bit out of breath.

I grab my translation sheet and pencil to understand some of what she just said. I immediately get the words "Harold" and "midnight rounds" but need to write down the rest. The first word is "you" and then "need," Followed by some little words and then "Harold after midnight rounds."

"Lucy, I'm not going to ask you why right now, but after you eat and are a little stronger, I'll have to know what this means," I say as I leave the room.

Walking into the dining room, I announce, "Lucy is awake, and she's hungry! She's swallowing just fine and wants soup and fluids. The red juice and ice cream, please. I'm off to find Donna to let her know. I'll help Lucy eat instead of Harold."

I notice Harold is very quiet now down the hall. Heading out the doors to the nurses' station, I can see Donna down the hall on A-wing with her med cart. Although helped by prednisone, my joints are far from being back to precrisis. Walking all the way down A-wing seems like more exercise than I'm able to do just now. A better idea is to wait and let Donna come to me. All the aides are in dining rooms or resident rooms assisting with supper. With Donna busy and the nurses' station empty, I decide to snoop at Lucy's chart.

Realizing I don't know Lucy's last name, I find our room number to identify which chart is hers. In the most recent nursing notes, Donna has charted that she expects Lucy to expire tonight or tomorrow. The stated probable cause: stroke.

"Stroke, my ass, Donna," I mumble.

Lucy's last name is Storm. I wish I could dig further, but Donna is making her way closer, close enough to catch me snooping. It's a nasty no-no, reading a resident's chart—except for nurses, doctors, and the state inspectors, that is. Oh yes, and social workers and many administrators of the nursing home. That's practically everyone except me. I would continue to wait for Donna, but she's so pokey. I trek down A-wing to meet her just as she is coming out of a resident's room, and I lean on her cart for support.

"First, hands off my med cart, next, what do you want?" she says, thoroughly annoyed.

"You really know how to turn a fine moment into crap, Donna," I say. "Lucy is awake and wanting food. She's much weaker, but alert."

"No food until I assess her swallowing," Donna says, asserting her authority.

"I already did that. She's swallowing thin liquids with no problem, and I ordered her soup, juice, and fruit or ice cream. Come to her room and watch her eat soup, Donna."

"You will not, I say not, give any food to Lucy! Do you understand? If you do, I will have the police remove you from this facility," she says, shaking her finger at me.

"Okay, okay, no food for Lucy. Understand, she's awake, she's hungry, and after you assess her, I'll help her eat," I say, walking away miffed.

On my way back to our room, I tell the aide to hold up on Lucy's tray until after Donna sees her. When I turn in, there's Lucy, alert and sitting up, looking like she expects more than me empty-handed.

"You have to wait until Donna puts her fingers down your throat before you get to eat! She threatened to call the cops and have me removed from the nursing home if I so much as touch your lips with a spoon. While we have time to waste, how about telling me why I should see Harold after midnight rounds?"

"7-0-17-14-11-3 22-8-11-11 4-23-15-11-0-8 -13. 8 11-8-10-4 24-14-20 1-4-19-19-4-17 22-7-4-13 24-14-20 0-18-10-4-3 18-12-0-17-19-4-17 16–20-4-18-19-8-14-13-17"

"I'll have you know, Lucy Storm, I was never dumb! Let's see, I go down to see Harold after midnight rounds and …"

"1-4 18-20-17-4 19-14 22-4-0-17 2-0-17-12 2-11-14-19-4-18."

"No more. I have to decode this … You liked me better when I was dumb, and he will explain. Do I have it right? No, let me try again. You liked me when I asked smarter questions. I really don't get that last part. Wear warm clothes? Really? Are you coming with me to Harold's room?"

"8 22-8-18-7," she says with a faraway, wistful look.

"I'll do this because it seems very important to you. I want you to relax, eat some food, and get big and strong, Lucy girl. But still, wear warm clothes? Really, you'd think I was going traveling. Do I have to tell you its summer?

"13-14!"

"You're a woman of few words, and that's another good thing. Well, well, here comes Donna the RN. Make nice and swallow like a good girl," I say as Donna pushes her med cart into the room.

"Well, Lucy, I see you're back once again. Let's have you swallow some water for me. If that goes down without choking, we'll try your medication. I know your roommate already gave you some water, but you have to swallow some for me as well," she says, filling a glass of water.

Lucy holds onto the glass with both hands, drinks several ounces, takes a deep breath, and finishes all the water.

"No choking, no coughing. Good for you. Yes, you can have some soup and the other food Ms. Doe here ordered for you. Please remember, Lucy, your roommate is just another resident. She is not your private nurse. I want you both to understand this before there's real trouble."

Lucy looks at me and raises her eyebrows. I accept her challenge and am ready to clue Donna in when Lucy's tray arrives. Much more important that Lucy eat than I have fun telling Donna what she can do with her rules. Donna gives me a look of smug satisfaction. *Another day, Donna*, I think, *you and me.*

Pulling my chair up closer to the head of Lucy's bed, I begin spooning the homemade, delicious soup our kitchen serves. Lucy purrs, relishing each spoonful. Donna retreats, leaving me with medication and disapproving looks. The aide soon enters with my tray and leaves us with a smile. After they're gone, Lucy clutches her spoon and nods toward my tray.

"Okay, I'll eat too as long as you keep the spoon moving," I say, pushing my chair back to my bedside table. Fearing her reaction, I'm finding it impossible to tell her that Wirm is back in his old room or, for that matter, that Harold is displaying escalated agitation. Even though I would like to ask her how the two events are related, I'd sooner cut off my arm if it contributed to further endangering Lucy's health.

She understands my thoughtful silence and says, "18-19-14-15 22-14-17-17-24-8-13-6 0-1-14-20-19 12-4 8-12 5-8-13-4."

"I can't figure out how you so easily read me or how your mysterious mind knows everything that happens behind the doors, good and evil, but I have this sneaking suspicion I'm going to. I'm not sure I can stop worrying, sister. Can you?" I say.

By the time supper is over and Lucy is drinking the last of her red juice, I realize how dog-tired I am. Lucy is too, from the looks of her. Thinking about changing my clothes, I get the navy sweat suit, the first clothes of my adventure, out of my closet. Lucy nods with approval at my selection.

"Warm enough, Lucy?" I say.

I put on Lucy's call light for tray pickup and her night cares. Preparing to get in bed myself, I wonder whether I'll hear the aides making midnight rounds. I have the good sense to be at least a little afraid of what will happen after—and excited too.

With many sighs, Lucy is assisted into bed. The overhead light goes out, and except for the hustle of the aides in the hall, the wing behind the doors quiets for the night. I feel the weary tension of this day slide away into dreamless sleep.

Part Six
Child's Play

When the night is dark and scary,
and the moon is full and creatures are a flying and
the wind goes Whoooooooooo, you better mind
your parents and your teachers fond and dear,
and cherish them that loves yah, and dry the orphans tears
and help the poor and needy ones that cluster about,
or the goblins will get yah if yah don't watch out!!!!

—James Whitcomb Riley, "The Little Orphan Annie" poem

Between the dark and the daylight,
When the night is beginning to lower,
Comes a pause in the day's occupations
That is known as the Children's hour.

—Henry Wadsworth Longfellow, "The Children's Hour"

Chapter Fourteen

"9-0-13-4, 9-0-13-4!"

"I'm awake, Lucy. I'm awake," I say, trying to decipher my surroundings into some coherent reality. Finding my way around in the dark, I make my way to the head of Lucy's bed. Putting my hand on her face, I follow my fingers and plunk a kiss on her forehead. "I don't know what you're getting me into, but give me a dose of Lucy luck, will ya?"

Lucy murmurs touching Jane's hand with a squeeze for luck.

Every move I make sounds like I'm trying to get caught. Opening and closing our room door makes enough noise to raise the dead. Staying close to the hall wall, I venture about eight feet, or as far as the next room, before taking a breath. Feeling pretty stupid holding my breath, I try to concentrate on stopping my heart from beating so loudly. My sneakers squeak like I just walked through water. Even my sweat pants swish as my fat thighs rub together. Progressing to the next room, I think my heart actually does stop when I realize someone is standing in the doorway. I almost give a frightened scream before I recognize Otto Jener. "Jesus, Otto," I say with my hand over my heart to keep it from imploding.

He puts his hand on my shoulder and whispers encouragingly, "Jesus Christ." I pat his hand on my shoulder and continue down the hall. Before I get to Wirm's room, I cross to the opposite side. The last encounter I want is with big-mouthed, dead-eyed Wirm. As quiet as a lumberjack, I traverse the eight feet to the next resident's door.

Shun Lady is sitting in the open door in her wheelchair. "Congratulation, mercerization, avocation," she whispers. Courage immediately fails as my heart skips several beats and paralysis freezes me. It takes several seconds for my brain to give the "move" order. With a small wave and a glance across the hallway at Wirm's room, fearing the Shun Lady woke him up, I pass the next two rooms quickly. Lucy, Otto, and the Shun Lady were all awake as if to say good-bye. I shudder at the realization that they may know a lot more than I do. I'm not sure why I forge ahead, but the compelling need to satisfy Lucy keeps me focused.

As I reach Harold's door at the end of the hall on tiptoes, the desperate chant rattling around my brain is "He's asleep. Oh dear God in heaven, I hope he's asleep." I want very badly to turn around the way I've come and hunker down in bed as though I never left it. A very pale, thin arm snakes out of the partly open door, takes hold of my wrist in a strong viselike grip, and pulls me into his room.

"Harold Brown, you son of a bitch, you're going to give me a heart attack!" I say, nearly crumpling to my knees in a dead faint.

"You made enough noise coming down the hall. It's a wonder you didn't wake up every resident in the building," he says with probity.

Without awareness I've been turned around and unceremoniously plunked on the bed. Lowering my head toward my lap in an attempt to recover, I realize a dim light is coming from the bathroom. Harold is sitting on his Adirondack chair, still holding my wrist tightly. That he spoke to me in a coherent sentence is finally penetrating my confusion.

"So all of a sudden you can speak to me?" I utter as if this is the most important thought in my head. "Oh, forget that, why are you hurting my wrist?" I demand to know why I've been suckered into coming here in the middle of the night. The only reason I'm here is to humor Lucy. "Now let me go!"

"Close your mouth before the jig is up!" he hisses, leaning close to my face. "I can't let you run away. Now stand up and lean against this wall. Now move over so I can stand next to you. Jane, I'm not going to bite you. Face the wall."

"Harold, what am I doing here?" I say, feeling ridiculous standing shoulder-to-shoulder with him, my nose touching the wall. "This has all been good fun. The joke is on me. Now I really have to leave. I bet that witch Donna put you up to this!"

"Jane, stop talking. Empty your mind and focus beyond the wall. Now! Walk into the night," he whispered in my ear.

Of course I do what he says. I don't know why. I just do it. Harold continues to grip my wrist, but I barely perceive the pressure. Suddenly, anxiety hiccups in my throat as I feel like I'm coming apart, cell by cell. I'm able to see Harold's hand on my wrist, but not the rest of my arm. There's a fog like a corona surrounding the space in front of me. A prodromal warning assaults my psyche, much like what I've always presumed a cerebral hemorrhage must feel like—minus the pain, thank God. Seconds or hours pass; I'm not sure which. Conscious thought is all but impossible. Lost in the ephemeral blackness with seemingly no way back, I float forward, or maybe I'm falling down.

My first punch of reality is my sneakers thudding on concrete. Next is light rain and wind on my face and, oh, the starless sky. Trying to find some balance, I realize I'm no longer attached to Harold. Flailing my arms, I manage to find equilibrium.

Harold is standing several feet from me on my left. Turning his gaze toward me, he says, "Quite a rush, huh, Jane? First time it feels a lot like dying. You'll get used to it."

I am barely able to choke out words. "Since it's never happening again, whatever that was, I don't plan on getting used to it. Now I'm leaving back through the door I didn't come from!"

"If you turn around, you'll see there is no door to go back through," he says emphatically.

"Harold what kind of crazy stuff are you feeding me? Now what happens?"

"Say anything you like, Jane. Whether you admit it or not, this is why you're here: the story. It's all about the story and pushing Wirm into oblivion so the people of this town will be free of his murderous evil once and for all. You, Jane, with my help, can do this. Lucy is back there confusing Wirm's mind to give us a chance to get out of here. She can hold him for about thirty minutes. By then we need to be away from here," he says sagaciously.

We are standing on a sidewalk that leads to nowhere. The portal I was forced through is now a stand of trees and underbrush. It's not exactly summer out. Feels a lot like fall. The fierce wind is blowing a light mist in my face and whipping the treetops with howling vengeance. There's a dim streetlight where a driveway leads to a two-story building. Looking more carefully, I recognize the building as the town's medical clinic run by possibly the most sarcastic doctor that I ever had the displeasure to work for when I first got my degree.

"That's old doc Massart's clinic, isn't it? Then right where we're standing will be the nursing home. Right? I'm going nuts, Harold. Right here will be the nursing home. I left my life back there! From all the pictures of Massart's clinic I've seen it was build in the 1930's when Doc Massart was a young man. Judging how new the building looks, this has to be the 1930s." Taking Harold by the shoulders, I frantically shake him and scream, "Where's Lucy? Where are my children? Where's my life, Harold?"

"Oh, stop being so dramatic. We're not lost in time, you know. Because we have nothing else to do, let's get outta here," he says, walking toward the streetlight.

I don't know what to do. Should I follow him or just stay right where I stand until he eventually comes back? He says Wirm is coming. What will Wirm do to me out here with no protection? It's an easy decision: follow the crazy guy. *Lucy, I'll get you for this*, I think. *You wacky broad.*

By now Harold has turned left, heading toward the paper mill. I huff and puff to catch up.

"I knew you would come to your senses," he grumbles.

"Since you have no senses to come to, I'm leaps ahead of you, Harold Brown," I say.

"It's all about the story. It's all about Wirm," he repeats.

This must be some kind of mystery-speak. Without a doubt, I'm going to follow him. It seems I cannot, according to the two conspirators, abrogate my duty, which will remain unclear until Harold decides to enlighten me. Mumbling these thoughts under my breath, I'm forced into a walk-run to keep up. One probability, with all this body heat, is that I will not feel the cool autumn-like wind pushing at my back.

This is not the Harold down the hall, lost in dementia. Some other mystical being inhabits his body, enabling him to practically jog down the streets of old Cre Falls without getting winded.

Yes, old Cre Falls. Certainly not the Cre Falls I recognize from just yesterday. Stopping to stare at what was Maud's Bar before modernization occurred in the late seventies, I'm speechless. I must be hallucinating or having a complete mental breakdown. According to this duplicity, Maud's was Fred's Nickel Bar in this time, whenever this time is. What's more, it started as a clapboard lean-to. A weak yellow light shines through mostly dirty windows. Parked out front on the street is a Chevy, vintage 1930-something. Born in 1936, I'm not sure when this car was made, but before Harold and me, I'm certain.

Harold is standing at my side, watching me. "Don't let what you see freak you out," he says. "Just print this in your memory for putting on paper later. Let's push on before this incredible journey gets the best of you. We're off to find wheels."

"Sounds like we're going to steal transportation. Sure, nothing like getting caught for grand theft auto in 1930. I wonder where the county pokey is? My final memory is going to be behind bars instead of behind the doors. Harold, I don't know where we are?"

"Keep up, Ms. Doe. We're almost there. We just need to turn in this alley … and there she is, raring to go!"

There, looking like the Junker I remember, resting and rusty, is my old Toyota. It's the very car that pulled this old bag to the Crow's Nest Motel. When I parked it, I was sure its motoring days had ended. I assumed the police towed it to the junkyard after they found no evidence clinging to the old girl. Why, or how, it showed up in this alley is beyond me. Harold's plans for its use also elude me. I am more than sure it won't start. Furthermore, I'm positive that the gas tank is empty. Optimism never started any car of mine. I find myself wishing the thing would miraculously come alive so I wouldn't have to chase Harold to whatever inimical destination he's pursuing.

"Come a little closer, Jane," he says, standing next to the hood. "Getting this car to run will take both of us."

"Yeah, sure, and all the magic you posses. I'm no mechanic. The most I know about cars is turning a key and putting the transmission in drive. Speaking of keys, the cops took them away from me at the motel. That fact really limits the possibilities," I say now leaning on the hood.

"Ah, you of little faith. Didn't we walk through the wall of the nursing home and magically end up here in old Cre Falls? Take a leap of faith, Jane. Open the hood and put your hands on the carburetor," he says, looking for the hood latch.

"Speaking of, I demand an explanation about all of that. The pull for the hood is in the car on the driver's side. The word 'hood' is printed on the lever. This is such an exercise in futility. Let's just go back, Harold. When the crew finds us missing, I'm sure the able Cre Falls police will be hunting our sorry asses."

"No going back. Not until we have the story, girly," he says, opening the driver's side door with a scraping screech and pulling the lever.

After Harold comes back around and props up the hood, I'm surprised to be looking at the Toyota's engine. I don't know where I thought the engine would be, but there it actually is. This discovery doesn't bring a lot of comfort. An engine with no spark or gas continues to be a standstill wreck. If I understand correctly, I'm now supposed to say a blessing over the engine while the power in my hands cures its ills. Maybe I should kick the tires and curse. At least I wouldn't feel quite so stupid.

"Okay, Harold. Here goes!"

Placing the palms of my hands on what I believe is the carburetor, I say, "Knock three times if the answer is yes."

The rumbling beneath my hands as the engine catches blows me flat on my fanny. Not in my wildest imagination did I believe this old car could start, but that I just started it by placing my hands on it is too much for me. Sitting on the wet ground, getting the seat of my sweat pants wet as the car knocks, pings, and groans, I put my head in my hands while waiting for it to cough out, dispelling the notion we are driving anywhere.

"Let me help you up, Jane. We have places to go," Harold says, offering his hand. Opening the driver's side door, Harold says, "Get in. You're driving."

Turning to Harold after he has settled himself in the passenger's seat, I say, "I really hate to be the chink in your armor, but as I remember, the passenger door wouldn't open without a crowbar. Obviously, now it does. And I no longer have a key, and still the thing started, but just because this rattletrap's motor is running doesn't mean the gas fumes will get us out of this alley …" But they do.

"I know we're not out for a joyride, Harold. Want to give me some idea where next?" I maneuver the car onto the street.

"You know how to get to Sawyerville? Take a right onto the highway and a left one block down on Library Road. Take Library straight out of town. The road gets to be little more than a cow path, so be careful," he says.

"We have a big problem here. If I meet townies driving around, not to mention people walking, this Toyota is years and years away from this time. It's dark and all that, but we'll be spotted as an alien spacecraft. This Toyota will not be able to outrun the constable, you know," I say, noting the bubble of fear sound in my voice.

"Not to worry, Jane. We're not even noticeable. You just drive; I'll take care of everything else."

The gravel road ends about four blocks from the highway. Without a doubt, Harold knows the landscape. After the gravel road, the way out of town becomes a path with two tire tracks and brush. I will have to drive into the brush, scraping the sides of the car, or play chicken if I should meet another car coming toward us. The fact that the gas gauge is on empty doesn't halt progress up the cow path. No moon lights the surroundings. There are no houses on either side of this path. Of course, this isn't the Falls I remember. Worse, we're in no-man's land, farther and farther away from a safe place. There is no way I could turn this car around if I had to. I say as much to Harold, who just shrugs without comment. The wind continues to buffet the driver's side of the car, and light rain hits the windshield. Fallen leaves swirl in the headlights. There are times in life when instinct screams, "This is going to be bad," but some force prevents rational turnaround action.

While I am lost in these thoughts, Harold startles me out of my nightmare. "Watch for a drive on the left," he says.

Turning cautiously into a rutted, muddy drive, I spot a cabin on the top of a slight rise. From what I can see in the headlights, the cabin is made of hued logs chinked with some brown material. The front porch roof is sagging. A path from the porch leads to a dooryard with a garden area to the left. The yard is craggy with ruts and weeds. A discarded rusting wheelbarrow is turned on its side. No light shines in the cabin window. The place looks forlorn and abandoned. A sliver of the moon slides out from beneath a cloud, giving the cabin a diabolical, haunted look.

Knowing where I am floods me with terror. There's no way I could mistake this isolated haven of horror. It's just as I imagined, or just as the old codgers at the downstairs round table described it.

"Okay, I've seen it. Let's get out of here. If you think I'm going to be able to handle seeing this story, your brain is a wasteland. I'll back this car all the way to town if I have to, Harold!" I say, attempting to swallow the bile that floods my mouth.

"Turn off the headlights. The people in the cabin can't see us, but Wirm can. Be ready to get out of the car when I say so," Harold says, scanning the stand of trees on either side of the car.

I turn off the headlights, and just as suddenly, the car's motor quits. "Oh, this is a good time for the car to quit. Now we're stuck here. I'm not who you think I am. I'm just a bored old bag who decided to risk everything for a better book. Whoever you want me to be, you're totally mistaken," I say, pleading.

With the car lights out, I can no longer see his face. For a surreal moment I feel left alone in this horrible place with the prospect of facing an incestuous baby killer, and he says Wirm is here and will be able see us. I hunch down, pulling my collar up, expecting to see Wirm leering in the window.

"Harold, talk to me. I'm going to freak out if I have to sit here much longer enduring your silence. What are we waiting for, sunrise?" I say.

"There! Look over to the left by the garden. Can you make out Wirm's outline?" Harold whispers.

I couldn't see anything and doubted Harold could. Just when I was going to tell Harold he was seeing things, the ursine thing I was looking at moved. Then all was still. We waited. Wirm waited. The rain was more of a mist now, driven in swirls by the howling wind.

"They can't see you, Jane, and no matter what happens, no matter how badly you want to change what happens, do not try to interfere! The story you're here to witness has already been written in the past. You will see two Wirms. The one standing by the garden is as real as we are. He knows we're here and will want to hurt you or kill you if you give him the chance. He won't touch you as long as you don't let go of my hand. I have the cross Father Jim gave me. He fears it more than he wants you dead. Now, Jane, get out of the car!"

On the edge of a hysterical cliff, my hands are shaking so badly I can't open the car door. Outside, Harold opens the door for me and reaches in for my hand, helping me out. In his other hand he holds an ancient-looking crucifix. Harold pulls me forward up the rutted, muddy driveway before I can change my mind and run back.

Wirm is still standing at the edge of the garden with his arms outstretched, beckoning me to come. "So you're here for the show. Come stand by me; we'll watch together," he barks. "What do you need that pisser Harold for?" His voice becomes a chorus of several voices coming from the open maw of his mouth when once again he coaxes me across the dooryard.

The glow of a lantern appears on the porch, carried by a man in work coveralls that are grease-streaked and muddy. His other arm carries a bundle of white rags. This must be old man Heyfeld, I deduce. Heyfeld puts the white rags on the ground. I watch as the bundle moves and a tiny white infant's hand reaches out. The infant wails in discomfort, kicking aside the rags that confine it.

"Stupid girl! Got herself knocked up again. Born another mongrel hell child," he mumbles, setting the lantern on the ground next to the child. Picking up a shovel, he begins to spade the damp earth in front of him.

I know the story. He will kill this baby just like the last if I don't stop him. Not able to pull my hand out of Harold's grasp, I mew, horrified.

"Harold, let go of me. I can save this one. I know I can. For God's sake, let go of my hand!" I cry.

Making good on his promise, Harold grips my hand even tighter. "You can't do anything to change the story!" he shouts.

From the trees at the end of the dooryard, the Wirm of then walks up to the hole Heyfeld is digging. He laughs and offers the baby killer a paper bag with the neck of a bottle sticking out.

"Here, you ol' fucker, take a break," Wirm says, handing the bottle over. "Where's that whore daughter of yours? Night's young. We could have some fun before we have some fun. Whatcha say? It's not neighborly having both those girls to yourself. We'll shut the brat up and do the girls later. Work for you? Ha, sure it does," Wirm says, punching Heyfeld on the arm like they were old comrades.

Heyfeld inspects the neck of the bottle sticking out of the bag drooling on the front of his coveralls. "Just what a feller needs old friend, a bottle break."

Just at that moment, a painfully thin girl slips quietly out of the cabin door. With hunched shoulders and a beaten-dog appearance, she hangs her head in submission. Dressed in a threadbare homespun shift, she is barefoot. Taking a cautious, unsteady step toward the naked infant lying on the ground, she stretches out her arms.

"Please, Papa. For the love of God, don't kill my baby. Let this one live," she pleads, picking up the baby from the ground and clutching it to her flat chest.

"You beg for this evil seed. It's little more than a dog. If I wasn't so busy you'd be on your knees, begging for the cock that begot this monster. You can always spread your legs and get another one, you whoring girl. Shut up or I'll make the hole big enough for both of you. Then your sister will have me all to herself," he says, taking a long pull on the whiskey bottle Wirm gave him.

He reeks of cheap whiskey and strong unwashed body. His clothes are stiff with filth. His salt-and-pepper hair is long and plastered over his triangular skull. His unkempt beard hangs to the top of his sternum. He appears to have no neck as he hunches over, lifting shovel after shovel of damp earth out of the grave.

She sobs as she holds her newborn but doesn't attempt to run away. I scream at her to run, but she makes no indication she can hear my frantic call.

"She's more afraid of him than what he'll do to the brat," Wirm says, still rooted to his same spot by the garden. "He'll kill her as fuck her, and she knows it. Are you liking what you see, Jane? Wait, it gets better."

Turning, Heyfeld staggers to the girl and snatches the infant from her arms. Startled, the baby starts to cry again. He picks up the pail and staggers back to the newly dug hole. The hell-bound bastard puts the baby in the pail and drops it in the grave. Then, upon finding a rock that fits his fist from the pile of turned earth, he bashes the baby's head twice with force enough to crush its skull. The crying is silenced at once. The killer father picks up his shovel and starts to fill in the tiny grave with soil. The only sound that breaks the silence is soft, hitching sobs.

The Wirm of then doesn't have to encourage the killing of the oldest daughters second child. For that matter, when Heyfeld killed the youngest daughter's first child a couple months back Wirm was there to help his old friend. All three babies were sired by Heyfeld and born to his daughters. He and the devil are in league, sharing the same evil spirit. Wirm pats Heyfeld on the back and says, "Fine job," before turning and walking into the woods the way he came.

Horrified, hand over my eyes, I retch. I vomit again and again. Not really able to internalize what I've seen, I beg Harold to help me back to the car. Never, for the rest of my life, will I forget the sound of the rock smashing the skull of that infant.

"No stomach for the fun?" the Wirm from our time taunts across the dooryard. "Hey, what's she doing? Heyfeld, stop her!"

Just because the devil can read scripture doesn't mean he can pretend to know what God knows, including how this story ends. For that matter, Wirm doesn't care or have compassion for his victims of the past. Only thing is, Wirm doesn't like not knowing; makes him question his power to influence and perpetuate evil.

The girl picks up the shovel, and while her father pats the dirt in place over the grave, she hits him with more force than her skinny arm possibly could have, at least without help from someone.

"You'll die too, Papa!" she screamed, hitting the back of his head again and again. He fell on top of the little grave, oozing blood and gray matter from the fatal gaping wound.

The girl turns to the cabin door. "Momma, Lizzy, bring your shovels. Let's plant him in the garden before the sun comes up. Over by the pumpkins, I think," she says more to herself than to anyone listening.

I am stunned, speechless, and paralyzed, rooted to where I stand. Harold too looks stupefied. Like Wirm, Harold is a voyeur of the stories and can only lead Jane to them. Harold didn't see this coming because he didn't know.

Two women, one a mere girl, appear from the cabin with shovels in hand. Without a word, they pass Wirm and begin to shovel another grave.

Harold pulls my arm, shaking me out of a daze. "Run, back to the car. We have to get out of here before Wirm's attention shifts from the women with the shovels to us. Wirm didn't see the girl having the gumption to kill Heyfeld," He says, moving me to the car as quickly as possible. He pushes me into the driver's side, and before I can find my voice to ask how we will start the engine, he is standing in front with his hand on the hood. The other hand still grips the cross. The engine roars to life. Nothing can surprise me, or so I think. Harold crashes into the passenger seat and shouts, "Go!" I rapidly back down the incline, turn, and spin the wheels, spitting gravel. I set the car racing toward town like the devil is chasing us, because I think he is.

Shock has set my teeth clattering against one another, making it impossible for me to ask the important question. I look to Harold, hoping he will read my mind and tell me where to go next. Wherever we go, nothing could be as bad as the place we left. Already, I cannot believe what happened back there.

Harold says, "Let's get the car back in the same alley. The cross stays in the car to protect it until the next time. I know you want to talk all this out, but you saw what I did. Work it out on paper when you get back to your room. The only justice that will come from this is the truth—the truth that has never been told."

Harold has given me the only explanation I'm about to get. I've been coerced into this nightmare, and I feel exposed and threatened. Besides that, I'm in shock, cold, and damned uncomfortable. He wants to talk about the next time—the next time! What I want to hear is how I get back through the nursing home wall. How do I walk out of the past into the present?

Upon turning into the alley and stopping, I automatically reach for the key to turn off the motor. But I know now that when I get out and close the door, the car will quit by itself. Turning to Harold, I say, "Now what? I need a clue here. If the cross stays in the car, will Wirm catch up with us?"

"He could. Don't start without me. We'll have to make a run for it. Once we're a couple of blocks from the nursing home, Lucy will be able to pick up Wirm's mind and delay him until we're safely inside. If we ever get separated, go to the Catholic Church. Father doesn't lock the church, and Wirm will never follow you in there. I'll look for you there as soon as I can," he says, making a move to leave the car.

Outside, the wind has calmed. The only sound is the thudding cadence of our shoes striking the pavement. My heart pounds with the fear that Wirm is breathing down my neck. Past the mill, turning right to the sidewalk that goes nowhere, I cling to a tree to catch my breath. The nursing home has not miraculously appeared. In front of me are brush and a grove of trees where the nursing home was.

Gripping my wrist, Harold nudges me forward and says, "Focus beyond the trees, Jane. See through the brick and wall to where you want to be. Let your mind take you there."

Again, I feel my cells splitting apart and acute nausea from the vortex. Coming back to myself, I lean my back against the wall. Harold is at my side. Letting go of my wrist, he slides into his chair. "Do-da, do-da," he mumbles. "Get a gun." I walk out of his room into the deserted hall. I notice the clock in the dining room as I pass. It's just minutes after twelve. Pausing to stare at the clock in disbelief,

I am now sure I dreamed Harold, the car, and the terrible cabin scene. I certainly do not believe that I walked through the nursing home wall and ended up in Cre Falls's past. The only explanation for my standing out here in the hall that my mind will accept is sleepwalking. This has never happened to me before, but then, I have never written a book before. Rational thought, that convincing voice in my mind, is forming a reality I can accept. I'm aware that nothing in the recent past proves I'm mentally stable, but to believe what happened and end up standing in the hall looking at the clock, finding only five minutes have passed, is far and away totally nuts! This is totally out of the realm of a stable mind—and to think the psychiatrist is making rounds soon.

I slowly turn to look back down the hall to Harold's room, and my breath catches in my lungs. Muddy footprints lead from Harold's door to where I stand, gawking. As I look down at my mud-encrusted shoes, a silent scream forms in my mind, threatening to overwhelm the slender grip on my sanity I've been hanging onto. Unable to remain standing on my jelly, shaking legs, I sink to the floor. No nurse or aide is going to believe Harold took a stroll and made muddy footprints down the hall. Cleaning them could be very difficult, even though I can't locate one painful joint. Sitting on my butt—not a position easy for me—I remove my shoes. Housekeeping will blame the mess on a night-shift aide. I'm really reluctant to have that happen. It's totally against my principle of accountability and all that, but it is convenient. Getting up off the hall floor is as simple as getting my feet under me and standing. I don't remember being able to perform that gymnastic feat in more than twenty years. For that matter, a faint memory of running up the street from the car (with Harold just keeping up) dries up all my spit. Oh my God, oh my God.

Mercifully, the hall continues to be deserted and without sound, which I find disquieting. Usually, snores, grunts, and murmurs are as much a part of the night sounds as the residents' calls for help. It crosses my mind in a panic, I may be alone behind the doors. Carrying my shoes, I head for my room. If Lucy isn't in her bed where I left her, then I'll deal with it.

"Lucy … Lucy," I whisper as I enter the dark room. "Damn, you'd better be here. If you're not, I'll never talk to you again."

"15-11-4-0-18-4 1-4 16-20-8-4-19 22-8-17-12 8-18 1-0-2-10 8-13 7-8-18 17-14-14-12," Lucy says in a rush.

Snapping on my bedside lamp, I search for the code sheet I left on my table. I translate the first few words and discover she has told me to be quiet. The audacity of that woman after all I've been through. Just as I am about to give Lucy what for, I hear a groan and a thumping noise. He's back.

Chapter Fifteen

Wirm kicks his door open. Moving into his room, he farts and shits his pants, chortling with self-satisfaction. True, he didn't wring Harold Brown's neck or rape that damnable inquisitive broad, but he sure had them on the run. Who knew she could sprint so fast? *Arthritis, my ass*, he thinks. Well, she's not going anywhere anytime soon. Too bad the whoring daughter killed his worthy cohort. Still, the effect was stellar. Most troubling to him is that he doesn't remember the killing happening back then. The killing of Heyfeld is disconcerting. For the first time in his existence, he wonders what else he may have forgotten and how that may change where this current story ends. The possibility of not fulfilling his purpose, his reason for being, slits an opening in his confidence. *What am I thinking?* He asks himself. That could never happen. He is, after all, Wirm, never beaten. He is the always-voracious procurer of those who lust, who are lost in greed, and who falter from the protection of the Father. He especially searches for the lost. Cre Fall's population of plus or minus four thousand has always been enough to keep him occupied—and, not to forget, never challenged. Until now! With this last thought, he puts on his call light; time to get a lucky aide to freshen him up. "You know I love the attention, don't you?" he whispers to the darkened room.

The smoky odor in his room is sulfurous, the hot spew from hell. If the aides were asked, which of course they never were, all of them would say the most disgusting job (the one job they would most like to pass on to anyone else) is perineal care on Wirm. On night shift, an aide answers his light with a partner. The unwritten code is to never answer Wirm's light at night alone. The aides gossip about actually seeing smoke rise from his bowel movements, about the smell being so bad that tears roll down their faces. The night aides say his dead, white hand snakes out and touches them, causing momentary loss of time. The one thing they all agree on is that they should never answer his light at night alone.

True to the code, two aides open the door to Perry's Alzheimer's Unit on their way to answer Wirm's call light. One observant aide notices the muddy footprints on the floor.

"That's odd," she says. "This muddy mess on the floor just stops. That's really weird. We'll have to leave a note for housekeeping."

With no time to ponder muddy footprints, they head for the dreaded Wirm cleanup, both of them thinking that they can't catch a break tonight.

Practiced, one aide opens his door, they both take a deep breath, and the other aide snaps the light on. Leaving the door open, they work in concert, eager to get the job done with little or no conversation.

"Come here. You know you love your Wirm," he croons.

I smell noisome fumes penetrating the hall, the walls, the rooms, and my nostrils, causing the bile to rise in my throat. I can hear the gagging and retching of the aides caring for Wirm. Getting out of bed to peek out in the hall, I see two aides supporting one another, walking slowly down the hall. Assaulted, tearful, and looking green in the gills, they're mumbling the same protest over and over: "Never … I'm never going to take care of that pig again." One aide tearfully says, "I'd rather get fired!"

Feeling unbelievably wide awake, I decide it's better to write than to toss and turn the rest of the night. Gathering my writing things on my overbed table, I roll the table across to the dining room. Positioning my chair below the dining room alarm button, I feel reasonably sure I can get help quickly should that succubus down the hall threatens me. Taking some time to read back a couple of pages and get in the mood, I realize today that there are more revealing tidbits in these pages than I care to have discovered by someone from this snoopy staff. As it is, I'm sure it won't take long before someone pokes their head in to find out what I'm doing, clacking away in the dining room this time of night. So friend, Harold, here's the first story.

> "9-0-13-4, 9-0-13-4!"
>
> "I'm awake, Lucy. I'm awake," I say, trying to decipher my surroundings into some coherent reality. Finding my way around in the dark, I make my way to the head of Lucy's bed. Putting my hand on her face, I follow my fingers and plunk a kiss on her forehead. "I don't know what you're getting me into, but give me a dose of Lucy luck, will ya?"
>
> Lucy murmurs, squeezing Jane's hand for good luck.
>
> Every move I make sounds like I'm trying to get caught. Opening and closing our room door makes enough noise to raise the dead. Staying close to the hall wall, I venture about eight feet, or as far as the next room, before taking a breath. Feeling pretty stupid holding my breath, I try to concentrate on stopping my heart from beating so loudly. My sneakers squeak like I just walked through water. Even my sweat pants swish as my fat thighs rub together. Progressing to the next room, I think my heart actually does stop when I realize someone is standing in the doorway. I almost give a frightened scream before I recognize Otto Jener. "Jesus, Otto," I say with my hand over my heart to keep it from imploding.
>
> He puts his hand on my shoulder …

I am absorbed in my writing as I clack away on my typewriter, so I jump, startled, when an aide opens the dining room door. "What are you doing out of bed, JD?" she says. "I'd really like to know what you're typing on that machine?"

So I have a new nickname, do I? It seems JD, for Jane Doe, apparently. Oh well. It's kind of endearing, actually.

"I'm just passing a sleepless night. You want to know what I'm writing. It's poetry. Do you like to read poetry?" I say, hoping not.

"No, actually, I don't, JD," she says. "The first complaint I hear that typewriter is too noisy, I'm shutting you down. Okay? The psychiatrist … what's his name … Dr. Sturges makes rounds at one o'clock today and you're on the list. He's kind of cute. He has big brown hypnotic eyes. Rumor is he can spot a fake right off the bat. Get it? Batty or not."

As she turns her back on me, I decided to try for some staff information on Wirm. "Got a minute?" I say before she can walk out the door.

"Yeah, just about," she says, turning around and looking annoyed.

"What's the story on Wirm?" I say before she can blow me off. "I heard you and your friend having a fit about Wirm's toilet habit. He gives me the fright nights. How about you?"

"I'm not supposed to talk about another resident, but boy, I'm with you there," she says, rolling her eyes up to the ceiling. "Wish Perry would transfer him out of here. We all know she won't—money, money. I'm going to refuse to take care of him next time he messes his drawers. Let the nurses do it." She was beginning to rant.

Trying not to waste time on discussion of the picked-on aides and taking advantage of her willingness to talk, I hurriedly ask, "Where did he come from? Has he been living here long? I wonder where he gets his money from—I mean, to afford this place."

"I don't know for sure. Donald has been working here the longest, and he once said Wirm has been walking the streets of Cre Falls for as long as he can remember. He said that Wirm never had family that he knows of. I've been working here for five years, and Wirm just showed up one day. Kind of like you, JD," she says with a chortle.

"Know anything about his money or where he came from before he showed up in Cre Falls?" I say.

"Nope. He probably gets his room and board from the state. Enough. I gotta go. What are you doing, writing a poem about him, JD?" she asks before scurrying away.

So much for information, I think Lucy and I will visit the round-table boys downstairs tonight. Armed with a little more knowledge and ready to ask thought-provoking questions, I may learn more. At the very least, Lucy will get off the floor for a little R and R. I'm all about wrapping this writing session up and getting some sleep. I must be awake for the dazzling, brown-eyed psychiatrist Dr. Sturges.

Chapter Sixteen

Sleep comes easily and is dreamless. When I do wake up, having slept through breakfast, I'm astonished no nightmares plagued my sleep. Rolling on my side to get a feel for how much cooperation I am going to get from my joints, I see Lucy is up, dressed, and looking sassy.

"Hey, Lucy," I say, yawning. "Two things to do today: one, psychiatrist comes today; two, my plan is to get the pages of my book to the deceased resident file in Medical Records for safekeeping. With you as my lookout, I figure it will be a piece of cake. The secretary takes her break about ten and doesn't lock the door. That gives me about fifteen minutes. What do you say? Are you in?"

"18-20-17-4," she says, giving me her most tolerant smile.

"We're just like Thelma and Louise, right?" I say, wondering whether she has any idea who Thelma and Louise are.

"11-14-20-8-18-4," Lucy says, turning her attention to the day aide, Pat, who is walking into the room.

"Are you talking to yourself, Lady Jane? Don't think for one minute that's going to fool the psychiatrist. You missed breakfast, so I'm here to offer you cold cereal, juice, and coffee," she says in her "pity pout" voice.

More and more, I feel like a patronized child. To stir things up, I say, "No to the cold breakfast. I want hot cereal, juice, and coffee. Oh, and toast as well."

"Ha, if you insist on that, you'll have to make instant oatmeal and toast in the dining room by yourself. Kitchen is already working on lunch, Lady Jane—or JD as you're now being called, I've heard," Pat says, looking gleeful at manipulating the conversation.

"You're on," I say, deadpanning the look on my face. "If I burn myself, you get to write up the incident report for the state." Getting out of bed and reaching for my robe and slippers, I'm prepared to make my own breakfast.

"On second thought, Queen JD, I consider it a privilege to get you a hot breakfast myself," she says, retreating to the hall.

"So, Lucy, could you stomach some more oatmeal? Looks like I'm stuck with eating some whether or not I want it," I say.

Just as I'm about to robe up and go find nutrition, Pat delivers a tray with something under a cover to keep it hot. I say thank you to her back because she doesn't waste time making a hasty retreat. I salute Lucy with my spoon and remove the plate cover. What I find is a bowl of cold cereal, milk, some sugar packets, and a note that says, "Enjoy." I have to give the girl points for sticking to her guns, and to show her no hard feelings, I dig into the cold cereal. Lucy giggles and shakes her head.

Getting the pages of my book together, I put them into my manila envelope, just about filling it. The pages are adding up. My goal is to walk out of here the end of March next year with a finished book. The probability that the book will not be done by that date or that I will not walk out of here at all is a thought I can't get my mind around. A chill travels up my spine when I anticipate someone finding these pages. I haven't intended to claim written ownership of this envelope, but I have a change of mind. Printing in small letters, I write, "Anyone opening this envelope without permission from JD will face prosecution and will be sued." I hope that statement will at least prompt anyone who finds my stash to return it to me. Dreamer! Nevertheless, I'm sure my hiding place is the best.

"Hey, Lucy, what do you think? Do you think the book will be safe in Medical Records? I just can't think of any other hiding place. I considered taking a trip down to the basement to have a look around, but I'd have to do that at night. Frankly, the thought of Wirm following me scares the bejesus out of me," I say.

"13-14 1-0-18-4-12-4-13-19," she says, with lots of emphasis on "No."

"Got it. No basement. How about I take it out of here the next time Harold grabs my wrist and stash it in the car? Not a bad idea, huh?"

But putting the manuscript in the car would mean losing complete control over it. The car cannot be relied on. Okay. Medical Records it is!

Fifteen minutes later, Thelma and Louise—Louise riding shotgun in the wheelchair and Thelma the holdup crook of the deceased file drawer—are on the move.

"Lucy, keep your number-numbing mind on Wirm. We don't need any surprises or the ghoul sounding the alarm," I say.

"11-4-19-18 3-14 8-19," she says, excitement coloring her cheeks.

"Time, Lucy," I say, gathering up the manila envelope. Putting it on Lucy's lap, I wheel her into the hallway. The medical records secretary is still at her desk, pecking away at her computer, so I wheel Lucy down to Harold's end. He is not sitting in the hall, but I can hear him muttering unhappily in his room. I poke my head in his door cautiously to be sure he isn't in a state of undress and then announce we are coming in. At once Harold calms down. Lucy has that effect on Harold. As always, they sit side by side, not saying anything; however, I have the distinct feeling the story of our midnight escapade is being told. Watching for medical secretary movement down the hall, I notice Wirm's door is closed.

There she goes off for morning break. Quickly, explaining to Harold we need to go, I turn Lucy's wheelchair around and head down the hall. "Remember, Lucy, give a loud warning if you think any staff is heading into Medical Records," I say, retrieving the envelope and heading into the office.

I close the door, locking it from the inside so I won't be surprised. I could always use the excuse I wanted to use the telephone. Finding the deceased file is simple because the file cabinet is labeled exactly that. Not locked, the bottom drawer opens easily, and as luck has it, there is more than enough space behind the last file. Putting the envelope in, I cover it with a couple of files. The files are out of place, but I doubt this drawer sees much activity. The file dates are almost ten years old.

Just as I am about to open the door, Lucy lets out a squeal. "7-4-11-15!" she exclaims. Just as I feared, Wirm is bent over Lucy, squeezing her shoulder, breathing in her face. I step out of the doorway into the hall and am immediately standing by Lucy's wheelchair. Wirm pushes me aside hard enough that I fall against the wall. Before I can stop him, he has Lucy by the shoulders and is lifting her out of her wheelchair. Screaming for help, I run at Wirm and smash him in the face with my fist. Roaring, he drops Lucy to the floor and turns to face me. Fury and hatred contort his face into pocked, oozing sores. The fetid smell almost makes me swoon to the floor by Lucy. Screaming once again for help, I shake my head clear of the fog that has filtered into my brain, and I bring up my knee as hard as I can between his legs. My knee sinks into his groin flesh like the tissue is mashed potatoes. He pushes me to the floor, laughing. Curling myself around Lucy in a fetal position, I try to protect her from the kicking blow I know is coming.

It seems nurses and aides appear from everywhere. Looking at the number of shoes at my eye level, it seems to be a crowd. They successfully back Wirm down the hall. He bellows, "Those whores attacked me! I'll get you for this, you no-good floorflusher. Take your hands off me. Nobody touches the Wirm. Nobody!"

Sitting, I cradle Lucy in my arms. Her carotid pulse is strong and not tacky. She does not seem to be in pain, but she still hasn't opened her eyes. I whisper in her ear that Wirm is gone and we're all right. Down the hall, Harold is out of control and agitated, yelling and ranting. The hall behind the doors looks to be in complete chaos: at least four aides, Donald the orderly, and two nurses all converging on Wirm's room.

"Oh, Lucy, God help me," I whisper. "If you're hurt, it's my fault. I shouldn't have put you in harm's way just to hide the book. We have to change our room away from Wirm before he really hurts you."

Opening her eyes, Lucy murmurs, "13-14 22-4 2-0-13-19."

"If you're okay, let's get off this floor," I say, admiring her tenacity.

"Can we get some help here? Hello? How about us?" I yell at the crowd down the hall.

A nurse and two aides come to our side but refuse to move us until we get checked out for broken bones. That assessment also includes a quick check for other injuries. The aides get me to my feet and next assist Lucy back into her wheelchair.

Mary, the day shift RN, says in a voice without compassion, "I'll take a good look at your skin for bruising after the aides get Lucy in bed. I'll also want to know what provoked this incident. Good thing the psychiatrist is making rounds today. You, Jane Doe, will have to tell him about this thing between you and Wirm and how Lucy is involved."

Sitting on my bed, I try rehearsing what I will tell Mary and the psychiatrist about Wirm and his attack. Let's see: we were coming back from visiting Harold, and didn't hear Wirm coming up behind us, when he reached out and pushed me against the wall. He grabbed Lucy's shoulders and lifted her out of the wheelchair. Trying to defend Lucy, I punched him in his face. Wirm let Lucy slide to the floor and pushed me back. Before I could react, he pushed me to the floor by Lucy. We had no contact with Wirm before the incident and in no way provoked him to attack us. All of this is easy to tell over and over again. I'm sure no one witnessed me coming out of Medical Records except Wirm, after Lucy yelled for help. I can visualize the empty hall. I'm sure no one but blasted Wirm saw me! That's the story I'm telling, and I'm sticking to it (except for the part about Wirm seeing me come from Medical Records).

When I tell it once again to Lucy out loud, she says, "12-0-17-24 22-8-11-11 2-0-11-11 19-7-4 18-19-0-19-4 14-13 22-8-17-12."

"Okay then," I say. "I hope Wirm gets evicted to the psych ward in Marshfield. If they don't believe my story, I'm going to have to think of some way to protect us."

Knowing that Wirm, the devil's spawn, saw me leaving Medical Records does little to bolster confidence that my story will hold up to scrutiny. The psychiatrist, Dr. Sturges, is already in the building, probably being briefed by Nurse Mary right now. He will come in here armed with Mary's perception of the incident, colored by that lying slimeball Wirm. As I sit on pins and needles, my colossal fear is that "old brown eyes" Sturges will see through my fatuity and write orders to remove me from this wing—or worse, out of Cre Manor on *my* way to Marshfield. Leaving Lucy vulnerable to Wirm is out of the question. I'm going to have to convince Sturges I'm daffy and definitely well placed "behind the doors," but charm him into believing Wirm is malevolently motivated to cause trouble to all residents, not just Lucy and me. That tall order, I'm not sure I can deliver. As the clock of doom ticks, I really wish talking to Harold was possible. But my wish is too late: Sturges is in the hall with Mary. Here he comes, ready or not!

Dr. Sturges appears in the doorway, a not very tall man, perhaps five feet six or so, but handsome. He indeed has big brown eyes framed by lacy dark lashes. *Unusual for a psychiatrist*, I think. He wears an immaculate white lab coat with his name on the breast pocket and a blue starched dress shirt with a striped blue tie, together with tan dress trousers that touch the tops of impeccably shined dark brown shoes.

As I size him up, I notice Lucy doing the same. I'm sure my jaw has dropped open, and I snap it shut at once. Lucy chortles with a piquant smack of her lips. Realizing that old we are but dead we are not causes a very rare flush to my cheeks. All in all, this is not a good beginning to my evaluation for a permanent address behind the doors. I'm sure I would fare much better with a less good-looking, old, tired psychiatrist with a bored seen-it-all attitude, or at least with a "if it's not broken, why fix it" approach.

"I'll see you after talking with Wirm in the dining room," he says, his baritone voice startling me. No "Hi, my name is"—just right to business. Apparently, Mary has filled him in with her gossipy report on me, and he's up to the challenge.

"Look, Mary," I say as offhandedly as I can manage without stuttering. "The dining room is already filling up with the lunch crowd. Not a very good place to protect my privacy rights, do you think?"

"Good of you to be so helpful," she says sarcastically. "I'm sure the doctor can meet with you in your room as well. Okay with you,

Randy? I'll get an aide to move Lucy to the dining room." I notice the flirty emphasis on his first name.

Turning to address Mary, he says, "I prefer a more neutral setting, but her room will have to do. A half hour is all I need to get Wirm's side of the incident." Signaling to me with his hand in a stop position, he continues, "See to it that she stays in her room, Mary."

As an aide comes in to transport Lucy to the dining room, he retreats with Mary down the hall.

That command was certainly unnecessary. Just where does he think I'd go? I'm sure he said that to threaten me into compliance. I know my tendency in such situations is to rebel. I have a feeling this stance will get me nowhere. I need to fight my instincts and aim for acquiescence and spacey nuttiness. Or maybe I should tell the unbelievable truth. Maybe I should tell him I can understand and talk to Lucy, walk through Harold's wall into the past, start a car without a key by touching the carburetor, witness the killing of an infant in this town in the 1930s, and come back with mud on my shoes for proof. All this is more than just nutty, but a version could work.

Suddenly, a buzzing in my head turns into a woman's loud wail. My eyes cloud up, and I can't make out the room in front of me. The wailing becomes acerbic. Time and space become a presage of looming blackness.

Part Seven

The Pernicious, Myopic Past

Tell me where dwell the joys of old, and where the ancient loves,
And when will they renew again, and the night of oblivion past,
That I might traverse times and spaces far remote, and bring
Comfort into a present sorrow and a night of pain?

—William Blake

Chapter Seventeen

As my vision becomes clearer, the wretched wail gets louder. Not twenty feet in front of me, kneeling on a gravel driveway, is the source of the wailing noise that is blowing out my eardrums.

The full moon is high overhead, casting a shadow of the kneeling woman. A large brick farmhouse is set back from the driveway, flanked on the right by a manicured field bathed in moonlight. The quintessential red barn built into a hillock is at the far end of the driveway. The barn door hangs open. Nearly inaudible over the crying, the barn door screeches on rusty hinges and bangs against the side of the worn barn wood. Nothing is discernible in the black doorway. It is a maw of inky blackness that seems to have no end.

This nightmare is so familiar. If the woman lifts her head, I will recognize her. Fear turns my blood to an ice flow. I shouldn't be here. I shouldn't know this place and the woman crying out in profound grief. Oh God! I shouldn't know she has a gun. I do know there are two children in that farmhouse asleep who need her. I try to call to her—"Remember your sons who need you!"—but the shout remains in my head. I remain mute. I notice that I do not cast a moon shadow like she does. I am a ghost. I am her future.

Slowly she rises from the gravel. Screaming, she shakes the pistol in her right hand at the moon. Her wailing becomes angry shouts. "I'll kill her for doing this to me!" she shrieks. She moans, "I'll kill her for taking him. I swear, I'll do it." Her words turn into sobs, and staggering, she barely remains on her feet. Regaining some composure, she walks toward me.

Barely in a whisper have I addressed her. "Oh, I know you. I was there when this pain pierced your heart. It was I who swore to kill that whore, Kathy, for taking the one we could not lose. How could he become part of her life? How could he say he loved us like a sister? Like a sister! He said he had another life. He had other children. He said that it was a relief that we knew. What relief? There was no relief. Not for me then and not for me now. Not for my two boys." How fortunate Marie, my daughter, would not be born for years to come.

She walks toward me. Rivers of tears streak down her face, making lines through the road dust that clings to her skin. Stopping five feet from me, she points her finger. "You! Stay out of this."

Staring straight at me, she takes car keys out of her left jean pocket. Turning, she does a sexy swagger up the driveway toward her parked car, singing "Bumpity, bump bump," waving the pistol in her right hand.

I scream after her, "No! Don't do this! Use your head. If you do this, you don't have a future, and neither do I! Please, Jane, *think*!"

With her hand on the car door, she stops, staring at the open barn door. I can't see what she's looking at. Bending from her waist, she screams, "Go away! You can't make me kill her. You're nothing to me but an evil monster!"

She looks at me with a wide but crazy smile. "I will hurt them both another way. I will be the kindest, sweetest friend to him. I will torment her with my accepting friendship with him. All who see me will admire my courage and condemn his infidelity." With her hand on her heart, she sobs. "My boys will grow up putting me on a pedestal. They will call me better than him and call her a whore."

Putting her forehead on the car door, she wails in anguish. Turning, she walks up the sidewalk to the kitchen door. Looking back at the open barn door, she lifts her chin in defiance and yells to some unseen presence, "My day isn't over! Do you hear? My day isn't over until I say it ends. You, beast, will be back for me another day. I'll be ready. Don't claim my soul for him yet."

I'm sure now that somehow we defeated Wirm this time. It's because of this bleak night that Wirm's mark follows me. For the first time I get it. I'm not here just to write a book. I'm here to help pay a debt. I'm here to wipe my soul clean, to help Harold and Lucy get rid of Wirm. I'm here to stop his history of crime and his hold over the people of Cre Falls.

I turn away from this nostalgic farm where my boys and I lived all those years ago. I'm so temped to follow my heart up the stairs to their bedrooms for one look at their sweet, innocent, sleeping faces. *I'm sorry, dear ones, for what you will have to face tomorrow*, I think, *but your mother has found strength to help you.*

I feel the night swirl away from me, the present merging with the past as I seem to have one foot in each. I will meet the psychiatrist with new armor. In order to help Lucy and Harold, I must keep Wirm down the hall behind the doors. I will do as Harold asks, gather the facts of Wirm's crimes, and give Cre Falls police the opportunity to solve cold cases that were, until now, totally unsolvable. I know Wirm was standing in the barn door, even though I couldn't see him. He was there trying to push her, me, into evil that would have destroyed our lives and the future of the children. I resolve to do all that I can to send him back to hell.

Snapping awake and straining to focus in the bright light of the present, I see Lucy perched in her wheelchair in front of me. "I thought you were put in the dining room for lunch," I say, wondering what has caused her to appear so nervous and intense. "What's up?"

"19-7-4 15-18-24-2-7-8-0-19-17-8-18-19 0-13-3 12-0-17-24 0-17-4 7-0-21-8-13-6 0-13 0-5-0-8-17-4 7-8-18 22-8-5-4 22-14-20-11-3 19-0-10-4 0-22-0-24 0-11-11-14 7-4-17 12-14-13-4-23 8-5 18-7-4 10-13-4-22," she says, nervously eyeing the door.

I decode and decode as fast as I can. "Oh boy! You don't know how badly I need this bit of *flagrante delicto*, Lucy mine. Having this information, I bet we could have a window installed in our room or get passes to the poker room downtown. Save my lunch tray. If this interview goes well, I'll get to eat lunch yet."

Lucy raises her eyebrows, enjoying a bit of self-righteousness. When the aide was gossiping about Sturges this morning, she mentioned that his wife was loaded. Seems she comes from old money. I'd put money on the fact wifey doesn't know her good doctor is messing with Mary who-who.

"This is poetic justice, Lucy. I could come out of this without having to throw away psychotropic medication he's sure to order or, worst case, getting removed from this hallowed hall. He's never going to believe you told me, but I'll use that to tweak his nose hairs. I'm sure he'll spend until I'm too old to care trying to figure who in the grapevine told me. High five, Lucy." I turn upon hearing a noise at the door. "Oh, here he comes," I whisper. "Showtime!"

As Dr. Sturges graces our door, chart in hand, he looks annoyed at Lucy. "I thought you were taken to the dining room, Lucy. If I want something done, looks like I'll have to do it myself," he mumbles, turning Lucy's wheelchair toward the door. Just as he's about to push her across the hall, Mary intercepts them.

"Didn't I tell the aide a half hour ago to get Lucy out of her room?" she says, touching doctor's hand. "I'm so sorry, Randy. I'll take her from here."

Dr. "Brown Eyes" Randy watches as Mary wiggles away before turning toward me. He pauses for a short second, as though adjusting his thinking before confronting me. The corner of his mouth is pulled down in a smirk. He looks as confident as a fox in a hen house. After walking into our room, he closes the door behind him. Crossing over to a chair, he sits, crosses his legs, and balances his clipboard on his knee.

"Before we begin, you will give your complete name," he says. "I will not tolerate any of your childish lies. You have manipulated the staff of this nursing home long enough. As your future here is up to me, I will have your complete cooperation, or your future is not going to be here. Do I make myself clear?"

Holding his stare without blinking, I sit silently contemplating his probable contempt for my not answering. Our staring contest ends with me looking away.

"You not answering my questions is not an option, and it will not go well for you. You understand this facility is relying on me to solve multiple problems you have caused for yourself and the residents living on this hall."

"My name will not pass my lips to your pen under any circumstances," I say with little emotion. "Ask other questions, or this interview is ended."

There is silence for what seems an eternity and then the intake of air to signal he has weighed his options and is ready to begin again. "All right, I will come back to the question of your name," he says calmly. Making intense eye contact, intense enough to make me want to giggle, he says, "What were you doing in the Medical Records room this morning?"

"I was not in Medical Records this morning!"

"Mr. Wirm says he observed you coming out of Medical Records before you assaulted him," he says.

"That lying sack of evil wouldn't tell the truth if you were his brother. The truth is, I had turned to close the Medical Records door, which had been left open, when Wirm attacked and shoved me into the wall. Before I could recover, he was lifting Lucy from her wheelchair by her shoulders. Of course, I came to Lucy's rescue by hitting him in the face. Just so you know, and you can write this down, I called for help before trying to rescue Lucy. The rest, as they say, is history."

"Mr. Wirm says you're writing a book. Where is this book?" he asks with a raised eyebrow and a smug look.

"Whatever I'm writing is none of your, or the staff's, or Wirm's business. I demand and will exercise my right to privacy. I do not give you permission to pry into my privacy," I say, raising my voice and noting the startled look on his face.

"If you do not reveal your name, I will seek a court injunction to search your room," he says threateningly. "I might add, the court will rule in favor of my petition. I will prove it is in the best interest of my patient. If the judge insists on questioning you, it will be under oath, and you will have to reveal your name and address before being allowed to live here; so either you tell me, or you tell the judge. Either way, you *will* answer the question."

I listen to his threat with my head bent, looking at my hands. A full minute passes in silence before I raise my head to look him straight in the eyes. "Before I'm forced to talk to the judge, you will be required to testify in divorce court. How are you going to enjoy supporting Mary and your lifestyle as Cre Falls's leading psychiatrist? Once your wife takes your bank account and her money, Mary doesn't seem worth it, does she? Oh yes, I will tell your wife and offer proof."

His face turns beefy red. "Who told you this?" he sputters. "I demand to know who is spreading this ugly gossip."

"Ugly for sure. Gossip no! You and Mary should be careful discussing details of your tryst where you're likely to be overheard—details I can prove," I say.

Again, silence echoes, as if he is weighing his options. He finally comes back to me. "What do you want from me to keep your mouth shut?"

So this is what Dr. Sturges looks like under stress. No longer the brown-eyed, handsome, confident weasel who entered my room, he now looks only like a weasel, nothing more.

"You know what I want," I hiss. "I want your report about the Wirm incident this morning written just as I say it happened. No mention of a book. You *will* report to the nursing staff and anyone else who has expressed concern that I do not know my name. I want you to delete all medication orders you have written dealing with my psychological status. And you will secure my residence behind the doors with Lucy and me sharing a room. See to it that your orders go unchallenged until I challenge them myself when I'm ready to be done here. In three months when you're scheduled to see me again, we will talk about the weather or about baseball, but not about any of this."

He puts his pen in the breast pocket of his lab coat, stands up, and walks to the door. To his back, I say, smugness dripping from my voice, "Oh, and doctor? Tell Mary I'll have my lunch tray in my room, reheated, of course. Thank you for being so in love with your wife's money. How perfect for both of us."

He leaves without another word. I just make it to the bathroom before fear empties my stomach.

It never occurred to me that Sturges would petition the courts to force me to reveal my name. I'm sure that the doctor went straight to Mary from my room and that they have already narrowed down who may have overheard them. Realizing that they might have been wrong in their assumption that Lucy could not repeat what she overheard in the dining room, much less tattle about their affair to me before Sturges saw me, must have left them speechless. Surprisingly, the validity of what Lucy said went essentially unchallenged in my meeting with Sturges. However, I feel sure that Mary will defend or deny the affair to Lucy and me and make some threat before she goes off shift. She will find ways to make my life miserable, but that will be small potatoes compared to going to court.

As I make plans to see Harold tonight, Lucy is escorted back from lunch. Not surprisingly, Mary is pushing her wheelchair, looking pale. She glares at me over Lucy's head, her mouth turned down. Her lips are thin, giving her face an instant aged look.

"I can't imagine where you two got your information about Dr. Sturges and me, but if it gets to the gossip mill, you can expect repercussions," she says, lowering her eyes.

"Mary, Mary," I say. "Why would I lose the golden egg? You can count on me to keep my mouth shut as long as you and the good doctor keep out of my private life. If you find you cannot do this one little thing, I promise you, Mrs. Sturges will hear from me posthaste. Oh yes, one other thing: I will read your incident report. It will not be filed with the state without my signature. By the way, where's lunch, Mar?" I turn and give Lucy a wink.

"An aide is bringing you a cold lunch because you waited too long with your request. It will have to do. The incident report is not finished," she says, turning to leave.

Once Mary is gone, I turn again to my friend. "Lucy, if you hadn't gotten that sizzling information to me before Sturges questioned me, I'd be in sorry shape, I say. How did you get back to our room before the good doctor left Wirm's room?"

"8 22-7-4-4-11-4-3 12-24-18-4-11-5," she says proudly.

"You did? You wheeled yourself? As I live and breathe, Lucy, I should never be surprised by you. You certainly saved my hide." I am about to say more, but the aide shows up with my lunch tray.

"You're getting good at cold food, JD," says the aide. "You want to order supper now and save the suspense?"

"Yum-yum," I say without enthusiasm.

After she leaves, while I survey my tray, I say, "Two things, Lucy. You and I are taking a walk downstairs to sit with the boys after supper, and just before midnight, I'm going down to see Mr. Brown. This Wirm thing has gone to a new level of danger for you and me. If Harold knows how, we need to stop that evil bastard. Agreed?"

"0-6-17-4-4-3," she says, nodding. There's a grave look in her eyes, followed by a stillness that is so haunting I shiver a little.

Lucy will be napping soon. I intend to keep an eye on our door from the dining room while trying to get some pages written. Feeling an urgency to capture Wirm's threat in the pages of my book, I decide to stop nibbling on the poor excuse for lunch and organize the afternoon's work. Telling Lucy as much, I dig out the Underwood, paper, and some notes I made earlier.

"Lucy," I say, "you know how to yell if you need me. You relax and take a nap. I'll be watching from the dining room. After this morning's fiasco, I don't think he'll take a chance on getting caught in our room this afternoon, but I'll be watching."

It wears on my heart to see her little white head nodding off, so I put on her light for help to bed and take myself over to the dining room, positioning my chair in full view of our door as promised.

Reworking the last page from my previous writing session, I can visualize the next pages taking shape. Soon, I'm embroiled in the emotion of the scene at my farm. Fresh grief washing over me, I relive and write that moment in time that went on to define the rest of my life. Understanding now that Wirm was the mendacious creature lurking in the barn, using feral evil to influence me to perpetrate a crime that surely would have destroyed my life, I no longer wonder what force drew me here. I thought bumping through life with happenstance glimpses of where I've been was enough to justify old age and the complacency that goes with it. The egocentric scenario where I would just go to the source and write the Cre Fall's stories and then have the children safely take me back to my apartment, where I would die contented, was never in the cards. As much as I thought I was manipulating events, I'm the one who has been manipulated by the devil's bastard son, Joseph Wirm. Harold

Brown and Lucy are compelled to defeat him. I can only wonder whether this story, now my story, has already been written.

So I clack away on my old typewriter, now and again checking the open room door across the hall, losing myself in the story. When at last I become aware of the time and the noisy operations of the nursing home changing shifts, I have written many pages. The purpose of writing this book has metamorphosed. It is no longer my story but the stories that will stop Wirm.

A nurse's aide—I think her name is Nancy—comes into the dining room with a permanent marker in hand. Curious, I watch her remove my name from the seating chart and pen it in a the table away from Lucy, Otto Jener and all.

"So, ah, why is my dining room seat being changed?" I inquire.

"Mary's orders," she says. "Mary says you need to socialize with other residents and stop focusing solely on Lucy. Better for you and Lucy, Mary said."

"Give this message to Mary. I'll give her five minutes to change me back to my old table. You also tell her she's interfering again. Make sure you emphasize 'interfering.' If this is a problem, tell her I expect her to show up with her side of this argument in five minutes. Five minutes," I say, sounding more annoyed than I actually am.

Well, so this is how Mary intends to get retribution. I put on my best aggrieved face, expecting Mary to show up any minute, and I am not disappointed.

"You cannot override my authority with the aides," she announces the minute she has two feet in the room. "The change is now part of your and Lucy's care plan. You will be compliant."

Rising from my chair, I say, "Your interference in my life is noted, Mary. You report this to your lover. I was more than serious when I told you to back away from my personal life, which by the way includes any resident I wish to socialize with. Especially Lucy. I'll wait here for just another five minutes for your decision before I take action. You may end up leaving your job, but I will continue to live behind the doors with Lucy as my roommate!"

Her face flushes to a deep red, and prominent neck veins bulge. Before trusting her voice, she turns to the seating chart and writes my name in large black letters next to Lucy's on the chart. Turning with a glare, she storms out of the room.

This day is beginning to get my goat. Confrontation, believe it or not, is not my strong suit. Constantly being on guard is going to be tiring. This incident was easy. Getting caught walking through Harold's wall at midnight will really land me in hot water. I just never know when some resident will take a turn for the worse, and the hall will have staff running to the crisis. I need a plan. After today, the spotlight is shining on me. My activities will not go unnoticed. Oh, swell!

What a paradox. The stories are the book. Without the stories there would be no Wirm. Without Wirm, there would be no need for me to write this book. Without Wirm, I wouldn't be here playing "Jane Doe, the 'behind the doors' reluctant eradicator of devil spawn" with my two cohorts (and all the others behind the doors I recognize as co-cohorts).

I race (race may be the wrong word) my writing things back across the hall to look in on Lucy and get washed up for supper. God willing, unlike the last two meals, supper should be hot. Whatever is served, I'll be at Lucy's table. Making a mental list of residents I can trust in case I need to get out of the hall in a hurry tonight, I vow to be prepared. I know there are Otto and the "Shun Lady."

When I finish, Lucy is beginning to stir. She sleeps so soundly it scares me. I can barely perceive her chest rising. It takes her several seconds to reluctantly open her eyes. This afternoon she clings to sleep as though opening her eyes for one more supper is too much.

"Rise and shine, lady," I say, more concerned than I want Lucy to know. Watching her struggle up from wherever she goes in deep sleep reminds me how vulnerable she is. Hearing my voice, her eyelids flicker open. Immediately, a small smile plays the corners of her mouth.

Stretching, she murmurs, "22-4 13-4-4-3 19-14 18-4-4 17-0-11-15-8." Checking my code chart, I ask, "Ralph who? Where does he live? Behind the doors? I don't recall a Ralph back here.

"17-0-11-15-8 12-4-0-17-18 19-22-14 3-14-14-17-18 3-14-22-13 5-17-14-12 7-0-17-14-11-3. 7-4 3-0-19-18 8-13 7-8-18 17-14-14-12."

"Ralph Mears? I know who you mean. The guy with the red face and very white wavy hair. The one that always wears bib overalls. That guy?"

"24-4-18," she says, rolling her eyes.

"I'll have to talk with him after supper before we take a stroll downstairs. Want to come along?"

"18-20-17-4," she says emphatically.

Although I'm still reluctant to accept my destiny, the more I learn of Wirm's influence on the citizens of Cre Falls, the greater my responsibility to help stop him. I'm just an old lady and not a very physically fit one at that. Ralph may not be willing to help us, but if I don't ask, the answer will always be no. Not very confident and fearing for these old bones, I can no longer hide behind the doors, trying to convince myself that if I don't look, Wirm will go away.

Every time Harold and I take a trip through his wall, I will have to get a written copy of the story, with leads to evidence, to the cop shop and the newspaper. Sooner or later, I'm bound to get some interest, starting with the 1930s baby killings. I'm thinking the safest way to get copies of the stories out of the building is the mailbox downstairs. The best plan might be enlisting a very trusted person from behind the doors to carry this mail. I cannot be seen stuffing the mailbox without raising suspicion.

"Lucy, I'm going to take story number one to Medical Records and beg a couple of copies. She will probably want money, but I can pay. You know, I could use a key to that office. You think I could pinch one?"

"19-17-24 13-14-19 19-14 6-4-19 15-8-13-2-7-4-3 24-14-20-17-18 -4-11-5," she says.

"First, a couple of copies," I say, gathering the 1930s baby-killing story, and I head out the door.

The medical records secretary is sitting at her desk, clacking away on the computer keyboard. The nameplate on her desk identifies her as Gail Reece. Looking up, she asks, "Can I help you?"

"I want two copies of these pages. I know how to make them myself, and I can pay for the copies," I say.

Seemingly not surprised at my request, she says, "Ten cents a copy. Be careful you don't jam the copier."

I did not think for one minute that getting copies would be this easy. All my adrenaline preparing to argue why I need the copies, wasted. Getting on with it, I get the job done in little time. Eight pages in hand, I ask her if I can buy two plain envelopes as well.

Gail looks up from her work. "Eighty cents, plus one dollar for two envelopes. Do you need stamps?"

"Yes," I say, reaching in my pocket for the two dollars and fifty-four cents. Stamps, I should have thought of stamps to cover the request for envelopes. My heart is thumping in my chest. Because I am such an object of interest, Gail will probably mention I was in here making copies to the charge nurse. Oh well, deed done.

Before I can get out the door, Gail says, "Just a minute." Ice shivers up my spine as I turn to face her. "Before you leave, Mary asked if you would read this incident report and sign it. Since it must go to the state tomorrow, could you take care of this now?"

Standing in the doorway with one hand on the frame, I take the report from her hand. Mary has dictated a carefully worded report with the slant of blame on Wirm. The last paragraph details Wirm's visit and my own visit with Dr. Sturges and the fact that no new medication orders were written and that the doctor wants a "wait and see" approach. Sure, wait until he kills Lucy and me and see how he does it. The man's an idiot. Nevertheless, I sign the report.

As I turn and leave, I note that I didn't see loose keys lying around Gail's office. Not that I had a chance to see much. Nursing must have keys for this office. I remember seeing keys hanging on a board behind the nurses' station. That's my target for a key to the Medical Records door. For now, when I need copies, I'll just ask. If Gail refuses or asks too many questions, I go for the nurses' key.

Lucy has already been assisted to the dining room when I arrive to hide my copies. Putting them between the sheets in my bed will keep them safe while I eat supper. Giving Lucy a thumbs-up as I arrive at our table in the dining room, I feel like the sleuth star of "behind the doors."

As I'm pulling out my chair, Otto nods my way, and the Shun Lady, looking away toward the door, murmurs loud enough for me to hear, "Persuasion."

"They know, Lucy. They just know," I say in awe. What kind of convoluted reality am I living? I'm not willing to believe in telepathy. However, I do believe I can pass through Harold's wall, witness a past event, and start a car by touching the hood. Telepathy, though—I don't think so. But something is stirring inside me.

"3-14 13-14-19 5-14-17-6-4-19 19-7-4 12-20-3 14-13 24-14-20-17 18-7-14-4-18," she says.

"Okay. Mud on my shoes, I was probably sleepwalking. Telepathy? I don't think so, honey. Yet, I have no idea how Lucy knows about my muddy prints down the hall.

"You know, Lucy, I was thinking, we could play Scrabble," I say, raising my eyebrows up and down like Harpo Marx. "Think about it, a word here and there. It might give us a number break. What do you say? I can ask activities to get an electronic game."

"8-11-11 19-17-24 0-13-24 19-7-8-13-6," she says, mirth turning up the corners of her mouth.

"I'll talk to the activity aide tomorrow," I say.

Immediately after supper, I wheel Lucy down to Ralph Mears' room. We find him sitting on the side of his bed, his supper tray still in front of him. I forgot dining room trays come up first. Ralph is having supper with his shirt off. Covered with white curly hair, his bare chest and arms are surprisingly muscular. His small paunch belly just hangs over the waistband of his coveralls, the straps hanging down too. What's more startling, his bare skin is a coppery tan. His face is, as I remember, flushed. The shock of white, thick, wavy hair is remarkable, but well, a muscular bare chest is certainly titillating at Ralph's age. I'm left speechless.

He looks up from his tray and greets us without making an attempt at covering himself. "What are you ladies doing so far from your room?"

Realizing I am staring, I manage to find my voice. "We're sorry to interrupt your supper. I forgot room trays come up last. We can come back later if you like."

He says, “I know why you’re here, so you may as well stay and talk it out. Say, Lucy, it took her long enough to get down here. Been expecting you.”

“Lucy only mentioned your name today,” I say somewhat defensively.

He gives me a long, disbelieving look. “You know, Miss Doe or JD or whatever you call yourself, this Wirm thing is way bigger than you. All of us who know are sure you can’t do this with just Harold and Lucy. We may not be able to do what Harold does, or Lucy for that matter, but we can watch your back behind the doors. Only thing is, you have to ask for our help, or Otto, the person you call the Shun Lady, and I are left sitting on our hands”

“So I’m asking,” I say. “How can you help Lucy, Harold, and me?”

“For one thing,” Ralph says, sighing as if we are finally getting down to business, “Otto and I can watch the hall.. We can watch out for Lucy when you can’t. Another thing, we can hide you,” Ralph says all in one breath.

“Oh yeah,” he says, looking suddenly embarrassed as he glances down at his own bare chest, “the reason I’m so tan is I work in the residents’ garden whenever I can. That’s most days from early spring to frost.”

Realizing that he has read my mind too, I say, “Ralph, how do you do it? Read my mind? Otto and Shun Lady can do it too. Lucy is really good at telling me what I’m thinking. Playing Scrabble with her should be very one-sided. But no matter how I try, I can’t read anyone’s mind. I’d really like to know what Wirm is thinking.”

“For one thing,” he says, “better you don’t. You could open your mind to Wirm. But if that happens, Lucy won’t be able to protect you against Wirm invading your mind. He would know exactly what we’re talking about right now! Lucy’s able to protect your whereabouts in the nursing home and about as far as the car. He’s been trying to get past Lucy and her blocking ability for more years than I’ve lived here.”

Confused, I say, “That doesn’t tell me how the four of you do this trick, though. Did you just wake up one morning, and the next sound you heard was someone’s thoughts?”

"Not exactly," he says. "Well, shall I tell her, Lucy?"

Lucy nods with a faraway look in her eyes. She reaches over to Ralph and covers his big paw with her ivory, veined small hand. The tensing of Lucy's body makes me dread what he thinks I need to hear.

Ralph gets up from his bed to close the door and begins pacing back and forth. Putting his hands on the back of Lucy's chair as if to steady himself, he says, "Lucy's story is for another day, unless you can get Harold to tell you sooner. Okay, ladies first, I guess. Shun Lady was happily married to one of Cre Falls's lumber barons. I need to mention here that he was also a lawyer. After years of wanting children, she gave birth to a little doll of a girl. When the baby was just a toddler—two or so, I guess—she was walking on Main Street with her father. Most people on the street say he pushed that beautiful little girl under the wheels of a pulp truck. His story was that Joseph Wirm pushed her. The money story was she pulled her hand from her father's and tripped, falling into the path of the pulp truck that then dragged her for two blocks under its wheels. The jury verdict, after a lengthy trial, freed the husband.

"Lydia was never the same. She flipped her lid for a while. She did quite some time on the fourth floor in Marshfield Hospital before being admitted here recently. Actually, it was Lucy who saved her—made her understand that Wirm would not go unpunished for his part in her little girl's death. We would wait, Lucy said. Help was sure to come.

"Only thing, thereafter, all Lydia would do is rhyme and say shun words. She was admitted behind the doors recently. Lucy and Harold knew Lydia Weimer made perfect sense, and she could read minds: Perhaps because of the shock, perhaps because her brain made other pathways. Our Lydia is a very special lady. You can count on her help when you need it."

Grief and anger punch my heart. Wirm, you son of a bitch. Sour acid fills my mouth.

"Okay, okay," I seethe. "What about Otto Jener?"

"Yeah, Otto," he says. "You need to know that everyone who knew Otto thought he was a prince. Otto's the kind of guy everyone likes. He and his wife were married for twenty years. He had a good job at the paper mill. Nice little house. No children. Otto never said why.

"He worked the p.m. shift, getting home about half past eleven. I remember it was Friday night when I heard cop car sirens racing up Fifth Avenue. Like most people up that late, being two blocks over, I ran over, following the sirens. When I got there, three cop cars were parked in front of Otto's house. One of the cars was the state cops. I thought for sure someone was dead. By this time a crowd had gathered on the street in front of Otto's house. I started to get nervous when I realized no ambulance had responded.

"The cops brought Otto out the door handcuffed. Otto looked like a beaten dog, eyes looking at his feet. When they brought him past me, I whispered he shouldn't worry. I would get him the best lawyer. I tell you, what he said confused me.

"He said, 'Jesus Christ.' I also saw he was dragging his left leg some. The crowd was shocked silent. Before they took Otto away, another cop came out of Otto's house with Billy the mechanic, who worked up at Fair Auto. I can tell you, Billy had a reputation for being fast with the ladies. Billy had his pants on, but that's all. He was yelling, 'He almost killed me! You saw him with that big hunting knife!'

"The crowd went nuts, chanting, 'Fast Billy' and things like that. But even above the noisy crowd, I could hear a wicked laugh. I immediately went home and called attorney Berk. I told him about Otto and to meet me at the Cre Falls jail right away. Berk and I go back a long way. Berk went to meet him at the cop shop first. The clink was full of people all talking at once. No sign of Otto. I figured they were holding him in a cell. Berk demanded to see his client. Chief said it wouldn't do any good. All Otto would say was 'Jesus Christ.' He said if attorney Berk wanted to know what had happened, he better ask Otto's wife.

"That's just what we did next—or rather, after Berk ordered that no one was to question his client while he was gone. All the lights were still blazing when we got to Otto's house, so we boldly walked up to the door and rang the bell. Otto's wife came to the door wearing a bathrobe, with a belt loosely holding it together. She looked a mess, with hair hanging in her face. Berk came straight to the point. He said he wanted to ask her some questions. I noticed he didn't say he was Otto's attorney.

"This is what she told us near as I remember: She and Billy were having one of those affairs, seeing each other when Otto was at work. Billy was different this night, she said—drinking, she thought, even though she didn't smell liquor on his breath. They were in bed making love—wild, rough love—when Otto opened the bedroom door with his hunting knife in his hand. Even after Otto yelled at him, Billy wouldn't stop. He kept showing Otto his stiff dick, taunting him. Otto grabbed Billy by his hair and was going to slice his throat when something strong seemed to knock the knife out of his hand. The wife didn't see anything, but she heard a weird laugh. All Otto said was 'Jesus Christ,' and then he picked up the telephone off the nightstand and dialed the cops. The cops came and cuffed Otto. Took him out the front door and told Billy to get his pants on.

"She said all this without a hint of remorse. Not a tear. Berk told her Otto was in jail, and he would be representing him. She called Berk an SOB and told us to leave. When we got back to the station, an ambulance was taking Otto out on a stretcher. Doctor riding with the ambulance said Otto had a stroke. He said Otto was dragging his left side and was aphasic. All Otto could say was 'Jesus Christ.'

"Days later, I went up to the hospital to see Otto. He was sitting up in bed when I looked in his room. When he saw me, he said, 'Jesus Christ,' in a tone like he was glad to see me. I told him about his wife saying she thought someone else was in the room when he opened the door and saw Billy. He just nodded and said 'Jesus Christ' again, in a knowing way.

"He was admitted to the nursing home behind the doors a few weeks later. The only two words he has ever said since that night are 'Jesus Christ,' but always in such a way we know exactly what he means. Right, Lucy?

"I don't know how Lucy did it, but she helped Otto understand that Wirm was the third person in that room with Billy and his wife. Since then, Otto has been the mind-welding gent you know. He and Shun Lady's only reason for living is to help you and Harold get Wirm.

"Now you know everything Lucy and I know," Ralph says, jerking me to the present.

Trying to process Ralph's stories, I innately know they're true. Our pasts are all linked to Wirm and some horrible moment in time, mine included. We've assembled a behind-the-doors crew for a showdown. Only one goal exists.

"Still," I say, "it seems that you and I have come out of our past encounters with Wirm pretty intact. What's your story, Ralph?"

Looking thoughtful, he says, "My story is simple. I was born reading others' thoughts. I have more controversial traits than innocent mind reading. Wirm raped my mother sixty-five years ago. I am the son of that crime. Really, JD, didn't you recognize the wavy white hair?"

Suddenly, I find myself really looking at Ralph. Just as suddenly, I feel a scream bubbling in my throat. Jumping up, I take hold of Lucy's wheelchair. "We've got to get out of here, and I mean right now, Lucy," I say, furious with myself for putting Lucy in danger once again.

"Take it easy, Jane," he says. "Sit down. Do you think Lucy would have brought you here if I intended to harm you? Yes, I'm the son of that rape, but I'm also the perfect goodness of my mother. Her absolute pureness is what Wirm tried to destroy. Rising above her pain and disgust, she raised me to triumph over the evil that spawned me to become a part of this small army against him. Like Otto, Lydia, Lucy, and Harold, I will do anything I can to help you."

Calming my blood pressure enough to speak, I say, "I don't fashion I'm any good at reading true character, but I trust Lucy with my life."

Looking into Lucy's eyes, I see only calmness and strength. She sighs as if a weight has been lifted off her shoulders, as if sharing the burden has at last given her the right to relax.

"Okay, Ralph," I say, "if you're good enough for Lucy, who am I to argue? Harold and I need all the help we can get. The three of you watching out for Lucy is gold. I'm counting on you. One thing … okay, maybe more than one thing, I really don't care how old Wirm is, but what I want to know is, how long has he been leading the people of Cre Falls by the nose? Why hasn't someone, like the four of you, stopped him before this? I don't care about why me. What I'm asking is, why now?"

"We tried, Jane," he says with a look of deep shame. "Every time we tried, someone close to us got hurt, an aide or another resident. Wirm, like the five of us, has been waiting. Wirm has been waiting for you. We waited for the one who could defeat him, not as you think, with words on a piece of paper, but with all that's holy, like putting a cross against his forehead. Something like that. Wirm has been here a long, long time. Way before the 1930s baby killings. Do you know why he lives here at the nursing home? He likes to watch us. He likes knowing we're watching him. He thinks the older we get, the less able we are to defeat him. We, on the other hand, know that what will fatally damage him is experienced memory: Old memory!"

Stifling an ironic laugh, I say, "That's us for sure. We at least fit the old part." Holy Joe, just when I figure out a way, I have to find another way to deal with the bastard. The next thing Ralph will tell me is the stories, as I write them, reveal too much about our identity and more. What I'll do is rewrite the story using just the details that will lead the powers that be to find evidence against Wirm. Maybe only a holy cross can hurt Wirm, but an investigation into his past can keep him off balance.

Speaking more to Lucy than to Ralph, I say with some urgency, "We had better get back to the typewriter. I think I'll write a Wirm background and about what I saw back in 1930s Sawyerville."

Wheeling Lucy back down the hall, I glance at the clock in the dining room. It's almost nine o'clock. We talked with Ralph for the better part of three hours. It would take me more than an hour to write a presage of information to the Cre Falls Police Department and the *Daily Press*. Thinking about midnight, I'm less fearful of being out there than I am about getting through Harold's wall. Just the thought of passing through makes me grind my teeth. This hero stuff is sure hard on an old soul.

Getting my typewriter out and getting my thoughts straight takes me as much time as it does for the aide to get Lucy ready for bed. The aide yells "g'night" as she passes into the hall, quickly off to another resident's room.

Mocking her, I mutter, "G'night, Lucy. Don't wait up for me, girl."

With that said, I begin getting ready as much as I possibly can. After finishing a sophomoric synopsis of the Sawyerville story, I type a short graphic exposé on Wirm. Then a sneaking thought slips into my brain. What a dunce I was not to realize this sooner. I'm walking out Harold's wall at midnight. If all goes as suspected, I'll be in another time. A letter to the cops and editor of the newspaper in God knows what year would be worthless. If even read, it would be disregarded as coming from some nutcase. I'll have to mail the letters before going through the wall. Luckily for me, we are still in an era of "a box of rubber gloves in every bathroom." I put on gloves and lightly rub the typed sheets with the talc the aides use on Lucy when they do her cares. Hopefully, that will take care of any fingerprints. Addressing the envelopes and affixing the stamps I bought, I put away my typewriter and step into my slippers for the trek to the mailbox downstairs. If I can't avoid being seen—its ten fifteen, and the aides are sitting in the lounge working on charts by now—I will have to be ingenious. The stairs are outfitted with an alarm. I will have to take the elevator across from the nurses' station. My plan is to take two quarters and tell them I'm going downstairs for a soda.

After hiding the letters in the waistband of my pajamas and putting on my robe, I walk down the quiet hall and push open the doors. All of the evening staff is present, and they look up as I boldly walk to the elevator.

Alerted, the nurse says, "Where do you think you're going this time of night, JD?"

"Downstairs to get a soda," I say, turning away.

One of the aides gets out of her chair and says, "I'll get one for you. Do you have some change?"

Always my luck, a helpful aide. "No, thanks," I say. "I can do this. You're busy charting. Go back to work. I'll be right back."

Just as I am about to push the down button, the nurse says, "Wait a minute. I'll get your ten o'clock Tylenol. Save my feet a trip down the hall."

I feel very exposed standing in front of the elevator waiting, but hopefully, I appear calm. After what feels like ten minutes, the nurse holds out a medication cup with two white pills. I nearly choke swallowing the sticky pills, but I manage to get them down without a crisis.

"Now I really need a soda," I tell her, pushing the elevator button.

Once I'm in the elevator, the last sight I see is the nurse looking at me with suspicion as the doors close. She will probably follow her doubt and alert the downstairs nurse I'm coming, who will do her duty and follow me. "Oh, nice move, JD," I say quietly to myself. As I exit the elevator, I wonder whether it is perhaps an omen that the downstairs nurse is not at the station—although, as I predicted, the phone is ringing. Praying no one will run up to answer it, I freeze by the closed elevator doors. Fortunately, all are off attending to residents' needs.

The painted blue mailbox is on this side of the vestibule doors. The doors, being an exit, are alarmed. Looking like an escapee in pajamas, robe, and slippers, I quickly get my letters out of my waistband and open the mail slot. The slot door hasn't been greased in a lifetime, and the noise is surely enough to wake the dead. Quickly dropping my letters in, I close the door, hoping it's only the dead who heard me. Mail is still a big privacy issue in nursing homes, so I know only the mailman with a key will take the mail in the morning.

This job is not done until a root beer can is in my hand. Walking into the dining room, deep in thought about how dry my mouth is, I fail to hear the nurse come up behind me.

"What are you doing downstairs?" she asks, her voice bouncing off the walls.

Almost jumping out of my slippers, I stutter, "You don't have to sneak up on a person! You scared me out of my wits. Just look, I'm getting a soda. Even lowly residents on the second floor want a soda now and then."

Contrite now, she says, "I'm sorry I frightened you. We don't usually see residents in here this time of night."

A moment later, with the cold can in hand and nearly drooling, I say, "I'd better get back upstairs before they send out the warden."

Mission accomplished, I push the call button, opening the doors of the waiting elevator. Now sure of my luck, I can't help wallow in it as the elevator ascends. Lady of "BTD" strikes another blow for independence. So much for this small side adventure. Soon on to the real thing. Terror pushes back my fleeting confidence and grips this aging heart. No running away. No closing my eyes. Some of this terror feels like excitement as I anticipate midnight.

Part Eight

Ding, Dong, the Schoolmarm's dead

"School's out, school's out.
Time to sing, time to shout!"

Chapter Eighteen

Midnight came way before sleep. Remembering Lucy's instructions last time, I put on warm clothes and sneakers. Wishing I had a flashlight doesn't make one appear in my hand, so I lean over Lucy, hoping for her benediction. Touching her face, I whisper, "See you soon, roomie," and leave the room before fear stops me.

As last time, the hall is deserted and silent. However, this time when I arrive at Otto's door, Ralph is standing with him. Both give me a silent pat on the arm. "Take care of Lucy," I whisper. Crossing the hall to avoid Wirm's room, I glance at his open door. No dim light from the hall penetrates the absolute blackness of the space inside. *Oh, woe is me*, my mind screams. What if he's waiting for us outside? Shun Lady, whom I now know as Lydia, is sitting in her wheelchair, filling her doorway. Pale, with her mouth grimly downcast, she appears anxious and fearful. As I pass her, I say in my mind, "You and me both," knowing my thoughts are easily read.

Creeping silently toward Harold Brown's closed door, I hope that I will find him asleep and that this night will pass with me doing the same. But no, as I carefully open the door, his steely hand latches on my wrist, pulling me in.

"Harold! Not so tight. You'll cut off my circulation or, worse, break my wrist," I say, wincing. "I take it you're expecting me? Let's get this mind-bending night over with."

Harold remains as silent as the room. As he pulls me to face the wall, I can't help muttering, "No foreplay, Harold? Shame on you." The words barely slip off my tongue before my mouth snaps shut.

The whirling vortex catapults my body to the other side, rearranging my cells as it pushes me forward.

Harold's voice sings in my head: *Be with me Lord when I'm in trouble. Be with me Lord, I pray.* I don't stop to wonder what he's doing in my head. His singsong, childlike voice is disturbing, but it's a thread I latch on to.

The passing through takes longer than before, I'm sure. Landing outside, I wither, and the soda I mistakenly drank earlier rises from my stomach like a fountain. I sink to my knees, retching.

Harold leans casually against a tree, watching me spew root beer. "Use a leaf to wipe your mouth, and let's get going," he says.

His compassion is overwhelming. The vertigo has zapped my strength. What I want to do is curl up in a fetal position and play dead. But I realize that if I don't move now, Wirm may be the answer to that prayer. I choose trying to get on my feet versus the ugly alternative.

Moaning while my stomach clenches, I say, "I know, I know, before Wirm knows we're gone. Right? When I passed his room, his door was open. His room had an empty feeling. He may be waiting for us."

"Highly unlikely, Jane," Harold says. "Lucy would have alarmed us. Lucy and the others are jamming his radar for now. We should make for the car before he starts looking for us. Let's go, Jane, or is it JD now?"

Rising from the damp ground, I sucker-punch his arm. There is no path leading away from where the nursing home will stand in the future. A thick stand of mature trees and a mossy-carpeted forest floor leave me completely disoriented. Harold, on the other hand, knows his way around the trunks of very large trees—trees I know weren't here the last time we passed this way. A narrow, scarcely traveled path emerges that only allows us to walk single file. Struggling to keep up with Harold in the moonless dark, I don't see the river until we're nearly getting our feet wet. The trail alongside the river leads to a wooden bridge of questionable sturdiness. Before I have time to wish once again that I had a flashlight, Harold has moved forward, without hesitation. Quickly crossing, he pulls me behind him. After the bridge, the path widens into a rut-filled road of sorts. Clapboard buildings line Main Street of Cre Falls, a Cre Falls of a long, long time ago. I fear my dread is esoteric.

Harold turns and says, "The car is up ahead, more out in the open now. The buildings that will form the alley haven't been built yet. This is bad for us. We're going to be easy to spot. I'm counting on you to get the car going immediately. I'll get the cross from the backseat."

There it sits in the knee-high weeds. I would recognize the red, rusted jalopy anywhere. This is really antiquity. The road in front of the car is wood plank. I don't know enough to place plank roads in the past history of Cre Falls. *Is this Cre Falls or Kansas?* I wonder as I approach the car.

"Where in the hell am I, Harold?" I say, laying my hands on the hood. At once the engine vibrates, coughs, and catches. Without asking, remembering the last trip, I know I am expected to drive. Sliding in the driver's seat with Harold riding shotgun, I put the transmission in drive, and as expected, the car negotiates the bump onto the wood road.

Not even glancing at the gas gauge, I say, "Which way, Harold? And hold on to the seat of your Depends; this is going to be a rough ride." I suspect that this will be the last bit of humor to come from my mouth for probably ever as Harold points right up the washboard road. After two more right turns, the road becomes gravel with a hard-packed surface. Driving north, following Harold's pointing finger, we pass a small settlement of a few houses and a bar. Harold, my guide, mentions this is Bittercreek and points us onto another gravel road to the right. The smooth ride is over; this road is much narrower and filled with holes and ruts. As the Toyota straddles the middle and left shoulder, trees brush the car. The little jalopy clutches the road as we move steadily northeast. The headlights penetrate the inky black night only a few feet in front of the car. Harold sits hugging the cross, arms crossed over his chest. His face is cast in a ghostly glow from the dashboard lights. I think, *I'm not only old, but an old fool to put myself in this demonic car with speak-no-evil (or speak-not-at-all) Harold clinging to a talisman.*

"Harold," I squeak, "I want you to tell me where we're going. I know that son of bitch is probably in hot pursuit, but did he get your tongue too? Come on, the night is scary enough without your silence. What ya thinking?"

After some moments of continued silence, Harold says, "Hard to explain the exact where or the time. I'm sure you don't recognize any landmarks, but you should get some gist of the direction. Northeast of Bittercreek should put you in mind of the flowage."

"The Tombaugh Flowage?" I'm aware of it, from my younger days in Cre Falls. It is a bewildering acreage of vast forests, swamps, and chains of lakes for miles. A settlement of tree-huggers squatted on the land, clearing it and trying to farm. I do know when that was. Then it became a favorite place for sportsmen for fishing and hunting, always with a guide. It's been said that men have gotten lost somewhere in the flowage, never found.

I say, "Why the flowage, Harold? Don't we have enough unsolved crime in Cre Falls? We're talking miles here on way less than good roads. Getting up there, not getting ourselves lost, and getting back with or without Wirm's constant threat is taking much too big a bite out of crime for me. Let's turn around and find a safer murder closer to home."

"We'll be all right," Harold says. After a moment, he adds, "Stop worrying."

How comforting, I think. "Harold, trusting you is taking more confidence than I have in practically anyone I know. And I have to tell you, I don't have trust issues. A rusted jalopy and—I'll take your word for it—a saving cross is where I have to put my faith. I don't know; that just doesn't inspire much confidence."

Keeping the car's balancing act going, running one wheel in the center and one on the narrow shoulder, strains what driving skills I have. We keep moving on through the night like a small ship on a choppy sea. It seems like hours have passed, but Harold's right: time has no meaning. I think Harold is praying. He's either talking to himself or praying.

To add to my visual limitations, zigzag bolts of white lightning race across the sky, imprinting on my retina, followed by thunderclaps that vibrate the steering wheel. Trees, bending nearly to the ground, crowd what is little more than a cow path as gusts of wind warn of the rain that surely will soon reduce our slow going to a stop. I fear stopping. We cannot and will not stop.

"Trust the car, JD," Harold says between claps of thunder. "Take your hands off the steering wheel. Relax. Just be a passenger. The car will do the work. When I tell you to turn left, you can get back to driving."

Sure the car will turn sharply and crash into a tree or a colossal, left-behind ice-age boulder, I take my hands from the wheel and cover my face with them. By this time, tired numbness has spread between my shoulders. Harold leans over and pushes my shoulders back against the car seat. Letting my spine melt into the fabric and foam, I realize that my feet have given up control of the pedals. For better or worse, the car is driving us. I let my hands fall limply to my lap, and I'm not really surprised when the car slows down to let a family of porcupines cross. Suddenly, the clouds let down sheets of rain. The drumming on the roof is deafening. Wind-driven rain on the windshield makes the road obscure. Still, the car chugs up the road without a pause.

"Harold, how is all this possible?" I say, closer to asleep than awake. "How can the car that died in the parking lot of the Crow's Nest Motel end up magic? Not to mention the old bag that rode the rust bucket into town. I don't feel changed. I mean, I do feel somehow younger after I pass through your wall. Maybe not younger, but my joints are less sore, less stiff."

"Oh, I think we were chosen, more like picked, a long time ago," answers Harold. "Our lives crossed Wirm's, and somehow, unlike so many others, the six of us were able to protect ourselves. The time to pay the piper is now, or so Wirm would lead us to believe. I just think all of us were brought together at this time and place to end his possession of Cre Falls's people. And of course, don't you feel we're not alone?"

"I really lack your insight, Harold. Most of the time, all I'm doing is protecting Lucy and myself—and I must say, not all that well. Despite knowing we must do something, I can't figure out what that is. I pray we're not alone in this fight. It's like fighting the playground bully, only his father is the bully behind the bully. If we get sand kicked in our face, I hope we're able to kick back."

The car stops next to a road that leads to our left. Taking back the steering wheel, I can almost palpate the car's reluctance to move forward. Harold nods and points ahead up a small hill. As I urge the Toyota up the incline, fear quickens my heart. The road ends abruptly in a turnoff. The dense forest ahead of us is dark and foreboding. Flashes of lightning hardly make a show under the umbrella of close-growth trees. For a minute, neither of us moves. Harold holds the cross tighter to his chest, humming "Be with Us, Lord."

Chapter Nineteen

There's no preparing for what's to come once I open the car door. The blatant fear on Harold's face matches the raw terror that I know must show in my own grimace. If the car's engine had not quit, I would be putting the transmission in reverse, making a coward's run for it. Filled with dread, I reach over to touch the cross clutched in Harold's arms. No electric holy juice quakes my hand. I take up Harold's litany: "Be there when we are in trouble. Be there, I pray, oh Lord."

Harold finds his voice. "Let's go now! Pay close attention. This isn't going to be easy. He's here already. Waiting."

"Oh God, oh God, oh God," I mutter, opening the car door.

Harold is waiting in the weeds in front of the car, facing the dense forest. When I round the car to stand by his side, he latches on to my hand. With the cross tucked under his other arm, he drags me into the primal forest. I have no sense of where the path is that Harold is descending, but I try to keep my balance, periodically tripping over huge exposed roots hidden in the cloistered dark.

"We cannot get separated, but if we do, remember the way back to the car. Do not wait for me! Go back the way we came. Wait for me in the Catholic Church. Don't leave the church until I get there, no matter what happens," he cautions.

I'm about to say, "How will you get back without the car?" when he turns, putting his hand over my mouth. "No more talking," he whispers.

Piqued at being told to shut up, I'm barely able to keep from shouting at him. But I do what he says because I'm scared to death. The gloomy, ink-black trees shriek when a lightning bolt strikes the upper treetops. The smell of ozone and wood smoke is brief because pelting rain snuffs the fire.

Harold abruptly turns right. I nearly miss his signal to get down because I'm preoccupied with trying to memorize the way back. Pulling me to my knees, he points at a swaying light making its way through the darkness ahead of us. The light proceeds through the trees, illuminating a small clearing about twenty feet in front of us. A stand of trees and underbrush surrounds the clearing. In the center is a huge oak tree. Hanging from a lower limb is a gutted deer carcass.

As the man holds the lantern higher, the glow illuminates him, but his face is shadowed in a bristly beard, making his age indeterminable. He's wearing a greatcoat made of some sort of animal skin, making him appear bulky. Talking softly to a woman holding his arm, he pulls her forward.

She is covered from neck to ankle by a cloak of some heavy-looking material, wool most likely. The hood covers her head, obscuring her face. Walking by the man's side, she is much shorter than him. Abruptly, she hesitates on the edge of the clearing, removing her arm from his, and covers her mouth with her hand.

Sounding acerbic, he says, "Now, now, marm, 'tis only the venison I kilt this morn. It's dead. Can't hurt you none."

"Ah, Barney," she says, reaching to touch his face affectionately, "you don't have to call me 'marm' when we're alone. The dead deer frightens me, love. Can you take it down and put it out of sight?"

Jerking away from her touch, Barney says, "Nah, the wild critters will get it, sure. May hap they get you too."

"Barney, where will I sit? The ground is wet and cold," she whines.

From the edge of the clearing, a high falsetto voice mimics the woman. "I'm frightened of the dead deer. Where will I sit? Ha, I'll get my ass wet. Barney, oh Barney, what about the lump?"

I try to sink into the wet ground. "God, it's Wirm. Harold, it's Wirm," I whisper. By this time I'm soaked to my skin, and cold is seeping into my bones.

Harold says, "It's not the Wirm that knows we're here. That one is here too. I just don't know where."

In the circle of the lantern light, Barney has removed his greatcoat and is spreading it on the ground, away from the hanging deer. Under his coat his homespun shirt stretches the buttons, revealing a muscular chest. Suspenders hold up what look like leather britches. Large, meaty hands untie the woman's cloak. As he pushes down hard on the woman's shoulders, she half-sits, half-falls on top of the greatcoat with a look of discomfort on her face.

"You don't have to be so rough, Barney," she complains. "Why did you lead me way out here in the woods? Not many folks go out on a night like this. Your ma and pa will be at church for hours. Why couldn't we go to the barn where it's at least dry? Please sit, Barney. See, I made room for you."

Towering over her, his hand still on her shoulder, Barney says, "If Ma and Pa catch us, they skin me alive for sure, marm. Out here, no one hear us. Ya tell me about the catch again."

Raising her voice, she says, "Sit! I can't talk to you way up there. You don't have to call me 'marm' when we're not in the schoolroom. Call me Abby or darling when we're alone. When we're married, you'll use my proper name, won't you? I'm going to call you Bartholomew. I'm thinking we'll be married before the baby shows. That won't be long now. Already I'm getting side looks when the baby makes me sick in the morning. Preacher will be back this way early next month. You'll marry me then, won't you? Tell me. Why don't you sit with me?"

Wirm makes himself visible, stepping into the clearing. Leaning against a mammoth virgin oak tree, he purses his lips and begins whistling "Ding-Dong, the Witch Is Dead."

"Oh, Bartholomew," he continues, "the school witch gonna get you if you don't watch out. She will strap you to her bustle. No more drinking and hunting with the boys. The lump will be just like her, howling all the time. Life's over, Barney. Hey, boy, got your hunting knife? Do ya?" Wirm roars with laughter.

Digging my cold fingers into the wet earth, I feel my heart stall. Wirm whistling a tune from *The Wizard of Oz* must mean this is the Wirm chasing us, the Wirm from our time. I feel Harold shudder.

Swallowing the bile that threatens my throat, I say, "Can they hear Wirm, Harold?"

"No. I have a feeling the Wirm of then is repeating what he said to Barney a long time ago and the Wirm of now was the one who called Lucy to tell her the Flowage story. The whistling is a new thing. He's whistling for our benefit—to spook us. As hard as this is going to be, JD, watch carefully for evidence the law may have missed when Lucy sent them searching. Already we have more than they had. We have the guy's name. There he is, by the path. See him? Look by the path that Barney and the woman came from. It's the Wirm of the past."

Following Harold's pointing finger, I find Wirm standing at the mouth of the path with his arms folded across his chest. The two Wirms appear the same, both with wavy white hair, both dressed in blue pullovers and brown slacks, both with dark shoes. It's like seeing twins from the past and future. Looking for some difference, I notice that the Wirm from our present is wearing a ring. I can't see a ring on the past devil. Once again a bystander, I'm without the courage it takes to witness yet another Wirm slaughter. Whatever evidence the law might have missed will surely go unnoticed by me. Yet I need to write something significant to attract interest if I want someone to investigate the unsolved crime I'm about to witness. No longer fooling myself—the woman will not live, and her unborn baby will die with her—I feel tears of grief hot on my face. Wiping the tears with the back of my hand, I notice Harold's lips moving in a silent prayer.

Taking his hand off her shoulder, Barney walks to the dead deer's side. Removing his hunting knife from its sheath, he slices through the rope around the deer's neck without drag on the knife. After the deer falls to the ground, he runs his thumb gingerly across the blade, testing the honed sharpness. Satisfied, he replaces the hunting knife. Dragging the deer carcass toward the trees, he disappears from sight.

"Barney? Oh, Barney," the woman calls out, "Please don't be gone long. Please hurry back. I don't want to be alone."

"What'd I tell you, Barney?" Wirm says, chuckling. "That bellyacher will suck you dry. A man's got a right to dip his wick without it becoming a jail sentence. You have to take care of this little problem while you got her alone. There's more like her in every hayloft."

Walking silently, Barney once again appears at the edge of the clearing. He shakes raindrops from his shaggy head, or is he trying to get Wirm out of his brain? I can't be sure.

Screaming in my head, I keep pleading with God to change Wirm's words, to use the good in Barney to save the woman and the baby. *Can none of this be changed, God? Is there no way to stop the carnage? Where are you, God? A little help here. A little help here,* I plead.

Barney walks back to the woman and sits behind her. Reaching around, he covers her mouth with his hand. "Quiet, woman," he cautions her. "You'll wake the devil himself."

She leans against him, snuggling into his warmth. "Barney, it's so much better with the deer gone, but your hand stinks of dried blood. Can you clean your hands with wet leaves? Thinking of you touching me with deer blood on your hands makes me want to lose my supper. Can you do this one thing for your darling?"

As Barney gets up, a small voice is there with him again. "Hey there, Barney," Wirm says. "This devil is already awake. Do you really have to listen to this wench? Deer blood on your hands, oh my. How would you like to eat her liver, Barney? Yum, good eats." Wirm puts his arm around his shoulder. "When is the last time you tasted young liver cooked on the campfire?"

Barney mutters as he moves his hands in the wet leaves. He runs his hand over his hair as if contemplating something. Hearing this, his companion calls out.

"My darling, who are you listening to?" she asks Barney, tipping her head as if trying to catch a distant sound. "We are here alone, right? Oh, please tell me we're alone."

Barney turns to meet Wirm's eyes. The pivotal point of no return comes while Barney stares deep into the hollow blackness of Wirm's eyes. As Wirm sucks Barney's weak soul from him, all moral resistance scatters. The smirk that moves across his face is brutal. In a hissing voice he says sitting, "No telling, woman."

Barney's hunting knife appears in his hand faster than I can follow it. I can't stop my screams as I watch Barney pull Abby's hood off, revealing her long hair. She is only able to grunt, "Wha—" before he grabs her hair, pulling her head back and exposing her creamy-white throat. Knife in hand, Barney makes one swift slice across her throat with his left hand, cutting through her sternocleidomastoid and tracheal cartilage, slicing the external jugular vein across to the external carotid artery. A wheezing gurgle escapes her severed windpipe as her head falls forward, blood pouring onto the bodice of her dress and pooling on her lap. Barney continues holding her shoulders, preventing her torso from falling forward. Her head remains attached to her body only by the intact cervical spine. Barney gets up to his knees, allowing her body to tip on its side. He and Wirm stand looking down at her, as Abby's lifeblood pools on Barney's greatcoat.

"Blast," says Barney. "Her blood will ruin my coat for time and always."

Wirm whispers in his ear, "Burn it, Barney. But first, finish the job."

He walks into the woods and retrieves the rope from the neck of the deer. Tying the rope around her feet, he drags her body over to the tree. After he hoists her off the ground and secures the rope to the low branch, her hair nearly touches the ground. He appears dazed for a moment, before his eyes begin rapidly searching the ground by his ruined coat. Barney spots the knife where he laid it. Wirm casually walks over and picks up the knife and returns it to Barney's side.

"Here it is, Barney boy. Not to worry, all's well. Take the rest of her. Now!"

Even as I retch bile, I can't take my eyes off the bloody scene in the clearing. As she hangs from the limb upside down, Abby's neck wound gapes open. The lantern barely casts light on her shadowed face. Blood streaks down her face into her blond hair and drips onto her cloak, which has slipped to the wet ground. In slow motion, her dress falls down her body, inside out, covering her face. Thanking God for that small mercy, I turn my face to Harold's shoulder and sob.

"No more, Harold," I say. "I can take no more. I'm leaving before insanity takes my mind."

"JD, it's not over," Harold barely whispers over the sound of the rain. "Hold on a little longer, just a while longer."

Still standing next to the huge oak tree, Wirm of our when gestures with his finger across his throat, hanging his tongue out the corner of his mouth. Whooping with glee, he does a shuffle-ball-change dance and says, "I'll dance on your grave too, girl. Yours and all the bastards that challenge me. See what I can do?"

Unable to stop myself, I stand. Shaking my fist at him, I yell across the clearing, "You don't scare me, Wirm! It's your grave the six of us will mark. All of Cre Falls will celebrate your death."

Harold yanks my arm, returning me to my knees just in time for me to see Barney cut the clothing off the dead Abby. Her clothes fall on top of her cloak, leaving her naked except for boots on her feet. Barney has tied her feet to the branch and wrapped some of the rope under her arms and around the tree, hugging her body close to the trunk. He stands staring at her naked body. Passing his hand over her pubis mound, he sighs wistfully. Taking his knife, he begins to gut the body, taking care to scrape out the womb cavity. Carefully snipping the internal organs from the connective tissue, he works silently. He removes the liver before opening the sternum, making sure the liver is not contaminated by the pile of intestines on the ground. He then turns his attention to the removal of her heart. Tied to the tree trunk, the body jerks only a little as he tugs and cuts. That accomplished, he shows very little fatigue. His attention to the body momentarily forgotten, he collects rocks to make a fire pit. Passing back and forth from the woods to the fire pit, he collects a mound of firewood in a very short time. Producing a sulfur match from the pocket of his breeches, he kneels and cups his hands to encourage the small flame. As the flame grows, he adds twigs and then larger pieces of wood. Dancing shadows flicker off the body as the fire lights the grotesque murder scene. Barney returns to the woods yet one more time, returning with a green bent branch. Drilling the branch into the ground next to a rock, he positions the branch over the fire, a practiced task. Returning to the fire with the liver, he starts a hole in the side with his knife and screws the branch in firmly. Positioning the liver over the fire far enough from the flame to avoid burning it, he turns his attention to the guts piled on top of her clothing. He picks up the corners of his greatcoat and begins to pull them in toward the middle of the pile.

"Hold up, son," Wirm says. "How about adding her head to that pile?"

Barney looks up at him and nods as if in a trance. He stands and walks to the tree. Taking his knife from its sheath and gripping her hair, he severs the head from the cervical spine. Still gripping her hair, he transports the head to the pile of body parts he intends to bundle in his greatcoat.

I'm an old lady and a coward—big revelation. Before Barney partakes of his campfire feast, I'm going to be gone from this clearing, Harold or no Harold. The scene in front of me is a physical assault. I don't believe there can be any more carnage to witness. I'm sorry, Abby. Your murder has gone undetected all the years since your stroll in the forest with Barney. I refuse to believe that my telling your story will pin your killer's name to this scene and that long-awaited justice will be yours. Ah, Abby, I'll tell your story, hoping it will help, but I'm not sticking around to find more evidence.

As I am about to stand up and run, Harold's pale arm snakes up, and he grasps my wrist. Locked in his steely grip, I'm forced to stay in the clearing and endure. "Stay put, JD," Harold hisses. "Barney and that bastard Wirm will make the next few minutes' pure hell, but it will be over soon. If you leave now, Wirm will follow you back to the car. He wants to get you alone more than anything. He kills you, he wins. Look, Wirm has changed positions—nearer to our way out of here."

Sure enough, Wirm is now standing by the tree behind my left shoulder. A few more steps, and he will be blocking our way out. If I had run blindly, Abby and I would have met in heaven. The way I figure it, thanks to Harold, he'll have to wait until later.

The preternatural scene from the past is a display of a cozy campfire—a burly young man and his white-haired companion with his arm affectionately around his shoulder, waiting in silence for the fire to cook their meal from the kill. Harold and I are spared from the aroma of cooking liver. We are spared from hearing the sizzle and spit of meat juices dripping into the fire.

The horror etched in Harold's face and the tears making rivers down his cheeks must mirror my own. The breath has been knocked out of my lungs, causing me to make gulping sounds. Black spots dance in front of my eyes, and the possibility of fainting feels like a God-sent blessing. Harold raises the hand that is not grasping my wrist and delivers a stinging slap to my face. My lungs suck in a deep breath, saving me from the relief my mind seeks. Dry heaves rack my body, and bile burns my throat. I know I'm going to die here in the woods on this damp ground. I will surely cheat Wirm out of the fun. My heart and mind will not allow me to continue life after this debauchery. Harold and the others will have to go on without me.

Harold turns my face into his shoulder and holds me there gently. He murmurs, "You'll be okay, JD. Be tough. Hang with me just a little longer."

Unable to utter any words to indicate that I'll be all right, I lift my head with resolve to do the job I came here to do. I look up just in time to see Barney unsheathe his knife. Moving the cooking stick away from the fire, he slices a piece of meat and hands it to his evil mentor like a good student. He slices another piece for himself and holds it up, nodding in reverence. They eat in silence, licking the juice off their fingers. Barney repeats the ritual again and again until they are sucking what is left off the stick. As if by some unseen signal, they both stand and make their way to the bundled carnage. Barney hefts the bundle off the ground, and they both head toward the path from where Barney and Abby emerged, when Abby was a living schoolmarm pregnant with child and hopeful for a future with her baby's father.

Barney, carrying the bundle, leads the way into the forest, with Wirm following. Harold follows suit, dragging me to my feet and crossing the clearing. I think for a moment that we are going to make a run for the car, but I soon realize we are actually going to follow them. As we step into the trees, a fog cloaks the forest floor. Looking down, I cannot see my legs below my knees. By this time,

I'm gripping the belt that holds up Harold's jeans. Shuddering, I know nothing below the earth, or following behind me, could make me lose this grip on Harold's belt (except maybe if my hands were cut off). I can almost feel his icy hands around my neck or my back being stuck with a knife as I stumble after Harold. The storm having past, a weak moon shines through the trees, and I soon see it reflected on a mirror like surface. This sick funeral possession has made its way to a lake or wide river. The water appears thick and oily, and patchy fog is swirling over the surface.

Harold quickly darts behind a mossy tree trunk, pulling me with him. Standing to Harold's left, I see Barney crouching down and striking his flint, trying to light the lantern. His impatience at not succeeding is expressed in curse words. Wirm chuckles with amusement at the pique of his student. Lowering himself on his haunches next to Barney, he points his finger under the raised globe of the lantern, and a flame, fueled by the sulfur of hell, leaps to the end of his extended finger, lighting the lamp. Barney, watching Wirm, screams and screams. His horrid cries echoes across the lake. Too late, sagacious Barney sees the truth. Recognizing the devil at his side, Barney screams Abby's name to the night that cares little. Suddenly aware of his greatcoat bundle by his side, Barney scrambles to his feet. Fear now his impetus, he moves quickly to the shoreline, where a dugout canoe is tied to a tree. Placing his innocuous bundle of horror into the center of the canoe, Barney wades back to untie the rope. Stepping into the birch dugout, Barney retrieves a paddle and pushes off from the shore. Nearly in silence, he paddles twenty feet from the shoreline. With a practiced stance, he lifts the bundle over the side into the inky water. With the help of his paddle, Barney pushes the bundle of carnage under the water. After several seconds, it bobs up, floating. The lake is listening as he yells his frustration. Paddling back to shore, he retrieves large boulders from the shoreline and paddles back to the errant bundle. Leaning precariously over the side of the canoe, he slides several boulders under the rope that holds his greatcoat together. Her guts (minus her liver), the encapsulated womb holding their child, her head, heart, and lungs, and the clothes that covered her nakedness, all wrapped in his greatcoat, sink to the bottom of the watery tomb to become fodder for the bottom feeders. Barney, screaming to the lake that doesn't care, paddles away to a destination unknown. What Barney doesn't realize, and what I saw, was that his hunting knife slid from its sheath into the water at the shoreline when he came back for the boulders. There, protected by the bottom silt, it is waiting to become evidence of Abby's murder.

Searching the shoreline, I can no longer see Wirm. I was focusing on Barney in the canoe and did not notice when Wirm disappeared. I also realize Harold no longer grips my wrist. Moving out from the tree trunk, I hurry to the shoreline, where I last saw Barney's knife slip into the water. Getting on my hands and knees, I dig into the sand and small shore pebbles. Shoes kicked off, I wade into the icy water up to my knees and work the bottom as I walk slowly back to shore. Without success, I move over three steps and wade out again. By the time I have repeated this process three times, my teeth chatter with cold, and my feet have become blocks of ice. Wading back to shore discouraged, I yelp with pain. Reaching down to feel my wounded right foot, I feel the hilt of Barney's knife. From the little I can see the blade is clean and sharp. The hilt is covered with some kind of leather with the imprint of the owner's hand. I have a name and the weapon, a killer and his knife. Limping to shore, I slip into my shoes and start searching for Harold.

"Harold, Harold," I hiss through chattering teeth. "Show yourself, Harold. Where in the hell are you?"

Slicing through the absolute stillness of the forest, Wirm bays, "He's gone and left you for me, JD. Ran away like a little boy, he did. Come on. Let's get this over with. You're going to love my worm."

The cold is nothing compared to my racing heart. Clutching the rusty knife, I move from the shoreline behind the first tree I reach. Leaning my forehead into the rough bark, I whisper, "Harold, you son of a bitch, how could you leave me?"

Moving to the right so I can see around the tree, I notice the moonlight filtering through the canopy of leaves. The clearing is all shadows and spotty, weak light. Wirm is standing exactly at the head of the path, my only way out, his arms outstretched, beckoning me. Behind him, standing stoically still, is Harold, his face bathed in moonlight. Clearly, the problem is, how do I get past Wirm and to Harold? Unable to move, I am rooted to the ground with fear. I can see no way around Wirm unless I leave the clearing, taking my chances in the forest. Harold is not looking toward me, but staring at the tree we were hiding behind before I made a dash to the lake. Reading Harold's mind is completely impossible for me. Despairingly, I search Harold's face for any clue about how to do this. Wirm continues to mew his invitation to hellish torture. Trying to understand why Harold didn't wait for me behind the tree, I curse my fuddled brain. It must be that he had to get to the path before Wirm blocked our way out. How do I get around Wirm before he discovers Harold standing behind him? Looking at Harold, I try to figure out what's different.

Oh my God! Harold doesn't have the cross. His arms are empty. Praying I'm right, I figure he must have left it behind the tree for me to find. If Wirm turns and discovers Harold without the cross, Harold is dead. Making as much noise as I can to keep Wirm's attention, I race to the tree, pick up the cross lying by the trunk, and run screaming straight at Wirm. Recognizing I intend to bludgeon him with the cross, Wirm vanishes. Harold hasn't moved. Gently taking the cross from my hand, he nods. Gripping my hand, he turns to leave this godforsaken place. As my feet awaken from the numbing cold of the lake, the wound from stepping on the knife begins to burn. Limping at Harold's side, I feel giddy. We're leaving. I'm actually getting out of here, and not without a story, not without finding evidence of the schoolmarm murder up on the flowage and convincingly putting Wirm at the scene.

I'm not foolish enough to believe getting back to the nursing home is going to be a piece of cake, but I still feel overjoyed to be walking away. Picking up the pace, Harold must sense something. Sort of remembering the way out, I limp faster to keep up. Weaving between trees, cutting right and then left, I'm able to see more than on our way in because the storm has blown over. My ragged breath makes hearing sounds of Wirm closing in impossible, and Harold shows no sign of slowing down. Harold still clutches the cross to his chest. Now and again, I reach over to run my fingers over our savior. No doubt now that the cross has power to protect us. I can only wonder whether it's the cross that runs the car. My right sneaker squishes as we hurry out of the forest to the car. The warm, wet feeling means that there is probably blood pooling. A welcome site for my sore eyes, the car appears rusty red in the moonlight. Standing in front by the hood, hands touching near the hood ornament, I mumble, "Start, you bugger." The car roars to life.

Like a deer startled in the headlights, I stand in front of the car with my back to the trees for a moment too long. Icy hands grip my shoulders. Fetid breath wafts past my ear as he pulls me back against his chest. With his cheek against the side of my head, Wirm growls, "Do you think I'm here just to relive Bartholomew's moment in hell and let you escape back to my town to spill your guts? Time has come to know who I am."

When he turns me to face him, his features have changed. His face is pocked with oozing craters on dead white skin. His mesmerizing eyes hold my gaze without allowing me to look elsewhere. Deep from the coal-black depth, his torture, murder, and rape of screaming victims enter my mind. A silent scream issues from my brain. Opening the black cave of his mouth, he pushes out his long, pointy tongue, dripping ooze from hell. Putting both claw like hands on the sides of my head, he reaches out toward my face with his lapping tongue. Droplets of sizzling acid strike my face, immediately creating corrosive burns.

Struggling to fight him, to move my feet, to save what sanity I may have left, I fight against his prodigious strength. As my strength wanes and my knees weaken to the verge of collapse, I am held up only by his claws squeezing the sides of my head. His tongue laps closer and closer.

I just barely hear the car's engine rev, cough, and rev louder. It pushes me from behind, and this is all I need to turn and push back at Wirm, causing him to momentarily lose his balance. Reflexively putting my hands out to break my fall, I plunge Barney's rusty knife into Wirm's soft, spongy gut. A cry explodes from Wirm, and he loosens his grip, freeing me. Rolling off his body and pulling the knife with me, I wiggle on the ground beyond the left tire not a moment before the car lurches forward, pinning Wirm under it. Having the presence of mind to move while I can, I scramble to the driver's side door. Flinging the door open, I throw myself in, pulling the door closed behind me. The car tires spin and bump as I back out of the turnaround and head back the way we came.

Once I feel that we are rolling away toward safety, I let the car take over and start raining accusations on Harold before looking over and realizing that he is slumped against the dashboard, not moving. The cross has slipped from his arms and is lying on the floor. Sliding across the bench seat, I take Harold by his shoulders and put his head on my chest. Even though the inside of the car is cool, his forehead is bathed in sweat. Putting my nose by his mouth, I smell the fruity breath of acidosis. "Not now, Harold," I whisper. "I don't have anything sweet to raise your blood sugar."

Harold tries to move but is able to move his arm only a little. At least he is not yet in a coma. I look through his pockets, attempting to find sugar of any kind. Failing that, I open the glove box. Nestled in the corner is a lollipop. Certainly not mine, obviously Harold's. Quickly pulling the wrapper off, I open his mouth with my finger. Luckily, his mouth is moist and will absorb the sugar. Holding the sucker in his mouth, I pray for signs that he is reviving. The soothing rocking of the car as we bounce along calms my overextended nerves until I slump my head on Harold's shoulder, and we in effect hold each other upright. I close my eyes, asking the powers that be to keep me awake while I hold the lollipop. Someone in my past told me that if you want to stay awake, you should sing and sing as loud as you can. In the silence of the car, I sing the "Lollipop" song: "Lollipop, lollipop. Oh, lolli, lolli, lolli. Lollipop, lollipop." I sing it over and over. Just when the song is threatening to stop working, Harold stirs.

"Will you stop singing that stupid song, JD?" he mutters. "Can I hold that sucker myself? You have it nearly down to my tonsils."

"Harold! You're okay! You are going to be all right, aren't you?" I say, gushing, not like a schoolgirl, but like a foolish old woman. My inability to express myself combined with nervous exhaustion has me blubbering. Not able to produce a worthy word, I slide back across the bench seat after untangling myself from Harold. "I think

I killed Wirm with Barney's knife," I say softly. "I stuck the knife in his gut when I fell on him, just before the car ran over him." My admission should be met with high-five congratulations, I think. Instead a roaring silence ensues. So I say much louder, "Did you hear me, Harold? I think I killed Wirm."

"If you think Wirm is that easily killed, don't you think I would have done it long ago?" Harold's voice is somber, filled with a hollow sadness. "For our sake, you did slow him down, though. We should get out of these forsaken woods before he pulls himself together enough and follows the scent. Are you all right? Did he hurt you?"

"He sprayed drops of spit on my face that still burn," I say. Turning toward Harold, I ask, "Can you see if he burned me badly?"

"I can see red dots mostly on your chin and the left side of your face," he says.

"If I have to explain, I'll tell the nurses I have a case of adult-onset acne," I say, chortling. "Was the sucker enough to get you out of crisis?"

"For now. I will have to get something better as soon as I can," he says. "Good thing you slowed Wirm down. Maybe we bought some time."

I put my hand gingerly to my face, grimacing. Not burning as much, the lesions now are maddeningly itchy. Concerned about infection, I force my hands to not touch my face by gripping the steering wheel as hard as I can. My clothes are still soaked through, but it's only now that I'm noticing I'm wet at all. My right shoe continues to feel warm and squishy. My foot aches like hell, but no matter—I still have the knife.

"Harold," I say, my voice quivering, "my fingerprints are on the handle of the knife. And if plunging the knife into Wirm's abdomen killed him, my DNA is mixed with his on the blade; I cut my foot on the knife blade when I was looking for it in the water. Oh, Harold, if I wipe the knife clean, the evidence from Abby's murder will be lost too, and this horror story will have been for nothing."

The silence from the passenger side is deafening. "Harold, no comment? I could go to prison for killing Wirm!"

"Clean it," he says, sounding much stronger. "But my money says Wirm is still alive. Even so, you don't want to be connected to the knife. Clean it and send it with the flowage story to the cops. After all this time since Abby was murdered, there can't be much on the knife to connect Barney to her death. We'll get Wirm, JD. We will keep doing this until all the stories are told, and I know we'll find a way to send him back to hell. But if you keep stepping on knives and getting acid spit in your face, I may have to recruit another partner."

"Fat chance, Brown. If you continue to take your dates to the stormy flowage and force them to watch carnage, good luck convincing another old fool to follow you," I say, almost laughing.

The full moon creates a vestige of shadows in the thick pines alongside the logging road we are traveling. All of the shadows look like Wirm. Fear of Wirm has become my mantra. It is now a living, breathing way of life. Harold and Lucy have assuaged the horror of Wirm for an unimaginably long time and have bravely waited for the cowardly Jane Doe to come to their aid. This insanity is surreal. That I have come to believe in the magic of this car and cross is so unlike the woman who lived and believed only in the reality of the world she touched. The doppelganger Wirm that exists in the phantasm of the stories Harold drags me to is enigmatic. How will any cop read my story and believe Wirm is the instigator, the predator, of all the cold cases, especially those as old as the murder of Abby, the flowage schoolmarm? All of these thoughts crowd my mind as the car and its beleaguered passengers, looking our part in the horror story past and present, get pulled along toward warm beds and oblivion. Wirm catching his prey just as safety looms, forces its way to the front of my mind, causing steel claws to climb my spine.

The road home seems to take so much longer. Just as I become aware of the puddle of drool I've left on the steering wheel, the car makes a left turn toward Bittercreek. The car's noises as we turn left onto what will be a highway in our future and then home of Cre Falls sound like hopeful music. Even the car's engine stops coughing and piston-pinging. Not exactly purring, the car engine smoothes out, and though not flying low, we pick up speed on the improved road.

"Harold, are you still with me? Next stop is the alley," I say. The relief, as my eyes threaten tears, is almost overwhelming.

"Here ... still," Harold says in a weak whisper. "You'll have to help navigate home, JD. My legs are too shaky to get me there on my own."

"Oh God, I hope I can help us up the road," I say, not at all sure I can. The Catholic Church and the nursing home are about equal distances from the spot where we leave the car. Given a choice, I'm going west through Harold's wall. If Harold has other ideas, I'll have to ignore his protests and drag him.

The car bumps down the corduroy street, stopping in exactly the same spot. Heart racing, I extract Harold from the passenger side and instruct him to hold on to the open door as best he can. Maneuvering to the front of the car, I reach out and touch the warm hood. After a whispered word of thanks for saving me from Wirm, I promise to get Harold home. The engine sputters, and the world becomes absolutely quiet. Moving back to Harold, I check that the cross is lying on the front seat. Harold puts his arm around my neck, and I circle my arm around his waist. Bearing some of his weight and limping beside him, I trudge back the way we came.

I try not to imagine what we must look like—drunken derelicts, the woman with wild white hair and soaked navy sweat suit limping beside a painfully thin, hunched-over man, arm clinging around her neck for support. Still we manage to find a rhythm of one foot in front of the other. Fear fills me as darkness gives way to moonlit shadows and as we cross the bridge and find the nearly invisible path where this horrible story began. So close, but not there, my knee buckles. Harold and I slump to the ground.

"Harold, we have to get up," I say. His ear and my mouth are conveniently proximal. "Wirm can't be far behind."

When the moon casts light on Harold's pale face, it shines with perspiration. The front of his shirt is soaked with rain or dreaded sweat. The effort of trying to get back to safety has caused a blood-sugar drop again. Getting to my feet in a panic and with great effort, I try to get Harold upright. He's weak as a noodle and dead weight.

"Nooooooo," I cry. "Please, Lucy, help me get Harold home! Please, Lucy, talk to him; Wirm's not far behind, and we're in trouble."

Harold moans and opens his eyes briefly. Bending and putting my arms under his in a hug, I slowly lift him to his feet. As I slip my arm around his waist, we start off again. Harold is trying to lift his feet, but mostly I drag him up the trail to the place where I think I remember coming out. Holding Harold's wrist with my free hand and still keeping him on his feet is very awkward, but I drag him one more step closer to the underbrush.

Just before the magic happens, I can hear Wirm baying like a hound far too close. We're sucked into the swirling vortex. Pulled into Harold's room, I swing him around, landing him hard in his chair. Without wasting time, I run to the dining room. Incredibly, the clock in front of me again shows five minutes after twelve. Knowing there are sandwiches left over from the eight o'clock snacks, I quickly grab a couple and find red juice. My shaking hands find sugar packets on the counter. Dashing back up the hall, spilling red juice from the pitcher, I pray I'm not too late. Harold is still sitting on his chair, head slumped toward his chest.

Harold's glass is on his bedside table. Pouring a small amount of juice and adding two packets of sugar, I swirl the mixture. I lift Harold's head up and put the glass to his mouth. Holding his mouth closed and stroking his throat, I watch his Adam's apple bob with a first swallow. After repeating the process until all the sugar-laced juice is gone, I pour more juice without sugar. Helping him swallow is easier this round. I wait impatiently for a first sign that he's coming to. About five long minutes later, Harold opens his eyes, not the Harold I walked through the wall with, but the agitated nursing-home Harold. He stares at me with unseeing eyes. Kneeling beside his chair, I offer him a bite from the sandwich. He eats hungrily until most of one is gone. Agitation grips him. "Do-da, get a gun. Do-da, run, run," he chants. That must be my signal to move. I'm sure I hear Wirm moving around in his room.

"Too close this time, Harold. I'm gone," I whisper.

Quietly, my heart in my throat, I creep down the hall past the monster's room. Scanning the hall floor behind me, I'm relieved to find no bloody shoeprint trail follows me. Harold's loud agitation will surely alert staff, but hopefully not before I get out of the hall and safely behind our door. Sudden panic grips me just as I'm about to turn the doorknob. Light from inside our room filters out underneath the door. Being in a wet sweat suit and looking like something the cat dragged in is sure to get me busted. I have no plausible explanation for why I'm out of my room or why I'm in such a disheveled state. Putting my ear to the door, I cannot hear voices. Perhaps the aides are helping Lucy to the bathroom. At a loss as to what to do next, I notice the linen cart in the hall by the dining room door.

A workable way out presents itself: shed my clothes, put on a hospital gown off the linen cart, and towel drying my hair. I can stash my wet clothes in the dining room garbage can until I can go back for them, and I can pick up a snack in there while I'm at it. Grabbing a hospital gown and towel off the cart, I also lift a pair of white socks out of a resident's clean clothes bin. Changing behind the dining room door and tying my wet things in a bundle, I drop them in the trash. Getting another half sandwich out of the refrigerator, I boldly cross the hall and open our door.

The scene by Lucy's bed stuns me. Otto, Ralph, and the Shun Lady flank her. Otto is holding Lucy's hand, and Ralph keeps his hand on Lucy's forehead while softly muttering words of encouragement. "It's all right, Lucy," he is saying as I enter. "They are back now. Harold is going to be fine. JD took care of him. It's okay now—relax." Shun Lady is sitting in her wheelchair at the foot of Lucy's bed, looking pale with worry.

I close the door quietly, motioning Ralph away. He moves back from Lucy's bed. Concerned, I take Ralph's place and lean over Lucy's face. "Harold is out of danger," I whisper. "Open your eyes and look at me. We're back. You can let go of Wirm's mind. We made it back okay, thanks to you once again."

Lucy's eyelids flutter several times and at last open. She breathes a deep sigh, and a trace of a smile tugs at the corners of her mouth. Apparently she mistrusted the reports from Ralph and was waiting to hear my voice before allowing Wirm to become aware that Harold and I are safe. Just as Lucy opens her eyes, Wirm curses Lucy in a barking voice down the hall.

Lucy chortles before putting her hand over her mouth and pointing with her other hand at Ralph, who is lewdly staring at my bare behind. I had forgotten the back of these blasted gowns are open and revealing. Clutching the opening together, I glare at Ralph, giving him my best chilly look, and head to the closet for my robe.

Once again in possession of my dignity, I say, "One thing, Ralph: if I happened to still be young with a firm ass, you would faint."

Having been caught in the act, Ralph's jaw still hangs open. Shun Lady has covered her mouth with Lucy's bedspread to hide her laughter, and Otto merely says, "Jesus Christ," with a hint of admiration.

"Enough, all of you," I scold. "Have you decided what to tell staff when one or all of them bust through that door to find out who organized this party? Harold's down the hall making enough noise to get their attention. As a matter of fact, that should happen soon. All of you, scram. I have to clean my bloody foot before it's infected and try to do something with the acid burns on my face." Holding up my hand to stop the protests, I say, "I can't explain now. Talk to all of you tomorrow. Now get!"

As soon as enough time has passed for the others to be safely in their rooms, I quietly make a dash back to the dining room to fetch my wet clothes and my prize evidence, the knife. Just as I close our room door, several staff members burst through the double doors and hurry down the hall. Peeking out, I watch them head for Harold's room. Harold's agitated voice is playing second fiddle to Wirm's barking curses directed at Lucy.

I take down my plastic wash bin and head to the bathroom, turning out the overhead light on the way. Lucy is already breathing softly. *Poor dear*, I think. This night must have exhausted her as much as Harold and me. Filling the plastic washbasin halfway with warm water, I sit down on the toilet to peel off my now-dry, encrusted, bloody sock. It hurts like a son of a bitch coming off, but the wound is actually only an inch long. It is fairly deep with ragged edges, though. If I was so inclined, it would be difficult to stitch. Easing my foot in the warm water, I muffle a moan. With soap and a clean washcloth, I wash the wound as clean as I can, clenching my teeth against the pain. Luckily it does not start to bleed again. Now for a look at the acid burns on my face. I'm not too shocked, looking at my fatigued, worn face in the mirror. The red, round marks almost look like freckles. Well, too large to be freckles. More like acne. That's the story I'll use tomorrow if anyone is interested. I wash my face, comb my hair, and brush my teeth before leaving the bathroom to find something better to sleep in besides this glamorous hospital gown. Before getting into bed, I put the knife in my typewriter case and find a plastic bag for my wet clothes. Marching out into the hall, which is now quiet, I throw the bagged clothes in the trash cart. Returning to bed, I am prepared to be awake the rest of the night, with the horror of the flowage playing over and over in my already crowded mind. But I slip easily into dreamless sleep.

Chapter Twenty

Invigorating, restorative sleep is not beyond the attainable, despite the myths about the elderly, one of which says, “The one thing older folks do not do at night is sleep, especially nursing home inhabitants.” I wonder what the quotable people think—that we have wild sex all night. This thought amuses my waking brain as I stretch, catlike. I feel amazingly restored and invigorated. I'm perhaps a little manic with plans for a new day in captivity: write the story, mail the knife, finish chapters of the book, hide my pox-marked face from nursing. My ebullience suddenly falters, and I snap up at the waist. Last night's real-life safari jolts me out of insipid morning dullness.

Seeing Lucy stir in the bed next to me, I say, “Okay, Lu, how do I explain red acid dots on my face? Oh, and probable infection in my foot from a wound I cannot expound on. Can you help me out, numbered friend?”

Lucy hee-haws with delight. “19-4-11-11 19-7-4-12 13-20-17-18-4-18 24-14-20 22-4-17-4 18-19-0-13-3-8-13-6 7-4-7-8-13-4 0 2-20-22”

I have become adept at translating Lucy's number speak, and her humor sets me giggling. When I can control myself, I say, “And where, dear friend, do I say I found a cow to stand behind? Have any other ideas?”

“13-14,” Lucy says.

Getting out of my bed and reaching over to the end of her bed, I tweak her great toe. The expression on Lucy's face immediately changes from amusement to wide-eyed wonder when she looks at me. Puzzled at the changed expression, I scurry to the bathroom. After taking a brief moment to look at my face in the mirror, I sit down hard on the toilet seat, covering my face with my hands and breathing in shallow gulps.

The red acid burns no longer mark my face. They're gone, just gone. No scars, no nothing. Same old face that looked back at me before Wirm's spit splashed my skin. I shakily stand before the mirror again. The red pits have not reappeared. Come to think of it, the side of my right foot no longer hurts either. I sit back on the toilet and remove my right sock. Like my face, the wound on the side of my right foot where I stepped on the rusty knife is gone. The skin appears to be smooth—no redness, no scar, nothing! Just like the red pits on my face, my right foot is healed. Fear knocks against my chest. If this is a miracle, why am I afraid? Evil did those things to me. Surely God's goodness healed them. Still filled with wonder and fear, I walk out to face Lucy's questions.

To my amazement, Lucy asks nothing. She holds my hand, and her calmness releases my anxiety. Her other hand caresses my healed face. Lucy nods and smiles. "6-14-3," she says.

"I need to see Harold—see if he survived the night. I'll stop by Ralph's room to ask him to mail the knife and the story when he goes out to work in the garden tomorrow. One thing less that nursing can catch me doing," I say. "Meet you in the dining room for breakfast."

The hall is a hive of activity as aides scurry from resident to resident, doing morning cares. Wirm is bellowing, maybe because of my healed skin miracle, or he could still be verbally assaulting Lucy. Passing as close to his door as I dare, I say, "What's the matter, Wirm? Life behind the doors getting to be too much for you?" Hurrying on to Harold's room before Wirm roars back at me, I duck through the door. Harold is still in bed, with the sheet covering his head. For an instant, I fear he's dead. Then the sheet is sucked in and blown out, proving he's breathing. Snatching the sheet off his face, I'm ready to chastise him for making my heart stop when wonder stops my world once again. Harold's face is glowing with the most beatific smile, mischief sparkling in his eyes.

"Harold Brown, you look like the cat that swallowed the canary. "Did you get a get-out-of-jail-free card?" I say admiring Harold's mischievous look.

"Look, Harold, no red pox marks. My right foot is healed as well. What do you think it means?" To this Harold has nothing to add.

"I'm not making this visit just for show-and-tell. I'm here to encourage you to eat all your breakfast. It sounds like Wirm is in a sucky mood this morning. I'm thinking that's why you're in such a good one. Eat your breakfast, friend. Talk to you later."

I hardly give him a chance to utter even one "do-da" before I'm out the door. Blowing him a kiss, I head a few doors down to Ralph's room. Poking my head in his doorway, I see him coming from the bathroom. Bare-chested and with a towel around his neck, he appears nearly ready for breakfast.

"Ralph, get a shirt on and come to the dining room for breakfast. I'll get Otto, Lucy, and Shun Lady to save you a chair at our table. Just a word of caution: be careful not to talk about last night in front of staff. Oh, and so you're not too stunned, face and foot are healed. No trace of Wirm's inflicted burns on my face, wonder of wonders. See you there." I say this all without leaving him a breath to protest.

I intercept Lucy in the hall as she is being wheeled by an aide to the dining room. "I'll just be a minute to get presentable. Ralph will be sitting at our table," I say, loud enough to get the aide's attention.

Stepping up to our bathroom mirror, I meet the challenge of what to do with my face with an ambiguous shrug. Wash it, comb my hair, brush my teeth, and call it good. However, this morning I pause to stare at my image in the mirror just a little longer than usual. My cheeks look sort of smooth, less wrinkled. My eyes look clear, shiny even. I must say, I look rested, healthier. As I am pulling on knit pants and a top, I hear the aide in the hall announce that trays are up. I leave my room feeling a close sense of family, a comfortable feeling of not being alone.

As I turn the corner into the dining room, my people, my supporters, are seated at table eight. Lucy, Shun Lady, and Otto are waiting for me. Knowing Ralph will be right along; I get a tray and pour five cups of coffee from the coffee service. Heading for the table and my friends, I realistically know there are hard, dangerous times coming. But for just now, this moment, I'm confident. Not invincible, just confident.

Startled by my feelings that they are my family, this is home, and this is where I belong, and by the lack of the compelling need to escape back to the life I ran away from, I feel my hands tremble. Shaking enough to spill coffee into the tray I'm carrying, I recognize the hot, humid days of August are here, and I feel anxious that the book isn't nearly done. The stories are not nearly told. Wirm is as free a devil as there ever was. This cannot be the time for complacency. As I approach my friends, I hope they will shake up the warm fuzzy feelings I walked in here with and push me faster than ever toward the duality of my roles: truth writer and Wirm slayer. I smile at that thought, Wirm slayer indeed.

Sitting down in my chair, I look at their faces one at a time. All three of them appear quiet, serendipitous. Calmness reigns. Lucy, staring at my face, only nods her acceptance. Otto attempts to hide a smile that twitches at the corners of his mouth. Shun Lady, not to be outdone, murmurs softly, "Complexion."

From behind my chair, Ralph's voice makes me turn. "You going to hand out that coffee or drink all of it yourself?" he inquires with a smirk.

Taking a cup of coffee off the tray, Ralph sits in the empty chair next to mine and says, "So is this a meeting of the 'behind the doors' irregulars? It might as well be 'behind the doors' rebels. I do say, JD, you look a lot better without Wirm's marks on your face."

Just as I am about to reply with sarcasm, an aide plunks my breakfast tray in front of me. Realizing that I have a voracious appetite, I set about discovering what is for breakfast. I lift the dome lid covering my plate, and the smell of three pancakes deliciously fills my nose and the hunger center of my brain. There is bacon too. And we have not red juice but orange juice and more coffee. I smear butter on my still-warm pancakes and reach over to help Lucy do the same. After cutting up Lucy's pancakes and drizzling syrup over them, I hand her fork over to her. Unable to put off my appetite longer, I dig in, cooing with every bite. Taking a brief moment to look at my tablemates, I notice they are doing the same. With a determined look on her face, Lucy is managing just fine. We eat in a companionable silence until Ralph clears his throat to get attention.

"So, JD, when will the package be ready for me to deliver to the mailbox?"

"I was thinking before supper or early tomorrow morning before breakfast. When do you think it would be easier to deliver?" I answer, unsure of how we should get this rather sensitive task done.

Without skipping a beat, almost as if we are in a business meeting, Ralph fires back, "Tomorrow morning during shift change. The staff is very busy during that time, and they're used to seeing me down there getting ready for garden work. I get my tools lined up and check the activity sheet to see who has signed up to help me. You know, JD, a little garden work wouldn't hurt you at all. We're starting to pick tomatoes; a favorite time."

The man with a plan wins, and it makes me smile. "Thanks for the invite, Ralph, but the book has to come first. I wouldn't have to be asked twice if you offered a share in the eating, though. I'll get the envelope to you after the unit calms down. Before ten o'clock. How's that? You cannot be seen putting it in the mailbox. Already staff is noticing that the five of us are hanging together more often."

Helping Lucy with her juice and with scraping up the last of syrup and pancake bits, I feel sad that Harold can't be here with us. I know that's dangerous thinking. Harold has gone to great lengths to hide his rational self from anyone curious. Today, I plan to write, get the knife ready to send, and talk to Harold about stepping up the midnight presage into Wirm's past. It's more than time to get on with what we have been called to do. I have no clue what makes this night the one over another, but I intend to attempt to understand. I rather think Harold has no control over where our destination will be once we move through his wall. Another mystery is his knowledge of the landscape, the place in time, and the implacable darkness that he's able to navigate without hesitation. Without Harold, the chance to expose Wirm and the cold crimes of Cre Falls would be lost. Of course, the book will end, and I will walk out of here, catching some sort of transportation home. Flapping on the outer edges of my consciousness are fleeting thoughts about what I will do when time comes to leave and I cannot leave my friends behind. I cannot face that question. Not now. Not when there is so much that needs to be done.

While I was daydreaming, an aide must have removed Lucy's tray. She has her left elbow on the table and is supporting her chin on her hand, looking far off at something I can't see. The skin on her face is so translucent, it sort of glows. Her blue eyes are sparkling, and the irises are rimmed in navy blue. Eyes like Lucy's are eyes I remember noticing on babies. I wonder whether she has any regrets—maybe that she didn't risk falling in love again after Steve's accident. I know his name is Steve because she often mumbles the numbers of his name in her sleep. When I asked, Harold said only that a log fell on him. He made the cryptic telling of that story rather banal, and I just couldn't bring myself to ask Lucy about him. Watching her gaze at some distant memory, I wonder whether she's recalling a horrific Wirm moment in her past. Lucy, apparently feeling my eyes on her, hisses softly, as if confirming my conjecture. Although the shiver of her thin shoulders indicates the memory is ineradicable, the shiver nonetheless bolsters us both into action.

"Are you ready to face the day, Lucy my friend?" I say, chasing the look of recent fear from her face. Otto and Shun Lady are already leaving. Ralph bolted as soon as the aide collected his tray—no lingering over breakfast for him. I do notice that Wirm hasn't graced the dining room this morning. A silent prayer that he is sick crosses my mind. I still hold out hope that the knife made a fatal wound.

"11-4-19-18 6-14," Lucy says.

"I'm on it, Lucy," I say, pushing her out the dining room door to our room.

I really need to get this day started if Ralph is going to get the envelope tonight, I think. If he gets caught, I plan to cut his suspenders and have a great laugh when his coveralls fall down. No, I plan to do much worse. I realize I'm still not able to completely trust him. I suddenly wonder whether Wirm's absence from the dining room is connected to the fact that Ralph (who doesn't usually eat there) had breakfast with us. I wonder whether the two of them ever cross in front of each other—and if not, why not? I'll be sure to watch Ralph for any unusual activity.

Chapter Twenty-One

Without a lock on the bathroom door, I hurry at cleaning the knife. Although not rusty and corroded, the knife is in good shape. Hopefully it will hold up for laboratory testing. I remove all traces of my bloody foot. Examining the handle, I think better of removing the leather covering. Using latex gloves makes it simpler to scrub the knife without cutting my hands. I dry the knife with paper towel and put it back in my manila envelope. Feeling very clever, I put the envelope back in the bottom of my typewriter case, checking out the meager stack of dwindling funds. Maybe tossing my shoes wasn't the best idea. When I go to Medical Records for stamps, I'll have to use the phone to call the shoe man who brings samples here for fittings.

Blowing a kiss to Lucy, I head to the dining room, pushing my typewriter on my bedside table in front of me. The dazzling August sun is blazing through the windows, warming my still-frozen joints; whether they were frozen by terror or the icy water of the flowage, I'm not sure. While I sit front of the window, the welcoming warmth seeps into my bones. Before I allow drowsiness to render the morning lost, I decide to make a trip to Medical Records for supplies.

I knock lightly. The medical secretary doesn't answer, so I open the door without announcing my name. She is sitting behind her desk doing computer work.

"I would like to call Mark the shoe guy," I say, holding up my slippered foot. "My shoes are nowhere to be found. I really don't need to bother the activities person. I think I can do this myself. Oh, and I need a bunch of carbon paper and stamps please."

"You know, Miss Doe, this is not your private supply store," she says, eyeing me with a rather annoyed expression. "Just happens I have an old folder of carbon paper left over from sometime in the last century that I'll gladly get rid of. Stamps, you will have to pay for. Is twenty enough? You will have to look up Mark's phone number. He'll want to know your shoe size and whether you have enough money to pay him. From here on out, solve your supply problems with activities. That's what they get paid for." She offers me the Cre Falls phone book.

"How about a couple of manila envelopes too?" I reply, taking the hefty book. "If you'll do this for me this one time, I'll be set for a while, and I promise that I won't bother you for a long, long time."

"You sure are a bother today. Get your money out," she says.

A few minutes later, with phone call made and supplies in hand, I thank her and hurry out before she asks too many questions. I think what I'll have to do in the future is resort to stealing this stuff when I hide more of my book in the bottom drawer of the file cabinet.

Like a crash of thunder, I remember that I left my typewriter vulnerable, sitting on my bedside table in the dining room—my most private possession just sitting there, waiting for someone to walk away with it. What's wrong with my head? Either my brain is getting soft, or my new disease is Alzheimer's.

When I get to the dining room, Mary, my day RN nemesis, and that new aide are leaning over my typewriter, having a quiet conversation. From the doorway I ask, in a voice way louder than needed, "Mary, what did you say the phone number of the ombudsman is? I want to report a violation of my privacy."

Startled, the guilty pair turns to face me. Red-faced and stuttering, they move away from my bedside table.

"We were going to return your belongings to your room," Mary sputters. "I didn't give you permission to use the dining room as your personal office. For your information, we were not violating your privacy. Can't even open the damn thing."

"But you tried. My typewriter has a special lock to keep nosy nurses and aides from disrespecting my property," I say, walking into the room and getting in Mary's face, challenging her to confront me further. "And for your information, Mary, this room is for all residents and family to use without permission from the nursing staff. Look up the policy and be sure to inform your aides where the boundaries are."

Looking embarrassed and eager to escape, the aide mumbles a soft "sorry" and backs toward the door. Mary, on the other hand, looks rooted to the floor with a lot more on her mind. Giving way, she says, "Next time, Jane Doe, you won't make it out," and she follows the aide into the hall.

The jolt of her words leaves me clinging to my bedside table, with the wind knocked out of my lungs. My mind, almost my entire body, flashes back to a gravel road and a clear view of a driver in a red convertible. I remember a snaky tongue tasting the aura of a little girl, myself, the child of my dreams hidden behind a hillock. *Next time*, he mouthed, *next time.* I know him to be the same demon hiding in the barn cajoling me to commit murder.

Lowering myself into the chair in front of my typewriter, I sit, stunned. *Could Mary and Wirm be* … I can't even allow the thought; impossible. Mary is a terrible geriatric nurse who should not be allowed to take care of patients, but in league with Wirm? The possibility is staggering and certainly poses a daunting problem for Lucy, Harold, the three behind-the-doors regulators, and without a doubt, me. She could easily screw up Harold's insulin. Too much could surely kill him. If she is a danger, the only way I can protect him is to check his blood sugar after breakfast and lunch, which means I will have to steal an Accu-Chek and supplies off the nurses' medication cart. First, I'll talk to Harold or Lucy about Mary. It could be that I won't have to do any of this. Actually, I could buy diabetic testing supplies from the drugstore.

Putting this out of my mind for the moment, I proceed with the book, starting with the flowage story. I use the carbon paper to duplicate only those pages I want to send to the police: the ones about Wirm's involvement, the actual murder, and the cover-up.

Time flies, and before I know it, lunch trays are coming up. Taking my work back to my room, I continue writing until Lucy returns from lunch. A quick "see you later," and I am back in the dining room, writing page after page. Even if I have to write all night, Ralph will have the envelope to mail in the morning before going to his garden work.

The story continues to go well. The telling is so painful at times. The nausea returns, and during the telling of Abby's death, I sob. I only just control the fear as the words spin from memory to paper. The telling of Abby's murder has exorcised the awful deed that has been buried beneath the icy waters of the flowage and that is now awakened on my pages. For the second time, I wonder what the aftermath of that night might have been. Rumors of her pregnancy probably surfaced, I suspect, and as time passed, it was thought reasonable that in her humiliation, Abby would have secretively left the community, her employment, and all of her belongings, never to be heard of again. I question the rationale of this thinking. But this backwoods thinking would have been justified in those times. The men, while drinking together, must have gossiped about Abby getting "what's come her." I can imagine the kinds of things they said—"why, her a schoolmarm and all, spreading her legs like a whore" and "served her right." Barney carried Abby's truth to his grave, until now.

As I fight to stay on task, supper is delivered and cleaned up. Lucy and I communicate in a look as we pass each other from room to dining room. Evening resident cares commence with their usual assault of noise in the last hurrah of the day. I'm tired and dehydrated. The story is incomplete. Outside the dining room, the hall has become still with only an occasional door closing. The nursing home is preparing to sleep. As I slip into an adrenaline-induced haze, the story takes on a life of its own. The words I type seemingly come from an ethereal place located up at the flowage. Page after page stacks up on my bedside table. In the dim light of this isolated space, I forge ahead, unaware of time as the pages pile up.

At long last, awareness seeps back. Aching with exhaustion, I pull to my feet and take one hesitant step, still holding on to the back of my chair. It's past midnight. Fifteen hours of inactivity has made my joints so stiff that taking another step seems impossible. Hunched over the back of the chair, I push it around the room, one step at a time. Recovery is slow. Pushing the chair away from me, I try to walk without help. Slowly my joints begin to respond as I make my way back to my bedside table and the stack of pages. Out of time for a reread, I separate the originals from the carbon copies, selecting those pages that describe the scene of Abby's murder and implicate Barney and Joseph Wirm. Handling the pages with rubber gloves, I put them in the envelope along with the knife I've wrapped in paper towel. Sealing the envelope and addressing it, I wipe it clean with toweling. After pushing my bedside table out of the dining room and across the hall to our room, I walk up the hall to Ralph's door.

Opening the door as quietly as possible, I move into Ralph's room. A dim wedge of light shines into the room from the hall. A dark form outlined by the night light of the window causes me such fright that my screech is soundless.

"So, JD, what took you so long?" Ralph says. "I've been waiting forever for you to show up."

Taking great gulps of air in an attempt to settle my hammering heart, I step into the room and turn on the overhead light. "Holy Joe, it's like fright night around here," I say, still trying to get in control. "You don't have to sit in the dark, scaring me half to death, you know," I say, raising my voice a notch. "I just finished writing, and by the way, I've been working all day," I say in a tone that sounds like whining.

The overhead light is hurting my red, irritated eyes, and I'm swaying dangerously on my feet. The only place to sit is next to Ralph on the bed, so I continue to stand, reaching out to the doorframe for stability. Holding out the envelope, I say, "This—in the mail tomorrow morning. If you let it out of your sight before mailing it or get caught in the process, I plan to make you pay dearly."

"Oh sure," Ralph says. "And you were expected in Harold's room five minutes ago. Try to keep the racket down. The walls have ears."

"Oh no, you don't, farmer Ralph. I've done all I'm doing tonight. You tell Harold I'm going to bed. Just get that envelope in the mail posthaste in the morning," I say, turning to leave.

"Harold didn't say please, JD. He said, 'Tell her as soon as she delivers the envelope.' I'm just the messenger, lady. It sounded important."

"Okay, okay. I'll take care of Harold. Mailing the envelope is your next job." Turning to leave, I wonder what's up.

Chapter Twenty-Two

My exhaustion is palpable. I'm limping with a sore left knee. Not only is walking the thirty feet to Harold's room torture, but I also may fall, which would cause all kinds of wretched nursing home bother. Plus, the commotion would surely bring Wirm into the hall. When Harold realizes the shape I'm in, he will dismiss me for the night. Lying down being the only comfort I can imagine, I make my way past Shun Lady's room. Her light is still on. Are we all suffering from insomnia tonight?

The exception is probably Wirm. A cloud of silent pollution emanates from his open door. When I stop to stare into the stygian darkness that is his lair, a shiver causes me to think someone walked over my grave. I'm sorely tempted to turn around and put Harold on hold for one more day. It's only foolish old lady ego that prod my aching feet on toward Harold's room.

No light frames Harold's closed door. Undoubtedly, I will find him sitting in the dark, ready to propel me through that familiar killing vortex. Gingerly, expecting an electric shock, I turn the doorknob, crack the door, and peer in.

"Harold," I say in a hissing voice, "I have to rest now! Too much is just too much. Harold, do you hear me?"

"I hear you, and so does everyone else. Get in here before that dog bites your ass," he says, chortling. "We have places to go."

Slipping in and closing the door, I whine, "I'm not going! You just run along and get the story, and after eight hours of sleep, I'll be happy to write it. Oh, don't get killed while you're at it, okay?"

Watching him rise from the Adirondack chair, I know my whiny lament will not hold water. Resolve gone the way of a good night's sleep, I meekly approach his side, waiting to be catapulted through to the other side of the wall. I'd rather slug him, but he can't go alone. So without pause I take hold of his hand and raise my right hand to the wall.

The vortex is bone-crushing. For sure, this time I will come out on the other side dead. Nausea churns in vertiginous swells. Interminable minutes later, I reach out for some solid object to cling to. Thorny vegetation scratches my arms and pricks my clutching hand.

Harold, standing away from the thorn patch unscratched, says, "You really need to do this better. Only you would find the rose bushes."

"I will come with you, stick a sucker down your throat to keep you from diabetic coma, and even half-tolerate your sarcasm, but I refuse to be your old-lady sage because you say so," I say, pulling loose from the thorns sticking to my shirt. "How did you not land in the rose bushes? I recall holding your hand before sinking into oblivion."

"Don't make me fire you, JD. We have to find the car. Remember where we left it?"

"Where we left it? Check your recall, you old coot. The last time I saw the car was only twenty-four hours ago. I need you to know I'm running on practically no sleep and almost no food, and I'm in big-time need of pain medication for this damned arthritis. So go ahead and fire me, you ass. I'll gladly be back in bed before Lucy rolls over twice," I quip, completely frustrated, tired, and close to tears.

"When can I make you understand that it's not about you coming here to write a book? It's about sending Wirm back to the hell he came from. Then and only then will you be fired from this job," he says with quiet impatience.

"Okay, okay. Don't get your tighty-whiteys all in a bunch, old man. Ready when you are. If we hang around here any longer, Wirm will be the next thorn in our ass."

The reminder that Wirm is probably inches from us gets me moving away from the invisible door that brought us here. Following Harold's lead, I walk down the nursing home sidewalk. Unlike other trips, where underbrush made walking out to the street difficult, this time I am sure we are headed into a more modern Cre Falls.

The weather is almost balmy, tropical-like. The paucity of rotting summer flowers is made pungent by humidity. Rare after-sunset heat makes the odor sensual instead of offensive. August heat lightning lights up the sky a few hundred miles away. The pismire of mill muck soon replaces the cloud of perfume as we trot past.

"Harold, slow down," I pant. "I'm not a sprinter. What's your hurry? I had to throw away my shoes, and my slippers are too big for running down the street."

Harold stops and turns. With a look of bored impatience, he says, "You're tired, you threw away your shoes, you landed in the thorn bush, *and* you're no sprinter. Catch up, Jane! Getting caught out here by Wirm would certainly add to your litany of complaints."

With great effort I tag along, slippers slapping the pavement. Still, wonder of wonders, I'm walking on a paved street. It's one of those rare summer nights—warm enough to go without a sweater, humid, and with a perfect breeze keeping the mosquitoes from eating me alive. Almost palpably, a vapid whisper of hidden dangers swirls with the humid air.

Without a doubt, it's a Cre Falls I remember. I know this street I'm thudding along. There's Maud's place, still boarded up. Up Main Street, all of the buildings mysteriously appear frozen in a time when I walked here. I suspect I'm going to know the Cre Falls people up ahead—people, I fear, doing God knows what to God knows who.

Catching up to Harold, whose expression is exactly as I picture it—long-suffering—I take his arm and mutter in his ear, "This is going to be something, huh, Harold? Are you sure we can come out on the other side of this one?"

Irritatingly, he doesn't answer. Silently he leads me to the street where the car is sheltered in the alley. Touching the car's hood, a habit now, I lean over and kiss the hood. "Car," I whisper, "please take us where Harold wants to go and, for the love of God, back where my bed waits. I thank you, car." The car's engine is purring like some giant cat. Reluctantly, I slide in the driver's side, and the car rolls out of the alley.

"This car's engine is still clicking off heat from the flowage run. So where are we going, Harold?"

"Not far this time," Harold says quietly. "Be prepared to be offended and frightened. Best prepare yourself to run like hell. Wirm is already ahead of us. The car needs to be at the crossroad, out of the way, so we will have to walk up the other road to the trailer. When all hell breaks loose, run like your life depends on it. It probably will. Leave those floppy slippers in the car, or you're sure to break your neck."

Run like my life depends on it? Break my neck and Wirm already ahead of us? Oh God, it sounds like party time to me.

"Harold," I mutter, fear lapping at my resolve, "you can go this one alone. I'd rather go back or go anywhere else but here."

The car does a circuitous route past the mill and doesn't slow as we pass the nursing home. I have to bite my tongue to stop myself from yelling out as I look longingly at my refuge. Harold, the bastard, is giving me an all-knowing smirk. I think he finds my discomfort funny.

"You wouldn't jump out if your pants were on fire," he says with a touch of truculence in his voice.

I'm not counting, but I think maybe in six blocks the car turns right on River Road. High above the Cre River on steep banks, River Road winds into dense underbrush and scrub trees and, just as Harold predicted, a fork in the road. The car swings to the shoulder, stopping under thick overhangs. Twinkling lights from a house filter through the trees. More than reluctant to get out of the car after Harold's warning, I try to waylay the inescapable next step. Shoving the cross in the back of my pants and leaving my slippers on the driver's side floor, I plunge into the offensive danger Harold has promised.

I am intrigued by what I could possibly find offensive. I've lived in a generation of "you can't have enough reality hit your face". I've nursed the human body in every state of failure. Of course, there's being saturated with the infernal gutter-mouth television, since freedom of speech includes allowing the overused word "fuck" to be used often and wherever. At this juncture, I find it impossible to believe I can be shocked or offended. I don't think I've even been grossed out since I was in my twenties.

Mumbling this defensive position while I cut through the underbrush, I follow Harold down the grassy road toward what looks like a doublewide 1970s trailer house nestled in the woods, with lights blazing out every window. A black pickup truck, a small sports car, and a motorcycle are parked one behind the other. The motorcycle is blocking in the cars. Loud music with thumping bass vibrates the air. No need to sneak up on this party.

Harold leads the way to the second set of windows. "So we are not going in the front door to join the party? I sure as heck am not going to see in this window for the peep show," I say, standing on my tiptoes.

Harold is busy looking for something to stand on when he discovers several cement blocks under the trailer. He is just strong enough to haul two over and position them under what must be the living room window.

Harold tries to say something, but I can't hear a word over the music. He touches my arm and points toward the window. Slowly, I step on the cement block and gaze into the trailer. The insidious scene before me is out of a pornographic movie, but in this movie I can call all of the actors by name. This is from a time when I lived in this town.

Dancing with Wirm in the middle of the living room is one totally nude Linda, a lawyer's wife. I don't know her personally, but I recognize her face. My face blazes with embarrassment as I watch her gyrating, suggestively pumping her hips, rubbing her ass against Wirm's crotch. She laughs, holding her pendulous breasts and pointing them toward a man sitting in a chair in front of her.

I know that man to be the banker, Mr. Wyman. He's holding a mirror on his lap with a line of white powder. Leering up at Linda, he reaches out and jiggles her breasts before dropping his head to the mirror.

Across the room, Sharon—a nurses' aide I knew—is sitting on Lester's lap. Lester was a schoolteacher when I was in town, but what grade I can't remember. The kitchen chair allows her to spread her legs out on both sides. While she humps him, he is sucking on her breast. With a look of exaggerated excitement, she reaches sideways to fondle the erect penis of the naked man standing on her left. I inhale sharply as I realize the naked man standing there is a person I've dealt with many times as a nurse—the undertaker from a nearby small town. He was well known at the nursing home when I worked there.

Straight across from my window, standing outside and looking in from the opposite end of the trailer, Wirm is enjoying the peep show. His tongue is flicking in and out in time with the music. His eyes burning with evil, or perhaps desire, he gives me a licentious look. The pervert.

Standing in the doorway of the front bedroom, which opens onto the living room, is a young man with an early VHS camcorder. The black camera is balanced on his right shoulder as he spans the horrific scene. He's dressed in blue jeans and a black leather jacket with engineer boots on his feet. I'm sure Jake is the motorcycle rider because I know this story. Jake's family lived less than a mile from my farm. He takes the tape out of the camera and slowly creeps to the front door. Surprisingly, he drops the tape in a trash basket sitting by the door. Making a great effort not to be seen, he slips out the door and heads for his motorcycle.

How the partygoers manage to hear the motorcycle when Jake guns the engine is unknown to me, but they're instantly alert. Linda grabs for clothes, and so do the two naked men. The previous loud music is replaced by everyone yelling at once. What I hear easily through the window are shouts of "Get him!" Mr. Wyman yells frantically, "The truck—hurry!"

Wyman, Lester, and Wirm run for the front door, with Linda close behind. For whatever reason, Sharon is slowly dressing. She's in no hurry to leave the trailer. *Probably stoned and so moving slow*, I think.

I suddenly realize that Harold is pulling on my sleeve, desperately trying to get my attention. "This is when we run like hell for the car, remember?" he yells. "Come on! Let's go! Leave the window! Hurry!"

Absentmindedly brushing off his hand, I say, "Wait a minute. I want to see what Sharon does next." Just as I'm saying this to Harold, Sharon goes over to the basket by the door and slips the VHS tape into her purse before leaving the trailer on foot. I know she is heading to the nursing home for night shift as a nurses' aide. When I worked as a nurse, she was a CNA. One evening shift while we were working behind the doors, she confided in me about her rehabilitation in a mental health hospital for a breakdown she had suffered.

Snapping out of my curious inquiry, I step down, and with urgency Harold and I run past Sharon to the car, which immediately roars to life. I take my place behind the steering wheel. Harold's anxious need to catch- up is contagious. We're losing the taillights of the truck, already turning left off River Road onto Highway 152. As I watch the truck turn, Linda's red car turns right.

"Harold! Quickly, which way? Who do we follow?"

"Follow the truck! It should turn right on 15," he says, holding the dashboard.

"Car, car, faster, faster," I plead. "We're losing the truck!" No sooner have I said the words than the car doubles its speed, taking the right onto 15 practically on two wheels.

Having turned north on 15, the truck continues heading out of town. At the last cross street, I see the motorcycle up ahead, coming in our direction in the other lane. The truck makes an almost too fast U-turn. Jake, on the motorcycle, is only ten feet ahead of the truck. He must have thought that he could double-back, buying some time. I watch in horror as the truck moves into the left lane, directly ahead of us, and swerves hard into the motorcycle. Jake has no chance. He loses control, and the bike goes down. Skidding on the gravel shoulder with half of his body under the bike itself, he hits a huge boulder marking a driveway. The head-on crash is not with the motorcycle, but with Jake's head. The motorcycle slides, and Jake's now-rag-doll body flips and flops, losing momentum. Both the motorcycle and his body come to a rest, right in the middle of the driveway.

My hands press against the driver's side window. I scream in horror as the car screeches to a stop across the highway from the crumpled motorcycle and Jake's bleeding, broken body.

I feel as though I'm screaming underwater and cannot take a breath. My mouth is open, but no sound comes out. Harold pounds my back and shakes my shoulders, trying to get me to take a breath. With a deep sob, I'm able to breathe, and the screaming in my head stops. Still, I can't get my mind around the carnage across the highway. The men are out of the truck, including Wirm, searching Jake's effects. I know they're looking for the incriminating tape.

"We have to go now. We can't risk Wirm getting ahead of us," Harold whispers in my ear.

I realize he is sitting with an arm around my shoulder, and the other arm is holding my hand, trying to help me get control.

"Oh, Harold," I croak, "we can't go back until I find out what Sharon did with the tape she fished out of the wastebasket. I know she is going to the nursing home. We have to pick up her trail before we lose her. We have one chance to use this tape as evidence to prove who killed Jake. I think Wirm will be busy for a while."

"Remember, JD, we have to return the car to the alley and get back to the nursing home on foot after we do what needs to be done. All that takes more time than we have. It will be risky."

As I wonder whether the posse we rely on back at the nursing home is strong enough to hold out longer, reluctance hangs between us like the humid air that is making us sweat. The risk! What if there isn't enough time? "God help us," Harold whispers as the car rolls forward.

"No, Harold, absolutely not," I cry, reading his thoughts. "You are not going to drop me off to follow Sharon while you park the car and walk back alone. That has been Wirm's aim all along—separate us and we're as good as dead. Let's just do this and run like hell."

The car turns left on Highway 152 toward the mill and the nursing home, slowly retracing our earlier route. I spot Sharon nearing the driveway to the nursing home. She's walking along slowly with the confidence of the righteous. I have this screaming urge to run her over and take the tape from her.

"Pull over. I'll get out here. Harold, stay with the car in case we were followed. Car, don't let him move from this spot until I get back," I say, opening the driver's side door and patting the roof for good measure.

Crossing the highway, I fall in behind Sharon. My thoughts run to what she could possibly get out of being part of the porno gang. If I can prove who killed Jake, at the very least she will be implicated in his murder. When the tape comes to light, she will lose her family and freedom.

I follow as she reaches the employee entrance, punches the time clock, and walks down the hall toward the first-floor nurses' station. The nurse listening to a recorded report does not look up as Sharon passes. She walks past the dining room and turns into the activity area. To the left are round tables and activity areas, and along the back wall, flanked by bookcases, is a collection of approximately two hundred VHS tapes. Sharon's hand reaches out for the row of tapes at eye level. Quickly I count the number of rows down and watch as she counts four tapes in from the left. Pulling this fourth tape out of its case, she replaces it with the tape from the trailer. She puts the tape she removed in her purse and leaves the activity area. Not able to recover the tape now, I note where the tape is again and turn to leave, feeling sure I can find it after Harold and I get back.

As I run out the way I came in, my heart bangs against my ribs. I rush up the driveway and across the highway to the waiting car, where Harold sits waiting, his head in his hands, mumbling. I think he's praying. I jump in and screech, "Go, go!" and I'm still pulling the door shut as the car makes a two wheel U-turn. Minutes later, the car races into the alley, where it will hide until the next time, and suddenly stops, throwing me into the dashboard. With no time to think about head damage, I scramble from the car, feet running before they touch the ground. Harold is on my heels and gaining fast.

The thrum of my bare feet on the pavement repeats the mantra "faster, faster." The pavement is starting to become wet from the rain the heat lightning warned about. I feel like I'm young again.

Part Nine

She Dwelt among the Untrodden Ways

She dwelt among the untrodden ways
Beside the springs of Dove,
A maid whom there were none to praise
And very few to love:
A violet by a mossy stone
Half hidden from the eye!
Fair as a star, when only one
Is shining in the sky.
She lived unknown, and few could know
When Lucy ceased to be;
But she is in her grave, and oh,
The difference to me!

—William Wordsworth

Chapter Twenty-Three

I have to get back through the wall and get to the first floor to retrieve the tape. Standing next to Harold in front of the wall, getting through can't be fast enough. The vortex is relentless and vertigo grips me as I lose myself in its pull.

Once in his room, Harold slides easily in his chair as I reach past him to open the door. Knowing his dementia will not allow for questions, I say moving quickly towards the hall "I have to get that tape."

Running down the hall not stopping to look at our room, I only slow down for seconds to make sure I won't be seen heading for the elevator. The nurses' station is empty. The elevator ride down takes seemingly forever.

Still barefoot I make as little noise as possible. The first floor nurses' station is empty, but I can hear someone down the hall talking loudly to one of the first-floor aides. Staying close to the dining room windows, I creep slowly toward the activity room door. Just as I'm reaching for the doorknob, a bony finger taps me on the shoulder.

"Just what are you doing prowling around in the middle of the night? Trying to sneak up on me with your shoes off?"

Turning around, I face one of the night-shift aides, lucky me. Putting a finger to my lips, I shush her. "I want to get a soda. Can't sleep. Please don't tell the nurse I'm off the second floor. I'll get the soda and be gone before I'm missed. A soda and I'm gone."

She sighs, seeing the lie in my eyes, I'm sure, and turns in the direction of the nurse down the hall. Fear loosens my bowels. If I'm caught, there will be no tape, no evidence of who killed Jake. Just as she turns to walk down the hall, a call light goes off, and the ringing sounds like a fire drill in the quiet hall. I watch her quick footsteps for only a moment before I make tracks in the opposite direction.

"Fifth row down, fourth tape in. Fifth row down, fourth tape in," I whisper to myself over and over until I am standing in front of the VHS tape case. I count down and over and remove the tape, but it occurs to me that I still have one more thing to do before flying out of here. Going over to the VCR player, I put the tape in and push play. There on the screen is the trailer's living room, with all the actors wallowing in debauchery.

Ejecting the tape and putting it down the front of my blouse, I move as quickly as I can toward the first floor elevator.

"Dear God, dear God," I plead. "Please get me back in time." The penalty for our not getting back before Wirm will break Lucy's mind barrier. I knew that this is what I was risking when I took the time to go for the tape.

After I slip through the doors I need to quietly move up the hall pass Wirm's room. Fear crawls up my spine. Not only is he in there; he is pacing and cursing with each step. I hear something about "fucking four-flusher" as I slide softly by his door.

Back tracking back down the hall the door to our room is not open when I get there, but the room light is on. Touching the doorknob is like touching a live electric wire. I breathe in and tell myself, "Take things in small doses—one small thing at a time. See them slowly. If it's a slaughter, I'll never handle it!"

Lucy is in her bed with her eyes closed. Her blankets are tucked under her chin the way she likes them. She is as pale as the pillowcase her head rests on. Her dear face sports a deep grimace. I can just perceive the blankets moving as she labors to breathe. The room is absolutely silent. Otto and Ralph stand by, and Shun Lady sits in her wheelchair with her head in her hands. They shift to make a place for me at the head of Lucy's bed.

Her skin is icy cold as I slide my hand to her neck to feel her carotid pulse. Thready and weak, her pulse is difficult to palpate, fading in and out. I look up in disbelief at the faces of my friends.

"She's dying. For the love of God, she's dying!" I wail. "Why are you just standing here, watching her die? For God's sake, what happened? Why didn't she use her numbers to protect her mind? Why weren't you here to protect her? God, God, what did he do to her?"

Otto reaches for the top of her blanket and lowers it to her waist, revealing her folded hands. Her fingers, all of them, are shades of blue and black. They are swollen sausages about to split. That freak Wirm broke all of her fingers.

I ran through the door and up the hall to Wirm's room, screaming. "You son of a bitch, come out here and fight with me! You son of a bitch! She's going to die, and you know if she does, so will you! I promise, so help me God, I'll kill you!" When I get to his door, he's gone, and I don't stay around to find out where.

I ran back down the hall. "Help me!" I scream. I push through the doors, and there behind the nurses' station is none other than Mary, sitting and charting some nonsense. "Mary, you have to help me. Lucy is hurt badly. Wirm broke all of her fingers. She needs an ambulance right now! Please, Mary. Please, Mary, help me," I yell frantically. "Wirm did this!" I sob. "He hurt her, and if we don't do something right away, she's going to die."

Mary slowly looks up from the patient chart she is working on and gifts me with an evil smirk. "Good luck with that story," she says. "Lucy fell out of bed and landed hands first. You're right, Miss Doe. Lucy is going to die, and all your frantic lying is not going to help her live."

That's when I slap her—hard enough to leave a red mark on her cheek and hurt the hell out of my hand.

"You bitch! I'll call the squad myself!" I spit at her. Looking around for the wall phone, I am starting to walk past the desk when two nurses' aides take hold of my arms and firmly turn me back down the hall to the doors. I'm screaming and kicking but too weak to get out of their grip. Without ceremony, I am escorted back to my room and told the consequence of not staying out of the hall. Otto, Ralph and Shun Lady have retreated from my room rather stay and have to answer more questions.

Fear clutches my chest as I hear Lucy moan, knowing I can do nothing. I put on Lucy's light, hoping Mary will respond with pain medication, cold packs, anything to comfort her. Minutes go by with no response from anyone. Poking my head out the door, I holler for Mary.

She saunters up the hall with a med cup in her hand. I'm still in the doorway when she approaches, reluctant to let her by except that Lucy needs what's in that cup.

"You get back by your bed, or I'm not entering this room, and Lucy will not get this acetaminophen."

"Acetaminophen!" I shout. "For the love of God, Mary, can't you see she needs much stronger pain medication than acetaminophen?"

Mary cranks Lucy's bed into a sitting position, causing Lucy to moan and grimace with pain. She puts the two pills in her mouth and holds a cup of water to her lips. "Take a drink and swallow these pills, Lucy," she says, clearly annoyed. Lucy swallows with coughing and sputtering. Mary then turns on her heels and leaves the room. Lucy is still sitting up in the same painful position.

After lowering the head of her bed, I go into the bathroom. Drawing water as cold as comes out of the tap, I soak and fold washcloths. Lucy moans again as I place the cool washcloths over her swollen, broken hands. This time she opens her eyes and looks at me. In her cornflower-blue eyes I can see acceptance. She is allowing the pull of death to take her. Her body relaxes, and her wonderful little chin lifts in defiance.

I sit by her, holding as much of her as I dare. Unable to stop sobbing, even as my tears fall on her chest, I cry, "Lucy, don't give up. Please, Lucy, don't die. I can't do this without you. Please, live for Harold. He needs you here. Without you, Wirm wins."

Lucy's little voice whispers, "No, Jane, you will never let that happen. All my life I've lived for this fight. Let me go now. I'm ready."

Her words are a testament to the fact she's dying. These first words are probably the last I will hear. No more numbers.

I let go of her to make my argument again, but my words stop in my throat.

Lucy's eyes are closed again. Her respirations become slow and labored, with twenty to thirty seconds between each inhale. I need no stethoscope to tell me her heart is beating wildly, trying to push more oxygen to her failing organs. Her pallor starts to gray. Her legs mottle as blood leaves the periphery. My heart breaks as Lucy's heart fails. At the last moment before death steals her, before her last breath, I feel the protection and unconditional love given once before to the little girl hiding behind a hillock. I recognize this same wonderful feeling of protection illuminating Lucy's face, and her chest does not rise again.

Movement is impossible for a long moment. I am frozen to her last breath. I want to go with her. I want to be where she is. I'm ready. I'm ready. Lucy, I'm ready to be with you. It feels like my time, but it's not. I have to kill Wirm before I sleep. No, first I have to bury Lucy. First, her body must go to church.

Intuitively, and all too soon, Mary appears in the doorway. There is no way to stop Mary from doing the after-death nursing duties consistent with her job. I sit on my bed with my head in my hands, willing my mouth not to betray me.

Mary puts her stethoscope on Lucy's chest and feels for a radial pulse by lifting her wrist. Satisfied with her assessment, she says, "The funeral home will be here to pick up her remains in a half hour. In the meantime, her aide will be in to do last cares and choose the dress and under things Lucy will wear. I warn you to not interfere." With that she gives me the look that is supposed to keep me in line and leaves.

"I'll be dammed if I let Lucy leave here one minute before I'm ready to give her up," I mumble at our empty doorway.

Otto, Shun Lady, and Ralph (with Ralph helping his two friends into the room) quietly take their places alongside Lucy's bed again. Eyes red and puffy, faces etched with grief and disbelief at their loss, they lovingly touch Lucy's face and lightly touch her arms.

A nurses' aide arrives, pushing Harold in a wheelchair. She starts to say something, thinks better of it, and backs out of our room. Ralph positions Harold at the head of Lucy's bed and proceeds to close the door. All eyes are on Harold as he stands, pushing the wheelchair back away from him. Tears stream down his face and drip off his chin. He murmurs her name over and over. "Ah Lucy, my Lucy, my friend, my companion," he whispers, shoulders shaking with grief. I want so badly to confess my responsibility for the delay in our getting back, but Harold stops me with a finger over my mouth.

"You know what we have to do once Lucy is in her resting place," Harold says, inviting no argument.

He is about to say more when outside our door a noisy, egregious protest fills the hall. Seems the men of the downstairs round table are fighting the staff to be able to pay their respects to Lucy in no uncertain terms. The door opens, and Charlie, Fred, Jim, and four or five others from the round table file in.

"Who done this to Lucy?" Charlie says. "We heard downstairs it was that no-good son-of-a-bitch, Wirm. Why'd he want to hurt her? Fred and Jim are ready to go down the hall and call him out. What say we all go? 'Bout time we stomp on that no-good heathen. Sorry for the bad language, ladies."

Harold holds up a hand and says, "We can't change what's happened. No point in the bunch of us getting kicked out of this fine nursing home. Fred, Charlie, you know your family can't take you home. We have to take Lucy to church. Then we'll watch for Wirm to squirm. If we need help, boys, Ralph here will contact you."

One by one, they pay their respects. More than a few openly weep. More than a few pray. More than a few curse Wirm to hell.

Fred is the last one to leave. Hugging me, he says, "We'll all want to be there. You send Ralph with word on the arrangements. We can't trust the staff to let us know in time, so you send Ralph." With a nod he walks out, saying to the aide in the hall, "Okay, missy, it's your turn."

Lucy is sent off with her good blue dress, under things, and a pretty blue hair clip. The undertaker promises he will make arrangements with the church and says she is to be interned next to Steve. Lucy not only provided enough money, but also left instructions of her wishes. Now she is simply gone from our sight. Only the spirit of her presence and the time she graced us with her love is left. Far from hugging each other, Harold, Otto, Shun Lady,

Ralph, and I clutch each other as we watch Lucy's retreat on the gurney through the doors.

Two days later, all who love her are shuttled, in several trips, by the nursing home van to the Catholic Church. We file into our pews much like an eighth-grade catechism class. I don't want to be here. My friends wish they were anywhere else. We pass by Lucy's coffin in the narthex. She looks beautiful in her blue dress, but dead, not like she is sleeping. We don't really have to be here. We could have stayed at the nursing home, but this is what friends of the deceased are supposed to do.

I let my mind wander; I imagine the six of us are sitting on the shore of a beautiful blue lake. Here, too, we've come to say good-bye to Lucy, but only when she's ready. When she's ready to go find Steve and her new life, we'll know it's time to let go. Her blue eyes twinkle with anticipation. There's not a trace of pain on her lovely face. Harold gets up and turns to help Lucy stand. She brushes his hand away and nimbly gets to her feet, like a very young Lucy. She just waves her hand a little and walks toward the shoreline. Lucy turns toward us once more and whispers, "Never good-bye, always I'll be seeing you." With that she simply vanishes.

A squeak from the hardwood pew jolts me awake. Tears rolling down my face and audible sobs cause me to cast down my eyes in embarrassment. Looking at the floor, I see my shoes are wet and sandy. Harold's next to mine are the same. The rest of Lucy's funeral will be easier to tolerate for her compatriots left behind now that she's truly gone.

Father Tom, dressed in a black chasuble, begins the requiem mass for the dead with a solemn chant for the repose of Lucy's soul. The melody is quiet and mournful. Father has a wide girth, tonsured hair, and a kind, open face. His love of the spoken mass is easily discernible as he proceeds in prayer, inviting all of us to join in the response. His homily proves he knew Lucy's heart, and he refers often to her bravery. His last sentence, spoken directly to the five of us left standing, is "Leave vengeance to the Lord your God." With that, he blesses Lucy's closed coffin and walks down the aisle, leaving the church.

The pallbearers line up on either side of her coffin and begin to roll it toward the double doors. Tradition has it that we follow. We are afforded a last glimpse as her coffin is assisted into the waiting hearse. No longer can we see her, or touch her, or laugh at her sense of humor. I find no words to explain the profound loss I feel.

The ride back to the nursing home is silent. Our grief is as palpable as the debasing fear of Wirm has ever been. "Sorry, Father, we are honor-bound to confront Wirm," I say quietly. I follow this thought with a prayer, ending in Jesus's name. Not one of the others expresses approval, but mercurial anger and resolve replace the profound sorrow.

Part Ten

Will the Wirm Squirm?

"BAD MOON"

HANGING ON THE HORIZON
THE BAD MOON FEELS NO PAIN
AS IT PUSHES THE SKY IT'S RISIN'
IT FLOODS THE LANDSCAPE WITH STAIN

THEIR LITTLE GROUP HUDDLES BENEATH IT
REVENGE ON THEIR LIPS, FEAR IN THEIR HEARTS
STERN WARNINGS OF FAILURE, PAIN TO INFLICT
THERE WILL BE NO AFTER ONCE THIS STARTS

WHERE DOES THIS STORY END?
THE BAD MOON KNOWS
IT WAITS TO RISE AGAIN
THAT'S WHERE THE
BAD MOON GOES.

—JUDITH J. THIER

Chapter Twenty-Four

Not wanting to be alone, the five of us who are left meet in my room. The silence is broken by all of us talking at once, all of us pledging to do the unthinkable: kill Wirm. Make him pay for what he did to Lucy.

Harold, the wise leader, stops the chatter with a raised hand and a stern voice. "Ah, come on, I haven't heard one plan that will work. We have to walk out of here, hope he follows, do the deed, and come back alive. And it has to be a simple plan. No complications, no heroes. We'll get one chance at this. Ready? Put your hearing aid in and pay attention."

The next morning, a Saturday, four of us simply walk out the front door with families taking their relatives out for the day. Ralph pushes Shun Lady's wheelchair, and I help Otto manage with his quad cane. Harold instructs us to walk to the car, get in, and wait for him. He will not hear me when I plead with him to come with us. He says go, and we do.

I do not leave empty-handed, however. Tucked into the stretchy top of my pants, the tape goes with us. I will get this to the police somehow. I'm determined not to fail. The price paid for this tape will always be too much.

The streets of Cre Falls are Saturday-busy—people busy running errands, not really seeing the faces on the sidewalk, passing without making eye contact. Our progress is slow and halting, with several curbs as obstacles. Shun Lady and Otto are enjoying being out, gawking at the Cre Fall residents and Ralph muttering comments about new construction and the like. Once again, I'm impressed by how Otto seems able to understand Shun Lady's shun-word commutations when I barely follow what she is saying.

Ralph, having taken the lead, announces our pilgrimage is ending, and the alley has been found. The car, its red paint faded to a nondescript rusty red with true rust spots on the hood and door panels, is where Harold and I left it, snuggly in the alley. I approach the car and rest my hands on the hood, expecting the engine to roar. The car remains silent, as though waiting for Harold's blessing.

Ralph helps Shun Lady into the backseat. Opening the trunk, which gives a loud shriek, he folds her wheelchair and stows it. Helping Otto open the back door is a challenge. I try to help him move away from the door, but his quad cane is planted in front of the door. Otto just will not move until Ralph kneels down and inches Otto's cane and feet away from the door so that the latch can be opened. Easing Otto into the backseat after Ralph's help is a simple finish. Ralph gets in shotgun, and I slide in behind the steering wheel. Having done that, we settle in to wait for Harold.

The waiting is interminable. The conversation inside the car is like white noise. First, we are on fire to enact our revenge on Wirm. Slowly some of the steam morphs into quiet utterances of fear for Harold. The malevolence that we know is Wirm is such a threat to Harold, we fear he will get hurt or worse. Even that quiet prayer-like conversation fizzles to silence. An hour becomes two, and still, we wait.

One thing we can count on is that every two hours or less, Shun Lady becomes restless and announces her need to use the bathroom. Knowing the urgency, I put my hand on the door handle and say, "I'll help you, Shun Lady."

Ralph stays my hand. "Stay where you are, JD. I'll get this one. Shun Lady can get pretty heavy when you have to bear all of her weight."

I watch as he opens the back door and slides his arm around Shun Lady. In a very practiced way, he lifts her up in his arms. I open my door in case he might need help. Turning, he trucks down the alley to the side of a building. I wonder how he is going to manage this, but he turns down her clothes and underwear and holds Shun in a crouched position. Turning his head, he whistles a haunting tune. I feel ashamed that I suspected Ralph was not the person he claims to be and rather was allied with Wirm.

As Ralph slides Shun back into the car, she says, "Nothing like an empty bladder, right, Otto?"

My jaw falls open, and for a second I am speechless. "Wait a second!" I croak out. "Could you always do that? In all the time we've been together, you've only spoken shun words. But now, like Lucy before she died, you're making sentences. What does this mean? Does this mean Otto can walk? Shun, can you walk too? Lord help me, I think we're all going to die."

"That story hasn't been written yet, JD. It's a bad moon we face. Some of the mist has lifted. You can understand me, and no, sadly, I can't walk. Dear Otto can't walk any better either, but we will find ways to help. Now, I have so many things to tell Otto. Time is short. I want say the words 'I love you' before it's too late." Otto and Shun put their heads together and begin mumbling.

I turn and watch the sun begin to set. As I gaze off into the distance, fear for Harold becomes hard to escape. I turn and ask Ralph, "How long do we wait for Harold? When should we go back to find out what happened to him? Do we stand a chance against Wirm without him?"

Ralph looks at me with determination. "We wait. We can't go back. We don't stand a chance."

The sun rapidly sinks into a sunset on the horizon. As the tension in the car mounts, I know too many hours have passed for Harold not to be in trouble. Opening the car door and announcing that I have to find him or go mad, I expect all kinds of protest. But my companions remain silent, giving me the permission I need. Fleeing the alley, I head back the way we came. Hoping I will not have to go back as far as the nursing home, I look at every building and alley. I focus on finding Harold but am fearful of finding Wirm instead. Too late, I realize I should have given Ralph the tape. If I didn't come back, he would know what to do with it.

"Shit," I exclaim when I finally see what part of me knew I would find all along. Standing with his face against a red brick building, his body bent, Harold is barely being supported by the wall. I hurry to his side, my heart slamming against my chest wall. He looks so broken. As I put my hand on his back, he turns to face me. His face is bruised and bleeding. His left eye is swollen shut. The red welts on his neck where he was almost chocked to death look angry in the fading light.

Turning his good eye on my face, he says, "Help me! Hurry! He's coming. We need to be there before him."

"Be where?" I almost say, but I hold back the questions. Slipping my arm around him, I start to move us back the way I came. Movement is slow, and he winces in pain with every step. With a great deal of effort, we reach the alley. At once Ralph is by Harold's side, bearing most of his weight. I open the passenger door so that Ralph can help him into the car. Harold winces again when he attempts to sit. Moaning, he is able to sit upright.

"Ralph, get in front in the middle," Harold says, his voice scratchy and hoarse. "JD, start the car. We have to be outta here before Wirm turns down this street."

Once Ralph and I are in, I put my head down on the steering wheel and say, "Car, start. Get us where we have to go and be quick about it."

The motor roars to life, and the car moves quickly down the street, making a left at the intersection and heading for the highway. Minutes later, we turn right on the highway and then take a quick left after two blocks. Without hesitation the car turns right onto a grassy road. I am sure that if Lucy were here, she would know where we are going. I can only guess at this point. The road is rough, and Harold moans in pain with each jolt. Ralph has his arm around Harold's back, holding him upright. The two lovers in the backseat are silent. I envy their closeness and the ease of their love even in this moment of peril.

Harold has a patina of sweat covering his face, and he's short of breath as he fights the pain. I fear Wirm has injured some internal organ. My most compelling fear is that we're going the wrong way. We should be headed to the hospital. When asked, Harold whispered, "No." And when Harold says no, it's no, no matter what. As we drive, Ralph produces a bottle of water—where he got it is anyone's guess. He wets his handkerchief to mop Harold's face, alternating the patting with sips of water. In my pocket I have several lollipops. I unwrap one and give it to Ralph to hold for Harold. He certainly doesn't need a low blood sugar crisis now.

After ten or so minutes, we turn left, and the car guns the engine to climb up a bumpy incline. We come to a stop in front of a run-down cabin that has seen better days. The car's headlights shine on the cabin's windows, which look like empty eyes, judging our right to be here. The front door is half off the hinges, and it screeches as the wind moves it back and forth. Peering into the darkness beyond the open maw of the swinging door is like looking into an abyss. The front yard is clumps of dry grass and barren areas where nothing seems to grow.

After a long pause, Harold opens the passenger door. Not moving, he stares at the scene before him. For a long time, none of us stir, clinging to the security of the car. All eyes seem to focus on the screeching cabin door, expecting Wirm to slither out of the depths of hell. All of us in that moment examine the fear of our own spiritual profundity. The bad moon sails above, staining the landscape. Fighting paralyzing fear, I open my door, stepping into my worst nightmare.

Harold and Ralph say together, "Stop!"

Using the car door for support, Harold lifts his body to stand. "Don't go any further! Stay next to the car! Make sure you're touching part of the door JD while Ralph helps Otto and Shun Lady get out. You're the one he wants mostly." Harold orders.

Wirm—the man in my nightmare of the eight-year-old girl on the lonely road, the figure standing in the barn door on a farm long ago, the ghost that haunted my life as a nurse in Cre Falls, the horror that ruined the lives of dear Otto and Shun Lady, and the monster that killed Lucy and beat the hell out of Harold. That Wirm is now standing in front of the gaping maw of the cabin door with putrescent, squirming maggots spewing out of his mouth as he roars my name.

"Harold, what are we going to do? He'll kill all of us!" I scream over the roaring Wirm.

"Would I come here without a plan, JD?" Harold asks. "Ralph help Otto and Shun Lady lay on the ground. Directly in front of the car is a cement well cover. It will be the most difficult thing we've done yet, but we must move the cover to the left off the well opening. Otto, Shun, and Ralph will lay on the ground, pushing on the right side of the cover; JD and I will thread the rope through the ring in the middle and pull from the left side. Now everyone move!" he yells.

The well has to be as old as the cabin, but it is no less heavy due to its age. Harold throws me the rope. With my heart pounding, I leave the side of the car door and cross in front. Lowering to my knees, I crawl to the cement cover and locate the ring. Threading the rope through the top, I tie the best knot my damaged hands can manage. Throwing the other end of the rope to Harold at the car, I crawl to the left side of the cement cover.

Harold shouts, "Heads up! When I say go, try to move the cover."

Harold crawls to my side, out of breath and grimacing. How can he do this? The pain will be too much. Before I'm able to even think, he shouts, "Go!" and I'm standing, pulling with more strength than I ever thought possible. Harold's hands are bleeding from the rough rope. He wipes them on his pants one at a time, attempting not to lose traction. Across from me, I can hear Ralph, Otto, and Shun Lady pushing and grunting. I jerk the rope several times, thinking this will start to move the cover. It does not budge. At the cabin, I hear Wirm screaming with laughter in between the taunts of how he will bury us in the well as soon as we move the cover out of the way. Harold is now laying face-down in the dirt, barely conscious. In my frustration I scream at the well cover. "Move, you son of a bitch, move!"

Falling face-first in the dirt next to Harold, I whisper, "We're doing this all wrong. Are you listing to me, Harold? I'm going to tie the rope to the car, and it can pull the cement cover right off the well. Get ready to move when Ralph comes to help you.

"Ralph, Ralph, do you hear me? Get Otto and Shun Lady away from the back of the car. Then come and help Harold. You and I need to tie the rope to the car. Now, Ralph. Hurry!"

Crawling with the rope end in my teeth, I approach the front of the car. Just under the car beyond the radiator is the exhaust system. Ralph joins me on the ground. Winding the rope around the pipe, Ralph ties a strong knot. I understand the apprehension radiating from his eyes. The exhaust system could pull off, disabling the car for good.

In the smallest voice I ask, "Is there anything else we can tie it to?" But I already know the answer. "I'll sit in the driver's seat and encourage the car not to break apart. Ready. Let's do this!"

I can only guess the car headlights shining directly in Wirms eyes keeps him from racing across the well to finish us off, or he has a more sinister plan, but he hasn't moved from the doorway.

I slither around the car to the driver's side door, trying not to be seen. God, help me! Standing, I quickly open the door and slide in. Placing my hands on the dash, I begin my prayer. "Please, God, help us and help the car pull the well cover off. I say this prayer in sweet Jesus' name. Amen. Now, car, start your engine and pull! Pull!"

The car roars to life. Without any more encouragement, the car's tires dig in. Gravel and rocks fly from the churning tires. I hope my friends are well away from the spewing gravel. Slowly, inch by grinding inch, the well cover moves. Slipping out of the car, I back step, using the door as a shield. I really underestimated the circumference of the well. It must be at least four feet across. Now that the cement cover is moving, I have no idea what to do next. When the car stops, the cover is pulled well away from the well.

Closing the car door, I walk to the edge of the well. Loose gravel spills down into it. It seems to fall for a long time before I hear the splash of water. Wirm is standing across from me, not four feet away. His bright eyes flash in the moonlight. Like the doorway of the cabin, his mouth is a gaping black maw. The skin on his face is unlined, translucent.

He shakes his fist, and the roar coming out of his mouth echoes from the depths of hell. "You, Jane. You fucking whore! You did my work for me. I will see all of you down at the bottom of this well for your Saturday night bath."

At that, he lunges across the open well. I scream even before I realize he has a hold on my ankles and I'm losing my balance. Arms flailing, I crumble to the ground. Slowly, Wirm's weight is pulling me into the well. Digging in my nails, trying for some purchase against sliding, I scream for Harold and Ralph who move quickly from the front of the car. But it's too late. My feet and legs slip over the lip of the well. As my legs dangle, I try to make my abdomen and chest serve as an anchor on the surface. My bleeding hands are slimy, failing to catch any hold on the bare ground. I grope and grope, but all I come up with is dirt. As my upper body starts to slip over the edge, I know this is where I'll die. Harold and Ralph grip my arms, trying to pull me up. They too slide over the gravel, trying for any purchase. Just as I lose sight of them, my arms slip from their grip. But at the edge of the well, my hands find the rope, partially buried in the earth. Exhausted and without hope, I almost welcome the water below.

Wirm is losing his grip on my ankles. Grabbing the rope with both hands, I swing my legs, hoping he will fall. My screams echo down the well as Wirm begins to climb up my legs, holding on to my pants. Dear God. Oh my dear Lord. Even with his hellish ability to see the future, Wirm has made a mistake. My pants, like the pants of my peers, have an elastic waistband.

With the help of the car's headlights I can just see my pants slide down over my rump as Wirm pulls even harder to pull me down in the well with him. My pants continue to slide down my legs. His nails rake the skin on my legs as he descends to my feet. I drop my eyes to the drama below. With nothing left to get a hold of, Wirm finally falls, bellowing until he hits the water. He is glaring at me as his head slowly sinks beneath the black water at the bottom of the well. Mesmerized by the ripples in the inky, thick water, I'm sure I will see his cadaverous hand reaching for me.

Harold and Ralph are looking over the edge of the well, telling me over and over again to hold tight. Slowly, I am dragged up by the rope. A couple of times my hands start to slip, but I resist trying for a better grip. My mind is doing the reacting, not my body, which comes up out of the well with no muscle integrity left. I flop on the gravel like a caught fish, lying flat on my face. Harold and Ralph turn me over and get me to my feet.

Harold whispers, "You have to get out of the way. The car has to pull the cover back over the well. We need you to help the car, JD. Up you go. You and the car are the final effort."

I don't understand "final effort." Panic swells in my gut as I cling to the door of the car before getting in. The car makes a growling engine noise as it laboriously pulls the cement lid over Wirm's grave. My mind melds with the car. I can feel its courage as its strength falters. The car's engine is spewing steam, threatening to blow before the cement lid covers the well. I rest my head on the steering wheel. Instead of pleading with the car, I summon and try to pass on the last of my strength not taken by the well and Wirm. As if with a sob, the car pulls harder, until the cover slips in place. The car heaves a sigh, and the engine puffs one last blast of steam just before it falls silent. It slips from me with a tug, leaving me feeling empty once again.

Finding the cross on the empty seat next to me, I take it in my arms. I somehow know what has to happen next. Slipping to the ground from the open driver's seat door, I crawl under the car to the center of the cement cover. I place the cross on the cover, and I'm not sure what happens next or how long I lie there. When I again become aware of my surroundings, I think I might have passed out. I close my eyes tightly and then open them again slowly. My vision clears, and I'm able to see with amazement that the cross has burned itself into the cement cover. The well is sealed. The impossibility of Wirm escaping the well leaves me with the most overwhelming sense of peace.

I push myself up to a kneeling position and then to my feet. Shakily, I make it next to the car. In the distance I hear my friends clapping and hooting at the moon. My laughter sounds hysterical in my ears, but I'm laughing. I feel the night breeze swirling through my crotch and suddenly become painfully aware that I'm standing in my white old-lady bloomers scuffed with dirt, with no slippers or even socks. My lily-white legs are streaked with blood and ooze where Wirm clawed me. Looking down at the damage while Harold, Ralph, and friends catcall, I remove my light jacket and tie it around my waist, pulling it down to cover most of my embarrassment. I snicker at my condition.

Admonishing them for their insensitivity, I tell Ralph to remove Shun Lady's wheelchair from the trunk of the car. It's a long walk back to town. Removing the tape from the front seat where I stashed it, I announce, "What to do? Where to go? We'll figure it out on the way."

Since I'm now the one with my bloomers showing, I walk out in front, giving them a good look at my barely covered ass. It's difficult to believe this long night has passed, but dawn is beginning to break on the horizon, making the road and my backside easier to see.

No words are uttered, only the occasional snicker. When I turn and look at them struggling down the road, I realize we resemble lost, homeless souls on parade. Harold's face is black-and-blue from the beating Wirm gave him, and he's limping a little from a sore leg. Otto limps along haltingly, with Ralph helping him over the ruts. Shun Lady, who has so much talking to do, is stone-silent. Ralph, doing his best to keep our little band moving forward, turns every now and then to convince himself that no one is following. The oozing scratches have broken open on my legs now. Warm blood trickles down to my bare feet.

Suddenly we were all talking at once. We seem to agree in unison that our only refuge is the Catholic Church. Father Tom will grudgingly help us if we can put together a plausible story. We agree that the most difficult questions will be these: Why do I have no pants, how did I get the terrible leg wounds, and who beat Harold black-and-blue? Oh, and what are we doing running away from the nursing home? These are all incriminating questions that cannot be honestly answered: because we killed Wirm.

We reach the cross street as the morning sun reveals our identities clearly. We do not turn right to the highway but limp straight to the church. As luck would have it, the church is unlocked. More luck: Father is at the altar preparing for the early Sunday mass. We file in the back pew, waiting for him to turn around and notice that our motley crew is not a group of early mass–goers.

Finishing up, Father turns around. As he tries to make sense of the sight in the back pew, the startled gasp leaves no question that we are in for it. Before he can make up his mind to go to the phone in the sanctuary, I start to bawl with great hiccupping sobs, not entirely fake. I think about all that's happened. Lucy is dead; my legs burn; after hanging in the well, I feel mentally deranged; and I'm scared to death that prison might be my next stop. Father comes down the aisle to sit in the pew ahead of us. Turning to really give us the once-over, he holds up his hand in the "stop" position, clearly meaning, "Do not speak."

He heaves a sigh. After contemplating our condition, he says, "Only one of you will speak, and this better be good."

My sobs dry up immediately. It is Harold who painfully comes to his feet and proceeds to tell the wildest story ever told. It is so good he makes a believer out of me.

Wirm beat him up because he got in Wirm's face and accused him of killing Lucy. When he was knocked down on the floor, I came to his rescue. With Ralph's help, we all stumbled into my room. In the hallway, Wirm called for nursing help. Mary accused us of doing something to Mr. Wirm once again and then made failed attempts to take Wirm to his room. We knew at once the staff would not protect us. By this time Otto and Shun Lady were in the hall. We decided to make a run for it. With Ralph's help, we got down in the elevator and out the door with the Saturday visitors. Walking away, looking innocent was nearly impossible. Ralph put Harold on Shun Lady's lap and pushed them up the sidewalk as fast as he could. Otto and I followed. After we turned in front of the mill, we headed for the highway. Ralph stopped to help Otto catch up, and I stayed where I was to see if we were followed. Soon, they were several blocks from me, and I started to run to catch up. Not watching where I was going, I tripped and fell on a wood pallet left on the sidewalk. Many nails were sticking up, which ripped my pants and gouged my legs. When I fell, the tight pants I was wearing split up the back. Holding my pants together, I limped behind the others. We decided not to stop but kept going for fear Wirm was following. We came to Eagle Park and hid in a line of trees. We stayed there, unsure of what to do, until this morning, when we felt sure the priest would help us.

Story told, Harold sits down and looks at Father with the quintessential innocence of someone completely crazy. But I believe him, and moreover, so does Father. I will slug him for the "tight pants" comment if he ever heals from his bruises. For the first time my gut stops fluttering, and I feel we can get away with what we did.

Father hustles us back to the rectory with instructions I am to take a shower and put antibacterial ointment on my wounds. He leaves rather large sweat suit bottoms for me to wear and asks Ralph to make coffee and feed us some of the fellowship doughnuts. He assures us he will be back after the first mass. He also demands that we not leave the rectory.

Minutes later, I am showered, dressed, and ready for breakfast. Shiny face, clean hair, sugar, and coffee, oh my. The tape, I discovered when I undressed to shower, was not lost through all this. It was lodged safely in my bra, where I put it before leaving the car, and is now sitting in front of my coffee cup. I contemplate who I can get to carry this incriminating evidence to the police. The only solution I can wrap my brain around is that Harold and I take a trip tonight to deliver it ourselves. Dangerous, yes, but the hard part will be to convince Harold that after all we have been through, we still have one more thing to do. I can no longer stick the tape in my waistband because Father is rather rotund around the middle, so I do the next best thing. I stick it back in the strap of my bra. While I was in Father's bathroom, I filched Tylenol in numbers large enough to cause kidney failure. By the moans and groans, every one of us is hurting, none more than me.

Father returns from mass. I want to touch his holy hand or run to the confessional, but I know I will never be sorry for killing Wirm. Snapping out of my moment of repose, I meekly follow my friends out the door to the waiting church van. We ride in silence until Father parks and leaves the van to open the back sliding door.

Harold says quietly, "Remember the story. All of us, separate or together, we tell the same story. I may not be with you as I am now, but tell the same story I told Father."

Father has known Harold this many years and has kept his secret. Father will keep Harold's secreted other self until one of them dies, knowing Harold has reasons that include Wirm.

Standing at the front door of the joint, a pseudo-affectionate term I have come to use for the nursing home, is not only security but also the director of nurses and all kinds of administrative personnel. I don't think they are there to welcome home the runaways. They greet us with acrimonious open mouths. Residents gawk from doorways. Some cheer, "You go!" and "You're our heroes!" We are immediately escorted to our rooms and told to stay there. Instead of sitting on my bed wringing my hands, I decide to take a nap. By this time, I am out of adrenaline and near collapse from exhaustion.

Rudely waking me, Mary barks, "Get up, sleeping beauty. You're next. Pee if you have to. Then follow me."

Still groggy from not enough sleep, I go to the bathroom and do exactly as I'm told, except I stay long enough to splash cold water on my face and change out of Father's enormous sweat pants. The videotape is hidden where anyone could find it, but it will be safe enough for the time being.

Mary leads me downstairs to the director of nursing's office, smirking and telling me I am really in for it this time. Ignoring her should be easy, except I can't let her get away with harassing me. I say in my most mocking voice, "If you had been doing your job, Wirm wouldn't have beaten the hell out of Harold." As I say Harold's name, he appears, being pushed out of the director's office in a wheelchair, very, very agitated. He's shouting, "Get a gun, get a gun!" We do not make eye contact. I brush past him, wordlessly.

In her office the director of nursing, or DON, has stationed security staff in chairs around the room. Her secretary has a recording device to catch my every word. Prudently, and I'm never very prudent, I decide to answer only the questions asked and not let my temper betray me.

She asks if I want a glass of water before we get started. Before I can answer, she pours one. Looking me straight in the eyes, she says, "Did you remove Harold Brown from the nursing home and away from its restricted lands?"

"Yes. On Saturday morning. I'm not sure what time. I'll answer your next question to expedite this hearing. Because Wirm beat the hell out of Harold, and Mary had no intentions of helping him. She was so concerned with Wirm. Ralph and I had to lift Harold off the floor and take him to my room out of harm's way. We continued out the door and away from here with Otto and Shun Lady."

"I'm told you didn't enlist the other staff to help because you and Ralph decided only the two of you could protect Harold. Is that correct?" she asks in a pedantic, accusing voice.

"Yes," I say and no more.

"Do you understand that by removing Harold, who is protectively placed in this nursing home, you have made a serious legal breach of the policy in place and can be prosecuted for your actions?" She thumps her desk to make her point.

That does it! The hair on the back of my neck stands on end. "Any nursing home that is so negligent as to allow a resident to do to Harold what Wirm did and have one of the staff, an RN no less, ignore the beaten resident on the floor deserves to be sanctioned by the state. We moved Harold to safety. Fight that!"

Red-faced, she says, "I will report this incident to the state board. You will tell the people in this room where you went after leaving this facility?"

"Do what you have to do," I say. "I would do it again in a heartbeat to save Harold."

"All right, all right," she says, her voice rising to match the anger in her eyes. "We'll hear the rest of the story."

"We walked out with the Saturday visitors to that park by the Catholic Church. We hid in that wooded area by the picnic tables and waited to see Father. Church was busy with people coming and going. Besides, we were afraid Wirm followed us. Sunday morning, we went to the church as soon as the doors were unlocked. The rest of the story, you know," I say.

"One last question, and you had better give the absolute truth, or I will refuse to help you in the future," she says threateningly. "Where is Wirm? He has not been seen since Harold left the nursing home. What have the five of you done with Wirm?"

My heart stops. Here comes the lie. "The last time I saw Wirm was the back of him headed to his room on Mary's arm on the second floor of this nursing home, behind the doors."

"And what, in your opinion, provoked Wirm to hit Harold?"

"I don't know," I tell her. "I wasn't in the hall. I left my room when Ralph hollered for my help." The other half of the lie.

"You may leave," she says, dismissing me. "You're confined to your room until this investigation is over. In the meantime, figure out your answer to how you ended up without pants."

As I leave the room, Ralph is waiting in the hall for his turn. Funny how a lie becomes truth when the actual truth is terrifying. As our eyes meet, I recognize the dogged determination. Shun Lady can't give credence to the lie, and Otto will only say, "Jesus Christ," so the lie is mine and Ralph's to defend. *Stay strong, my friends*, I pray as I walk down the hall.

Upstairs in my room, I pull out my typewriter to capture the DON's perverse reactions during my questioning. The paper is not even in the roller when she bursts in my room, demanding my supposed book.

"You will give up to the investigation what you've been typing on that decrepit typewriter right now," she demands.

I hand her the blank sheet of paper that I was planning to use. "Here you go," I say, knowing I have truly made a mortal enemy.

"I'll get you. No one gives me the slip. No one!" she says, leaving in a huff.

As I am standing in the doorway, thinking that the trays should be up soon, Ralph lumbers down the hall. He gives a slight nod of his head as he passes. Since he's being escorted by security, that will be my only confirmation that he repeated the story well. The hard part is upon us: waiting. Waiting for the police to show up, handcuffs in hand with my name on them, or for Wirm to resurrect from the well and show up behind the doors, or for life to just go on as before, waiting. Waiting for something to happen.

The evening wears on. Supper is a marvel—I mean, really delicious. I easily could have eaten two of everything. Even prisoners get to eat. Washing up and slipping into bed fully clothed, I set my internal alarm for midnight.

I dismiss the aide when she asks if I need anything, and she closes my door. Down for the night? Not so, little girl.

At midnight I startle awake from a nightmare about the well. Only this time, Wirm pulled me down into the waiting water. Dear God, will this ever end? The tape is under my pillow in a manila envelope. Reaching for it and pulling socks on my feet, I head for Harold's room. The ambient night light fills the hall. The place is as quiet as a tomb. I'm scared to death to cross in front of Wirm's door, so I cross to the opposite side of the hall to slip down to Harold's room. Oh, I pray Harold is ready for this.

Harold's room is as dark as a cave. The only light is from the night-shaded window. I find him sitting in his Adirondack chair. Touching him, I realize he is ready in his street clothes, shoes too. "We do this, do we, Harold?"

"Did you think for one minute I'd let you do this alone? Save all the chitchat for later. Now let's go."

I give him a hug, surprising him and myself, before we reach out for the wall. Holding Harold's hand, I feel the vortex take us like a vacuum, with the nauseating swirling. As in the past, my landing is less than graceful. This time I land on my butt, legs splayed out in front, and my head nearly touching the sidewalk. Harold, as always, stands next to me, as though flying through the wall is the most natural thing to do.

"Okay, JD, up off your ass—the world waits for no klutz. I hope you have a plan. I think our biggest danger is that pickup waiting at the curb, whose occupants may want to take that tape from us after bashing in our heads. Remember, we just walked into the past. This is unlike the stories we went to. The people in this adventure can see, smell and talk to us. They can also kill us".

I stand up, brushing off the detritus from my classy sweats. I mumble several curse words, not the least of them "fuck." "No walk in the park for us, huh, Harold? No pleasant walk to the police station and back without getting our heads bashed in? Really?"

"Stop swearing like a sailor. I have a plan." We walk around the back of the nursing home turn right and cross the road to the old clinic. The truck is parked facing the mill. "I think we can get across without being seen."

"Okay, Sampson, then how do we get across the river?" I ask, taunting him in a churlish voice.

"We'll figure that out when we get there, lady. Follow me."

He takes off through the rose bushes to the back of the nursing home. Following him, once again, rose thorns scratch every surface of me not covered, including my face. I try to pick my way through, but Harold is getting ahead of me. The nursing home during this time did not extend landscaping any farther than visitors could see; consequently, the back was brambles and underbrush. Without shoes the trek is torture. The black windows of the residents' rooms stare down, accusing me of more transgressions. Hubris will not allow me to ask Harold to wait up. Limping, I reach the corner of the building and think for a moment with relief; *At least it is not raining.* Harold is already running across the lawn down a knoll to the road. As he looks back to give me the "come on" sign, he looks very exposed under the streetlight. I wait as he crouches down and runs crab-legged across the road to the old clinic. Holding my breath, I wait for the porn stars in the pickup to see him. It seems like an hour before I get the courage to move, but when I do, I run like a deer, falling headlong down the knoll. As fortune would have it, I'm flat on my face when the pickup engine roars. It makes a U-turn and barrels up the road past the old clinic. Once it has passed, I run across the road like a teenager. Harold reaches out from the bushes he is hiding in and pulls me to him. I'm breathing like a wind tunnel, and my heart hammers against my chest wall.

With my tongue stuck to the top of my mouth, I'm not able to sputter a word. Harold chooses not to pause. He heads for the mill wood yard. Suddenly I know how we are going to get across the river: the train trestle over the dam. My brain screams, *Oh God, oh no, I can't do that.* Still, I scramble across the wood yard into the swampy reeds. The cement buttress stands as a monument to mill man's achievement. Harold scrambles up it like a monkey using the handholds. He silently encourages me to follow when he reaches the top.

I'm not a lightweight. Pulling up my weight using the strength of my arms will be an experience close to dangling down that cursed well with Wirm hanging on my legs. Nevertheless, if I'm going to get across the river, I have to try. Mimicking Harold's right-hand, left-hand pattern, I begin to pull myself up. I will never climb a mountain, and I know if I have a future, I'll never feel the need again. Wondering how far up the buttress I've managed, I peek up to the top. Not far enough. Halfway is a stretch of my imagination. Harold is sitting on the cement edge, feet dangling over, watching my slow progress. Gritting my teeth, I think, *If he says anything when I get to the top, I'm going to push him off.* Right hand, left hand. Right hand, left hand. Right hand, left … Suddenly, Harold is leaning down, in my way. Before I can admonish him for slowing my progress, he strong-arms me to the top. Hefting my bulk over the cement edge is one of my life's most difficult feats, especially as I try to protect the tape tucked once again into my waistband. Wasting no time, Harold begins to cross the trestle holding on the crossbars. So I follow, scared enough to pee my pants. My stocking feet are slippery, and several times, my foot slides out while I hang on for dear life. Beneath me is the churning river, calling to me to let go. Harold has reached the other side, while I struggle far behind. Remembering all the "never will do again" promises I've made myself, I decide this particular "never doing this again" has taken first place.

Legs shaking, hands shaking, and with the taste of salty tears, I reach the other side and stand next to Harold. Nearly giddy with relief, I can't find the scathing words to admonish him. Instead I follow him down to the ground. As soon as my feet land on terra firma, Harold is once again ahead of me, plowing through the brush to the highway. After one hundred feet or so of struggle, the walk/run slows to easy footing. Along with ease in footing comes the feeling of exposure. Harold hunkers down before crossing the highway. My chance to catch up has come, and I hunker down beside him. Several cars pass, none of them the pickup.

Harold speeds across the highway with me on his tail. We continue to run two blocks to our right before turning into a yard with cover. There we wait again for the killers to find us. With hand motions Harold indicates we move.

Hiding where we can, we run through yards, managing to alert every dog. A chorus of deep barks, yips, growls, and whining has the neighborhood awake. So far no sight of the pickup. Our exodus takes us behind the police station. Resting against the building, we wait for whatever comes next. What comes next is a gunshot, the bullet cracking the stucco just above Harold's head. I screech and run for the side door of the station. Harold inches behind me, grabs the back of my pants, and drags me down to the sidewalk.

"If you want to die, make yourself a target—stand up," he whispers, putting his hand over my mouth. He reaches up and tries the door. "What do you know? It's locked. I don't know where that gunshot came from, but I think we have no choice. It's the front door or draw more gunfire."

"We never catch a break," I mumble. Staying low, I creep to the corner facing the highway. I do not have to put the envelope in the hands of a cop. All I need is a mail slot big enough to put the envelope safely into the police station, away from our pickup killers.

"Harold, I'm going to creep to the front of the police station. I'll try to find a way to get the envelope inside. If I don't make it, you're next in line. Cover me!"

"With what? Rocks?" he says.

That does it. I can't stop belly-laughing as I crab-walk to the glass door in front. Finding no mail slot puts an immediate stop to my cackling. I stand up, making myself the target Harold warned me of, and search the stucco by the door. Bingo. There, embedded in the stucco, is a parcel drop. Dropping the envelope in, I start to sink back down to the sidewalk, but just then, the blaring headlights of the pickup make me a stunned deer. Harold jogs up the sidewalk and grabs my arm, skidding me along the cement into the ornamental bushes. Another gunshot cracks the stucco right where, just a second ago, I was paralyzed by their headlights.

The gunshot piques the interest of the policemen on duty. Before being discovered, Harold and I scramble around the corner of the building. The on-duty officers burst out of the door, crouching, guns drawn, shouting, "You, out of the truck! Hands up or we shoot!"

Harold and I do not delay. Taking advantage of the opportunity the officers have handed us, we sprint away from the scene. We cross the highway two blocks down and turn right, following the mill fence. Giving me a "well done" pat on the head, Harold takes my hand. We walk hand in hand to the mill cross street that will take us to the nursing home.

"Parse my every word, Harold old man: we did it again. We delivered the evidence and managed to dodge bullets. As a senior team, we're invincible. Don't you think?"

"Take the old man out of it, and I'd say you're right as rain, JD," Harold replies.

Standing outside Harold's wall, I feel a profound sadness about this time ending and the world moving on. I want to ask him, "Where to now, Harold?" But I know the answer is one I cannot face. Not just yet. Instead, I raise my right hand and place it on the wall to suck me back. Harold follows, still holding my hand.

Back in Harold's room, he sits in his chair as though he never left. Feeling like the moment I lost is gone forever; I sigh and slip into the familiar hall.

Just as when I left, the hall is quiet as a tomb, not a soul in sight. Though I won't look, the clock's hands will be just after midnight, as before. I saunter down the hall on Wirm's side as if daring trouble to fine me. But it feels like my days of rebellion have ended. With nothing else to do, I go to my room, throw away my ruined socks, and slide between the sheets in my quintessential day uniform. Before sleep takes me, my mind taunts, *Take that.*

Chapter Twenty-Five

The pounding on my door jars me awake. Trying to climb to consciousness is once again like climbing out of that rakish well. The knock sounds again, this time with a voice from the hall.

"Throw your legs out of bed, JD," the aide instructs. "You're wanted by the DON on the double."

"On the double, you say. Come back in a half hour bearing coffee. I have a colossal headache," I say.

Sliding out of bed, I realize the headache wasn't a delaying tactic. My head hurts, my joints hurt, and the bottoms of my feet feel like I've been running around town without shoes. And so I have. I realize I deserve the other ailments as well. Thinking perhaps I can at least improve my appearance, I decide to try that first. If not, I guess I'm out of luck. A warm washcloth and a comb help, but not so much. I'll have to be presented to the DON barefoot. I don't even have any socks left to put on.

The aide is back knocking on my door.

"Come in if you have a pair of shoes and socks I can wear. I'm willing to wear some from dead people donations," I say, putting off the inevitable one more time.

I anticipate the reason for this meeting is that the story didn't hold up, and I'm going to jail, not for helping Harold escape, but for murdering Wirm. A self-defense plea may be my only saving grace. Assuming I will get off the hook is, I fear, naïve. Prepare for the worst and pray for a tectonic shift in my favor: that is what's left for me to do. Then again, I will never be off the hook. Lucy, Wirm, the well—all of it has marked this time and place for the balance of the years I have left. It defines who I am and haunts my dreams.

The knock on my door is back. This time the aide appears with a wheelchair and shoes on the seat. She has a coffee cup in her hand. "So I don't understand the word," she confesses. "Hop on and tell me on our way down. We're late!"

"I don't need a wheelchair," I say head pounding. "The meaning of the word is large. As in, I have a large headache."

"You can't walk in these shoes," she snorts. "Way too big. You'll fall over your feet. These are the only ones I could find. By the looks of you, a ride wouldn't hurt."

She's right; a ride wouldn't hurt. I acquiesce without another word. Getting into the wheelchair and putting on the clown shoes takes all my energy. I feel depleted of adrenaline and apathetic. Having lost my concern for why I'm being taken downstairs, I let my mind drift. If this is it, this is it; I have no regrets. Nothing I'm sorry for. Let the clown shoe fall where it will.

There sitting behind the desk is my DON with a big warm smile. This cat-who-caught-the-mouse smile is like cold water poured on my head. I'm paying attention now. As the aide wheels me up to her desk, I suddenly feel a chill crawl up my back.

Without preamble she spills out the words behind that creepy smile. "We found your family!"

I cannot understand her words. The sounds are gibberish in my ears. I cannot interpret the meaning. Anxiety bubbles in my chest. I must have had a stroke. "What did you say?" I manage to ask.

Again she says, "We found your family! Your children, Ms. Doe. Marie, James, and George will be here before dinner."

"You found my family? I don't think so. You mean my family found you. Isn't that how it happened?"

Her smile gone, she stutters, "Well, technically yes. You daughter called early this morning. She asked if Jane Dobson was a resident. She went on to describe you in detail. Jane Dobson is your name, isn't it?"

I've been made. I should be very grateful my children found my letter taped under my desk. But I am profoundly saddened to leave my friends, to walk away from this life I did not create—but nevertheless a life where I was so needed and loved.

"Yes, my name is Jane Dobson. This nursing home owes me a refund on my room rent. I'll be sure to leave a forwarding address before I check out," I say with a preachy voice.

Turning the wheelchair to the open door, I call for the aide. Before I can successfully make a getaway, the DON says, "The other matter will continue to be investigated. I cannot hold you here, but I'll know where to find you."

I wheel myself out the door into the hallway, flip off the clown shoes, and walk to the elevator barefoot. On the second floor, I stand before the doors that opened and accepted me at the start of this. Echoes of that drug-induced night of my admission rush through my mind; "Put her in with Lucy behind the doors," the night nurse said. As I push the doors open, the world I've come to love rushes at me. Pent-up tears sluice down my face. Staggering to my room half-blinded by tears, I don't know how I will face the hours before departing for my other life.

Forget breakfast. To occupy my time, I drag out the old suitcase. The suitcase open on my bed, I begin to clean out the closet. What I don't throw away will go back downstairs for donation; I'm going to take only the clothes on my back, my Underwood, and the manuscript. *The book!* I'll have to retrieve it from Medical Records across the hall first chance I get. If no chance presents, I'll have to create one. The friends will have to create a diversion in the hall. Shun Lady can fake a fall in which Ralph and Otto come to her aide, making a ruckus. Hopefully, the medical records secretary will come to the rescue, leaving the door unlocked. My chance will be slim. It's another unavoidable scenario that will probably get my friends in trouble. I'll watch the Medical Records door and take my chance if she comes out without locking up.

Lunch trays come up, and the aide informs me mine is in the dining room. Eating with my friends will give me a chance to involve them in my plan to get the book in my hands. Walking into the dining room with the realization that this may be the last time leaves me breathless. Nothing is secret in the nursing home. I wonder how many staff and residents know I'll be leaving with my family today. It will be interesting how many call me by my name.

No sooner does the thought go through my mind than the aide with my tray sardonically announces, "I have a tray for Jane Dobson." That answers that question. I raise my hand, knowing full well she announced my name for the benefit of all. Otto and Shun Lady come through the door, spot me, and head to our table. Otto puts his hand on my shoulder and gives me a knowing "Jesus Christ." Shun Lady wheels up to the table and with a sad voice says, "Destination." Of course Ralph sits down quietly and only says, "Jane."

"Yes, my name is Jane Dobson. My children will be here for me before dinner, so I'm told."

Ralph tucks into his food without further comment. The other two look at me expectantly. They seem to know I have something more in mind.

"Okay, you know I have an important favor to ask. I'd better get to it, or we'll miss lunch. You know I wrote this book, as unfinished as it is. Thing is, I put it in Medical Records in the deceased residents file drawer. Whenever the secretary goes on break, she locks the door. I need to get into Medical Records to get the book today, later this afternoon."

"You want me to pick the lock?" Ralph asks.

"No lock picking. It takes too long. What I want you three to do is set up a diversion just up the hall from Medical Records. Ralph, you could help Shun Lady to the floor. Make it look like she slid out of her wheelchair. Otto could do a bunch of distressed 'Jesus Christs,' and you, Ralph, could yell for help. That will get her attention, and she will come running on the fly. I will slip in behind her, get in, and retrieve the manila envelope with the book. My plan is to get back in my room before she sees me. I'll get rid of the envelope and return to the hall to see what's going on," I say with conviction.

"Could work," Ralph agrees. "It's a boring day anyway. I'd like a little action. What do you say, Otto? Shun Lady? You up for Jane's plan?"

Otto gives an affirmative "Jesus Christ," and Shun Lady says, "Action." They looked adoringly at each other and begin to eat.

I may be dumber than a doorpost. I could just walk into Medical Records and get the envelope, period, but the DON would certainly hear from the medical records secretary and be knocking on my door to confiscate it. Surely, she would hold it as evidence.

"We pull this off as soon as the hall quiets down before shift change. Remember, the action has to happen far enough from the Medical Records door that I can slip behind her. Ralph, I will watch the door to make sure she's in there. You will need to poke your head out for a thumbs-up." They nod in agreement and continue eating. By this time my food is cold, but I'm too hungry to refuse to eat it.

After lunch, I continue putting a few things in a bag for donation downstairs and throwing many things away. Suddenly, it strikes me that I still do not have shoes. Knowing the way to the basement, I can take my donated clothes down and look around for something to wear on my feet. I should get the aide to come with me, but since I'm not predisposed to asking for help, I will go and be done with it. The clock in the hall registers twelve thirty, plenty of time before our "action" in the hall. The nurses at the desk are usually busy or on lunch break at this time, so it should be easy to slip on the elevator without being seen. Taking the bull by the horns, I grab my bag and head out the double doors to the elevator. Apprehension sends chills up my spine when I see the elevator is coming up from the first floor with a rider. Quickly receding back behind the doors, I wait until the passenger gets off. Opening the door a crack, I see Mary's back as she rushes down another wing on some sort of mission. I move with lightning speed to the elevator and push the button for the basement.

The cobwebby basement is cool and damp. The door I want is to the left, down a short hall. Opening the door, I feel the wall for the light switch. A single light bulb in the middle of the ceiling lights the room enough for me to see well. I start to poke around, trying to be mindful of the time. Donated things are arranged on shelves pretty much by category, I notice. There are six or eight shelves almost to the ceiling. It is easy to recognize where they put the shoes. I pull out a pair that looks like they will fit and start to leave. My jaw drops.

There on the end of the second shelf are things from Wirm's room—some ugly, tattered pants and some shirts, along with a pair of worn boots with his name on the tongue. I try to remember what he was wearing the night he became one with the bottom water of the well, but I can't. To my horror, Lucy's things are folded next to his. I have just started to gather her things to put them somewhere else when the light goes out. My heart stops, and breathing is suddenly difficult. Certainly someone saw the light coming from under the door and, thinking the light was left on by accident, opened the door a crack and turned it off. Knowing exactly where I put the shoes I found, I retrieve them. In pitch-blackness, I move to where I think the door should be. Sure that at any moment someone is going to jump out at me, I feel the wall for the light switch. Finding it, I turn it on and leave, not bothering to close the door behind me. Hell bent for election, I scramble for the elevator to the second floor. The elevator door opens to Mary sitting at the nurses' desk.

"So there you are. I won't ask where you've been because I realize rules are not meant for you to follow. This is an order: put your shoes on," she says perversely. Getting up from behind the desk, she gives me a look of pure malice before heading for the elevator.

I nod my head and keep walking in an adrenaline fog. Once behind the doors, I glance at the clock. I don't know whether the secretary is in Medical Records or not. Undecided, I stand by the dining room door, waiting for her door to open, or for some sign she is in that room.

Not looking for me or waiting for my signal, Ralph comes out of his room, pushing Shun Lady's wheelchair. Not paying attention to my hand signals to stop, he continues down the hall. Nearly in a panic, I watch him lift Shun Lady and sit her on the floor in front of her wheelchair. Without a pause, he bleats, "Help, help! Shun Lady is on the floor!" Then he makes some theatrical grunts as he tries to soothe the now screaming Shun Lady. Otto immediately comes out of his room, yelling at the top of his lungs, "Jesus Christ!" I want to fall on the floor laughing, but the secretary is out of the door and on the fly, leaving the door open. I quickly run for the door, closing it partway behind me. Opening the file, I snag my envelope and get out of there as fast as I can. The scene in the hall is calmer, and before I reach my door, two aides with a nurse close behind scurry down the hall to move the now smiling Shun Lady off the floor. I'm able to get in my room before the belly laughter takes over. With relief, I put my envelope in the typewriter case and return to the hall. Shun Lady is back in her wheelchair, pronounced unhurt, and Ralph is getting a tongue lashing for not being more careful pushing Shun Lady. *Ah, I'll miss them*, my heart whispers.

My heart also tells me I'd better say good-bye before the flurry of leaving. I approach Shun Lady in her room and kneel in front of her wheelchair. Holding her thin frame in my arms, I simply say, "Good-bye. I love you." With a sob, I get up to leave. She squeezes my hand and whispers, "Affection."

I walk across the hall to Otto's room. Taking him in my arms, I let my tears soak into his shirt. "Good-bye, my friend. I love you. Take care of Shun Lady and Harold." Of course my friend utters, "Jesus Christ"—meaning love, I know.

Ralph meets me in the hallway and holds out his hand as if to shake mine. I put my arms around him and get swallowed in his hug back. "Only you could have pulled off the action that well this afternoon. I'm so grateful. I will miss you and count on you to take care of the rest," I say, choking back tears.

Saying good-bye to Harold feels impossible. I know my heart will break. When I approach his room, Harold is ranting and raving in dementia. I cannot touch his mind or him. Head down in sadness, I know this is the memory of him I will take out of here.

Back in my room, I put on the shoes that I retrieved from the basement, which fit better than the clown shoes. My typewriter case fits in the open suitcase, and I put my white old-lady bloomers around it for cushion. Closing my suitcase is much like closing the door to the person I've become and opening the door to the person I left in that apartment. I was just a bored old lady. I don't want to be just a bored old lady. I want to be Jane Doe, the reluctant adventurer. Just thinking this makes the tears of self-pity flow. In the bathroom, I wash my face with cold water, comb my hair, and attempt to look like someone's mother. Now I settle on my bed and wait.

Chapter Twenty-Six

I easily fall asleep instead of keeping a vigil. Deep in dreams of running around the streets of Cre Falls, with dogs barking and gunshots, I relive the sweet moment of Harold holding my hand while walking back. I relive the car rides, the paralyzing fear, the evil of Wirm, and sweet Lucy.

As I struggle to wake up to voices I recognize, my face is wet with tears. Will I ever not cry? Will the fear of Wirm be part of my nightmares for the rest of time I call this planet home? Seeking to clear the cobwebs of sleep, I pull myself up to face the tongue-lashing from my children. Hopefully, it will be private without staff to fuel the fire.

Marie is the first to show herself in the doorway. As always, her beauty takes my breath away. Always I'm a little speechless when she voices concerns about my "behavior." Marie has a right way of doing things programmed in her cerebral cortex. She is both an artist and a true believer in order. She comes to me with her brand of unconditional love, heavy on the "Why didn't you tell me?" side. Our hug seems to go on for a very long time, with neither of us able to admonish or defend my selfish disappearance.

James doesn't waste time in tolerating his sister dominating his mother. He comes to me totally exasperated: "What if we hadn't been able to find you?"

Even though my murmurs of "I would have found my way back" fail to give him reassurance, still he does not ask why. My internal smile flares knowing my son; the Behavior Analysis always at work, wants to explain my behavior with just the right patronizing pedagogical voice of "even though she's seventy."

George is still in the hallway, berating an unfortunate aide with questions about my welfare and about why the nursing home didn't do a more complete investigation of my identity. He will badger that poor aide until someone comes to her rescue. That's George: he will fire out questions until he can deal with his reality. That done, he will be remarkably at ease (or as relaxed as he gets). This time I decide I must be the one to save the aide. In the hallway, I interrupt him with a hug and whisper, "I'm okay. Come in my room so we can talk." Taking his calloused hand, I lead him out of the hallway.

Marie brings the love fest to a serious level, saying, "We had to stop by the DON's office before coming to the second floor. She says there is an ongoing investigation that involves you, a guy named Harold, and the disappearance of a Mr. Wirm. She did say that you could be released without any problem, but addresses and phone numbers were needed. She also said you had some refund money coming. I gave her the information she asked for."

"Mom, she also said something about a book you're supposedly writing and asked if we would return it to her office to aid the investigation," James added.

Before I could reply, George let his anger fly. "Fuck that! What mom has belongs to her, and what she does with it is her own fucking business. What do you say we get the fuck out of here?"

"George! I'm sure you don't even realize that every other word you say is a swear word," Marie says, exhaling in his direction.

With that I indicate that my suitcase is all there is, and lead them out the door. It's a lot like dead woman walking. Sticking out my chin and with a little swagger, I push the double doors for what may be the last time. I do not even give the nurses' station a glance but push the elevator button for the first floor.

Marie timidly asks, "Isn't there anyone you want to say good-bye to?"

I say, "No, I took care of my good-byes before you arrived."

I lead them off the elevator and, to avoid the front door, take them through the employee break room to the employee entrance and into the parking lot. Waiting to have them indicate which car they used to come for me, I feel like a little kid waiting to be taken home from camp. Marie is apparently driving a four-door car I'm not familiar with. Unlocking the door with a keypad, she also opens the trunk. George stows the suitcase and gets in the backseat. I stand ready to open the opposite backseat door when my eyes travel to the second floor and then to Harold's window. There, his hand on the window as if reaching out, is Harold.

"Wait! Wait, I have to say good-bye to someone important. I'll be right back. Wait for me," I say, not giving any of my children a chance to stop me.

I rush back through the employee doors, into the hall, across from the first-floor nurses' station, and on the elevator before I think to breathe. I don't stop moving until I reach the double doors. Swallowing hard with heart in hand, I walk down the so-familiar hall slowly to Harold's closed door. When I push his door open, he turns from the window.

I slowly walk to him. He closes the few feet between us, and I'm in his arms. He gently lifts my chin, and I let him so I can receive his kiss. His lips are so soft. My heart leaps into my throat, constricting the sound of words I want to say.

Harold puts his finger to my lips, and I quit struggling for words. He murmurs, "Not good-bye. We'll see each other again. Look for the yellow paper with a map drawn on it. No questions now." He kisses me again, holding me tightly. Then he turns me toward the door.

As I leave his room, Ralph, Otto, and Shun Lady stand in front of their doors, each with a nod and a big grin for me as I pass.

I am going away less reluctant now because I know by some magic I will return. It isn't over yet. On my way back out to the car, I even stop by the nurses' station long enough to irritate Mary one more time. "See you, Mary. Don't think my time with you has been anything less than miserable." She glares at me and turns away.

Catch you on the flip side, my friends.

Lucy's Code

To crack Lucy's code, back up one number so that A becomes 0, B becomes 1, C becomes 2, and so on.

Acknowledgments

This book was written with the encouragement and nagging of my son Jon, who often said, "Get it done, Mom." Our creative car rides and bull sessions shaped this story. Bethany's editing kept me honest and able to internalize her constant corrections with the promise that the next book won't need as much grunt work. News flash: we're still friends after almost a year of many Saturdays spent at her kitchen table, poring over page after page. Encouragement came from many people, not the least from "Jerry down the hall," who turned out to be absolutely the best speller ever. Gagnon Creative Group captured the best design to help the story come to life both in the cover art and in the promotional materials. I thank Joanie, who read chapter to chapter and whose enthusiasm was a catalyst up to the point she heard the angels sing. I thank my benefactor Gary, who turned out to be a friend of writers, including me. And you—thank you, my readers, for going on a journey of stories. The story continues with the next round of tales in *The Wood's Portal.*

CPSIA information can be obtained at www.ICGtesting.com
Printed in the USA
BVOW07*0145140115

383195BV00002B/2/P

9 781491 750872